Death to the Novice Attorney

Death to the Novice Attorney

The Adventures of Pat Patton Series

Roger Fenton

Death to the Novice Attorney

OctopusPublishing

A Division of

Octopus Enterprises, LLC

P. O. Box 132

Covington, GA
30015-0132

Rev. 5 - 072018

Library of Congress Control
Number: 2013931575

ISBN: 978-0-9824433-0-9

Octopuspublishingcompany.com

Dedication

This book would not have been possible
without the help of my wife.
Thanks, Geleta, for encouraging and
helping me write this book.

Acknowledgements

My thanks go out to members of The Heritage Writer's Group, McDonough, GA, for their encouragement and help. Bruce Bailey (<u>32 Stories</u>, <u>Charley Traine</u>, <u>Little Breezy,</u> <u>A Tree For Santa</u>, on Kindle), Peggy Renfroe (<u>Black Valise</u>, <u>Blue Snake Running</u>, on Amazon), and Don Sweetenham (Bumps In The Road, Books 1 and 2) read and critiqued this work and their input is appreciated.

Many thanks to J. Steve Miller (<u>Sell More Books</u> and others on Amazon) for his comments.

A special thank you to Jim and Cathy Price for their review and helpful comments. Also a big thank you to Debbie Singley for her helpful comments.

Table of Contents

Preface

<u>Death To The Novice Attorney</u> is the first of <u>The Adventures Of Pat Patton Series</u>. Pat is an attorney who recently passed the Bar. A very hard worker, Pat completed college and law school without outside financial help. His next big hurdle is to set up a law practice, but he soon realizes he has no idea what he is doing.

Good luck comes when he is able to lease office space with an established attorney who is happy to help him. Bad luck comes when he represents the ex-wife of a cold-blooded killer in an adoption case.

We meet a somewhat immature Pat and his buddy, Eb, who love pranks, beer, and women. As the story unfolds, we see him growing up as he learns the world of prosecutors and judges while juggling armed robbery and other cases. Two people have a profound influence on his life: Shirley, the woman who loves him, and Skinny, a vicious sadistic killer, who hates him. Shirley wants to marry Pat while Skinny wants to murder him.

Much of what you read was derived from the author's actual experience with similar characters and events. However, his literary license allowed him to exaggerate, change, or totally fabricate some characters and events to make Pat's story more interesting. It also contains much humor and a tender love story.

Prologue

When Skinny was a young Griffin, GA, redneck, he was thrilled with the idea that he and his two brothers might become members of a secretive white supremacist organization, *The Brotherhood*. But, what great deed could they perform to prove themselves worthy of membership? They were young -- Skinny only 17, Jeb 18 and Jeffie a mere 13. What the brothers figured out was a surefire way to gain admission; in fact, they became legends in *The Brotherhood* because of what they did that very night. According to newspapers, the boys committed *a* "despicable and sadistic act of the first degree."

Meanwhile, on a farm outside Philadelphia, PA, Pat Patton was shooting at clay pigeons and working on a Cadillac engine in his 1939 Ford Coupe. His parents o n l y shook their heads after a teacher called about Pat playing another harmless, but sometimes frightening, prank. Membership in anything wasn't for him, but he did enjoy riding his motorcycle, being with friends, dating, hunting, and drag racing.

Years later Pat read in the *Atlanta Journal* of a man called Skinny, a well-known criminal, whose escapades and arrests were becoming more numerous and intensifying in cruelty. As a new attorney, Pat hoped he would not be assigned a case as complicated as defending Skinny, but he never expected to be defending himself *against* Skinny! However, when presenting his first case to a jury, he was to know fear so great it would send shivers through his body because Pat realized he was fighting not only for his life but also for the life of the woman he loved. He would find himself up against one of the meanest, sneakiest, criminals alive -- a psychopath who loved hurting and killing people.

CHAPTER 1

Early 1980 - The Big Guy

Skinny was having problems with a big guy at the Clayton County Jail. Otis Purswell was pushing people around and showing no respect for anyone. Skinny was watching a TV murder mystery in the day room, when Otis walked in front of him and switched the channel to a ball game. Then Otis started yelling, ranting and raving, because *his* team wasn't winning.

"Hey, man, I was watching a movie," Skinny bellowed.

"Too bad, mother! Now you're watching a ball game," exclaimed Otis, who kept his back turned to Skinny. He squatted down on one of the day room chairs, not meant for anyone weighing 300 pounds, and returned his attention to the game.

Skinny filled his cup with scalding hot coffee. He put the cup in his left hand and reached to grab another man's crutch, which had fallen on the floor. Things then happened very fast.

"Hey, big boy," barked Skinny.

When Otis turned around, Skinny threw the hot coffee in Otis's face and proceeded to beat him over the head with the crutch. Otis tried to cover up, but Skinny repeatedly hit him in the head, the arms, and the body. The beating opened up numerous cuts and Otis was bleeding profusely. The big guy slid off the chair onto the floor, arms and legs flaying. Repeatedly Skinny kicked Otis in the ribs. None of the inmates tried to stop it. They knew better and didn't want any part of Otis or Skinny. As Skinny kicked Otis in the head for the third time, three guards came running into the room. One of the officers slipped on the blood and went down. While another locked his arms around Skinny's waist, the third grabbed the crutch. The one mopping up blood, with his formerly clean and ironed uniform, grabbed Skinny around the legs, which caused Skinny to fall and land on Otis. Skinny's butt smashed down on Otis's face, breaking his nose, and the three officers landed on top of Skinny.

The big guy looked a lot smaller as he lay unconscious on the floor. Otis went to the hospital. Skinny went to the *hole.*

"Damn!" Skinny nonchalantly said in a cold, monotone voice to the officers on the way to isolation. "I messed up, man. The big guy. He's still alive!"

Arnold *Skinny* Anderson was certainly that - skinny. At 5'9", he weighed 135 pounds. He had dead-looking gray eyes, a crooked mouth, pockmarked face and a rough complexion. From his receding hairline fell very thin, straggly, greasy, brown hair that hadn't been cut for some time. He had been married twice and had two kids from his second wife, a boy 12 and a girl 10. He was now 40 years old, but deceptively strong for his build. His wife worked hard trying to keep the family together, however her waitress's salary would not go far. Skinny had framed houses when he wasn't drunk or high on something, or incarcerated.

Betty wanted to leave Skinny but was afraid because she knew he was dangerous. She was sure he had killed at least three men, but no one could prove it. Betty heard talk that Chuck Thomas had cheated him in a card game, so Skinny walked up to Chuck's front door, rang the bell, and when Chuck answered, Skinny blew him away with a shotgun. The blast injured Chuck's wife and one of the kids as well. Fear sealed their lips. If Skinny didn't get her, she was sure one of his Brotherhood friends would. The possibility that one of his victims might have a family and children would never enter Skinny's mind. He thought only of himself and had absolutely no conscience. Betty believed every word she had heard. He had beaten her several times and once she was in bed for almost a week from a beating with his belt. She also saw him knife a guy at a party. Luck was with the man, though, as he lived. Skinny escaped arrest because the man was afraid to tell who did it.

Everyone who knew Skinny was afraid of him, and of his *Brotherhood* friends. His two male siblings were no better. His older brother, Jeb, died at age 18, back in 1955, when he shot up the house of a black man. Apparently, the black man knew how to shoot back! Jeffie, the 13-year-old younger brother, idolized and followed Skinny and Jeb around, and even though he watched as his brother was killed, it didn't deter him from a life of crime. When the three of them committed murder and mutilation in order to gain entrance into *The Brotherhood*, the decision was as simple as deciding to go down to the river for a swim. Their sister, Charlotte, was the only one who steered clear of the law.

Arnold *Skinny* Anderson was uneducated but extremely intelligent, and cruel beyond belief. He started out getting enjoyment by torturing animals. He and his friends shot a farmer's cow numerous times with a .22 rifle and laughed when it went crazy with pain and took a long time to die. A long criminal history started with petty theft before he was a teenager, and detention centers did not dissuade him. Many other criminal acts followed, which put him in one jail after another. Criminal experience and cunning made him hard to apprehend. If caught again, he swore, "The cops will never take me alive."

However, on his last escapade, armed robbery, when three police officers showed up, his luck ran out. He was sure he could kill two of them but surrendered only because he believed the third would get him first. Skinny ended up in the Clayton County Jail where he was held for trial.

Through legal maneuvering he was able to stay in the county jail far longer than most inmates but he had his reasons for wanting to put off transfer to the state system. Eventually his time ran out, he was convicted, and transferred to the Jackson Diagnostic and Classification Prison.

* * *

Buzzzzzzzzzzzzzzzzzzzzzzzzz!
The noise was coming from the fifth floor of the Great Atlanta Underwriters Insurance Company, or *Great Atlanta,* as

the employees called it.

Dave was training John, a nerdy-looking new employee. Dave was 25 years old, an ex-high-school football player, handsome, built similar to a longshoreman and confident. He had been with the company for three years.

"What was that?" asked John. "I don't believe what I'm seeing! A fly is pulling a tiny sign through the air!"

"You aren't seeing things," said Dave. "If you look closely, I'll bet the sign says, 'I passed the Bar'. A flying announcement."

"How do you know what it says? It's too far away to read."

The fly seemed to be flapping its wings 1000 miles per hour but going through the air so slowly Dave could walk beside it. The drag of the sign slowed it down to the point it was almost impossible to stay in the air.

"I've seen them before. Look, here comes another. Remember me introducing you to Pat Patton, the guy girls say has Paul Newman blue eyes? He's the one who passed the Bar exam and will be sworn in next week. Pat intends to set up his own law office."

They walked to Pat's desk. He had his hand cupped, sneaking up on a fly, which had landed on some chocolate from a Hershey Bar strategically placed on his desk. Zoom! Pat's hand swept the big fly up and quickly closed. He carefully and slowly opened it and found the fly caught between the folds of his ring finger and the palm of his hand. He took his left hand and very carefully, so as not to injure the fly, got hold of its wing and took it out of his hand. He had already written a tiny sign, which said "I passed the Bar" in small letters on a piece of toilet paper. Glued to it was a piece of thread about one-half inch long. As the co-workers watched, Pat put a small dab of contact cement on the fly's tail and attached the thread from the sign. He held it there for about half a minute until the glue dried. When he let go, the fly walked around in circles for a few minutes as if in a daze. All at once, it took off, its wings flapping like crazy. It didn't appear to be going fast enough to stay in the air.

"Pat, you remember John?" asked Dave.

"Sure! Fellows, I'll be right back. I've got to wash my

hands after grabbing that fly."

On Pat's return, John asked, "How many of those flying signs do you have out there?"

"That was number five for the morning, but I only see three. The other two must have had heart attacks from overwork. Did either of you guys sell them a Great Atlanta life insurance policy?"

"No, Pat," laughed Dave. "But if they don't die of a heart attack, with the glue you put on their butts, they will surely die of constipation!"

John, his mouth open in awe, just looked at Pat.

Pat had the type of looks girls liked. His exercise routine of pushups, lifting weights and jogging kept him toned but not too muscular. At 30, he had learned how to be a *neat* dresser and always looked nice. In spite of his antics, he was a hard worker and had gone to law school at night, while also working part-time as, of all things, a motorcycle mechanic.

"Well, John," said Dave unenthusiastically. "We had better get back to work."

"Nice talking with you, Pat," commented John, shaking Pat's hand.

"Good luck with your new job, and listen to Dave 'cause he's a good guy and knows the ropes."

After they left, John asked with raised eyebrows, "And he's going to be a lawyer?"

"Yes, and I'll bet he'll be a damned good one and have an interesting career."

* * *

When Pat was born in 1949, his father owned an automobile repair shop and his mother was a homemaker who worked part-time at a bakery. Pat grew up with a pistol on his hip and a rifle or a shotgun in his hands. He loved to hunt and work on his car. Pat, alone, had done the engine swapping and rebuilding on the Cadillac-powered Ford. In his father's shop, he had access to an electric and gas welder, a lathe, drill press, air compressor, electric hacksaw, and almost any hand tool imaginable. He often worked late at night, listening to that wonderful 50's and 60's music.

Growing up on the farm was a good life, much better than the streets of Philadelphia. At one time, he had a pet crow, a cat, and a dog that all grew up together. The St. Bernard would walk over to the corner of the porch and go to sleep. Next, the cat would curl up against Berni. This was too much for Caw-Caw, who would hop over Fluffy and onto Bernie, make a nest with his feet on the dog's back, and take a nap with his friends. Pat always regretted that he never thought to take a picture. He loved animals, especially wild ones. However, he did not believe in keeping them in cages.

After high-school graduation, where they knew him as the class clown, he had good, clean fun, chasing girls and drag racing. None of his friends did drugs. Marijuana was big in the city but not quite catching on in the country. They drank some beer and smoked a cigarette or two. That was about it.

After less than two years at Penn State University, he received a draft notice. He always believed his lottery number would not come up; Uncle Sam thought otherwise. After basic training, he got lucky and got into a six-month electronics school.

While still in the Army, Pat met a girl and married, a physical attraction marriage that soon ended in a friendly divorce.

When Pat was discharged, his father's health was failing and Dad moved the family to Charleston, SC. Having no place else to go, Pat joined them and went back to college. He earned a degree in Business Administration and a year later moved to Atlanta to go to law school. The job at Great Atlanta allowed him to attend classes at night. Pat was able to buy a modest house through the VA because he did not have to come up with a down payment.

Because he knew that starting a new business would be a struggle, Pat saved enough money to live for three months while building his new law practice. He worked and paid for all of his college, as his dad's health problems had prevented financial help from the family.

After looking for some time, Pat had found an office in Jonesboro, which he rented from another attorney, and started buying used office furniture in anticipation of the big day. The attorney, Herb Butterworth, was a former assistant district attorney and agreed to help him get started, a common practice in that field.

* * *

"Hey, Pat," yelled Dave. "Go to lunch with John and me?"
"Where?"
"Downstairs to the sandwich shop."
"Okay. Be ready in minute."
They went down to a small lunch place in the Great Atlanta building. With one hour for lunch, they could not go far. Pat ordered his favorite, a ham and Swiss on rye, with lettuce and mayo.

"Pat also works part-time as a motorcycle mechanic?" queried John.

"Yes, in East Point, but he got fired. Pat loves to push the envelope. One day his boss called him into the office, chewed him out good, and told him he needed to grow up, gave him his paycheck, and told him to go home!"

Now more familiar with Pat, John asked resignedly, "What did he do?"

"They have a high-speed air-drill with diamond-tipped drill bits at the shop. Every time Pat would have a soft-drink, he would drill a small hole in the bottom of the bottle and replace it in the case with the empties. This went on for weeks until the day a representative from the soft-drink company showed up at the shop and said their company had traced the drilled bottles to that motorcycle shop, and their bottling machinery was being screwed up by leaking bottles. If it did not stop immediately, they would file a lawsuit against the motorcycle shop that could close it down. Pat made a wise decision to stop drilling the holes. Unfortunately, that did not stop him from being fired. You don't screw with a big soft-drink company."

"I thought he was still working there."

"Pat went back to the shop a few days later, apologized, and told the boss it would never happen again if he would let him come back."

"Yeah, I really screwed up that time. I didn't realize how much it cost the soft drink company or how it could hurt the motorcycle shop," said Pat.

"Not trying to change the subject but that Gloria is a real jerk," commented Dave. "I asked her for a rubber band and she looked at me like I had asked for the moon. Her good looks have made her almost impossible to work with. She thinks her butt is made out of gold."

"Wrong," said Pat. "She knows it's made out of gold. She's always talking about herself, her dad and his money, her T-Bird, and the country club, not to mention her sailboat. She also caused so much dissention in her department that two of the girls quit. Gloria will gossip and tell lies about anyone if she thinks it will benefit her. I guess it worked because she got a promotion at the expense of her two co-workers."

"Who's Gloria?" asked John.

"How did you miss her? She sits two desks in front of you," answered Dave. "Hey look, she's in the take-out line - - the one in the yellow blouse."

"Now I know who you mean. I haven't talked to her yet, but I couldn't help noticing how well she is put together."

"Don't bother," chimed in both Pat and Dave.

"She needs to be taught a lesson in humility," said Dave.

"Let me think about it," commented Pat.

* * *

Gloria was late from lunch, as usual. That gave Pat an idea. He typed a few lines on a piece of paper and when no one was looking, put it on her desk. Hurrying back to his space, Pat innocently started back to work.

When Gloria came back, she read the note and looked around the room, appearing quite agitated. The rest of the afternoon she was not able to concentrate.

At quitting time, John walked over to Pat and stopped at his desk. "I've been watching Gloria this afternoon and she seemed really out of it. What did you do?"

"Nothing much."

"Come on now, tell me!"

"Well, it wasn't much. I just put a note on her desk that read: 'You think you got away with it; however, you will be exposed within a matter of days! It will be a payback for Ginger and Mary."

Gloria went numb, looked around, and would not talk to anyone.

"The way she freaked out, Gloria must have a very guilty conscience," commented John. "I assume the two girls were the ones who left."

"Right on both counts."

Pat was really a very nice guy who would go out of his way to help most anyone and was well -liked in the department. However, people like Gloria tended to get him upset. Her lies caused two nice girls to leave the company.

CHAPTER 2

Late June - Jackson Diagnostic and Corrective Prison

Prison authorities transferred Skinny to the Jackson Diagnostic Center and Prison from the Clayton County Jail, where he had stayed for ten months after sentencing. The judge gave him ten years for armed robbery. He was lucky to get only ten, because he had a long record. At age 41, it was going to be tough, because Georgia could make him do the whole ten years.

All prisoners in the Atlanta area have to go through the Jackson Diagnostic Center before assignment to a regular prison. New arrivals get a physical exam and tests to see where they fit in the prison system. Prison officials base placement on the type of crime committed, health, age, education, abilities, violent nature, and likelihood of attempt to escape. From there, they send inmates to other prisons, or, in the case of lesser felonies, county work camps located all over the state. The old timers at Jackson, those who had been through the system more than once, knew of Skinny's reputation. About ten years earlier, he spent five years at Reidsville State Penitentiary for aggravated assault. Word gets around.

While there, another inmate decided to rob him of his *store call*. Prisoners who have money on the books are *called* out to go to the prison store. They may buy certain things, such as stamps, envelopes, candy, cakes, cookies and shaving needs. Inmates go to the store once each week and place their goodies in a see-through net bag, which they take back to their cells.

Tiny Jones, an inmate who weighed 275 pounds and

could bench-press 500 pounds, slapped the hell out of Skinny and took his store goods. He laughed at Skinny and cussed him out.

A few days later, Tiny was working out in the weight room. He was in the process of bench-pressing over 400 pounds, when Skinny struck like a bolt of lightning. He ran into the weight room with a large metal Master lock inside a pair of socks, one sock inside the other for greater strength, and the lock in the toe end. Just as Tiny lowered the bar down to his chest, Skinny struck!

Bam, bam, bam, bam! He repeatedly hit Tiny in the head with the lock. Blood was running down Tiny's face, a face that suddenly had a blank look on it. Although Tiny did not know where he was, he somehow managed to get the weight bar back onto the supports and struggled to sit up.

Bam, bam, bam! Skinny hit him again and again! The big man sat there like a big slab of beef while Skinny ran like hell. Tiny lived but was never right in the head after the beating. No one saw anything, which was amazing because at least 20 men were there.

From then on, no one, not even Tiny, ever messed with Skinny.

* * *

M House, Dorm 4, Bed 161 had a new resident. With 50 other men in it, M4 was run like a boot camp. They had inspections, head counts to make sure no one had escaped, and the men had to go through a *Sir, good morning, Sir*! routine. New inmates went into a dorm until they completed the tests and evaluations. After about four weeks, they moved to cellblocks with two-man cells until transferred somewhere else in Jackson, or shipped out to another prison. The average stay was six to twelve weeks.

Because he had been there before, Skinny prepared himself for his stay at Jackson. He figured he would be there for two months. He knew men who had been stuck there five times that long.

The first thing he wanted was a cigarette. There was a no-smoking rule for inmates going through the diagnostic phase. However, a prison black-market existed in cigarettes, for those willing to pay 10 to 20 times the original price.

Each dorm had six inmates called housemen. Their job was to clean up the dorm and bathrooms, buff the floors, wash the windows, and sell black-market cigarettes. Those not selected for the job could not wander around like the housemen. They had to sit on a hard floor elsewhere for hours on end while a warden inspected the dorms. Most inmates preferred working a job in prison to sitting on a hard floor.

Skinny approached Houseman Jerome.

"Hey, man, how 'bout getin' me some cigarettes?"

"Sure, man. It'll cost ya."

"How much?"

"You knows, man, them things are hard to get. If I gets caught, it'll mean my job, man, and I be stuck sittin' somewhere on a hard floor all day long, man."

"How much?" asked Skinny, again.

"Man, I gets 50 cents a weed, man."

"You want 50 cents for one damn cigarette? You must be crazy 'cause I can buy a whole pack for 65 cents on the outside!"

Skinny rebelled against those exorbitant prices even though a Brotherhood member had put money on his books.

Jerome saw the look in Skinny's eyes and said, "Look man, if you don't tell nobody else I duz dis fer you, I be sellin' you one fer 35 cents, payable in store goods or U. S. postage stamps."

Inmates were not allowed to have actual money.

"Deal. I got money on the books and we get store call tomorrow. Let me know what you want, man. I need five cigarettes."

"Man, I can only let ya have one until I gets paid."

"Okay."

Jerome handed him a cigarette that he had tucked into his sock. At the Diagnostic Center, they had to wear jump-suits that had no pockets. Just before they left Jackson, they were issued regular prison uniforms.

"When's light-up time?"

"After count, man."

"Anybody escape from here? It's been years since I been in this place."

"No way, man. This mother be a maximum secure prison. You know, with death row and the 'lectric chair and all, man."

"Yeah! Well, I only been here for two days and I know how I'd do it."

"Ain't no way, man. How'd you do it?"

"Don't wanna say right now, man."

However, Skinny immediately filled out a request form to attend GED class.

The next day he went to store call and got the items Jerome wanted.

"Hey, Jerome, I need four more 'cause I got the stuff you wanted."

"Cool, man."

Jerome took four more cigarettes from his sock and gave them to Skinny.

"When's light-up time, man?" asked Skinny again.

"Like ah says, count's not fo two more hours, but how 'bout now?"

"Great!"

There were four dorms in *M House,* arranged in a square with a hollow center. Inside the center was the guard shack, with windows on all four sides and a hallway going around the outside. The sides of the dorms that faced the guard shack had several large windows which enabled the guards to view all four dorms. At least two guards were on duty at all times. With this arrangement, two guards could keep an eye on four dorms at the same time. The inmates took advantage of the shift change, though, to smoke, among other things.

Skinny and Jerome went to the recreation room and watched the guards, who were in the process of a shift change. Now was the time to catch a quick smoke, as the guards would be busy and therefore lax in their supervision. Guards also tended to let problems go for the next guy's shift.

Jerome plugged in the floor buffer and turned it on. Skinny had a piece of a Brillo Pad twisted to about three inches in length and wide enough to touch the prongs of the male plug that went into the buffer. Skinny pulled the plug out about half way and put the steel-wool pad against the male prongs.

"Turn the mother on!"

Jerome started the buffer. Sparks flew from the plug as the Brillo Pad caused a short between the two prongs. Prisoners had found out the fine wires of the Brillo Pad glowed red-hot when shorted and would light a cigarette. Through experimentation, they also had found that using a fine wire pad caused only a limited short, which would not draw enough current to pop the circuit breaker. They had a half cigarette going almost immediately. Inmates never had time for more than half a cigarette.

As soon as smokers saw anyone head to the bathroom, after playing with the buffer for a short time, it was their cue to get a quick nicotine fix. Some went to bum a light and some to bum a puff or two. When they finished, the damage control team came in and went to work. Two guys had baby powder poured into the palms of their hands and would slowly blow powder into the air. When they finished, the place smelled like a nursery, not a smoker's lounge.

As he took a puff, Skinny's mind started to wander.

There I was in the hole they call the Clayton County Jail and my damn wife gets up her nerve to divorce me! Got a letter from attorney Herb Something-or-other. She's so stupid she didn't realize I deliberately had my attorney file several motions that allowed me to stay at Clayton longer than the normal time 'cause I figured it would be easier to escape from a county jail than a state prison. Wanted to get that damn woman and her worthless new husband but the guards watched me all the time, so I had no chance to escape.

She is going to pay and so is her attorney! The damn attorney talked her into the divorce. I just know it. I'll make sure she suffers before I kill her. And, that damn Herb will get to see his house burn down, hopefully with his wife and kids inside it! I'll show all of them mothers! And I damn sure will take out her new beau, too. That will teach them all a lesson.

CHAPTER 3

Middle of July - Great Atlanta

The big day was here! It was Pat's last day at Great Atlanta. "Tomorrow I'll be Attorney Patrick Patton."

Pat saw Gloria come out of a closed-door meeting in her supervisor's office with her blouse not buttoned correctly. Next a girl who had stood up to Gloria was summoned to his office and came out with tears in her eyes. She was fired.

Pat got the gang together and told them what he had in mind. They all shook their heads "yes."

First John walked up to Gloria's desk and said, "Ah, ah, I'm sure going to, ah, miss you."

"What do you mean, miss me?" yelled Gloria in a disdainful way.

"I'm not sure, but, ah, Dave overheard the general manager's secretary say something about your leaving, along with your supervisor."

Without saying a word, she got up and marched over to Dave's desk.

"What is that nerd John talking about? What about me leaving?" screamed Gloria. "What did you hear?"

"Well, I don't know how to tell you this, but common knowledge in upper management is that you will be gone before the end of the week."

"How did you find out?" demanded Gloria with venom in her voice.

"I was pulling a policy in the Records and I overheard the general manager's secretary talking to one of the girls."

"Well ... well ... what did she say?" blurted out Gloria.

At that point, Pat walked up to Dave's desk and said, "I can answer that, because I was there, too. It went something

15

like, "Gloria knows what she did and will be history by the end of the week."

At that, she marched off to the Ladies Room.

Pat went to lunch with Dave and John for the last time as an employee of Great Atlanta.

"John, did you hear about the mouse in the tube?" asked Dave.

"What are you talking about?" queried John.

"The tube is the message-sending system. Remember, it's the one I showed you? It is similar to ones the banks use to send your deposit to the teller at a drive-thru window. Pat almost got into some real hot water when he sent a mouse to the girls in Accounting. When they opened the cylinder, the mouse ran out of the tube, and the girls ran out of the room! They're still screaming."

"How'd you catch a live mouse?" asked John, looking at Pat in a strange way.

"Well, when I saw some mouse droppings, a trap was set. I got a ruler and an empty wastebasket. One end of the ruler was propped against my chair seat; the middle of the ruler was resting on the wastebasket's rim. I put sugar on the end that I suspended over the wastebasket. When Mr. Mouse ran down the ruler for the sugar, his weight tipped the ruler and he fell into the basket. The metal sides were too slippery for him to crawl out, thus one Mr. Mouse made Great Atlanta history."

All three laughed until customers stared at them!

* * *

Pat was sworn in as a member of the Bar. That afternoon he put up on the front of Herb's building the sign he had made a week earlier. It read, *Patrick Patton, Attorney-At-Law.*

Next, he had to go to the courthouse to place his name on the indigent list of the Court Administrator, who assigns attorneys to represent persons charged with a crime but are unable to afford legal representation. New attorneys signed up to get experience and bring in some money. Secretly, Pat was afraid he might get a murder case, when he barely knew where the courthouse was located. Yes, he had three years of law school, but it hardly prepared a person for the reality of actually representing someone in court. In fact, he had never been in a courtroom, except to get his divorce and get sworn in as an attorney!

Court-appointed lawyers were paid $50 per hour if they provided an accounting sheet. If the total was too much, the judge could cut the fee. Most attorneys accepted a flat $250 per case for a plea (no trial), $350 for a preliminary hearing and plea. You would not get rich but it helped pay the rent.

Pat learned his first court-appointed client was a man named Bobby McNew. Atlanta had a July 4th Chattahoochee River raft race which featured rafts built by college fraternities and civic organizations. The decorated rafts would float down the river past the cheering crowds that gathered on the banks and bridges. The Chattahoochee is not deep enough for the average powerboat but worked fine with rafts that drew little water. It became one big floating party. Booze and sex flowed as freely as the water and spectators on the bridges got a treat when college girls would pull up their T-shirts and show their boobs.

Bobby McNew was one of those spectators. He was some sight as he walked unsteadily, wearing a Bud T-shirt and a Red Man cap. As of last year, he could legally drink alcoholic beverages and he liked them all. Although he was not bad looking, he was not able to pick up a girl at this race.

His 5' 8" frame stood erect as he tried to peer over the heads of the crowd to locate his friends. However, his buddies had disappeared and he needed a ride home. The fact he had a wife and two small boys didn't seem to bother him. They would be fine because they all lived at his parent's house.

The day was turning out to be miserable ... he was not getting any sex. He did manage to get more than a few beers before his friends deserted him. He was hot and tired with no way to get back home.

Luck was with Bobby; he found a car with the keys in the ignition!

Aren't you supposed to take a car that is sitting there with the key in it? I need it more than the owner. You know, if the owner really didn't want anyone to take it, he would not have left the key in it. Right?

He looked around, got in the car and turned the ignition switch. The Chevy Camaro started right up with its V8 engine singing through two exhaust pipes. As he headed toward home, a glance at the gas gauge showed ¾ full.

"This is too good to be true!" he said out loud. A look in the glove compartment yielded enough change to buy two more beers, so he stopped at a convenience store.

Bobby drove around drinking beer and wondering what to do with the car. He also wanted money. The shop where he worked as a helper was closed because it was a holiday weekend.

Would they have any money lying around? If not, there are all kinds of tools I can take to a pawnshop. That's quick money.

Off he went to Clayton Auto and Truck Repair, Inc. He drove around the block to look the place over. This really was his lucky day -- no one was there. He knew the owners wanted to put in an alarm system. Lucky for him they never seemed to get around to it.

Bobby pulled around back, opened the trunk and took out the tire iron. After a few minutes work, he got the back door open. First, he went into the office and went through the employee's desks.

"Wow!" He found $137.50!

Now for the tools, thought Bobby.

He backed up to the door, got the trunk lid open, and proceeded grabbing tools and throwing them into the trunk. Air tools first, because they were expensive. Next came the hand tools. When he got what he wanted, just for the fun of it, Bobby threw a wrench through the boss's office window.

What fun!

Bobby closed the trunk lid then drove to the first liquor store he found. He bought two 12-packs of beer, a bottle of Jack Daniels, two bottles of wine, and six packs of cigarettes.

He lit up a smoke, opened up a can of beer, and looked for a pawnshop. Bobby pulled in at Honest Harry's Pawnshop, finished his beer and went in. He told Fred, a co-owner, he had been in the auto-repair business when he lost the lease on the building and had to close down.

The moron bought my story!

Fred allowed him $250 on the tools, which were worth at least $2,000. *What the hell; it's free money.* He took it and left. Fred turned off the intercom to the back room.

Unknown to Bobby, when Fred went to the backroom to get the money, he had the following conversation with Harry.

"Hey, Harry. You thinking what I'm thinking about that guy out there?" asked Fred, as they watched Bobby through a one-way mirror.

"He sure is stupid, isn't he? What a cock-and-bull story. Can we get rid of this stuff without getting caught?"

"No way, man. A lot of those tools have Social Security numbers engraved on them."

"Then why did you allow that lowlife $250 on the stuff?"

"Cause when we turn him in, it will take ten times $250 worth of heat off us with the cops in the future."

"Now you're thinking! You got all the info from his driver's license?"

"Yeah, and that dumb yoyo even had his birth certificate with him and I got that info! And a picture, too, as I was pretending to show him a camera."

"Good work. Now give him the $250 and get his license plate number before he drives away. I'll give the little piss-ant a five-minute head start before I call the cops."

Bobby was Pat's first client -- Burglary and Auto Theft.

CHAPTER 4

July - The Matchbook

Pat left the office and got into Max, his 1965 Mustang Convertible. It was 15 years' old but still a sharp car. It had a Hi-Power 289-cubic-inch engine with a four-barrel carburetor, four-speed shift on the floor, and was black with a white top. Not until after he bought the car did he realize that, in the hot Atlanta summers, black was the last color he should have bought. The aftermarket air-conditioner had to work hard on a hot day.

Now that he had the black Mustang though, he wouldn't think of getting rid of Max, and the girls also liked Max. It took a real muscle car to beat it in a drag race. Pat thought there was nothing like a convertible on a nice summer evening.

He lived in an older College Park subdivision in an all-brick house on a half-acre corner lot. It had a full basement that he had finished off into a recreation room. The rest of the basement contained a one-car garage long enough for a work shop in front of the car. The house had two bedrooms, one with a halfbath, a full bath, a living room/dining room combination, kitchen, a small den, which could be used for a third bedroom, and a small screened porch, which was seldom used because of noise from the Atlanta airport.

Pat drove Max up to the house and parked in the driveway because he was going out with his roommate and some fellows from the cycle shop. They were going to Atlanta's famous Stewart Avenue district. Everything was there -- Zayre's Department Store, a drive-in movie theater, J. D.'s Steak House, and a host of bars, nightclubs, and strip joints. His roommate Ebenezer, Eb for short, worked as paint and body man at a Ford dealership. He was going through a divorce and drank too much. Eb was born in East Point, Georgia, 28 years earlier and most of his family lived in the area. This was the opposite of Pat, who had no relatives in Georgia.

When Pat arrived home at 5:30 PM, Eb was already downing his second beer.

"Hi, Eb, I'm home!" exclaimed Pat.

"Hi yourself, and have a cold one 'cause I have a head start on you," answered a tall, good-looking man with dark hair dressed in a black T-shirt and jeans, smoking a cigar.

"Don't mind if I do."

"I got two TV dinners almost done. You want the Salisbury steak or the meatloaf?"

"I'll take the Salisbury steak."

"How did the first day at the law office go?"

"Got my first case today. I'm glad Great Atlanta is letting me work part time for the rest of the month so I have some money coming in besides my part-time job at Ted's. Of course, that's for only two weeks and then I'm a full-time lawyer."

"You glad you did it?"

"Sure am, but it's scary! Here I am setting myself out to be an attorney and I have no idea where to start. I don't even have my business cards yet. They were supposed to be in today. Now the office supply people say it will be Monday. I was hoping to pass them out to chicks tonight, maybe impress them."

"I feel like playing the drums. How 'bout it?"

"Why not?" replied Pat, as he walked to the piano. He was an accordion player and a self-taught piano player. As a result, he learned to cord with his left hand, then everything seemed to come out jazzed up. Eb was an amateur drum player. The two of them had a good time. After six songs and two more beers, the time was about 7:30. They still had about an hour until they needed to leave and meet the gang at Joe's Hide-A-Way.

"Hey, Pat, I feel like calling a redneck number."

"Okay, but you need to keep it short because I need about 45 minutes to get ready."

Eb had the ability to imitate most any kind of voice or dialect.

He looked in the phone book for names like Billy Bob, which usually indicated a redneck. That way he would also have the person's full name and address. Eb dialed the phone and motioned for Pat to pick up the extension.

"Talk to me," said a country-sounding male voice.

"Say, who am I talkin' to?"

"You got Billy Bob."

"Billy Bob. I'm sure glad I got hold o' you for you gone out!"

"What're you talkin' about? Who's this?"

"Billy Bob, you know Bubba's Roost, right man?"

"Yeah, what about it? I go dancin' there every Friday night."

"I was in der today and heard these two big hosses talkin' 'bout bustin' yer head, and you seemed like a cool cowboy to me, so I decided I'd give ya a heads-up warning."

"Hey, who's this and why do them dudes wanna bust this ole coon dog's head?"

Eb kept loudly spitting into his empty beer can.

"Well, thanks, partner. I'll be bypassin' Bubba's for a while."

Eb hung up the phone and they had a good laugh.

The boys got into Max, at 9:00, leaving Eb's Ford pickup at the house.

At 9:30, they went in the door at Joe's Hide-A-Way. Pat would go to a place like that only with a bunch of guys, because whenever you mixed guys, gals, and booze, safety was with a gang. Two mechanics from the cycle shop and two regulars who came into the shop sat at the table with six chairs. They had saved places for Pat and Eb.

"Be right back, Eb. Got to take a leak. Order me a Bud."

Pat was amazed at the urinal.

They must pay off the health inspectors, he surmised.

It consisted of a piece of rain gutter about *ten* feet long, nailed to the wall, and tilting down at a small angle, emptying into an open pipe that went down into the floor. At the other end was a water spigot you could turn on and sort of flush the rain gutter. Very sanitary.

Pat got back to his beer and friends. The talk turned to motorcycles, as it usually did, that or females, or possibly cars ...

normal subjects.

"Man, they sure improved the Honda 750 four-cylinder. It's really something! I can't believe the Japs made something like that. Sounds like a Grand Prix racing engine," said Pete, a mechanic.

"What are you going to do now, Pat? Your 450 is two years old, so ain't it about time you get you a 750?"

"Nothing much I can do. If I strike it rich in the law business, who knows. My 450 is paid for, and I've saved enough to live for about three months. I planned to have enough for six months but with the cost of opening up the law office and all, I won't be able to buy much of anything."

"Well, what have we coming in the door now?" asked Pat, as he saw six young women standing there, the staff rushing to arrange two tables for them.

Bars treated women like queens, because their coming in brought lots of guys who bought lots of beer. Pat was quick to pick out the one he wanted. She was about 5 foot 3 inches tall, of average build and average looks, but she had a very nice smile. Pat preferred small women.

His first wife had turned heads, both male and female, every time she wiggled her tail down the sidewalk. Although her face was not beautiful, it was attractive. However, her body was a sight to behold. The key factor was sex appeal. A woman did not have to be beautiful to have sex appeal. Either she had *it* or she did not. His ex-wife had *it*, and always dressed to kill. However, she would not clean the house or cook. She would leave dirty dishes and never wanted to vacuum, but was she ever good in bed! He did not take long to realize that a marriage based upon sex alone is doomed to failure. Later, he found out she was also a habitual liar. She would lie about anything. He had been too much in love with her body to see her faults. The marriage lasted a year and a half. Within three months of the divorce, she married a truck driver.

Pat also had a college experience dating another beauty. She was everything his ex-wife was, plus she had a beautiful face. She dominated the evening talking about herself and her family's wealth and power. Her father was a very successful businessman and a county commissioner. She had to be back at the dorm by 1:00 AM; he had her back by 11:00 PM. By the end of the evening, Pat was so turned off by her that even if she had started taking off her clothes, he most likely would have turned and walked away. He now looked for Miss Average Girl, because he learned they were much more fun to date.

The band played a slow song and Pat went over to ask the petite girl to dance. A big dude got there first, so he asked one of the other girls. She said "yes" and was very nice, but not his type. He kept looking at the other girl when he could and saw she didn't look too happy dancing with the big dude. The song was over. He had learned all of the girls were from Newnan, a town about 45 minutes southwest of him. The dude brought back his partner and she sat down. Eb had been with the blond in the group and was still talking to her.

When a fast song came up, Pat asked the petite one to dance, but she said, "No, thank you."

Shot down again, thought Pat, walking to his table.

The band had been playing three fast songs and then a slow one, so he was ready to charge the girls' table at the next slow song. Meanwhile, he asked another girl to fast-dance.

There it was! The band started playing *Twilight Time*. Wouldn't you know, again the big dude got there first. Pat's face lit up in a smile as he watched her turn him down.

Nothing ventured, nothing gained, thought Pat as he made his way to her table.

"May I have this dance, Miss?" he found himself asking.

She got up without saying a word and walked to the dance floor with him.

"I was hoping you would ask me again, especially because I told the jerk who just asked me to dance that I promised this one to someone else."

"Sure am glad I did," answered Pat.

"I'm embarrassed to admit it, but the reason I turned you down the first time is that I don't know how to fast-dance."

"Well, I'm not that great either, but I get by."

"Come on now, I watched you and Mary out on the floor and you did great."

"I would rather slow dance anyway. Now I get to hold you tight," said Pat.

24

When he pulled her close there was absolutely no resistance.

"What's your name?" asked Pat, as he pressed her thighs tightly against his. He felt stirring in his pants and hoped he would be able to walk off the dance floor without being too embarrassed.

"Sally," she answered. "What's yours?"

"Pat, and it is my pleasure to meet you, Sally."

They danced very closely for several minutes without talking very much.

The song ended and he took Sally back to her table. Pat liked her. He did not want to rush things. He planned to ask for her phone number when the next slow dance came up.

"Hey, Pat. How did you like her?" asked Eb, blowing out a cloud of cigar smoke

"Great! She really turned me on out on the dance floor!"

"I know, 'cause you looked like you had a tent pole in your drawers when you walked back to the table."

"That obvious, huh?"

"Afraid so, man."

Just then, all six girls got up and started to walk out.

No! She can't do this to me, thought Pat.

Then a miracle happened! Without a word, Sally threw a matchbook on his table as she walked by. He quickly opened it and saw a note that read "Sally, NU 461-7538."

Unbelievable. This only happens in movies.

"Pat, you and Eb going to the races Sunday at Lakewood?" asked Pete. "Bad man Bart will be there on his Harley and Gary Nixon on his Yamaha and Triumph."

"Sure, Pete," answered Pat, his mind not on the races. Bad Man Bart Markle was like no one else when he took a Harley around the dirt track at Lakewood Fairgrounds. He would go into the turns at 80 mph, sliding sideways, and spinning his rear tire with a rooster tail of dirt flying up behind.

One time Pat had seen Gary Nixon in a race where he stalled his Yamaha off the line and had to push the bike and jump-start it to get the engine fired up again. By the time he entered turn four, he was passing the leader. Nixon was that good. Tonight it was hard to think of either Markle or Nixon;

he had Sally on his mind.

The next day he planned to call her number. Now 2:00 AM, he had to get some rest because he had to be at the Honda shop at 9:00 AM. Saturday was a big day for the shop, doing as much business or more than two or three weekdays.

* * *

Visitation day at Jackson brought Skinny two visitors.

"Hi, man! Got some things out of the vending machine fer you -- a cheeseburger, chips, Coke, and an apple pie. Anything else you want?" asked Jeffie.

"No, but it sure is good to see one of my Brotherhood friends along with my brother Jeffie."

"We chipped in and put $250 on your books so you can have some good store days."

"You guys are family to me, Spider. Thanks."

"I never thought they would get you."

"Me neither. There were too many of them pigs. I almost tried it. I was sure I could get the first two, but I didn't think I could take out the third one before he got me. The other two would have been pork chops."

"I hear they got ya fer ten."

"Yeah, but I'm not stayin' that long, if you know what I mean."

"You got some plans?"

"Yeah. Gotta work out some details yet but my ex and her damned attorney are going to be in for a big surprise! Gonna burn that SOB out. Gonna kill my worthless ex and the new creep she married."

"Want us to take care of them fer you?"

"That's a tempting offer but I wanna look 'em in the eye when I pull the trigger. As far as Herb What-ever-his-name-is, I'll invite you guys to roast marshmallows on the embers of his burnt-down house."

"Still think you ought to consider us helping you."

"I know. I'd make the same offer if you was in here except I need to take care of 'em myself. You understand, man? When I check out of this place, I won't be able to see any of you

26

brothers 'cause the cops will be watching all of you. They'll figure that the first place I'll go is to one of you."

"How 'bout we key their car? Bust out a windshield? Something?"

"Hell, that would be fine with me. I want to do the rest!" informed Skinny with morbid finality.

"Skinny, you remember that creep, Wilber, who ratted you out?" smiled Jeffie.

"How could I ever forget him? Did he meet with an accident? Permanent like?"

"Something like that but better. I hear he lost his tongue, his ears and his pecker. Just a rumor, understand." Skinny smiled.

CHAPTER 5

Middle of July - Sally and Ann

Pat got up at 8:00 for a piece of toast and glass of orange juice, fired up his Honda and was gone. He got to the shop at 8:59, still trying to wake up and clear his head. Pat worked Saturday morning at Ted's. Motorcycles were not on his mind. Saturday morning was typical except for one incident. A young punk came in and started yelling at Pete because his cycle was not repaired on time.

"You sorry S O B. You s a i d it'd be ready this morning!"

"Look, buddy! Number one, I told you I would try to have it ready by this morning, not that it would be ready! Number two, if you keep cussing me out like that, it may never be ready!"

"Yeah, well I just might decide to kick your ass!"

"Bring it on, Dumbass!" invited Pete, getting hotter by the minute.

"You had better watch it because I know Karate!" threatened the punk.

"Yeah, well, you had better watch it because I know wrench!" cautioned Pete as he pulled out a large wrench from his toolbox.

The punk shut up and walked out. Almost two weeks later, Pete finished the bike.

At lunchtime, Pat called Sally, but she wasn't there. The female voice said it was the correct number, and that she was Ann, the one who d a n c e d with Eb.

28

Just then Sally walked in and Ann put her on the phone.

"Hi, Pat."

"I was hoping that the matchbook wasn't a gag."

"No gag. Some of the girls had to leave early, so I didn't have a choice."

"When can I see you again?" asked Pat.

"I'm not sure. Pat, I don't have a car and have to depend on Ann. You know, the girl you talked to a few minutes ago."

"She said she was the one who danced with Eb, right?"

"Yes, and she really likes him."

"Anyway, you don't need a car because I'll pick you up."

"No!" she responded a little too quickly and forcefully.

"You don't want to go out?" asked Pat, sounding dejected.

"Look, it isn't that. Maybe I could come over to your place, but Ann would have to come too 'cause she has the car."

"Can you fix her up with Eb?" asked Pat, not believing how this conversation was going.

"Just a minute and I'll ask her."

The silence for about 45 seconds seemed like 45 minutes to Pat.

"She said that would be fine. Are you and Eb busy tonight?"

"No!" blurted out Pat with growing anticipation.

Wow! I don't believe this, thought Pat.

"How do we get there? Wait and I'll put Ann on the phone for directions."

"Hi, Pat, this is Ann speaking."

He gave her detailed directions on how to get to his house.

"What time?"

"How about 7:00 PM, here at the house? We could take you girls out to eat if you like."

"Thank you, but we just want to come over to see you guys. That's ok, isn't it?"

"Sure. See you at 7:00."

"Bye," all chimed in, with Pat thinking, *this is too good*

to be true.

He called Eb, told him what was happening, that he would be home by 5:30, and to please make sure the place looked good. He would stop and pick up some beer and rubbers on the way home.

The afternoon at the shop went as slowly as a kid waiting for Santa on Christmas Eve but at last, quitting time. Pat jumped on the Honda and headed for the closest convenience store. He got two twelve packs of beer and six packs of rubbers. One could never be sure. He used bungee cords to strap the beer to the seat and away he went, arriving home at 5:40. He rode the bike into the garage, grabbed the beer, and ran up the stairs.

"Eb, are you believing our luck? We don't have to go anywhere. They're coming to us!"

"Right, and they're going to get what they're looking for! When the weather's hot and sticky, that's the time to dunk your dickie!" Eb, smiled, puffing on a cigar.

"You're too much, Old Bean. I'll put the beer in the frig. Say, the place looks good! Here's a couple of packs of rubbers."

"Thanks, man, and here's half of the tab," said Eb pulling out his wallet. "Let me know if it's more. How about a friendly bet?"

"What do you have in mind, Old Bean?"

"I'll bet I get some before you do!"

"You're on, Eb, but how will we know who got some first?"

"I don't know." Eb chewed on his cigar. "I'll have to think about it."

"I know! As soon as one of us is ready to put it to her, howl like a wolf."

"You got it, or rather they'll get it! "

They made sure the beds were made, had clean sheets, and mood music was ready to put on the Hi-Fi. Both of them took a shower and got ready for what they hoped would be a memorable night.

At 7:00, the girls had not arrived. At 7:15, still no

girls. Then at 7:20 the phone rang. They were lost and at a convenience store up the street. Eb had his Ford pickup out front, so they told the girls to stay put and they would be right there.

They jumped into Eb's truck, found the girls, and escorted them back to the house. Both were impressed with the house and the way it was kept.

"We must have taken a wrong turn or something," said Ann.

"That's okay, Honey," replied Eb. "What counts is that you're here."

Pat noticed Eb had a grin that covered his whole face.

"I'll show you around." Pat put his arm around Sally.

She turned to face Pat and threw her arms around him. He leaned down and his lips found hers. It was a long kiss and then they both smiled at each other. Eb took the clue and kissed Ann.

"How about a cold beer, girls?" offered Pat.

"Sounds fine," chimed in both girls at the same time.

"I'll get 'em," replied Eb, as Pat put on the mood music. Eb grabbed the couch and pulled Ann down beside him, which left Pat with the La–Z–Boy chair. He sat Sally on his lap and they talked, drank some beer, and listened to the music. They slow-danced a few times, then returned to the chair. About that time, all of them had to use the restroom. The girls got the master bathroom, and Pat & Eb used the half-bath off Eb's bedroom. Naturally, the girls went to the bathroom together.

"What do you think, Pat?" asked Eb.

"I like her, I surely do, but it's still hard to believe this is happening to us."

"Kind of strange, isn't it."

"Yeh. I don't understand why they didn't want us to take them out to dinner. Most women would jump at the chance."

* * *

"Well, what do you think Sally?" asked Ann.

"I like Pat, but I still can't believe I'm going out with a

lawyer. Pinch me."

* * *

"How about you, Eb? What do you think of Ann?"
"I'd like to get her in the sack! The sooner, the better!"
"I feel the same about Sally!" said Pat with a big smile.

* * *

"Ann, how do you feel about Eb?"
"If that hunk so much as tries to get me in his bed, I'm –
I'm – I'm going!" laughed Ann.
"Me, too, with Pat!"

* * *

As the girls came into the living room, Ann sat down on the couch with Eb, and Sally plopped down on Pat's lap.

Pat kissed Sally and at the same time put his hand on her breast. They were not large but felt good.

"I wish I had more for you," whispered Sally in Pat's ear.

"They're fine. I really don't like extra-large boobs anyway. Shall we go in the bedroom?" asked Pat with a mischievous smile.

"Sure."

He immediately became fully aroused but managed to pick up her 110 pounds and carry her to the bedroom without breaking anything. Eb and Ann were right behind them laughing and heading for Eb's bedroom.

He laid her on the bed and slowly undressed her, touching her all over. As he took off his clothes, she bent down and took him in her mouth, which felt like a bolt of lightning had hit him! After she sensed he was on the verge of a climax, Sally rolled over on her back for him to take her. They were both hot-and-bothered and Sally moaned as he gently stroked her pelvis.

Right before he entered her, Pat exclaimed, "You make me feel like an animal!" Then he let out a loud howl that penetrated the walls of the bedroom.

* * *

With the girls leaving sometime after lunch, they never made the races the next day.

"Man, you really messed me up last night!"

"What are you talking about, Eb?"

"It's like this. I got her in bed, and took off her clothes. Then she undressed me. I started kissing her breasts and put my hand between her legs. She was ready! Just as she spread her legs for me, and Waldo felt like he was as hard as a piece of steel, we heard this terrible loud noise! It was you howling like a wolf! She jumped up yelling "What's that? Did you hear that? What was that? It was all too much for the big boy and he went limp! It took another hour for me to get it up again!"

They both laughed.

"Let me tell you what I found out last night that isn't funny."

"What's that, Eb?"

"I was talking to Ann and found out why they didn't want to go out to eat with us."

"Why's that?"

"Because they are both married and didn't want to be seen in public with another man!"

"Wow!" exclaimed Pat.

"That ain't all, Buddy. Ann's husband is at sea with the Navy. Your girl's husband -- you won't believe where he is!"

"Where?"

"In jail for shooting up a b a r with a .45 automatic! And – he's about to get out!"

"Man, speaking of a bar, I need a Hershey Bar!"

Fun as it had been, they never saw the girls again. The guys hated that because they liked both girls... and what they had to offer.

CHAPTER 6

Middle of July - Bobby McNew

Pat got to his office around 8:00 AM because he wanted to get organized before Herb arrived. Herb usually got there between 8:30 and 9:00, and went through his morning ritual of tightening his belt and snapping his suspenders in place. Herb had been in law practice for 15 years and an assistant district attorney for about 10 years. He did dozens of jury trials, winning most of them.

Herb was an odd guy, who somehow did not make it big or fit in with the *in* crowd, even though he had both the ability and the experience to be one of the top attorneys in the county. He was a maverick who would not kiss anyone's butt. Herb, on occasion, came off as abrasive, but if you knew him, he was not that kind of person at all. He would go out of his way to help a new attorney who he had taken under his wing. Pat was an example.

About an hour after Pat arrived at the office, Herb came walking in, never in a hurry. The sun reflected off his glasses, and at the same time, off his balding head. He was two inches shorter and ten years older than Pat and developing middle-age spread.

"Good morning, Herb, how are you doing?"

"When you have a great wife and three wonderful kids, all mornings are good," replied Herb.

What a great attitude, thought Pat.

Rhonda and Julie came in about the same time as Herb. Rhonda worked full-time as Herb's secretary, and Julie was a girl who Herb brought in to work for Pat part-time. Later, when

34

Pat's business grew, she could be his full-time secretary.

When Pat looked at Rhonda, he saw a woman in her 40's, a little on the heavy side, wearing glasses, but with the appearance of being sure of herself. He had heard she was very loyal to Herb and had been with him for the last three years. They worked as a team and both knew and understood their roles.

What a gorgeous thing she is, thought Pat as he eyed Julie. *Got to be careful. She is married and it is bad business to mess with a secretary anyway. Herb said her husband was a cop, to boot.*

Julie looked to be a few years younger than Pat, and did she ever look good in a sweater! A natural blond, Julie was subjected to all of the blond jokes. Herb had told him up front that she had a jail record from another county. Driving home one night in a rainstorm, she ran a stop sign she did not see, hit another car and killed the driver. The judge gave her a ten-year sentence, three in prison with the remainder on probation. Julie actually served one year and was put on parole for the other two. She gave Herb permission to tell Pat about her record, as Herb had been her attorney. Herb said she was really bothered by having a record, but she was dealing with it the best she could.

Since Julie had never been a legal secretary before, Herb had agreed to let her help Rhonda for the first two weeks in order to learn the ropes. She would answer Pat's phone, if it ever rang, and Herb would pay three-quarters of her salary the first two weeks. She would then be Pat's secretary for as many hours per day as needed.

"Here's your business cards, Mr. Patton." Julie looked up from her 5'4" frame, only reaching his shoulders. "I picked them up before I came to work."

"Please call me Pat, and I appreciate your picking up the cards."

Good looking and efficient, too! What more could a boss ask for.

"Ok, Pat. I'll be training with Rhonda if you need me," announced Julie with a smile.

"Fine, I need to talk to Herb anyway."

"I heard that," snapped Herb , pulling on his suspenders. "Come into my office. What do you need?"

"Advice, mostly. I got my first court-appointed case and don't have a clue what to do with it."

Herb leaned back in his chair, pulled on a suspender, and said, "Tell me about it and let me see your file."

"What file? I have no idea how to make one up or what to put in it. They didn't teach us about that in law school."

"Look, first get a file folder, a two-hole punch, Atco clips, and labels. I had you buy all of these things. Right?"

"Sure, Herb, I got them yesterday."

Pat got a 15-minute lesson on how to make up a file folder.

Herb continued, "You will find that 90 to 95% of your criminal cases will not go to trial. Most of your clients don't want to face the exposure of the maximum amount of time in prison that the offense carries, so they will be anxious to plea to something less. That is if the DA is offering a good deal. If the maximum sentence is ten years and they offer eight to ten on a plea, advise your client to go to trial, as they have little to lose. Always remember - - if you take a case, do your best for your client, even if you can't stand him or her personally. This isn't a game."

Then he explained what Pat needed.

"That's a lot!"

"There is a lot more, but it's enough to get you started. Do you have the accusation?"

"Do you mean this?" answered Pat, while handing him a sheet of paper.

"Oh! They already indicted him. Now he's lost his right to a preliminary hearing. You could have asked a lot of questions at the hearing and got a good feel for the case. You could have seen how good the police officer did on direct and cross-examination."

"What do I do now?" asked a perplexed Pat.

Use one of my intake sheets for now. Get the folder ready and go see the Assistant DA assigned to the case."

"How do I know who it is?"

Herb picked up the phone and spoke to the secretary at the DA's office.

"Hi, Thelma, this is Herb. Say, who has the Bobby McNew case? Okay and thanks. Bye."

"You got Assistant DA Jack Wilson. He looks sloppy, and his shirttail often hangs out of his pants. He looks and acts a lot like Columbo on TV, but he has a mind like a steel trap, so don't let his looks fool you. The best approach with Jack is to level with him. Go to the DA's office and when you get back, I have a case for you. I told you I would feed you some cases here and there to help with the rent, so I have what appears to be an adoption case for you."

"Great, Herb! I really appreciate it. What's it about?"

"Last year I did a divorce for a client by the name of Betty Anderson. She is now remarried to a good man, and the new husband wants to adopt her two kids. She has a boy age 12 by the name of George, and a girl age 10 named Lorie. Betty was married to a real bad-ass by the name of Arnold Anderson, but they all call him Skinny. He's out of the picture now because he's in prison. I think he got ten years, and he almost certainly will serve most of it because he has a bad record. Here's a copy of the divorce and Mrs. Anderson's adoption intake sheet."

"Herb, thanks, but you know I never did an adoption."

"True, but then you never did anything yet!" laughed Herb. "Don't worry. I'll help, and you will need help because adoptions are complicated.

"On a serious note, law school never prepares you to be an attorney. They should do away with the Bar exam and require a law degree and a one-year internship with an established attorney or law firm. At least you would know where the courthouse is. You will learn more in the first year of law practice than all three years of law school," informed Herb with a snap of his suspenders.

"But, why are you giving me this case? She's already your client."

"When I told her my fee would be $750.00, or more if Mr. Anderson contested it, I could see there was no way she was going to be able to come up with the money. So, I took the liberty of telling her that a new attorney was coming in with me and he could do it for $350.00. She would need $150.00 for a retainer and you would give her 60 days to come up with the rest. In addition, there will be a $65.00 court cost, and some small expenses at the end for a certified copy of the final decree of adoption. They also will have to get new birth certificates for the children with their new last names on them. By the way, Rhonda has the $150.00 for you. Now get going and see Jack."

"I can't believe this! My first fee as an attorney and I haven't done anything yet!"

"Don't worry; you'll have a bunch of work to do before it's over."

"Thanks again, Herb. I guess I had better get over to see Mr. Wilson. I'm also going to have to inform Great Atlanta that I'm sorry, but I will not be able to work part-time for them after all. Herb, I just became a full-time attorney!" said an excited Pat.

"Someday you might wish you had stayed with the insurance company."

"Why?"

"Because I don't know a single old-timer attorney who likes what he is doing. Me included. This job will consume you."

* * *

Pat walked over to the DA's office, which was across the street. He found Thelma and asked to see Mr. Wilson. She picked up the phone, said something, and motioned for Pat to follow her.

"I'll take you to his office, Mr. Patton."

Thelma took Pat down a long hallway to Mr. Wilson's

office. It was not at all what he expected. It was small, could seat only two visitors comfortably, and was sparsely furnished. The room had only a desk, three chairs, and a couple of file cabinets.

"Mr. Wilson? I'm Pat Patton."

"I'm Jack Wilson. What can I do for you?" asked a man who looked disheveled and was about Pat's size and age. When they shook hands, his grip was strong, but just as Herb had said, his shirttail was hanging out. That made Pat smile.

"I'm pleased to meet you, Mr. Wilson. Herb Butterworth said I needed to be honest with you, so that's exactly what I intend to do. I'm a brand new attorney and although I don't have any idea what I'm doing, I'd like to get the best deal I can for my client, Bobby McNew."

"Okay", smiled Jack. "Let's see what the little turd has done."

Shuffling the papers, Jack said, "He does have a record, but nothing big yet. He's 22 years old, and has a wife and two kids. We got an auto theft and a burglary on him, but the burglary is not residential."

Glancing up at Pat, Jack added, "Residential burglaries carry a lot more time because they could develop into a violent confrontation with the homeowner."

Looking back down at the file, Jack continued, "Because you have been honest with me, I'm going to make him a deal he can't refuse. What does he want to do?"

"Sir, I haven't talked to him yet. I wanted to be able to tell him what your recommendation was when I went to see him."

"Still in jail, I see. About a week now. Do the little turd good to get a taste of jail. Okay. On the auto theft, five years' probation and a $500.00 fine. On the burglary, five years' probation and a $500.00 fine, and because his employer got his stuff back, we'll recommend that the sentences run concurrently. Oh, and he will have to pay for the window that he broke out of his boss's office."

"Let me get this straight. A total of 5 years' probation, and $1,000.00 fine. Right?"

"You got it. And, tell the little turd that if he doesn't take this deal, he's looking at 20 years on the auto theft and another

20 years on the burglary. You can also tell him he's got Judge Harold *Chain Gang* Musselman. I can tell you right now if he goes to trial and loses, the little turd is looking at a minimum of 10 years to serve and another 10 on probation. Tell him you twisted my arm. Make yourself look good."

"Yes, sir! Thank you very much, Mr. Wilson."

"Oh, Patton. Good luck, and here's the copy of the police report and his rap sheet you requested." Jack smiled as he handed them to Pat.

"Again, thank you, sir."

He hadn't requested anything.

Pat had trouble believing that conversation. Here he was, right out of law school, sitting down and talking about how much time a human being might have to spend in jail. What power attorneys have over people. Mind boggling!

* * *

He looked over the paperwork Jack had given him, found his way out of the courthouse and went over to the jail. The jailer asked to see his Bar card, but Pat had not yet received it in the mail. He did have the good sense to copy the number down and gave that to the deputy, along with one of his business cards. He told him he was in with Herb. That was enough to get him in the door.

The deputy led Pat to a large cell, with bookcases around the walls. They called it *the library*. He took a straight-backed chair and sat at a 4 x 8 foot table in the middle of the room.

"Clang!" went the big steel door as it shut. The noise was loud and echoed in the room. "Click!" went the lock as the deputy twisted the large key. What a strange feeling being locked in this place. And, the smell! Nothing smells quite like a jail. The strong odor of disinfectant, bleach, sweat, and urine was very noticeable. It was gloomy and a feeling of helplessness could take over after only a short time. A few minutes later, the deputy came back with a young man, opened the door, let him in, then closed and locked it again with another loud clang and click.

"Just yell when you're done," said the deputy as he ushered Bobby in the door.

Funny, but Pat almost expected him to look like a turd!

"Hi, I'm your court-appointed lawyer, Pat Patton."

"As you can guess, man, I'm Bobby McNew. Man, am I glad to see you! I gotta get out of this place!" said Bobby, rushing his words.

"Slow down, Mr. McNew. I need to get some information from you." Pat started to fill out the client's intake sheet. He asked Bobby to tell him what had happened.

"Man, it was like this. I went to the, you know, raft race with some friends of mine. We did a little drinking and those S O B s left me there. I had to get home. You understand, don't you?"

"Go on."

"It was hot, man. I saw this car there that had the keys in it and I just kinda got in and drove home. If the dude didn't want me to have the car, he wouldn't have left the keys in it, would he? That's about all."

"What did you do with the car?"

"I wrecked it about a block from my house. It still ran good enough to get it into an alley. Then I jacked it up and took the wheels and the radio. They don't know about that," he laughed. "I got away with that one!"

"How about your employer? What happened there?"

"I don't know what you're talking about, man."

Pat pointed to a couple of papers in front of him. "This police report from the DA's office has you ID'd by the pawn shop owners. You even gave your real name and showed them your birth certificate. Oh, and if that weren't enough, they got a picture of you pawning the tools."

"Oh!" Bobby acted surprised. "Well, you know, man, I was drinking and all, so maybe I forgot."

"Bobby, let me explain something to you. The offense of felony auto theft can get you 20 years, and the offense of burglary can get you another 20 years. Some more bad news, Bobby. The judge has the power to run the sentences consecutively, which means you're looking at a possible 40 years in prison!"

Bobby's face turned white.

"But, Bobby, the worst news of all is that the judge assigned to your case is Harold *Chain Gang* Musselman!"

"No! No! No! I done heard of him. Everybody in here's talking about him! That man will put me away forever! I got to get out of here! Man, you gotta understand. A big ugly dude in here has been winking at me!"

Taking Jack Wilson's advice, Pat continued the conversation.

"Look, Bobby, I checked your record before I came to see you. You have one, but not too bad. You are also married and have two little boys. You are only 22 years old and young enough to change."

"Look, man, I'll do anything, man. Just get me out of here!"

"As I was trying to tell you," continued Pat, who was now enjoying himself, "I explained all of this to Asst. DA Wilson . . ."

"Wilson!" exclaimed Bobby. "They say he don't lose no cases!"

"As I was saying, I explained all of this to Asst. DA Wilson, who wanted to put you away for at least 10 years with the Judge's blessings."

"Ten years!" blurted out Bobby.

"Let me finish, Bobby," said Pat, who was really getting into the role now.

"I told him I would spare no time or work going to trial on this case. Also a series of motions would be filed and there would be exhaustive discovery requests served on the DA's office, plus a lengthy trial if he didn't come off the 10 years!" said Pat very forcibly. He read about that in law school.

"Please tell me, man, did he?" broke in Bobby with a tremor in his voice. "Man, remember the big guy winking at me."

"Bobby, you keep interrupting me. After I told him everything, he thought about it for a few minutes, all the while sorting through his papers and looking at his . . ."

"I can't stand it, man! What did he say!" pleaded Bobby.

"Look, Bobby. I can leave and come back tomorrow. Give you time to calm down."

"No, Mr. Patton, please, please don't do that!" again pleaded Bobby.

"Then be quiet and let me finish. Ok, now where was I? Oh, yes. The Asst. DA thought for a while, looked at his calendar, looked at the file again, and made a new recommendation."

It was all Bobby could do not to interrupt Pat again, but he had learned his lesson.

"He said he was really too busy to contend with all that,

so if you agree to plea, he would go five years on the auto theft and a $500.00 fine. On burglary, five years and a $500.00 fine."

"Man, that's ten years and $1,000.00 fine!"

"Right, Bobby, but that's a lot better than 40 years, isn't it?"

"Yeah, but 10 years, and $1,000.00 fine?"

"Not quite, Bobby. Because I got him to agree to run the sentences concurrently, it's a total of five years. But, you still have the $1,000.00 fine. And I almost forgot, you have to pay for the window you broke out of your boss's office."

"How am I going to be able to do all that, man?" replied Bobby with a tear in his eye. "I'll be locked up for 5 years!"

"Shall I tell him we have a deal?"

"Yeah, man. I guess five years is a lot better than 40 years." said Bobby, reconciling himself to jail time.

"Look, Bobby. I really like you, and now that I know more about your case, I'm going back to the DA and read him the riot act! I'll be back later today."

"You mean you will fight for me? Like get in the DA's face and all?"

"That's my job, Bobby. I fight for my clients."

"Thank you, thank you, Mr. Patton! But, please don't make him mad!"

"See you in about an hour, Bobby."

Pat smiled and yelled for the jailer. He left and headed for a little sandwich shop across the street and had lunch. When he finished eating, Pat went back to the jail.

After the same closing clang and click of the door, Bobby was again brought into the library.

"Hi, Bobby."

"Mr. Patton. What did he say?" Bobby looked beaten down and ashen-faced.

"After I read him the riot act and he saw I was serious, he backed down."

"What did he say? What did he say?" pleaded a now-rejuvenated Bobby.

"Good news, Bobby. I talked him into probation. That's a total of five years to be served on probation and $1,000.00 fine." Bobby was so happy he jumped up, grabbed Pat's hand, and almost shook it off.

"I can't believe it! I'm going to tell all my friends about you!" exclaimed Bobby. "I was facing both a 20-year burglary and a 20-year auto theft and you got me five years' probation! You must be the best attorney in the county to be able to do that."

"Here's several of my business cards. Please pass them around."

"I sure will. Give me some more and I'll like flood the jail with 'em. Thanks, man! Thanks!"

Pat gave him another pile of business cards.

"One more thing, Bobby, and this is straight from Mr. Wilson's mouth. If you decide to go to trial and lose, you're looking at a minimum of 10 years to serve. You understand that?"

"Yes, sir!" answered a very happy Bobby.

"Ok, then I'll tell him we have a deal and get him to have it put on the judge's calendar as soon as possible so you can get out of here. And - stay away from the big guy with the gleam in his eye."

Pat left the jail in a very good mood. He was already enjoying being an attorney. What a slick deal that was! The *little turd*, as Jack called him, said he was a great attorney and this was his first full day on the job! He had never even been before a judge in his whole life except to be sworn in as a member of the Bar and when he got his divorce.

* * *

Pat went back to the courthouse and asked to speak to Jack again. Just as he said his name, Jack came out the door.

"Jack, Mr. Patton is here to see you. I was just about to call," said Thelma.

"Sorry, Patton. I can't see you now. Judge Musselman has summoned me."

"That's ok, Mr. Wilson. . ."

"Call me Jack."

"Ok, Jack, I just wanted to let you know we have a deal on the McNew case, and he wants to do the plea as soon as possible."

"Thelma, when is Musselman's next plea day?"

"Tomorrow afternoon at 2:00 PM."

"Can we get the McNew case on it?"

Looking at the calendar, Thelma replied, "Yes, Jack, there's room."

"Patton, be in the judge's courtroom tomorrow at 2:00 PM. You won't get a notice because of the short time-frame."

"I'll be there, and Jack, I took your advice on making myself look good."

"Yeah?"

"He thinks I'm Perry Mason."

Jack laughed and walked out the door.

What a great guy! thought Pat.

As Pat left the DA's office, he decided to check the four Superior Court rooms to see if any of the judges were taking criminal pleas. He was in luck as it was Judge Steve Lofton's plea day. Now he would at least have some idea what to do when he got into court on Bobby's case.

As he watched, he saw the Asst. DA call the case. The defendant and his attorney would go up to the podium, and the Asst. DA would read the charges against the defendant. The judge would ask the defendant several questions. As the plea progressed, Pat took notes. The judge wanted to know if the defendant was entering into his plea freely and voluntarily, had anyone threatened or coerced him into making the plea, was he under the influence of alcohol or drugs, was he satisfied with the representation of his attorney, and so forth.

He stayed and listened to another plea just in case he missed something. He also learned that the judge would ask the defendant what he did to make him guilty of the crime and either the attorney or the defendant could answer. Pat saw the attorney was the best one to answer because he saw a defendant him-haw around about his guilt, so the judge cut him off, and set the case down for trial. You don't want to go to trial before a hostile judge.

* * *

The next day Judge Musselman took McNew's plea with Pat answering for Bobby. After the plea, Bobby was taken back to the jail, met with his probation officer, and released.

That night when he was jogging, Jack Wilson was struck by

45

a hit-and-run driver and died at the hospital.

* * *

The next day Pat had Julie make a file on the Anderson adoption and he looked over several adoption files Herb had completed. Boy, were they ever complicated. A stepparent adoption was different from a relative adoption, which was different from an agency adoption, which was different from a third-party adoption. A foreign adoption was even more complicated, and way out of his class for now.

On top of that, unless the father consented, you had to find out if the biological father was the legal father or just the instrument of impregnation. Did he support the child, or have contact with the child within the last year, and if he did not, did he have a legal excuse, such as being in a coma or the mother was hiding the child from him? Was the father consenting to the adoption, was he a resident of Georgia, or was he an out-of-state resident?

Herb had told him that early on he should decide if he liked adoption cases, because he needed to do a lot or none at all. The law on adoptions was complicated and ever-changing, so you had to keep up with it by attending seminars and studying. Doing only one now and then did not justify the time spent on preparation.

* * *

Pat rushed from the office to Great Atlanta and informed his boss that, although he appreciated the offer of part-time work, he was too busy to accept it. However, he agreed to go over the files with Dave and John to make sure they were up to speed on them.

He found them at the new photocopy machine trying to copy a photo out of Playboy magazine.

"Hi, guys."

"Hi, your honor." Dave gave a flip of his imaginary hat.

"Your lordship," John used a triple-down queen's salute.

"Alright, guys, cut it out. I just told the boss that this will be my last afternoon here and I need to give you my open files.

"Gosh, thanks a lot." Dave faked a hurt look. "Just what we

need, more work!"

"Right, but Perry Mason here is going to lord it over us anyway," commented John as they walked to their desks.

Pat had a large box loaded with files from his desk.

"Here you are, big mouths."

"On a serious note, Gloria and her supervisor got fired this morning. The division manager, Mr. Watkins, walked into the supervisor's office unannounced and caught them in an uncompromising position. Watkins' secretary told us her boss got an anonymous letter postmarked Jonesboro."

Pat just smiled.

"You sure did some crazy things while you worked here," continued Dave.

"Pat's crowning achievement, however, was the delayed-action firecracker in the Great Atlanta executive washroom."

"Being fairly new, you've got me curious now. Just what is a delayed-action firecracker?" asked John.

"Tell him, Pat."

"I found out that a certain kind of heavy twine, if lit on one end, will smolder at the rate of about one inch every three minutes. So, if I take a firecracker and use about three and one-third of an inch of twine, my firecracker will go off in about ten minutes."

"I understand part of what you are saying.. How do you hook it all up?"

"Easy. You place a piece of twine about five inches long against the firecracker, with the required three and one-third inches above the fuse area. Then you wrap the firecracker fuse around the twine, and tape it to the firecracker. When the twine smolders down to the firecracker fuse, it ignites and goes off almost immediately."

"Man! You mean you actually put one of those things in the executive washroom?"

"Well, not at first. I had to work up to it. A few years ago I put a couple in a movie theater."

"You're nuts!"

"No, but you should have been there. The first few times I went to that theater, I noticed the side door was propped open a little with a book. I had two set for ten minutes, lit the twine, and tossed them in the door. A friend of mine went with me and we calmly went to the ticket window, bought our tickets, and got a seat at the other side of the theater. Then, if you will pardon my pun, we waited for the fireworks to start. It wasn't long until we heard two loud explosions! That wasn't the neatest part. It was the light. The explosions lit up the theater like two flash bulbs going off! You should have seen the ushers running up and down the aisles, opening the doors, and questioning people who had wet their pants. It was hysterical!"

Pat had painted a picture that made them all laugh.

"Then the washroom?"

"No. The first one was put under a can that went off under a moving car, but that's another story. Okay, the washroom. It happened last year. A mousey looking guy, Robert "Justin" Brown, an executive who works in personnel and never smiles, happened to be sitting on the can when one went off in the wastebasket. When the explosion was heard, people came running from all directions to see the stall door open and Justin Brown lying on the floor with his drawers wrapped around his feet! They never did find out who did it."

This brought more laughs from all of them.

"Say, he did my intake when I was hired," said Dave.

"He did the intake on many of the employees for years until the department got much larger and he was promoted," replied Pat.

"Well, Pat, I guess we had better get back to work."

After Pat left, John commented, "I still can't believe he is going to be a lawyer?"

* * *

Pat stopped and picked up a six-pack and a couple of Chinese take-out dinners and several Hershey Bars. After he put Max to bed, he walked up the stairs and yelled, "Hey, Eb, I'm home."

"I'm in the kitchen having a beer."

"You want the Mongolian Beef or the Pepper Steak?"

"The Pepper Steak. I heated up the oven so we can warm the food."

"Good. Let's do it and eat."

Pat told Eb about the office, the jail, court, and his visit to Great Atlanta, while they ate and drank beer.

After supper, they smoked a cigar and played a few songs.

"Pat, I feel like calling a Diamond number."

"Okay, Eb, but don't go too far with it."

Diamond was a telephone exchange where you first dialed the letters *DI* for the exchange in the West End of Atlanta, heavily populated with blacks. The phone book listed a last name as Lincoln. Eb dialed the number and when it started to ring, he signaled Pat to pick up the extension, as a female voice answered, with a heavy black accent.

"Hello, dis be de Lincoln residence."

"Say, baby, dis here be me."

"Who dat?"

"You know, baby. I done met you at the party."

"De one last Saturday night?"

"What be your first name again? All's I could member was Lincoln."

"Glenda."

"Yeah. Well, Glenda, you 'member me, I know."

"You be de tall one, light-skinned, mustache, and de Hawks cap?"

"Yeah, baby, dat's me."

"I was hopin' dat you be callin' me."

"Say, baby, when you going to give me some of that good stuff?"

"What's you be talkin' 'bout?"

"Baby, you knows 'xackly what's I be talkin' 'bout!"

"Hee, hee, hee, hee," squealed Glenda from way inside of her nose.

"Come on, baby, when can I meets you? And where can I meets you?"

"Look, I gots to go! Call me later, 'cause my ole man be pullin' up in de driveway!" Then she hung up and so did Eb.

"I got to get ready and go," said Eb.

"Go where?"

"A late hot date. You know, 'If the moon is bright and a man's not picky, the odds are great he'll dunk his dickie.'"

* * *

"Spider located Herb's late model van. We gonna do a job on it," said Hoss while taking a big chew of Redman.

"Nobody messes with a member of the Brotherhood!"

Three members of the Confederate Motorcycle Club, who were also members of The Brotherhood, followed Spider to where Herb had taken his family to the movies. It was crowded, so Herb had to park in back. This suited Skinny's friends just fine.

"I'll do the key work on it," volunteered Spider. "Zero, you cut the tires while Fatman pours a quart of Coke in the gas tank. Hoss, you be the lookout."

"Yah, the Coke should really do a job on that mother. Gum up everything real good," noted Fatman.

"I can't wait to see them come out of the movie!" Zero sneered.

The boys did their job and watched from a distance. They smoked a little dope and waited.

When Herb and his family came out of the movie, they saw their van with four flat tires, and the paint job had scratch marks along both sides of its entire length. Herb and Bonnie were sick when they saw it but it was not until later, when Herb tried to drive it home from the tire shop, that the fuel system stopped up and he came to a halt in the middle of Tara Boulevard.

Chapter 7

August - The Ming Dynasty

Julie Crawford got up and made breakfast for her daughter Mindy, who was nine years old and very intelligent for her age. Earlier, Julie's husband, Ralph, had left for work with the Atlanta Police Department.

"Hey, Mom, can I have some orange juice with my eggs and bacon?"

"I gave you a glass of milk. You want OJ, too?"

"Yes, ma'am."

"Okay, but you're now old enough to know where the refrigerator is located."

She filled her glass with OJ and looked at her mother. She was aware that her 28-year-old mother had a teenager's figure which men admired. Though she knew a little about *the birds and the bees*, she also knew more was going on than she was able to understand. Her mom was happy working at the law office for Mr. Patton, and she liked Herb as well. What really puzzled Mindy was that her dad put people in jail and Mr. Patton got them out! She did not understand how Mr. Patton made money as she heard her dad say that people in jail could not pay Mr. Patton.

Mindy was lucky to have such a good mom and dad and loved them both. She heard her dad talk about one of his bosses giving him a hard time. Her dad wanted out of the department but had too much time in, whatever that meant.

Mom said a man who parked in the same lot was giving her a hard time. Something about Mom taking *his* parking place. Mom said that no one had an assigned parking place and she parked there first. She said that he sure acted ugly toward her and even parked his truck so close that she couldn't get in

51

the driver's side. Mr. Butterworth had to get his car repainted 'cause somebody put scratches all over it. Grownups sure had a bunch of problems.

* * *

Julie was in the office, working on Pat's files, when he came in.

"Hi, Julie!"

Man she looked good today, but then she looked good every day!

"Good morning, Mr. Patton."

"Look, Julie, it's Pat. Remember?"

"I'm sorry, Mr. P..., ah, Pat, I keep forgetting."

"What's the matter, Julie? You sound down in the dumps. Here, have a Hershey Bar."

She told him about the man harassing her in the parking lot. She knew he worked for an insurance agency down the street because he went there every morning. She also told Pat about her husband's problems with Lieutenant Tomble, who gave him a hard time as often as he could. Her husband, Ralph, had more time in grade than Tomble, who was promoted over Ralph.

Pat asked a few questions, went into his office, and dialed his phone.

"Hi, Frank. This is Pat."

"How's the greenest attorney on the block?"

"Doing fine, but I need a favor from my favorite IBM computer hacker - - some info on one Lieutenant Antone Tomble, who works for the Atlanta Police Department. See if he has a Visa or Master Card."

"Hey, Pat. Heavy stuff, a cop and all."

"You can do it."

"I'll call back in about 15 minutes."

Pat looked out the window and saw *The Insurance Guy,* a small well-dressed Dapper Dan type, getting something out of his truck. Pat left the office and walked over to talk to him. As he approached the truck, Pat glanced at the distance between the truck and Julie's car. There were only a few inches, with no chance of her being able to get in the driver's side.

"Good morning, sir. Parked a little close to that car, aren't you?"

"Good morning to you, too, sir. Damned woman keeps taking my parking space." The man spoke in a high-pitched voice.

"I wasn't aware of parking spaces being assigned out here," answered Pat.

"They aren't, but I was here first."

"Isn't that going a little too far, parking her in like that?"

"Hell, no! She must think she's something because she works for some hot-shot attorney."

"Well, she works for me, so I guess that makes me a hot-shot attorney."

"Then tell her to stay out of my damn parking space!"

"Sir, because spaces are not assigned here, I'll do no such thing! However, we would both appreciate it if you would move your truck so the young lady can get in her car to go to lunch."

"It will be a cold day in Hell before I do that! I was here first!"

"Well, I tried," said Pat, as he turned away to return to the office. He made a point of glancing out of the back office window and saw *The Insurance Guy* go back to his office, without moving his truck.

Twenty minutes later Pat saw him go in the back of the coffee shop, which was on the same street as their office. The fronts of the buildings were on the main street of Jonesboro, directly across the street from the courthouse. Actually, there were two main streets because a railroad track ran through the middle of the town with a main street on both sides of the track. Pat's office was one of many buildings, which were connected to each other and covered the entire block, all backed up to an alley with parking for the tenants. *I   think it's time for a little lesson.*

He went out the back, looked to see if anyone was around, and took a plastic pill bottle out of his trunk. He removed two large roofing nails and put the bottle back in the trunk. Next, he double-checked Julie's car, and sure enough, there was no way she could get in the driver's side door although there was plenty of room on the other side of the truck. Pat placed one nail against the front tire and one against a rear tire in such a way that *The Insurance Guy* had to back over them in order to get out of the parking space. Pat returned to his office.

"There you are, Mr. Patton, ah, Pat. I've been looking all over for you. A man named Frank is on line one."

"Thanks, Julie; I'll take it in my office. Oh, by the way, how many men are in Ralph's department?"

"Around 12 or 13. Why?"

"Just curious. Thanks."

"Frank, sorry to keep you waiting."

"I know, you are now a busy attorney. Out working a tough case, right?"

"If you only knew, Frank. Did you get the info?"

"Easy man. He has both a Master Card and a Visa. I printed out a whole page of stuff on him. You want me to send it to you?"

"Please do, but I hope IBM doesn't find out about this. Right now, though, just give me the account numbers and his name as it appears on the cards. I'm not sure what I'm going to need, but this should cover it."

Frank gave him the information. "What are you going to do with it?"

"You know, Frank, maybe someday I'll have a computer of my own for my business. I know the ones out now are little more than toys, but wait a few years," said Pat, ignoring Frank's question.

"No way, Buddy! Do you have any idea how big these things are and how much they cost? No, they'll be limited to big businesses because they are the only ones that can afford them."

"I owe you one, Pal. Thanks!"

After he hung up, Pat thought, *A job for the great Eb,* and dialed his number.

"Paint and body shop. Eb speaking."

"This is Pat. You have a few minutes?"

"Sure. The boss is out sick today and I sort of took over."

Pat filled Eb in on what was going on.

"Yeah, Pat, I got the numbers. You say about 13 men?"

"Right. And what is a good expensive Chinese restaurant downtown that delivers lunch?"

"I think Julie mentioned two secretaries worked there, too. Make it five orders of Chicken Chow Mein, five of Pepper Steak, and five of Mongolian Beef."

"As good as done!" said Eb. He hung up and dialed the number.

"Ming Dynasty, can I help you?"

"Yes. Say dis be Lieutenant Antone Tomble speakin', and. . ."

"Yes, sir, I recognize your voice. We are always at your service, sir."

Wow, he must eat there often enough that this guy knows him! He said he recognized my voice as Tomble's. Man, I must be good!

"I decided to treat my staff to the very best lunch in Atlanta and I needs five orders of Chow Mein, five of Pepper Steak, and five of Mongolian Beef."

"Honorable Sir, would you like them to be deluxe with soup and eggroll?"

"Of course! Nothing is too good for my men."

"How do you wish to pay for this, Mr. Tomble?"

"Just put it on my Visa Card," said Eb giving him the card number. "Please put the receipt in the bag, and deliver it to Atlanta P/D, Second Floor, Room 208."

Eb called Pat back and said he didn't have any problems with the order. When Pat heard the whole story he broke out in a big smile. Sometimes things turn out unbelievably good. Eb came to his rescue again.

* * *

A short time later at the Atlanta Police Department, Second Floor, Room 208, a carry-out service man in a head-waiter's uniform brought in 15 Chinese dinners on a fancy cart with wheels.

"We, of the Ming Dynasty Restaurant, wish to announce that Lieutenant Tomble has instructed us to provide his staff with the very best lunch in the city of Atlanta. We have prepared lunch for 15, but I only count 14."

"Lieutenant Tomble is still in the Captain's office, so I guess one is for him."

"I can't believe this," said Sgt. Watkins.

"Man, look at all that food," said Det. Anderson.

"Wonder what got into Tomble?" said Det. Flynt, "He ain't never even bought us a Big Mac before."

"I will first serve the soup, then your choice of Chow Mein, Pepper Steak, or Mongolian Beef."

They all began to eat, wondering what was going on with Tomble. About this time the Lieutenant came in and was about to raise hell with everyone for having dinners on their desks.

"Thank you, Lieutenant"

"Very good, Lieutenant"

"What a surprise, Lieutenant!"

"Man, I 'preciates dis lunch, Lieutenant"

Tomble didn't know what to think! About then, the waiter came over to him with the 15th dinner and a receipt charging his Visa Card $296.25, plus tax, and a 15% gratuity. He was dumbfounded! That came to about $20 per person.

What de hell's going on! With half of de food eaten and de staff thanking me, I can't get out of it now. Better make de best of it, thought Tomble.

"That w a s v e r y n i c e of you, Lieutenant," said Sgt. Ralph Crawford, "And the food was really good!"

"It be's the least I can do for a good staff like I gots."

They all broke out with *For He's A Jolly Good Fellow*, and Tomble was actually getting embarrassed.

When Ralph got home that night, he couldn't wait to tell Julie what happened.

"And I had a full course Mongolian Beef Dinner, with soup, and egg roll, served to me by this fancy dressed delivery guy with hot Chinese tea and white cloth napkins! It was not on paper plates, but very nice china and real teacups. This waiter guy stayed until all of us were done and served more tea and then fortune cookies and some kind of cake. What a feed, but what I would really like to know is what possessed Tomble to do it?"

"Well, Honey, maybe he realized what a jerk he had become," said Julie.

"Not Tomble. It must have been something else, but I can't figure out what!"

"I wouldn't worry about it, Honey. After all it was a very nice gesture! It might be a better place to work."

"Maybe you're right. I really do feel good. Is Mindy asleep yet?"

"I'll check. You got something in mind?"

"After you check on Mindy, you'll find out what I got on my mind."

"Oh, my! Is that why they call you cops *dicks*?"

Ralph threw a pillow at Julie as she ran from the room.

* * *

The next day Julie went to work at 8:30 Aand noticed that at 9:00 the pickup that usually parked her in was pulled into another spot across from her. She could have sworn it was the same pickup she had seen last night sitting alongside the road with a couple of flat tires. Ah, it couldn't be, but it sure did look like it.

But, why did he all of a sudden decide to park over there?

Things were turning around for her and Ralph.

Pat came in from court around 10:30 and was in Herb's office when the phone rang.

"Pat Patton's office, Julie speaking."

"Hi, Julie. This is Eb. Is Pat busy?"

"He's in Herb's office, and I think Herb is giving him a new case."

"Just give him a message for me, okay?"

"Sure, let me get a pen, Eb. Okay, shoot."

"We have a double date Sat. night with some upscale gals and I just wanted to know if he might like to go to the Ming Dynasty for dinner. The food is good and the girls would love it."

"I wrote it down and will see that he gets the message."

Later, Pat came in with a new file.

"Got another case, Julie! Things are really going good."

"Eb called. Here's the message."

Pat read it.

Suddenly it clicked in Julie's mind, *The Ming Dynasty!*

"Pat, what do you know about *The Ming Dynasty?*"

"Why nothing, Julie." Pat had a big grin.

"You won't believe this, Pat, but *The Insurance Guy* didn't park me in this morning. Not only that, but I could have sworn he was sitting alongside of the road last night with a couple of flat tires. You wouldn't know anything about that either. Would you?"

Pat just kept smiling, but said nothing.

"Never mind. I don't even want to know!"

* * *

"There's her damn car!" announced Spider.

Betty Anderson Johnson was at a grocery store and had parked her car in the lot next to the street.

Three Harleys went by, each rider carrying a passenger with a brick in his hand.

CHAPTER 8

Middle of August - Moses

After plopping his 6'3" 160 lb. body on the couch and staring at the wall for an hour and a half, Sammy Joe Washington prepared to put on his Moses outfit. He had a good family, which loved him, though he had not been *right* since childhood, when hit in the head with a brick.

"I didn't mean to hit him! Just wanted to scare him, that's all," acknowledged the brick thrower.

Moses had lain unconscious for several days, and the doctors did not think he would make it. His mother, Mabel Moses Washington, had put him back in school, but he remained at a third-grade level, the grade he was in when injured. Mrs. Washington had enrolled Sammy in special classes, but he still did not advance. His mother had even transferred him to a religious school. Although he did learn some things about the Bible, he still did not progress. She was a good woman and tried to help him the best she could.

Sammy was now 23 years old and had a fixation on Moses, partially because that was his mother's maiden name. At times, he really believed he was Moses. When things were thrown up into the air, Sammy could not see them coming back down. He believed they went up to heaven. One day, Sammy gathered all of his Mother's silverware and threw them, one piece at a time, into the air. Many pieces were lost in the weeds.

He had another problem - - lighting filter-tip cigarettes, then standing them straight up on the filter-tip ends, placing them all over the house ... lit! His mother would find them on tables, windowsills, and most anywhere Sammy could find level. She was afraid he would burn her house down.

59

One time he was taken to the local hospital. His mother and aunt found him in the mental ward standing on his head in the hallway. Sammy was a nice guy, and harmless. The people in the neighborhood were used to him.

After staring at the wall, Sammy went upstairs to his room and took off all of his clothes, except for underwear. He had a pillowcase in which he had cut out places for his arms and head to go through. He slipped it over his head and put his arms through the holes like you would put on a shirt.

Next, he had a white towel that he wrapped around his head like a turban. Then came the sheet wrapped around his body to resemble a robe worn in the Old Testament days. Out of his closet came his special stick, which he had found in the woods. He had been told by a voice in his head to pick it up. It was very powerful, would turn into a snake, and the snake would tell him what to do, like in the Bible when Moses' staff turned into a snake.

He went downstairs and out the front door in his bare feet. When he had on his Moses outfit, he always went barefoot, even when it was cold outside.

* * *

Serpent and Rodent were two bad dudes who lived in the *hood*, about a block from Sammy. They were half-brothers.

Serpent got his street name because he threw snake eyes quite often when rolling the dice. He would lose his turn and his money when the two ones came up. Rodent got his name because he was a pack rat, never throwing anything away. His room looked like a trash heap. Both brothers looked upon people who worked for a living as suckers.

"Man, I be lookin' over dat bank, you knows, de Merchant and Farmer's Bank. They think dat they fool me, but I knows dey be havin' a big deposit Thursday afternoons aroun' 3:00 o'clock, to cover paychecks bein' cashed on Friday," said Serpent, his 210 lb. 6' tall frame not looking anything like a serpent.

"How much you think we can get?" asked Rodent who was 2" shorter and 30 lbs. lighter than his brother. At age 20, he was also a year younger.

"No tellin' but der must be thousands!"

"Man, a new set of wheels, and girls! Get high fer a week!" said Rodent.

"How 'bout we knock it off, Brother?"

"But, Serp, how we gonna do it?"

"I been in d e r several times. Piece of cake to knock over. Old guard, and d e y don't lock de safe door after d e armored car brings de money in."

"Guess they don't 'spect trouble in no small town bank."

"Guess not, Rodie. But, we needs another guy to do it. Two inside, and one in de get-away car."

"Man, I don't wants to give no loot to no one else."

"I thought of that, too, Rodie."

"You knows we can talk Sammy into anything."

"Give him a few hundred dollars. He don't know better."

"Yeah! I can steal us a fast car, a Camaro wif a 350 engine in it."

"Cool, man. You be's de get-away driver and me and Sammy goes into de bank. I be havin' a gun. I gives Sammy a knife, 'cause I don't trust him wif no gun. He might shoot one of us! We wear stockings over our heads, jus' like in de movies, and ..."

"And rubber gloves, too," interrupted Rodent.

"Right, brother. We don't wanna leave no finger prints. We needs to get spray paint and paint all de cameras we can find so dey don't get too many pictures of us on dem cameras. An, I needs a double-barrel shotgun -- a big mother! Sawed off, too! Scare the livin' hell out of dem mothers. And, a pistol in my belt. But, like I says, only a knife for Sammy."

"I can't wait! When does we do it?"

"Let's talk to Sammy first. I jus' saw him go by de house in his Moses suit."

They went running down the street and found Sammy preaching to a neighborhood dog.

". . . and I believe dat der be a dog heaven, so be a good doggie."

"Lo, Sammy," said Rodent.

"And he said: 'Bring forth two men from de promised

land,'" exclaimed Serpent.

"You be from de promised land?" asked Sammy.

"No. We messengers from you-know-who," continued Serpent. "We be bringin' a message from what was told us by an angel."

"Dat be right," echoed Rodent.

"He told us dat demons be takin' over de Merchants and Farmer's Bank, and be usin' de money to do sinful things. We been told to relieve dem of de money and I's to give it to de angel next week."

"Yeh, but he said fer us to give you $200 for helping out! We be payin' you out of our own pockets," announced Rodent with a slap on Sammy's shoulder.

"You talked to an angel? And, he said to give me $200? And, we takes it from demons what has it at de bank?"

"He also said dat if you tells anyone, and I mean anyone, 'bout dis, a lightnin' bolt will come out of de sky and you be nothin' but ashes!" said Serpent.

"Good thinkin', brother!" continued Rodent.

"What's you mean?" asked Sammy.

"We means dat we be thinkin' dat dis is a good way to fight demons," said Serpent.

"Right man, jus' tell me what to do, and I'll never tell anyone 'bout it. But, wait! I has to ask de Snake what he be thinkin'."

They both just looked at Sammy talking to the stick.

"The Snake thinks dat we should send a plague to strike dem down first."

"Tell de Snake dat the angel said dat if we did not do dis, dat you would have to throw him into de burnin' bush," instructed Serpent.

"No, not my Snake! He says okay!"

"We'll pick you up dis Thursday. . ."

"What be today?" interrupted Sammy.

"Dis be Monday. As I was sayin', we be pickin' you up Thursday, right after lunch. We gotta be at de bank right after 3:00. In fact, we needs to be der earlier to watch them bank people and go in as soon as de armored car leaves."

* * *

Pat was at the office working when Julie told him the Court Administrator was on the phone.

"Hi, Mr. Brown, this is Pat speaking."

"Pat, we have another one for you, but the judge wants you to go see him ASAP. He is pissed off at the guy and wants him in court this week to throw the book at him. But - - he wants the guy represented when he does it."

"What did he do, or allegedly do?"

"First of all his name is Buster Bradley. Second, the story is he owed his ex-wife a lot of back child support and when she threatened to have him arrested, he took a baseball bat and beat her car up so bad it died. It was an older car and I'm told he totaled it out."

"Aggravated Assault on a car, huh?" teased Pat. "Well, I guess I had better pick up the paperwork and go see him. I'm guessing he's still in jail?"

"You got it, or rather you're going to get it. The complaint, that is."

Pat went over to the Court Administrator's Office and picked up the paperwork on Buster, then went to the jail. The deputy took him to the library again. Pat was getting used to this, as he had been there several times before. He took a seat and waited.

"Click, clank," went the door. In came Buster.

"Click, clank," the big steel door closed. Then through the jail smell and noise, Pat could not believe what he was seeing! Buster was a big redneck, had his head shaved, an earring in one ear, and a T-shirt that said *Death to Everyone* with a skull and crossbones. Buster moved his six foot two, 245 pound body like Frankenstein, slowly, his black deep-set eyes glaring at Pat.

What am I doing in here, locked in a cell they call a library with this nut case?

"Man, I might as well tell you something right up front. They think I'm weird around here."

"Yeah?" asked a bewildered Pat.

"Do you know why they think I'm weird, man?" asked Buster in a loud crazy voice.

"No." Pat used a very submissive tone.

"Cause I was walking around with a sheet wrapped around me, man!" explained Buster with an arm motion like he was throwing a sheet around himself.

Pat listened with attentive disbelief but said nothing.

"Do you know why I had that sheet thrown around me man?" asked Buster in a louder, crazier voice.

"No, no."

"'Cause I didn't have no pants on, man!"

Pat just looked at him, not knowing what to say.

"Do you know why I didn't have no pants on, man?"

"No idea."

"Cause I'm a clean person man, and I wash 'em every two weeks!"

Get me out of this cell!

Pat managed to get the guy seated at the table and did an intake on the case. Both the child support and the auto damage charges were misdemeanors, meaning the punishment could not exceed 12 months in jail plus a $1,000 fine on each charge. That also told Pat the car was not worth much or it would have been a felony. The poor woman must have been getting by with a piece of a car when this creep beat it to death.

Pat knew he would face something like this eventually, but he did not think it would come this soon. He detested Buster for what he did to this poor woman but was appointed to represent him. Pat felt he had to do his best for Buster or not represent him at all. If he laid down on the job, he was not really representing him. Pat rationalized, and rightly so, that he was only one cog in the wheel of justice. The DA, or Solicitor in this case, was not playing games. He was trying to get Pat's client convicted. The judge or the jury would decide the verdict and sentence, not the attorney.

* * *

Pat went to see Solicitor Nevan, to ask if they could talk to the judge about Buster's case. Nevan was agreeable and they went to see the judge.

Judge Jim Price was in his middle sixties and did not

like fathers who refused to support their children.

Pat argued, "While 90 days in jail would make everyone feel good, it was not going to get money to the mother for child support."

The judge agreed with Nevan that Buster should have at least 90 days, if not more.

"And if he wants to go to trial and loses, I will give him 12 months on each count and run them consecutively! You can tell him to take it or leave it!"

"That goes for me, too!" agreed Solicitor Nevan.

"I'm calling this case for arraignment at 9:00 tomorrow morning. He can take the deal or he can demand a trial."

"But, Judge," said Pat, "that sounds like he is being punished for wanting to exercise his right to a trial by jury."

"No, son. I'm not punishing him if he wants to go to trial. I'm just giving him a discount if he doesn't."

* * *

Pat decided he had to take control and went back to the jail and explained that they had to go to the arraignment, which was where Buster would plead either guilty or not guilty. If he entered a plea of guilty, he would be sentenced to 90 days in the county jail. He would also be ordered to pay present and back child support when he got out. If he wanted to go to trial, his case would be put on a trial calendar in two to four weeks; he would lose and be given 12 months in jail on each count.

"But, why do you say I'll lose?"

"Do you have cancelled checks or receipts signed by her to show that you are paid up to date?"

"Well...no."

"And, a neighbor saw you beating up her car with a baseball bat, right?"

"Ah, yeah."

"And, you admitted all of this to the police, right?"

"Ah, yeah."

"And, this is not the first time you have been to court for back child support, is it?"

"Ah, no."

"You will be lucky to get 12 months if you go to trial and lose. The judge could give you another 12 months on the car charge, Criminal Damage To Property, and run the sentences consecutively! Just like he told me he would."

"What's that mean?"

"Let's see, 12 months plus 12 months equal 24 months. Two years, Buster! Two long years."

"Damn bitch! I should have knocked her lights out, too!"

"What?"

"So, you think I ought to plea, huh?"

"Buster, tell me what you want to do, okay?" Pat was trying hard to control his disgust.

"I guess I'll plea."

"No, you don't guess anything! You either plea or you don't. You are either guilty or you aren't."

"Okay, I'll take the 90 days."

* * *

The next morning Pat pled Buster out in Judge Price's court.

After the plea, he was talking to Herb.

"Even though I cannot stand the man, I don't feel like I did all I could for Buster."

"You could go back and talk to the judge. He can modify his own order without any type of a hearing within the same term of court. This is the July term, which includes July, August, and September."

"Herb, I would rather take a beating than talk to him again, but I will."

"Even if the judge will not agree, you will know that you did your best for your client. This is what I meant by either doing your best for a client you can't stand, or not representing them at all."

Pat went back to Judge Price, who said that if Buster could come up with $200 to buy school clothing for his children, then he would reconsider the jail time. Being the sorry bum that he was, Buster could not come up with $50, let alone the $200, so he stayed in jail. He was being punished but it was not helping his ex-wife or his kids.

Well, I tried, thought Pat.

* * *

On visitation day at Jackson, Skinny was surprised when he heard his name called out for a visit. He went to the guard who called his name and got a pass to go to the visitation area.

"Hi, Spider," said Skinny as he and Spider went through the ritual handshake.

"Hi, yourself, man. Me and the Brothers miss you."

"What have you guys been up to?"

"We been workin' on the cars of some of them friends of yours, if you know what I mean." Spider gave a sly smile.

"Tell me 'bout it. I need a good laugh."

"We got 'em good, Skinny. Me and the boys keyed the damn attorney's van, cut up all four tires, and poured a quart of Coke in his gas tank. We even put extra sugar in the Coke. So, when that stupid attorney got the tires fixed, it wouldn't be long afore the carb got so sugared up the motor wouldn't run."

"I'd love to have seen that!" laughed Skinny.

"You'll love this. Three of us rode by your ex's car and put a brick through the windshield. I think another one put a nice dent in the hood."

"Good job!"

"So, what's you been doin' here to keep busy?"

"Like I told you before. I'm not long for this place. Got my GED and a good job at the school. Got them suckers eatin' out of my hand. They think I'm reformed, like I'm just tryin' to help other poor inmates go straight. What a joke! I'm lookin' fer someone to help me get out of here. I don't have it all worked out, but I'll get out or die trying. And speakin' of dying, some people will have very short lives after I get out of this place."

* * *

Just as Pat turned into his driveway, a Snap-On-Tool truck pulled up in front of the house. It was George trying to sell him more tools. He knew Pat worked at the cycle shop and had stopped by on his way home. George lived on the next block.

"Yo, Pat! Need anything today?"

Pat had an account and the tool man would sell to the guys on time with 0% interest. The tools were expensive. However, they were very good quality.

"Matter of fact, George, I need a pair of curved needle-nose pliers."

"Come on into the house." George opened up the side door of the truck for Pat.

Pat looked through the pliers until he found what he wanted.

"I'll take these."

"On your account?"

"No." Pat
handed him a $100 bill.

"The law business must be treating you right. How much longer you going to twist wrenches at the cycle shop?"

"The way things are going, not too much longer. I just won't have time."

"Say, Pat, I got a hot phone number if you want it."

"Tell me about it, brother."

"Actually it involves two girls because they like to do it as a community event. You know, all four in the same bed. Or you and the two of them at the same time."

"You got to be kidding; you surely have to be."

"Not at all. Kim and Connie. Kim is the most attractive one. She has long black hair, nice body, about 25, but has a trash mouth. Connie is about the same age, reddish hair, average face, and a little on the plump side, but not fat. They both like to screw like minks and even provide their own rubbers. They won't let you near them without one. Want the number?"

"Are you serious? Does a bear shit in the woods? I have to see them for myself. Also I imagine Eb's getting horny by now, as it's been at least five days since he got any," said Pat laughing.

"Here's their number. Tell them George gave it to you.

They live together."

"You still see them?"

"Every once in a while, but my wife keeps a short leash on me. They understand."

"Thanks, George. I'll tell you how we made out."

CHAPTER 9

Late August - The Bank Heist

Serpent and rodent picked up Sammy in a stolen red 1980 Z28 Camaro that had only a little over 2,000 miles on it. The car was hardly broken in yet and the boys almost decided to go joy riding instead of robbing a bank. They were having so much fun with the 350-cubic inch high performance engine that they even stopped and bought a 12-pack of beer to celebrate.

"Let's see here now." Serpent drank a beer. "Seventh Street Stan got me a 12-gauge sawed-off double-barrel shotgun, and I got me a .38 Special revolver, too. Hmmm, and I gots a pump shotgun fer Rodent to have in de car. Look, Rodie, a Remington 12-gauge shotgun wif a sawed off barrel! And fer you, Sammy, I gots dis beautiful huntin' knife and a supersized can of green spray paint."

"Thank you, Mr. Serpent, but dis here knife and dem guns won't hurt no demons."

"Most likely not. We can use dem to get their money so dey don't do bad things wif it. You would like dat, wouldn't you, Sammy?"

"Yes, sir, Mr. Serpent. I sure would."

"Hey, Rodie, where did you gets dis neat car anyway?"

"I went fer a ride dis mornin' at de Chevy place and forgot to take it back."

Laughing, Serpent responded, "He forgot to take it back! You get it, Sammy; he forgot to take it back!"

They also forgot the car had a recognizable dealer's tag. By now, every cop in Georgia had it on his list of stolen vehicles.

"I sure likes dis sunroof. All you gots to do is push de button and open she comes," commented Serpent, eyeing some paper bags.

"What's in dem paper bags?" asked Rodent.

"I's stopped by de hardware store and gots us some roofing nails. See, if de cops be chasin' us, we can toss a bag of nails out de window of de sunroof and dey be gettin' flat tires and we be home free. Kool, huh?" Serpent had seen it done in a movie.

"Brother, dat sure is some kind of good thinkin'. De paper bags will bust easily when dey hits de road."

At 2:oo, they parked across the street from the bank located just outside of Riverdale. The armored car would deliver the money around 3:00. They wanted to be early in case the armored car came sooner than expected. However, three black men sitting across the street from a bank for an hour, drinking beer, was bound to get someone's attention. A bank employee had been watching them since they got there.

"Here comes de armored car!" yelled an excited Rodent."

"Good. It will only be 'bout ten minutes and dey be in and out again. Rodent, Sammy! Here be de pantyhose to put over yo heads. Trys it on before you be goin' in."

"Man dis is weird! Look at me," said Rodent.

"Good,'cause I can't tell who yo is. Sammy, yo looks good, too!"

"Hey, Serpie, why am I puttin' dis over ma head? I ain't goin' in de bank. I be goin' to pick yo guys up when you run out de door," commented Rodent.

"Dat's right, Brother, I be puttin' one on. Sammy, let's be puttin' on our rubber gloves, too. Dey should be comin' out of de bank what has de demons. Any minute now!"

"I gots my knife, but it won't be hurtin' no demons. Maybe I could paint 'em."

"How you gonna be paintin'....."

"Gonna be paintin' dem green, too!" interrupted Sammy.

"Say, brother, I gots a question."

"What's dat, Rodie?"

"Does we have time to goes to de gas station?"

"Why, man?

"'Cause I jus' be lookin' at de gas gauge and it be mighty low."

"Man, I can't believe dis! Why didn't you fill it up?" asked Serpent.

"Cause I didn't have no money, man!"

"Den it will just have to do."

"I be paintin' every demon dat I sees," said Sammy.

* * *

A teller inside the bank asked one of the armored car guards if he noticed three black men sitting in a car across the street.

"I was about to ask you the same thing," said the guard.

The teller told a VP, who was about to call the police just as the armored car left and the boys came in, wearing pantyhose covering their faces, and the legs were hanging down behind them. The elastic band for the waist was around their necks holding the pantyhose on. They were two of the most unlikely looking bank robbers imaginable with the exception of the sawed-off shotgun that Serpent waived around. He also had the .38 tucked in his belt and Sammy had a hunting knife and a large can of green spray paint in his hands while he babbled about demons.

A victim of too many gangster movies, Serpent shouted, "All of you mothers gets your hands up, 'cause dis here be's a stick up!"

He yelled as loud as he could, which was considerable.

"I come to do battle wif you demons!" yelled Sammy, as he spray painted the bank guard.

The people in the bank shivered with fear, as they had no idea what kind of lunatics these were.

"Gives me all de money you gots! I wants de money what come in dat armored car, too! Hands up or I be ventilatin' you!"

The frightened tellers gathered up all the loose money they had and gave it to Serpent in three bags, along with a red die bomb.

In the meantime, while Sammy was spray-painting all of the TV cameras he could find, three different tellers pressed their silent alarm buttons. Sammy spray-painted two of the tellers along with the security cameras. They freaked out as this hooded nut with a knife sprayed them. Sammy held one of the female tellers on the floor while the other two got the money. She had panicked and tried to run out the door.

"We gots de money. Let's get de hell out of here!" ordered Serpent, as he looked back at two green tellers and a green bank guard.

"And don't none of you demons try to come after us neither," said Sammy, waving his knife and spray can around, as he stopped to examine a picture of The Ten Commandments

"I said let's get de hell out of here!" repeated Serpent while looking at Sammy.

Rodent saw them coming and pulled the car up in front of the bank, and Sammy and Serpent jumped in. That's when they saw the first police car.

"Head for I75," yelled Serpent.

"Man, dem cops be right on our tail. Should I go fer da alley?" asked Rodent.

"Yeah, you knows where to turn."

"Man, der be three cop cars now!" exclaimed Rodent.

"Get ready to turn! Hold on, Sammy!" suggested Serpent.

The Camaro made a sharp left turn, then a right, followed by a left into an alley.

"I hopes you measured right, brother," questioned Rodent. Serpent had stolen some cable and cable clamps earlier in the week and measured a Camaro's height in a parking lot. He had previously measured the height of a police car. Serpent hoped he had strung the cable high enough for the Camaro to get under it, but low enough it would stop a police car. He had seen this done on a TV show. The cable went from one telephone pole to another, going across a little-used alley.

"Here we go," yelled Rodent. "Hold on!"

The Camaro cleared the cable easily, but the patrol car

behind him also made it through, minus blue lights, siren, and antennas.

"Damn, dey still be comin'!" yelled Serpent.

"I's be headin' fer de 'spress way," yelled Rodent.

The police still were on their tail but could not use radios, leaving the way clear for the boys to get on I75.

"Captain Keefauver, we no longer have contact with the patrol car that was on the tail of Willie (Rodent) Cason's car," informed the dispatcher.

"How did you get his name?" asked the Captain.

"He drove away this morning from Denton Chevrolet in a new Camaro he said he was test driving. He must have forgotten the salesman had asked to see his driver's license before he could go for a test ride. A car radioed in that the getaway car had a Denton tag on it. The salesman copied it on one of them machines that copies stuff. They said the picture was not great, but all of the printed information looked good.

"Captain, I've been following them on the map. I believe they are headed for I75." Lieutenant Keller emphasized I75.

"I think you're right! Put out an all-points bulletin on Willie (Rodent) Cason, and his half-brother, Jerome (Serpent) Smith, who is probably with him along with an unidentified black male," said Captain Keefauver.

"They'll have to get on I75 at the Hwy 138 Exit, but we have no way of knowing if they will go north or south," said Lieutenant Keller.

"Captain, we now have a patrol car at I75 and Hwy 138," informed the dispatcher.

"Good! Let's get some cars alerted both north and south, just in case."

Rodent managed to stay ahead of the pursuing police car and finally reached the expressway.

"Head north!" shouted Serpent.

"Oh, a cop car be ahead and is tryin' to block us!" cried Rodent.

"Get aroun' him! Sammy, get those bags of roofing nails back there and hand them to me!" yelled Serpent.

Rodent got around the police car and the officer took three quick shots at them, but missed.

Now afraid he might hit another car, the officer stopped shooting, got back into his car, and got on his radio.

"The suspects are headed north on I75 and just left the Hwy 138 exit."

"Why dey be shootin' at us?" asked Sammy. "All we done was take money from dem demons."

"Give me dose nails. Now!" screamed Serpent at Sammy, as they headed north on 75.

"Here dey is, Mr. Serpent."

Serpent took one of the bags and tossed it up into the slipstream above the sunroof. The paper bag burst when the roofing nails hit the road, and three out of the four police cars got flat tires. Dozens of other cars suffered the same fate! One police car was still on their tail, so Serpent tossed out another bag of nails.

"Gottem."

Now 5:00 PM, traffic was heavy before he tossed the nails out onto the road. There were hundreds of nails on the highway and traffic was jammed up for miles within a matter of a few minutes, creating Atlanta's worst traffic jam of the year, and maybe of all time. Serpent tossed out another bag. He was having fun.

Meanwhile, in the back seat, Sammy opened up one of the moneybags, which set off a dye bomb that covered everything with red dye. Sammy thought the demons were coming at him from the red gates of Hell. He threw the moneybag out the top of the sunroof and it made a red money snowstorm. People going in the opposite direction stopped their cars and ran to gather up the money. Now there was a gridlock in the south-bound lanes, too!

Suddenly, Sammy's stick came alive in his mind and he started swinging it at demons. One swing caught Rodent on the side of his head and he almost lost control of the car. Serpent grabbed the stick and calmed Sammy down.

"Dat crazy goofball threw a whole bag of money out de window," yelled Rodent.

"Dat's okay, We couldn't spend no red money no how," the more intelligent Serpent knew.

"Right thinkin', brother, we jus be keepin' on keepin' on!

But - keep Sammy still."

"We be home free! Nothing' be behind us!" yelled Serpent excitedly. Then he tossed out the last bag of nails for good measure.

"Yeah, brother, we did it!" yelled a jubilant Rodent.

"No demons after us either," claimed Sammy.

That's when they ran out of gas, just a quarter mile short of a road block, consisting of two 18-wheelers, 12 police cars, and a helicopter. They were caught with the money, guns, panty hose, knife, and an empty spray can of green paint.

"Captain, we got them," grinned Lieutenant Keller. "Three red men, in a red car, with a red interior."

CHAPTER 10

Early September - Kim and Connie

Pat had another busy day at the office. Now Friday and he was about to put the week behind him.

"Eb, I'm home." Pat set two six-packs in the refrigerator. Eb already had a six-pack cooling and had one in his hand.

"Well, what's on for tonight?" asked Pat.

"We could always call Sally and Ann."

"Yeah, and get shot by a jealous husband."

"How about we call a Diamond number?"

"You need to let those Diamond numbers alone. Someday you'll get your butt kicked good!"

"How about a redneck number?"

"You better let those alone, too. Call? Say, that reminds me. Snap-On George gave me what he says is a phone number of a sure thing. Let me find it. What time is it? Okay, 5:30. Maybe it's not too late to call them."

As Pat was telling Eb about his conversation with George, he found the number and dialed it. When it started ringing, he motioned to Eb to pick up the extension.

"Hello," a husky, sexy female voice answered.

"I'd like to speak to Kim or Connie, please."

"This is Kim. Who's this?"

"Kim, I don't mind saying you really sound good over the phone."

"Who is this, damn it!"

"Sorry. My name is Pat. I got your phone number from George ... the Snap-On Tool man."

"Yeah, I know all about his tool."

The boys did a double take at that comment.

"George told me you and another girl named Connie live together and I should give you a call."

"How do you know George?"

"He lives down the street from me and I also know him from the Honda Cycle Shop."

"Are you a biker?"

"No, but I ride and also work there part-time."

"Oh. What do you do full-time?"

"I'm an attorney."

"Really! You mean a real law attorney?"

"That's right."

"Connie, get on the extension. I'm talking to a real law attorney!"

"Good, because I have a roommate who is on my other extension."

"Hey, this is Connie."

"And this is Eb."

"And this is Pat, Connie."

"Connie, I been talking to Pat; he's a real law attorney."

"Wow! Where's your office?"

"In Jonesboro. Across from the Courthouse. I'm in with Herb Butterworth."

"I heard of him. He used to be a DA and sent a friend of mine to jail on a drug charge," said Kim with a frown.

"Pat, what do you look..."

"Wait a minute, Connie. I talked to him first!"

"Okay, but answer the question. You, too, Eb."

The guys described themselves, and the girls did the same. Of course they all lied a little.

"We were about to go out to Morrison's for supper. Would you girls like to join us?" asked Pat.

"Sure," responded Kim, semi-enthusiastically.

"Are we doing something afterward?" asked Connie.

"Anything you girls want to do is fine with us," added Eb.

"What do you have in mind?" asked Pat.

"Why don't we all come back to our apartment?" asked Connie, with another question.

"Sounds good to us!" agreed Pat, winking back at Eb.

"Get some rubbers on the way over," ordered Kim.

"What?" said Eb in disbelief, almost swallowing his cigar.

"I said stop and get some rubbers! We don't got no more, and we ain't going to do it without them," said Kim.

"That's right," stated Connie. "We're not on the pill and we don't want to get pregnant."

That makes two of us or I guess four of us, thought Pat.

"When the frost is on the pumpkin, that's the time for dickie dunkin'," said Henry Wadsworth Eb.

That brought out a laugh from all of them.

Neither Pat nor Eb had ever had a conversation like this, but they agreed to meet at Morrison's in an hour. The boys got a quick shower, and then each optimistically put three packs of rubbers in their pockets. When Pat and Eb arrived at Morrison's, the girls were already there. The only one who was mildly disappointed was Eb, as Connie, although not homely, had a plain look about her and was a little overweight. Kim was tall, built well, had an attractive face, beautiful long dark hair, and, as warned, a trash mouth. One thing Eb did like about Connie was her boobs. They were a lot bigger than Kim's, and hers were not small.

They ate, talked, and got to know each other. After supper, they went over to the girls' apartment. They each had a beer and the girls both sat on Kim's bed. Pat and Eb sat down with them.

"Well, did you guys bring some rubbers?" asked Kim.

"Sure did," said Pat and Eb together.

"Well, Connie, what are we waiting for?" Kim was unbuttoning her blouse.

Connie followed Kim's example. The boys looked in fascination as the girls stripped, not bashful in the least bit.

Pat and Eb took the hint and started taking off their shirts. The girls threw their bras at them. The boys did not make it home that night.

* * *

Pat went to the office Monday morning and Herb

confirmed the former Mrs. Anderson, now Mrs. Johnson, was coming in at 10:00 to talk about doing an adoption. Her new husband had been a father to the children for a year. Georgia law required the stepparent to prove that the natural father had abandoned his children before the court would terminate paternal rights. The Johnsons were meeting with Pat, and Herb agreed to sit in to help.

"Jeez, fellows. Mrs. Anderson and her husband are here already and it's only 9:45," announced Julie.

"Remember, Pat," said Herb, "half of what you do in law practice is covering your own tail. Keep a very good set of time sheets, describing in as much detail as time permits, all work done. I know it's a pain in the rear end, but you also need to make notes of every conversation you have with your clients. Sometimes your biggest problem is your own client!"

Julie showed them in and introductions were made all around. Pat, with Herb's help, explained the procedure.

"In order to have the stepparent adoption granted, the legal father must either consent to the adoption or have the court terminate his rights. Will he surrender his rights?"

"Hell, no!" answered John, who had known Betty and Skinny for years as a neighbor. "He never was a father to those two kids, but he'll hate me for doing this and feel like I'm taking them from him!"

"I'm glad he'll be in jail for a long time because I'm afraid of what he might try to do to us, or anyone who he thinks is a threat to him," said Betty. "He beat me and the kids. And, I do mean beat, many times. I'm scared of him, and so are the children. I heard he killed more than one person, and I believe it. Not only that but I recently got my windshield smashed by a brick thrown by some Harley riders. I feel in my bones that Skinny put them up to it."

"I could whip Skinny's butt in a fair fight but he doesn't know the meaning of fair. He would blow me away with a shotgun and think nothing of it. Just like Betty, I'm not ashamed to admit he also scares the hell out of me."

"Skinny? Is that the same guy I read about in the newspaper who got sent up for armed robbery?" asked Pat.

"The one and only. And - Skinny won't do a surrender."

"I'm glad I don't have to defend him, 'cause he sounds like a very bad dude!"

"You got that right!"

"Well, then we'll have to plan on how we'll do the termination. What do you suggest, Herb? Herb?"

"I was just thinking ... could Skinny have had anything to do with the trashing of my van? Come to think about it, witnesses say they saw some rough-looking motorcycle characters about the time my van got keyed."

"I wouldn't put it past him to have told some of his Brotherhood friends to do it. After all, you handled my divorce."

"Herb, what do you think about the termination?"

"Although it's much harder, we'll have to go for a termination of his parental rights. Believe me, this is not easy, and it should not be easy to take a father's children from him.

"The law says abandonment can be proven in two ways. First, did the father have significant contact with the children? Did he visit, write, telephone, send cards, buy birthday or Christmas presents, etc.? Second did he support his children, either by living with them or sending child-support payments? Both of these have to be for more than a one-year period."

"If he did not do the above," interjected Pat, you can add to that *without justifiable cause.* For example, he could have been unable to do those things because he was lying in a hospital in a coma."

"He hasn't done none of that in well over a year," replied Betty. "He wasn't in no hospital neither!"

"Well, Pat, it looks like we have a good shot at terminating his parental rights," said Herb.

"Any questions?" asked Pat.

"None I can think of," answered Betty.

"Okay. Come back after lunch and we'll have the paperwork done. After the adoption is signed, I'll have Julie take it over to the courthouse to be filed," said Pat.

The Johnsons were there promptly at 1:00 PM to sign the adoption paperwork.

"I'm glad that's done but I'm worried about Skinny's

reaction when he gets served. I know he's in prison but he has some dangerous friends on the outside," said Betty as she left. Her husband agreed.

Pat should have paid attention and thought twice before taking the case.

* * *

"Julie", said Pat, after the Johnsons left. "I'll be gone this afternoon on some personal business.

"Okay, Boss. You don't have any appointments this afternoon."

* * *

Pat pulled into the Fulton County Health Department parking lot. Although he lived in Clayton County, he was going to say he lived in Fulton. He didn't want anyone in Clayton County to know about this. Part of College Park was in Fulton County. Pat walked in the door and over to the desk.

"I need to talk to someone about a possible case of venereal disease."

"What's you got, son," asked an older nurse sitting at the desk.

"I hope nothing." Pat was embarrassed.

"What's ya mean by that, son?"

"Well, I don't usually do this, but a friend and I went out with two very loose girls over the weekend, and I'm worried I may have caught something. Like I said, I don't normally go out with that type of girl."

"Yeah, that's what they all say," laughed the nurse.

Pat felt like walking out, but he was worried. The nurse took him to a doctor who examined him but could find nothing. Next came a blood test.

"Son, no news is good news." The nurse winked at him. Now Pat was totally embarrassed. "What do you mean by that?"

"If you have something, we will notify you by mail. If not, you will not hear from us."

"Thank you." Pat hurried out the door. He went home from there and ate a TV dinner with Eb. At first Eb laughed, then it sunk in, and he began to have a worried look on his face.

"You think we're clean?" asked a concerned Eb.

"I sure hope so," answered Pat. "Pray I don't get a letter from the Fulton County Health Department."

Later in the evening, as they were drinking a beer and watching a Clint Eastwood Dollar movie, the doorbell rang. Eb looked out the window.

"Hell, it's them!" yelled Eb.

"Who's them?"

"Kim and Connie, friends of the Fulton County Health Department!"

"No! Don't answer the door!"

The doorbell rang, and rang, and rang.

Then it stopped and they heard two women screaming in unison, "We want some dick! We want some dick! We want some dick!"

"Eb, I've got to go to the door or the neighbors will have the police over here!"

Pat went to the door and Kim and Connie wanted in. He told them he had to go to bed so he would be awake for court in the morning, and Eb had to go to work early. They said that they were thirsty, so Pat gave them each a cold beer and finally got them to leave. As they left, they uttered a string of cuss words that would embarrass Satan.

CHAPTER 11

September - The Interview

"Hi, Brian," Pat greeted the Court Administrator. "I understand you have a case for me."

"I sure do. Sammy Joe Washington. You've got one of three bank robbers, or should I say *alleged* bank robbers? He's a 23-year-old black male with a history of psychological problems. He was caught with two other men trying to get away from the police. They hit the Merchants and Farmers Bank in Riverdale. You really have your work cut out for you on this one."

"Sounds like it to me. I read about the *Five-O'Clock Traffic Bandits in* the newspaper. From what I read, a lot of people were upset with caught in that traffic mess. A county full of pissed-off people could make jury selection very difficult. Herb's secretary, Rhonda, got a flat tire and was two hours late getting home from work and she didn't leave the office until 7:00 that night."

"Yeah, I know Rhonda and I both got caught in it."

"I take it Mr. Washington is in jail."

"Where else? The only reason I'm giving you a case this serious is because Herb promised to help you with it. Bank robbery is pretty heavy for a new guy."

"I understand, Brian, and I promise to do my best for Mr. Washington."

"I know you will. Good luck! Here's what I have on him." Brian handed Pat the file.

"See you, Brian," said Pat, over his shoulder, as he was walking out.

84

"And, Pat. Please see him today."

"I'm on my way."

* * *

This trip to the jail was far different from his first, as he now had his Bar card, knew most of the jailers, and pretty much knew the procedure. After he checked in, he had to get on the elevator to go to the second floor. Pat had more than one person tell him about the long, long ride from the first to the second floor. It was where an inmate could be beaten and no one would see or hear a thing. He heard that from clients and attorneys too many times for there not to be some truth to it. Getting smart with a cop, or spitting in his face, has consequences.

When he got to the second floor, Pat was taken to the library and took a seat. He could not help thinking about Bobby McNew and Buster Bradley. Bobby was out on the street, a ticking time bomb, while Buster was still behind bars.

I'll never get used to the jail smell.

"Click," he heard the door being unlocked. "Clang," it opened up.

In walked this tall, very thin, black man, with a dazed look on his face. He looked like anything but a bank robber.

Pat got up and offered his hand. Sammy shook it with a hand limp as a piece of overcooked spaghetti.

"Hello, Mr. Washington, I'm Pat Patton, your court-appointed attorney. Please have a seat."

Sammy sat down looking strangely at Pat. "Did they send you?" asked Sammy.

"You mean the Court Administrator's Office?"

"No, man, da demons, man."

"I'm sorry, Mr. Washington, but I don't understand what you're talking about."

"I took der money, man. Dem demons sent you, didn't dey?"

"No, Mr. Washington, no demons sent me."

"Is you sure?"

"Yes, I'm sure."

"Well, okay. If you says so."

"Let me start again. My name is Pat Patton. I'm an attorney, and the Court Administrator's Office sent me, not some demon, to represent you in court. Do you understand what I have just told you?"

"Yes, Mr. Patton. I understands."

"Good. You are charged, along with two other men, with robbing a bank. Do you understand that?"

"Yes, Mr. Rodent and Mr. Serpent. Dem and me took evil money from dem demons."

"Let's get this straight." Pat blinked his eyes and shook his head.

"You and two other guys robbed the bank, right? And their names were, uh, Mr. Rodent and Mr. Serpent?"

"Dat's right."

"Who are the demons?"

"Man, you know! In de Bible dey's angels and demons."

"Oh, okay. So you believe demons were in the bank?"

"Yeah, man. I done seed them! They look like people, but they couldn't fool me. No! No! They can look like anything. De last time dat I saw dem, dey was, ah, green."

"Can I call you Sammy?"

"Yah, Mr. Patton, dat's ma name."

"Sammy. What did the demons have to do with the money in the bank?"

"Mr. Serpent told me dat dem demons had money in dat bank. We had to take it, 'cause dey was going to do bad things wif it. 'Sides, Mr. Serpent was goin' to give me $200."

"Well, that was very nice of him because the police report here says $153,426 was recovered. It was in bank money bags marked Merchants and Farmers Bank. A third bag is missing."

"Dem demons was going to use dat money to do evil things! So I throwed one bag out de window fer de people."

"What kind of evil things?"

"I jus 'membered de lightnin' bolt! I can't talk no more!"

"What lightning bolt?"

"I can't tell you 'cause angels can call down lightnin'

bolts if they want to!"

"When I talked with the angel, he said it was a good thing to tell me and he wouldn't send down a lightning bolt to get you," said a quick-thinking Pat.

"Really?"

"Yes." Pat was gathering speed. "In fact, Gabriel told me Mr. Rodent and Mr. Serpent were really working for the demons. They may even be demons themselves."

"The real Gabriel dat talked to Mary 'bout de baby Jesus bein' born?"

"That's the one."

"Man. Dat's heavy! He said Mr. Rodent and Mr. Serpent were working wif d e demons? And if I tells you 'bout it, I wouldn't be struck wif no lightnin' bolt?"

"That's right." Pat was certain they had lied to Sammy to get him to do the bank job and keep quiet about it. Now he had to figure out a way to help this poor guy. Obviously, Sammy did not have the mental capacity to commit this crime.

"Is you sure it was Gabriel?"

"Yes, Sammy. Now please tell me all about it."

Sammy went on to tell Pat what Rodent and Serpent told him about the demons and the bank robbery. Pat asked him if it would be okay to talk to his mother and Sammy said "Sure."

Pat was taking notes and talking with Sammy for almost two hours. He left and went back to the office.

CHAPTER 12

October - Escape Plans

Skinny worked hard at Jackson, and in ten weeks, he got his GED (General Educational Development) diploma, sometimes known as a high-school equivalency diploma. He was on his best behavior. Not only did he get the GED but also he worked hard brownnosing the teachers and the director. As a result, he was assigned permanently to Jackson as an assistant to the Director of Education.

He constantly let the teachers and the director know he wanted to be part of changing men's lives through education. Maybe his little part would keep some young man from coming back to prison. Of course, this was all a charade.

What he really was doing was planning his escape, which he only thought about after receiving notice that the new husband of his ex-wife, Betty, was trying to adopt his two kids. Skinny was looking over the divorce and adoption papers and got very angry.

I'm going to get out, and when I do, they had all better look out! First, I'll burn down the damn divorce attorney's house. That would scare the hell out of all of them. Then I'll lay low for a little while. When the heat is off, I'll kill Betty, her new idiot husband, and that damn adoption attorney, Patton. Maybe that Herb Butterworth and his family, too! The adoption was all Patton's fault! He talked them into it. I can feel it in my bones.

There were only three successful escapes from Jackson in the last 20 years, all by trucks. One man hid in the garbage, and the other two, both at the same time, had made quick-connect devices, which allowed them to cling to the underside of a delivery truck. That possibility was all but eliminated now,

88

as a guard at the last gate would check under all vehicles with a mirror on a long pole with wheels on it.

The prison officials also installed a double-gate system to check all vehicles as they left the prison. You would drive through the first gate, usually with some other cars. Then a guard, who was in a tower about 30-feet high, electrically would close the gate. No one could get up there to force him to open it. You were trapped between two gates until the guards below were satisfied with their search and signaled the tower guard to open the outside gate. Escape would not be easy, but he thought he had a way figured out. It would take a lot of time, much work to implement, and a whole lot of luck!

Skinny simply planned to walk out of this maximum-security prison. He had watched prison personnel leave since the first day he got to Jackson. Before he could get outside from the school to the double gates, he would have to walk through an area consisting of four gates set up like a room with four sides. They were also electrically controlled, with a guard behind a glass window watching every move. That would put him in a box with gates on all four sides. The guard would open only one of the four gates at a time.

Another guard monitored more than a dozen TV screens, showing the hall going outside, the different cellblocks, the mess hall, and numerous other areas. Skinny would have to go down a long hallway to the final electrically controlled gate, with another guard behind a glass window, watching everyone who came in or went out. If Skinny got to that location, the parking lot was behind the last inside gate. He would have to find a car and drive through those last double gates with the guard in the tower. Freedom was just beyond that last gate.

Skinny's plan wasn't complicated. He would have to find a civilian or officer who was white, tall, and somewhat resembled himself. Most everyone weighed more than Skinny for their height. He didn't see that being a problem; he could make pads to put under his clothes, or rather under the civilian or officer's clothes he would be wearing. He also needed to make friends with someone in prison who had used disguises in their outside criminal careers.

All officers and civilian workers wore badges or ID

cards, which looked like a plastic credit card or driver's license with a picture. A hole was punched in the card. A spring-loaded clip and plastic retaining ring attached the card to their collars. He noticed people who had worked there for a while nodded to the guard on duty and walked to the parking lot. From there, getting through the last two vehicle gates to the outside was the next step.

I'm not sure how to handle the escape once I'm in the parking lot. I could drive the look-a-like's car, as I would have the car keys. I've got ways to make him tell what kind of car he's driving and where it'll be parked. What if he was friendly with a guard at the last gate? Maybe it would be better to fake car trouble and get a ride out with another employee. I'd be just a passenger and the guard wouldn't connect me with the victim's car. Gotta think about it. I also have to think about what I'll do to the person whose clothes and ID I steal. If I kill him, he can't talk. I got no problems with killing, but the prison officials will know who did it. If I get caught, it'll be the difference between five years for escape and possibly the electric chair for murder. I killed before and I'll do it again but I don't want them to catch me before my revenge is complete.

He went to work that morning, filling in for a tutor who was out sick. Skinny did that whenever he could, because a number of students came and went and he wanted to get to know all of them. He did favors for the guys, like getting them cigarettes, not because he was a good person; he was looking for a disguise man. Finally, he got a lead from another inmate about an expert makeup man, who had requested GED classes. Skinny put him at the head of the list and expected the inmate to arrive that morning. He had the power to do this, as he was the one who prepared the lists for the Director.

Skinny often subbed as a tutor, sometimes getting behind in his work, and stayed late to catch up. The Director thought he was dedicated to his job and it set precedence for him working late hours.

Dean Coverdale came into the GED class as a formality. He had an IQ of 140 and an equivalent of two to three years of college, but he had never graduated from high school. Dean was average looking, the kind who could get lost in a crowd, and was about 40 years old. He had not been in prison before. Not because he did not commit crimes; he just never was caught. He fully expected to whiz through the program in a few weeks, then sit for the test.

Skinny made sure he gave Dean the orientation speech himself. He sat Dean down and told him about the different education modules, times, and tests. The students covered math and English in these classes. A professional teacher covered science and other subjects in another classroom.

Skinny, in a sly manner, thought of how to ask Dean more about himself and what he did to get put in prison. He wanted to make sure this was the right man. He wouldn't have an opportunity to talk with Dean elsewhere. New guys lived in a different section of the prison than the permanent inmates. Skinny needed to get friendly with him in a hurry because he could be shipped out in as little as 6 weeks.

"You know, Dean. I went through diagnostics here. It's a pain in the ass. Being a permanent inmate ain't so bad.

"You know it, man. I hope I'm not here long. I only need a few weeks to study for the GED, and then I'm ready to go. I'm worried, man; I'm going stir crazy already!"

Gotta work fast, thought Skinny.

"Let me get your first book. I can talk to you more by pretending to help you with the book."

When Skinny came back with Dean's first book, the teacher was on the other side of the room helping a student.

"They gave me ten years to think about an armed robbery I did. How 'bout you?" asked Skinny.

"Man, I had 110 counts of forgery on me, but they could only make three stick. I was found guilty and got 20 serve ten."

"Ten years in prison followed by 10 years' probation is a long time. What were you forging?"

"You mean allegedly forging, don't you?"

"Yeah, allegedly forging," laughed Skinny.

"Georgia drivers' licenses for one thing. Checks for another. Credit cards. Birth certificates. Money orders. And so on," smiled Dean.

"I've got the idea," laughed Skinny. "What did you do

91

before that?"

"Believe it or not, I worked as a makeup artist in Hollywood, California. Octopus Productions to be exact. Made good money, too, until some expensive jewelry came up missing from some of the dressing rooms. They blamed me. Couldn't prove a thing. The description of the person seen going into the rooms did not look anything like me," said Dean with a silly smile on his face. "They fired me anyway."

"Pretty good, huh? With makeup, that is."

"One of the best, if I say so myself. Over the years, several unsolved bank robberies have been done supposedly by several different people. If you know what I mean," bragged Dean. "But I don't admit anything to anyone. Too many snitches."

"Very smart; I don't either. But you better believe if someone was to rat on me, they would be a walking dead man."

"Don't blame you a bit."

"I'd better let you get to work."

"Yeh, I need to look over this book to see what's on it before I take the test."

"Let's see your folder. This is a one-hour book. See here where it says 1.0? That means one hour. If you keep it less than that, make sure you pass the test. The time you see means the average person will take an hour study time to pass. If you can study less and pass the test, fine. But if the teacher sees you keeping books for 5 to 10 minutes when you are on an hour book, and then you fail the test, you will be kicked out of class."

"Thanks for the warning."

"I'll let you get to work now, but a little later I would like to talk to you about makeup. Okay?

"Sure, uh, what's your name?"

"Arnie, but everyone calls me Skinny."

"Okay, Skinny. I'll see you in a little while."

Dean would get a book, glance through it for five minutes, and take the test, making a 95 or 100, never missing more than one question.

"Hey, Dean. Want to eat lunch together?"

"Sure." Dean was flattered that a permanent inmate would take up with an inmate going through diagnostics. New guys in jumpsuits were considered beneath permanents.

"We're not supposed to eat together, but I know the guard and I think I can get him to look the other way. I run black-market goods in here through him."

"Cool, man!"

They talked and Skinny learned some basics of applying makeup. He intended to talk with Dean as much as possible in the next few weeks because Dean would be moved soon after receiving his GED.

Then Skinny got an idea.

"Say, Dean. How would you like to be a tutor after you take the GED test? Beats the hell out of sittin' in a cell all day waitin' to be shipped out. As a tutor, you would be in a dorm with lots of space. Some guys rot in their cells for months waiting and waiting. I could get you on easy!"

"Man, that would be great! Anything to get out of being locked up in that 6 x 8 cage all day. Man, I've got to find a way out of here!"

In two weeks Dean had completed all books needed to sit for the GED - - an unheard-of accomplishment. Most inmates took eight to ten weeks or more.

* * *

The night he passed the GED, Dean went back to his cellblock with a smile on his face.

After my buddy, Skinny, gets me the tutor job, I'll get out of this hamster cage and go to a working dorm where I can walk around and talk to people. Meanwhile, I gotta stay here for maybe another week or two.

Dean liked James, his cellmate, but he had to get away from the constant smell of burning toilet paper. Because inmates could not have matches or lighters, James had a wick going at all times to light the cigarettes Dean would get from Skinny. It was made out of six feet of toilet paper, doubled to three feet and twisted tightly. Once lit, it would smolder for two or three hours so a cigarette could be lit from it at any time. When it was about to go out, James would simply make another wick.

Only permanents could buy cigarettes but inmates found ways around that. James had been in prison before and liked to show off his knowledge. He was also quite a character.

James m a d e a paper s n a k e and got it after everyone w h o walked by his cell, and also the guys in the cell next to his. They pulled off its head, so James set out to get revenge. He took off one of his shower shoes and loaded it up with baby powder, then reached out of his cell bars and used the shower shoe to sling the baby powder into the next-door cell. In a matter of seconds the whole cell turned white, and the two inmates had trouble breathing for a few minutes. They all laughed convulsively.

Prison life was boring and you had to watch carefully when picking friends. Older inmates were usually okay but some of the younger ones could be dangerous.

Life Without The Possibility Of Parole is a sentence that should be eliminated, thought Dean. *A young guy who gets a sentence like that has nothing to lose. He is a real danger to inmates like me and the guards. If everyone given a life sentence were brought up for parole every five years or so, at least they would have some hope of getting out of this stinkin' place and would tend to behave. Some should have to stay in prison for the rest of their lives but that should be the decision of the parole board. Some people do change and, after a number of years, could be let out for a productive life on the outside. How much time is enough? The legislature mandates minimum sentences for certain crimes without taking the perpetrator into consideration. All are lumped into one category regardless of whether they are criminally minded or not. Minimum sentences should always be left up to the judge and maximum sentence up to the legislature.*

Inmates and guards have been killed in this place. I'm lucky to have friends like James and Skinny.

"What are you doing?" asked Dean, who watched as James took the state-provided toothpaste cap and twisted it tightly against his shower shoe.

"I'm making some ear plugs. This noise is too much for me. These blacks don't ever shut up." James bored a hole in the shower shoe with the toothpaste cap.

"Ever notice how the inside of the cap is hollow? It just happens to be the right size to make an earplug, which will fit in most people's ears. It knocks out about half the noise."

The most fascinating thing Dean saw was what James referred to as *The Inmate Postage Stamp Recycling Program.* The U. S. Post Office would love this.

James would place used stamps face down on the surface of his Speed Stick Deodorant, which was extended out as far as it could go. After a few hours, the envelope part could be peeled off the stamp without tearing it. The stamp was rubbed with toilet paper soaked with more Speed Stick or after-shave lotion to remove the post office cancellation marks. Then it could be glued to an envelope with toothpaste. Most all stamps could be worked this way but multi-colored Christmas stamps were the hardest to reuse. They tended to look washed out. Only in prison would it pay to work so long and so hard for so little. But many inmates had no one to visit them, write them, or send them money to buy things from the store. Stamps and cigarettes were money in prison.

Dean considered himself an artist when it came to makeup, but he was amazed at the talent locked up at Jackson. Several inmates sold envelopes, or handmade cards, so well done they looked like they were printed. Common pictures were a bear in a mailbox holding a heart or an open Bible with ribbons, doves, and roses.

M & M candy was used for color and a broom straw was the artist's brush. Medication came in plastic blister packs. The artist would place one M & M of the color he wanted in one of the small plastic bowls of the blister pack. A drop of water placed on top of it would allow the color to come off as the M & M was rotated with the broom straw. When the color was removed, the candy was eaten and the color used as paint. The painted envelope tended to be sticky, so baby powder was sprinkled on the palm of the hand and carefully blown on the envelope. The finished product was ready to sell for two or three stamps, a candy bar, or whatever the market would bear. Other inmates bought these envelopes and sent them to their wives or girlfriends.

Dean saw James work other wonders. A ballpoint pen would quit working. The ink cartridge, open end, would be stuck into a soft bar of soap. That caused pressure on the ink and it would write once more. Different color trash bags were braided and became beautiful necklaces.

Word got back to Dean that he was accepted as a tutor and would move to a permanent dorm.

"Out of this hamster cage at last!" yelled Dean to no one in particular.

* * *

This is my lucky day. James will be missed but Skinny is now my best friend.

I got him where I want him! thought Skinny. *He depends on me for cigarettes, advice, and most of all he wants to get out of here!*

CHAPTER 13

Late October - Pick'em-Up-Man

What a mentally draining day at the office.

A couple in a divorce case came in late in the afternoon. The case was supposed to be uncontested. The couple argued about the split of pots and pans, towels, and even the reversed rims for the van.

Pat finally told them, "You have three choices: One, agree now; two, go home and think about it; or three, I'll gladly act as a mediator at $100.00 per hour."

They still could not agree so they made an appointment to come back in two days.

As Pat drove home, his mind was on those clients. They didn't seem to understand an uncontested divorce was one in which the husband and wife came to an agreement on all issues, so the attorney could draw up an agreement, in legal terms, based upon the agreement of the parties.

Sometimes this job is really frustrating, thought Pat. *Time to turn on the CB radio and forget about them.*

"Yeah, good buddy, you got the Sheet-Metal King here," said a voice.

"Good to talk to you, King. This is Diamond Jim checking in," said another voice.

"And boys, this be the Pick'em-Up-Man, and I got the hammer down!" said a third voice.

As the conversations went back and forth, Pat was able to tell they were factory workers going home after a hard day's work. They talked about stopping off for a beer.

He learned the guy who called himself Pick'em-Up-Man fancied himself as a macho lady's man.

Time to have some fun, thought Pat, *but I need to be careful and not get caught because I might get my butt kicked.*

"S-a-a-a-a-y there, you darling Pick'em-Up-Man." Pat used with a heavy lisp. "This is the Gay Blade, come on."

"What!" said a voice.

"Don't b-e-e-e shy, Pick'em-Up-Man. You know darn well who this is, sweetie-pie," said Pat/Blade.

"You faggot, SOB! Get off this channel!"

"Why don't we have a p-r-i-v-a-t-e little rendezvous, while your buddies have a beer, you handsome Pick'em-Up-Man."

"Look, tight britches, if I get ahold of you, I'll kick your faggot ass clear across town."

"Oh, I just l-o-v-e it when you get upset! It turns me on!"

"Say, Pick'em-Up-Man, you don't have something going with the Blade, do you?" laughed the Sheet-Metal King.

"Yeah, P i c k ' e m -Up-Man. Sounds l i k e y o u two know each other," added Diamond Jim.

"Breaker, breaker. This is Dapper Dan. What's going on here? I'm on my way to Cleveland in my 18-wheeler and accidentally heard this conversation. I couldn't help breaking in! Sounds like Pick'em-Up-Man's got him a s-w-e-e-t tooth," said a hysterical Dan Adams.

This absolutely infuriated Pick'em-Up-Man!

"You damn queer. Come on out and fight me like a man!"

"B-u-t, b-u-t, sweetheart. You know I'm only half a man, and I do s-o-o-o want to see you again. But if you're going to act that way, I'm through giving my love to you. Ta Ta. Bye, love," and Pat/Blade put down the mike.

Pick'em-Up-Man was beside himself! He was in a rage because he was trying to fight an invisible enemy, and his friends were riding him. They called The Blade on the radio. Because Pat was getting close to home, he wouldn't answer.

* * *

The next day, Pat's mind was swamped. He had so

much going on at the office, he felt it was impossible to get it all done. He had gone to see a shrink at the Georgia Mental and Psychiatric Hospital in Atlanta about doing an evaluation on Sammy Joe Washington. Because it was a State-supported institution, the psychiatrists there would have to accept a subpoena to appear in court on an indigent case. They were paid by the State, so it was part of their job. To qualify as being indigent, someone had to have very few assets and show the judge there was no way she, or he, could pay for a defense. Showing that, the judge would declare the person *indigent* and the Court would appoint a defense attorney, the county paying the cost of the defense.

When Pat got to the hospital, he had in mind talking the doctor into declaring Sammy insane, therefore not mentally able to do the crime. After talking with Dr. Fester for about 20 minutes, Pat came to some startling conclusions.

First, he was not going to get a *not-guilty-by-reason-of-insanity* verdict. The good doctor was adamant that Sammy needed to be almost a vegetable to be declared unable to know right from wrong. Second, Dr. Fester, in Pat's opinion, was quite disturbed himself and needed his own shrink. That left a *guilty-but-mentally-ill* verdict to pursue.

Anyway, the good doctor agreed to see Sammy in jail and evaluate him. Frankly, all Pat expected was a report saying, "Yes, he is nuts, but he knew it robbing a bank was wrong, demons or no demons."

This was a case in which money could buy a lot. A man with money can shop until he gets the right shrink to say, "In my opinion, this man doesn't know right from wrong."

A psychiatrist with several degrees and published articles in well-known psychiatric magazines carries a lot of weight in court but is very expensive. However, the judge would never allow him to *shrink shop* on the taxpayer's money.

Pat would have to work with what he had. Now that he knew something about the case, it was time to see the DA. Pat would see him first thing in the morning.

An Assistant DA would represent the State in this case. In reality, a DA handled few cases and usually reserved the high profile ones for themselves. They needed to look good in the press to get reelected. That is - - when they were not out politicking. So, their assistants did most of the work.

Asst. DA Mark Kimbrough was assigned to Sammy's case.

* * *

When Pat got to his office, he called and made an appointment to see Mark later that day. Then he asked the girls if he could take them to lunch and they accepted. The answering machine could take over for an hour. He did paperwork until lunchtime.

Pat took Julie and Rhonda to the Brave Bull Mexican Restaurant. A waitress came to their table with some chips and dip.

"Hi, Pat. The usual?"

"Right, Sandy."

"What is the usual, Pat?" asked Julie.

"Special number two - - a burrito, rice, and beans."

"He always gets a Coke and cheese dip, too," added Sandy.   "I'll take the same," ordered Julie.

"Me, too," chimed in Rhonda."

"I'll bring them right out."

"You come here a lot, Pat?" asked Rhonda.

"At least once a week. I bring dates here, too. The food is good, the service good, and it's not too expensive."

"Like the Ming Dynasty?" asked Julie.

Pat ignored her but smiled.

"How's everything going with you, Julie?" queried Rhonda.

"Great, Rhonda! I can't complain, and all that good stuff. Especially between me and Ralph ever since his boss, Lieutenant Tomble, bought the whole office lunch. You wouldn't know anything about that though, would you, Pat?"

"Not me." Pat had a little boy innocent smile.

"Well, the guys really appreciated it and every one of them thanked Tomble for the lunch, and they now see him a little differently. He is a changed person and the guys like working for him. He actually treats Ralph like a friend now, and Ralph goes out of his way to help him."

"I wish Herb could've been with us today," noted Pat.

"I talked to him on the phone and told him we were going to eat here," said Rhonda. "And to come if he could make it."

"Well, speak of the devil, look who's walking in the front door," informed Julie.

Herb saw her waving to him, pulled on his suspenders, and came over to the table.

"Jeez," said Julie, "you must've heard us talking about you."

"Hi, gang! Just got out of court. I announced *ready* at the trial calendar call and darned if my client didn't show up drunk for his DUI trial!"

At that, laughter came easily. "How did it come out?" asked Pat.

"It didn't. The trial was put off so my client could serve five days in jail for contempt of court. I don't know what kind of reading they got at the police station, but he blew a 2.01 in the handheld machine. The trial next week should be fun now that he was found to be double drunk in Judge Price's court room. He might as well put a gun to his head and pull the trigger! He surely put the screws to his case now.

"Dis he have a good case?"

"Are you kidding? Heck, no! I tried to tell the fool to take the deal the solicitor offered, but no! He's going back to jail. I just don't know for how long."

"What's his defense?"

"*Lack of probable cause.* My client said he was driving just fine and the cop had no reason to pull him over. The officer is going to testify he was weaving all over the road and crossed over the centerline several times. Who do you think the jury is going to believe?"

"Well, you tried, Herb," smiled Rhonda.

"There's John Beaver." Herb pointed to a man who had come in. He wanted me to do some legal work for him -- I think a will, a trust for his kids, incorporation, and an adoption. There was one catch though. He wanted to teach me to fly, and give me flying time in an ultralight airplane in exchange for my services."

"And you didn't do it?" asked Pat.

"Hell, no! You won't catch me strapped i n a l a w n

chair with wings on it. That's what those things are. Except they have a lawnmower motor on them, too, which makes it worse. Not me!" Herb snapped his suspenders for emphasis.

"That's something I have always wanted to do!" Pat had excitement in his voice. "Do you think he'd be willing to offer me the same deal, Herb?"

"You're nuts!" exclaimed Rhonda.

"It sounds neat," said Julie.

"Probably so," continued Herb, "especially   if I say I'll help you do it."

"So what are you waiting for?" asked Pat.

Herb got up and walked over to John Beaver's table. They talked for a few minutes and Beaver shook his head *yes*. Herb returned to the table.

"Well, Herb, what did he say?" asked Pat with boy-like excitement in his voice.

"His deal goes like this. You start on his legal work this week and he is prepared to give you your first lesson this weekend, weather permitting. He'll be over here to talk with you in a few minutes. As I was saying, he is willing to give you lessons, see you solo, and give you ten additional hours of flying time. After that, you buy your own plane or work out a new deal with him. Also, he wants me, not you, to draw up a short contract with the above in it, plus a release from you in case of injury, and a clause saying if you break it, you fix it."

"I'll do it!"

"Okay, here he comes."

John Beaver was a talkative fellow, and full of smiles. He and Pat immediately hit it off. However, he said, "If you feel you know it all and endanger my airplane, the deal is off. Flying is very safe if you follow the rules, but very dangerous if you don't."

John was a businessman with several rental houses, and he worked for a major airline as a mechanic. He was going to adopt his wife's two children, twin boys age 9. Pat agreed to meet with them in the morning to intake the case, and he would start learning about ultralight airplanes Saturday afternoon. John kept his ultralight at Bellah Air Field, a private strip once used by the military to train pilots and parachute jumpers during World War II. The airfield was large, at over 200 acres, and had three main runways. John had his plane tied down under a hanger made out of tarps.

When it was time to go back to the office, they piled into Pat's Mustang and got there a little ahead of Herb. This was a teacher workday and he had a 1:30 appointment with the former Mrs. Anderson and children. She was already in the parking lot waiting on them when they pulled in.

"Hi", said Pat, "we just got back from lunch."

"I know. We're a little early, Pat, but better early than late. Right, kids?" asked Mrs. Johnson.

"Yes, ma'am," they replied in unison.

"Well-mannered kids," commented Pat.

"Come in and have a seat," said Julie.

They went into the office and Mrs. Johnson, along with the children, sat in the waiting room until Pat was ready for them. In a few minutes, Julie escorted them into Pat's office. The children's eyes lit up when they saw six stuffed animals sitting on Pat's credenza.

"George and Lorie, this is Mr. Patton," said Betty.

"Nice to meet you," said Pat, shaking hands with them.

"What are those animals doing there?" asked Lorie.

"You're not supposed to ask questions like that, Sis," admonished George.

"It's okay. All of these animals need a home and are up for adoption. You kids are going to be adopted, and your new father will be Mr. Johnson. After the adoption, your last name will change from Anderson to Johnson ..."

"Yea!" blurted out George.

"Me, too!" yelled Lorie.

"Great," said Pat. "Now to continue with what I was saying, you get to pick an animal you want to adopt. Then you ..."

"I want the bear! The girl bear!" interrupted Lorie.

"I think I'll take the gorilla, because they're strong," said George.

"Okay. Go get them. The other animals will have to wait for another boy or girl."

The kids went over to get their adoptees. Big smiles

were on their faces.

"You will be going into court to see a judge who will give your parents papers to show that Mr. Johnson is your new father and your name is Johnson. I am also going to draw up an adoption certificate for each of your animals, showing their present names and their new last name of Johnson. I'll sign the certificate as your attorney, my secretary will notarize it, and we will get the judge to sign it. It will say these animals are being adopted by you."

"Wow! said Lorie. "That's great."

"Now, kids, you have to come up with a name for your animals."

"I want to name my gorilla, ah, ah, yeah, King Kong. I saw that on TV."

"How about you, Lorie?" asked Pat.

"I'm thinking. I'm not sure."

"Or B o b b i e Bear," suggested Pat.

"You don't name a girl bear *Bobby.*"

"Lorie, Bobbie is a girl's name," informed her mother.

"It is? I didn't know that."

"You might like something that goes with bear, perhaps Bessie Bear, Barbara Bear, or Bonnie Bear.

"What are you going to name her?" asked Mrs. Johnson.

"I don't know."

"Bessie Bear sounds like a good name for a girl bear, Honey," offered Mrs. Johnson.

"Yeah, I think I'll name her Bessie Bear. My very own Bessie Bear!"

"Now, kids, you will both have to take care of these animals like your mom and dad have to take care of you -- make sure they keep their rooms clean, eat their vegetables, and get up in time to go to school every day. Are you willing to do that, kids?"

"Yes, Sir," said George.

"I love my bear and I'll take very good care of her," said Lorie.

"Betty, we have a termination hearing next week. Let me look at my calendar -- Tuesday at 9 AM. The kids don't have to be there. The judge will hear evidence that Skinny didn't provide support or have contact with the children for over one year. We have not heard from him yet and I think his time has run out. Yes, it ran out last Friday. On second thought bring them anyway, as I may be able to talk the judge into also doing the final adoption right after the termination hearing."

"What if Skinny doesn't answer or show up?"

"Then the judge will almost have to terminate his parental rights.

"Just a minute while I buzz Julie."

"Julie, please call the Clerk's Office to see if Skinny filed an objection to the adoption."

"The second hearing is the final one and the children need to be there. I believe we can get the judge to put on his black robe and let you bring your camera to take pictures. We will then go down to the Clerk's Office to file all the paperwork. Then kids, if your mother and father okay it, I will buy you both an adoption Coke."

"Yes! It's okay, Mommy?" asked Lorie.

"If you're good."

"A-h-h, Mom. You know we'll be good," said George.

Julie had stuck her head into the office. "Boss, I checked with the clerk and he was properly served but no objection was filed."

"Any questions, Betty?" asked Pat.

"No, sir.

"That's all for today."

* * *

Later that day Pat went to see Mark about Sammy's case.

"I take it the receptionist told you I'm here on the Sammy Joe Washington case?"

"Got the file right here, and to save you a lot of time, my recommendation is 20 years to serve."

"That's the max he could get if we lost at trial, Mark, and that almost makes me have to try the case. Sammy was used by two bad dudes and is mentally ill."

"I'm sorry, but our office is under a lot of pressure. *The Five-O'Clock Traffic Bandits* and all. Man, all those nails and flat tires have everyone mad for miles around. Not to mention the money they threw out the window that stopped up the other lanes of traffic. Hell, people are still getting flat tires from nails missed in the clean up! On top of that, we expect the press to follow this case like a hound dog after a rabbit. In fact, I'm surprised they assigned a novice attorney to this case."

"Herb will be working with me. The Lord knows I'll need all the help I can get."

"Yeah, we're both forced into a trial on this one."

"Is it true the other two agreed to plead out to the full 20 years?'

"Yes. They agreed with their attorneys that it would be a waste of everyone's time to go through a trial."

Pat shook his head. *Why not go to trial when you have nothing to lose? Who knows what might happen.*

"I really don't think Sammy had the mental capacity to hold up a bank and I saw Dr. Fester about doing an evaluation on him."

"I understand. With the discovery items, I've got for you an order for a psychiatric evaluation, signed by the judge. So go to it."

"Sammy claims he does not have a prior record. Is that correct?"

"True, and if this were not such a high-profile case, I could possibly go with 15 years, maybe even as low as ten."

"But, Mark, this guy is loony-toons! I've talked to him, his mother, and his aunt. Believe it or not, he thinks he's Moses. He walks around wearing a Moses outfit and carries a stick he thinks is a snake, and the snake tells him what to do. There's no way he is capable of robbing a bank. The other two guys led him on. I repeat, there is no way this guy is capable of robbing a bank!"

"Wrong! He just did."

"Touché, but you know what I mean."

"Yeh, I know. The police officers and the interviewing detective all think he's nuts. Ah, this is off the record."

"Okay."

"They all think he's nuts, but ..."

"I know," interrupted Pat. "Unless he's a vegetable, he knows right from wrong."

"You got it. Welcome to the real world of the criminal justice system. By the way, it's *Chain Gang's* case and he's up for re-election."

"Just my luck! Thanks a lot!"

When Pat and Mark were through with their meeting, Pat returned to his office dreading the day he would have to try this case in *Chain Gang's* courtroom.

* * *

Friday morning he met with John Beaver and talked more about trading legal work for flying lessons. He got the information he needed to get the release, will, adoption, trust, and incorporation going for John. They made plans to meet at Bellah Airfield at about 2:00 Saturday afternoon.

Pat had never seen an ultralight airplane up close and was excited about learning to fly one. A pilot's license was not required to fly an ultralight, so as soon as he was trained, he would be free to soar with the buzzards! The next day could not come soon enough for Pat!

That afternoon, on the way home, he turned on his CB radio. Pat talked to a friend on Channel 19, and then tuned around the band for other conversations. Sure enough, Pick'em-Up-Man, Sheet-Metal King, Diamond Jim, and MoPar Man were at it again on Channel 5.

Heads I will and tails...I sure will! thought Pat.

"Breaker. Breaker. S - a - y, Pick'em-Up-Man. You good-looking hunk. This is your sweetie, the Gay Blade. Come on," said Pat with a heavy lisp.

"Where are you, you damn fag!" yelled Pick'em-Up-Man.

"Come on, sugar. Stop pretending. Your buddies won't miss you for the little bit of time it takes to ... you know."

"Why you damn queer. If I find you, you're dead meat and will be lucky if you make the emergency room!"

"What w-a-s that you s-a-i-d about m-e-a-t?"

"Hey, Pick'em-Up-Man. We can spare you for a little while," laughed the Sheet Metal King.

"Yeah, go ahead, have fun," agreed Diamond Jim.

"What in the devil is going on?" asked MoPar Man.

Pat wisely put the mike back in its holder. He once again had created quite a stir on the CB radio. He stopped at a convenience store to get a 12-pack of beer. If he got just a 6-pack, Pat knew he would be lucky to drink two of them, as Eb would drink the rest. Eb wasn't cheap; he just drank too much.

In the store, Pat heard some familiar voices, which took a few seconds to register, but here they were in living color -- Pick'em-Up-Man, Sheet-Metal King, Diamond Jim, MoPar Man, and another guy he didn't know. He had noticed a couple of them had driven an old beat-up Chevy pickup truck with tobacco stains running down the driver's side door. The truck was parked three spaces from him. Each grabbed a 6-pack, then stopped at the magazine rack to look at girlie magazines. The temptation was too great. Pat paid the cashier and hurried out. He got in his car, took out a tablet and a rubber band from the glove compartment, and wrote a note.

"To Pick'em-Up-Man. Thanks for all of the good times! With all of my love, The Gay Blade."

Pat wrapped the note around a cold beer and fastened it with the rubber band. He made sure they were still in the store and not looking his way when he placed the beer on the hood of the truck on the driver's side and went back to Max.

As soon as Pat saw them going through the check-out line, he opened his car door, popped the trunk lid open, and pretended to be looking for something. Out they came. The Sheet-Metal King opened the driver's side door and saw the beer. When he read the note, the King burst out laughing and handed the beer and the note to Pick'em-Up-Man. As soon as he read it, he let out a string of cuss words that would do Kim and Connie proud. He looked around, saw Pat, and walked over to him, shaking his head and cussing.

Pick'em-Up-Man was a big man about 25 years old. His ponytail swung like a whip as he jerked his head back and forth. As he cussed, spittle squirted out between his bad teeth. His arms looked like a billboard with several tattoos on them.

Some lady's man! thought Pat.

"Hey, man. Did you happen to see the SOB who put this beer on the hood of my buddy's truck?"

"As a matter of fact, I saw a strange little guy in tight pink pants in that area, but I didn't actually see him put it there."

"Pink pants, huh? That fits. What kind of car was it."

"A bright yellow small car, you know, like a woman would drive. I figured it was his wife's car."

"Hell, y-e-s-s-s-s! It all fits. Pink pants. Yellow car! Did the queer SOB say anything to you?"

"Let me think - - he had his window down, and yes, he said something like, 'Ta Ta, bye my love.' But, that didn't make sense because he was looking at the store when he said it. He was backing up at the time. Oh, I almost forgot, he blew a kiss at the store."

Boy that was close. I almost started talking like the Blade when I got to the Ta Ta.

Pick'em-Up-Man started cussing again. The more he cussed, the more his friends laughed. Pat got in his car, started it up, and left. When he got down the road, he turned on the CB radio.

"--- you hear that, you queer SOB? You'll be sorry you were ever born, or hatched, or whatever! I know you're listening, Blade. What do you say to that?"

Pat picked up his mike and with a very distinct lisp said, "Love you, love you, love you, sweet Pick'em-Up-Man. Ta Ta! Remember what you told me last time we met. You said I was s-o-o-o good that you were going to give up girls. Ta Ta! Bye love!"

Finally, Pick'em-Up-Man used some of his 50 IQ brain and changed his tactics. He said, "You win, Blade. I admit I have to see you again. How about just you and me, behind the bowling alley, tonight at 10:00? Come on."

"You can't fool me, you sweet thing! That wasn't love I heard in your voice, Honey! Come on yourself."

"Okay, you damn fairy. If you want some of me, you'll be there with damn tinker bells on! Come on, turkey face."

"Now you've hurt my feelings, lover, but I know you have to play the manly role for your friends. Ta Ta, love!

Gotta' go now. Pat hung up the mike and turned off the radio.

He pulled into the garage and parked Max. Pat would ride his Honda to the airport in the morning. He would need his helmet when he was in the ultralight.

* * *

A new inmate was assigned to Skinny's dorm. He was a medical doctor who was in for killing his partner with a baseball bat. They called him *Doc*.

"Hey, Doc. Would you answer a medical question?" asked Skinny.

"Certainly. What is it?"

"Where do you shoot someone if you want to cause them the maximum amount of pain while killing them slowly?"

CHAPTER 14

November - Gertrude and the Adoption

Early Saturday morning, Pat was up and ready to go flying, several hours before his first lesson and a few weeks before he could solo. John had said he did not mind Pat getting there early and looking over the plane, and he could even sit in it as long as he did not touch anything.

When Pat got up, he went for a two-mile jog and then lifted weights for about 30 min. Nothing super heavy, just enough to get in good shape. He tried to do this three to four times per week. By 9:30, he had done his exercises, took a shower, and eaten breakfast.

Eb worked on Saturday for about six hours if he didn't have something planned, and today was a workday. Pat decided to go downstairs to his shop and reload some ammo. He had a .44 Magnum Ruger Blackhawk revolver, and when resting his arm on something solid, at 80 yards he could put six shots in a circle the size of a man's head. That is, if he used his hand loads. With factory ammo, he tended to get a flyer every 8 to 10 rounds that would be 2 to 3 inches outside the circle. Pat had a concealed weapons permit and often carried a gun.

At 11:00 he took the Honda for a burger, ate and got to Bellah Airfield by one o'clock. John had told the owner, Gordon Bellah, to expect Pat. As a new prospective pilot, Pat was in awe as he looked at the different makes of ultralights. Most were under hangers made of large tarps, hung over cables stretched between two trees. This was not a fancy airport.

Gordon came over and they talked a few minutes. He was in his late 80s, very thin and weathered looking, and wore old pants and a long-sleeved shirt. He lived in an old

111

singlewide mobile home at the airport, which was his whole life. Bellah Airfield was one of the oldest airports in Georgia. Gordon claimed he had flown with Lindbergh around Stone Mountain. His wife, Faye, was also a pilot. The airfield was grass, so it was a lot more forgiving on hard landings than paved runways.

Pat went over to the hangar Gordon had pointed out. The front was covered with a tarp held down by bungee cords. It had an elaborate system of ropes that joined together at one end and were on pulleys at the top. When pulled, they lifted the front tarp like a window blind. Pat opened up the front as John had instructed.

Inside was the most beautiful sight he had ever seen. John called her Gertrude. She was an Eipper MX, powered by a Rotax 440 two-stroke pusher engine, sitting on an aluminum frame. A pusher-type aircraft had the propeller located in the rear and pushed the plane through the air. She had blue fabric covering with red stripes on her wings and tail. The entire plane weighed just over 250 pounds.

John also had equipped the airplane with a ballistic parachute and a strobe light. He had told Pat because all ultralights flew slow and low, typically at 40 to 60 miles per hour cruise speed and 1000 feet of altitude respectively, normally all other airplanes flew above them. When another plane was above an ultralight, it was hard to see as it blended into the ground. Hence, the strobe light, which made Gertrude stick out like a black eye on a priest. It was designed to prevent a midair collision.

As Pat sat in the aircraft, he looked up and there stood John. Pat had been so deep in thought that he never heard him approach.

"What do you think of Gertrude?"

"She's beautiful!"

"Well, let's undo the tie downs and pull her out."

Gertrude was tied down to steel eyebolts embedded in concrete that was buried in the ground. A rope went to each wing and another to the tail. Pat helped John pull Gertrude out of the hangar.

"Before you ever fly her, you first need to thoroughly

check everything. Get in the habit of always starting in the same place and ending in the same place."

John showed Pat how to do a preflight inspection.

"The time has almost come to start this beast, but first you need to get familiar with the controls. Have a seat."

Pat got into Gertrude. Really, that's a misnomer as there's not much to get into. She was nothing but a bunch of aluminum tubes covered with fabric only on the wings and tail.

"It's hard to believe this plane will fly. When I look down between my feet, all I see is the ground. Not much around you is there?" commented Pat.

"Not much, but as to your first comment, on a 75° day, she will jump off the ground in less than 100 feet. The pedals control the spoilers, which destroy lift on the wings and allow Gertrude to rapidly lose altitude. They are little panels that you can pop up on the wings. Normally you will fly without pressing the spoiler pedals. To go up, pull the stick back, to go down, push it forward. That moves a horizontal part of the tail called the elevator. Left stick gives you a left turn and right stick a right turn. That moves a vertical part of the tail called the rudder.

"The handle on your left, if pulled, sets off an explosive charge, which deploys the parachute attached to the main frame of the airplane. It will let the plane and pilot down together. It is used only in case of a structural failure. I keep the handle locked when not flying. For a start, all I want you to do is taxi, very slowly. The throttle lever is on your left. Back is idle and forward speeds up the engine. Are you ready?"

"Yes!"

"Okay, put on your helmet. Ignition switch on."

"Check."

"Pump up the gas squeeze ball a few times and pull the choke out to the on position."

"Check. Pumped up, and choke on."

"Throttle advanced about 1/8th of the way."

"Check. Advanced 1/8th."

"If she starts moving, cut the throttle back some. To make a turn on the ground, you have to give her quite a bit of throttle for the wind from the prop to allow the rudder to control the airplane. Okay, here we go. Always yell *clear prop* so everyone knows to stand clear of the prop!"

"Clear prop!" yelled Pat.

John pulled the cord, just like on a lawnmower. Nothing.

"She usually starts on the third try."

Sure enough she did, and with a roar!

Pat let the engine warm up for a minute or so and then slowly advanced the throttle. Gertrude began to move.

I'm taxiing!

He taxied down to the end of the one-third mile runway and turned around. It was hard to get used to because Gertrude had a fixed-position front wheel, which was a simple tricycle landing-gear system, and he had to push the throttle all the way forward for a few seconds in order to get the front wheel to skid and the aircraft turned. Pat taxied down the runway and back several times, then came back and cut the engine.

"Getting used to the throttle and stick?"

"Yes. This is even more fun than riding a motorcycle!"

"Here come the guys. The wind will soon die down enough for us to fly. Did you ever see one in the air?"

"Not up close; just at a distance."

"You have about 30 minutes before the strip will be busy. This time I want you to put the elevator in the up position by pulling the stick back. Use the throttle to get the airplane to do a wheelie as much of the time as you can. The trick is to control the stick and the throttle to keep the front wheel up and off the ground, but don't get Gertrude in the air!"

"Okay. Here I go." Pat started the engine himself this time by pulling the starter cord as he sat in the seat. Wheelies were very hard to do at first, but after about 15 minutes, he was getting the hang of it. He taxied to John, who had been watching all the time, now talking to three other pilots, who had finished fueling and doing a pre-flight inspection on their airplanes.

"You did very good out there, Pat!"

"Thanks, John; I was having a great time."

"Okay, hop out. I need to gas her up and do another quick preflight. The wind has almost died down enough to fly. These planes are so small any wind over a few miles per hour will kick them all over the sky and make landing very difficult."

Pat got out and fueled Gertrude, while John did a walk-around preflight. John was a very safe pilot. The other pilots got into airplanes and fired them up. When John put on his helmet, Pat noticed he first put in earplugs. After hearing the noise from the engine and prop, Pat decided he would get some, too. John started Gertrude and got in line with the other ultralights, which were taxiing out to the end of the runway.

The first pilot lined up his ultralight for takeoff and ran up his engine. With 65° to 70° wether, the plane absolutely leapt off the ground. Then another and another took off. Finally, Gertrude's turn was breathtaking. Pat watched the pilots play around in the sky, flying here and there. They practiced emergency landings, sometimes with the engine cut off, and were having a great time. John did a few simulated emergency landings, from 500, 750, and 1000 feet, then landed and taxied over to Pat. He cut off the engine next to the hangar and prepared to put Gertrude to bed. Pat walked over to help him.

As John was preparing to get out, Pat yelled in alarm and ran toward the plane.

"John, stay where you are!"

"What is it?"

"A snake is coiled up right where you were going to step. My gosh, it's a copperhead!"

Pat ran over to the side of the hangar, picked up a cement block, and went over to the snake, which was still coiled for a strike. He raised the cement block high over his head and threw it down on the snake. John cautiously got out of the plane, but on the other side.

"Man that was close! If you hadn't have come out here today, I may have been snake bit. It gives me the creeps. I never saw one here before."

"Now, as a reward for saving your life, you're going to give Gertrude to me. Right?" laughed Pat.

"Not quite," said John, who also by now was laughing.

"Well then, I guess I'll hop on my trusty two   wheel

horse and head for home. I surely will."

"See you next Saturday, Pat. I'm going out of town, however, if you'd like to get old Gertrude out tomorrow afternoon, you have my permission. But, and this is a firm but, absolutely nothing more than what you did today. Oh, and when the guys get ready to fly, you put her away. A novice running up and down the runway with planes taking off and landing is too dangerous. As you saw, I poured the rest of the can of gas in her tank. It's almost full. Someone will be here by 3 o'clock. Please don't play when no one is here."

"I don't know what to say! I'd like to get familiar with the controls as fast as I can. I think riding motorcycles has helped the learning curve, but I see the safety aspect of not being alone."

"Well, have fun tomorrow, and remember - - if you break it, you fix it. Here's a key to the lock."

* * *

Sunday, Pat was back and practicing how to taxi, do wheelies, and become more familiar with the controls. That was really the name of the game - - getting used to the controls so you could react quickly in a tight situation. If you have to think about each move beforehand, you could wind up a statistic. That is something neither Pat nor John wanted. So far Bellah Airfield had zero fatalities.

* * *

Monday, Pat got ready for his first adoption and termination hearing.

Tuesday morning came and he checked with the Clerk's Office once again to see if an objection had been filed. His luck was running good, as the petition had not been answered or an objection entered by Mr. Anderson, who had been served in jail.

He found the Johnson family and reviewed what to expect. He assured them things looked very good. Pat wondered why Skinny never filed a response.

Little did he know that at that very moment, Skinny was

into the last stage of his plan to escape, and had worked himself into a steady low-level rage aimed at Pat, his clients, and Herb.

"Ready, Mr. and Mrs. Johnson? Ready kids?"

"We sure are!"

"The judge's secretary said he's ready for us, so let's do it."

They went into the judge's chambers. Judge Steven Lofton was 45 years old, trim, had dark hair, a big smile, and you could immediately tell he liked kids. Pat introduced his clients to the judge, who was now dressed in a white shirt, red tie, and black pants. His suit coat was hanging on a coat rack beside his black robe.

"Mr. Patton, you may now make out your case, which I believe is a termination hearing in which your clients are seeking to terminate the rights of the legal father. Is that correct?"

"That's right, Sir, and I do not believe the defendant is present, being incarcerated at Jackson State Prison. Judge, I checked with the Clerk's Office this morning and was told that an objection was not filed. The deadline for filing expired last week."

"Very well. Bailiff, sound the court room and the hall for Mr. Anderson."

The judge looked through the file while the bailiff sounded for Mr. Anderson. She came back and said, "Judge, no one by that name answered my call."

"Okay, Mr. Patton. I have established Mr. Anderson is not present, nor has he filed an objection to this adoption, according to court records. You can now make out your case."

Pat stood up and motioned for Mr. and Mrs. Johnson to do the same. Pat presented their case to the judge.

When Pat was done, the judge announced, "Mr. Anderson's parental rights are hereby terminated and the adoption is granted. I have looked over the order and signed it."

"Thank you, Judge. If we could indulge upon your kindness for a little longer, these children have some animals they would like to adopt."

"Okay, what do you have in mind?"

"Judge, this is the adoption of King Kong Gorilla by George Johnson and the adoption of Bessie Bear by Lorie

Johnson. Here are the adoption certificates signed by me as their attorney and notarized by my secretary. They're waiting for your signature.

"Kids, please raise your right hands. Lorie, your right hand, not your left. Do you both swear you will take care of these animals just like your mom and dad take care of you?"

"Yes, sir."

"And will you make sure they get to school on time?"

"Yes, sir."

"And will you make sure they eat their vegetables and keep their rooms clean?"

"Yes, sir." The children were now laughing, because they could see these were the same things their parents were telling them to do.

"That's our case, Sir."

"Very well. The adoptions are granted and I have signed the certificates."

"One more thing, Your Honor. Could we get you to put your black robe on and pose for a picture with the family?"

"It would be my pleasure."

The judge was no fool. There were three votes sitting in his chambers and more to come when they told their friends how nice he had been.

"Here's the file, Mr. Patton. You may take it to the Clerk's Office. Be sure to fill out an adoption certificate for each child and be sure to check the spelling of the names, because that is the way they will appear on the new birth certificates."

"Already done, Sir."

"Good luck to you. Bailiff, get the next case ready while we take a picture," instructed the judge while putting on his black robe.

They took pictures and went to the Clerk's Office to get the final paperwork completed.

"I can't believe it's finished. I expected to go to court again." Betty sighed a great sigh of relief.

"Me, too," agreed Pat. "The judge was being kind to us."

They took care of their business in the Clerk's office and Betty asked a stranger to take a picture of all of them, including Pat. Then they left the courthouse with big smiles on their faces.

* * *

None of them would be happy if they knew what Skinny was planning, as this day was the beginning of a nightmare!

A week later Skinny received a letter in the mail.

"I will find you! And when I find you, I will terrorize and kill you! Very slowly!" muttered Skinny in his jail cell as he reread the letter he had received from the Clerk's Office of Clayton County. Not only had he lost the rights to his kids but the damn judge also granted the adoption.

They stole my kids! I'll kill them both! That damn adoption attorney, too. And, burn down the house of the damn divorce attorney. They'll pay! They-will-pay! I'll see them burn in Hell! I'll make them all shake in their boots long before I pull the trigger!

CHAPTER 15

Middle of November - Shirley

Skinny made arrangements with Dean to work that night, telling him they needed to talk.

"Dean, were you serious about wanting to get out of here?"

"Hell, yes, man!"

"I got a plan. You interested?"

"Are you kidding? Fire away!"

"Well, I've been thinking about this since the day I got here. Over or under the fence is not good. Too much chance of being caught and maybe shot. No, the only way is to walk out of here. This is Wednesday, and there are two maintenance men who look a lot like us on the night shift. They come and go as they please. Their last night on this shift is Friday. That's when we go. They rotate every few weeks, but I have friends in the right places who can keep up with those things."

"You mean *this* Friday? Two days from now?"

"That's right, and tonight you're going to get a good look at the guy who resembles me. In fact, in just a little while. I called him about a light that's out in the closet. I hid a burned-out bulb several weeks ago and put it in the fixture. When he comes in, I want you to burn into your memory his face, build, walk, and speech."

"Sure, Skinny, but why aren't both of them coming?"

"Your guy is off sick tonight but will be back Friday," lied Skinny. "I got his face, build, walk, and speech burned into my mind. With the make-up lessons you gave me, I can make you look like him."

"Right, Skinny. I put all of our make-up things in the hidden box in the other room. I can't believe this. I'm getting out of here!"

"Just two more days, Dean, and your dream will come true!"

"Say, Skinny, how did you get all of this make-up in here anyway?"

"Got a guard in my pocket. I told him I sell it to the queers who put it on in their cells. In return, I fixed him up with two girls I know on the outside."

"You mean the girls cooperated? I mean, with you in here?"

"Dean, I got friends out there. I was a member of *The Brotherhood* on the outside. They were afraid not to do what I told them to do. Afraid one of those guys might show up."

"I understand. By the way, what is this *Brotherhood* you mentioned?

"Man, it is super-secret, but I can tell you this - - we had fun! Look around you, man! Look at all the 50 I. Q. blacks, and *they* run this place! I'd like to have a dollar for every cross I've burned in yards, every black church I burnt to the ground, every buck I knocked over the head, and every family we ran out of town. Several times we even went further than that! Much further, if you know what I mean."

"Yeah, man. I bet those were the good old days."

"You got the pads made up for me yet? The guy is at least 30 pounds, maybe even 40 pounds, heavier than me."

"Sure, man. I also put them in our hidden box."

"Quiet, here he comes."

"I understand there's a light out in here?" asked the maintenance man, who really did resemble Skinny -- a lot heavier but the resemblance was definitely there.

This will be a piece of cake, thought Dean.

Before he replaced the bulb and went to his next job, Skinny kept the maintenance man talking so they could both hear his speech patterns.

"You got that, Dean?" asked Skinny as soon as the maintenance man left.

"No problem. I wish they were all that easy. You need to

pad your cheeks some, though. From the inside, like Marlon Brando did in *The Godfather*."

"You got something to do the job?"

"No, but I will by the time we have to leave."

"Most people will clear out early Friday. As soon as they do, I want you to make me up. I'll call maintenance again and tell them we have a two-man job. We'll tie them up, knock them over the head if we have to, and I'll make you up while looking at the other guy's face. Then we're out of here."

"I can't wait!"

"Me neither. I hope he wears his jacket again like he did tonight. It covers up more."

"You're learning. By the way, did you get his name?"

"You bet. Larry Near."

* * *

Wednesday morning Pat went to the office for a short time before going to meet with Jalessa Johnson, a court-appointed client. He left the office, went across the street to the jail, and asked to see Jalessa. Attorneys had to meet female prisoners while standing in the hallway. A female deputy escorted a very large woman out of her cell.

Jalessa *could overpower the female deputy at will, as she could have been a defensive lineman, uh, linewoman, with The Atlanta Falcons.*

"Ms. Johnson, I'm Pat Patton, your court-appointed attorney."

"Hi, Mister Patton." Jalessa's hairy black chest contrasted greatly against the white low-cut prison uniform.

"Please call me Jal."

"And you can call me Pat."

She looked at him with bright intelligent dark eyes, put her arm around him, and said, "Say, Honey, you sure is a good-lookin' thing. You gonna be able to get me out of dis mess?"

"Let's talk about it, Jal. I only know what I got in the paperwork from the Court Administrator. Namely, three counts of forgery."

"Originally der was 33, but 30 of them was dropped," informed Jal with a sly smile.

"Yeah, because they want to go with three solid cases against you. They really want to put you away, or so the Court Administrator told me."

"You talk to da DA yet?"

"No, Jal, I wanted to hear your side of the story first. You're an old-timer, so I don't have to tell you that I'm on your side, and we have an attorney/client relationship. As you probably know, what you don't tell me could hurt you in the long run."

"Okay, Honey. De only type of these cases that worries me is de tire cases, and dat's de three dey kept."

"Please tell me what you're talking about."

"I was a-workin' wif a burglary ring. Let's say dat you was married and your house was broken into and your wife's checkbook was found. Dey would tear out a couple of checks where dey would not be noticed unless you was lookin' fer dem. Dey would sell me dose checks. I would go to my license man and have a fake Georgia driver's license made up wif my picture and your wife' name and address on it."

"Wow, that's a lot of trouble to go through, isn't it?"

"It's my job, Honey, and I made over $150,000 last year! How much did you make?"

"Not even a quarter of that amount but you're in here and I'm out there. I surely am."

"Dat's right, Honey but you be *existin'* and I be *livin'*. Lookie here. I'm a black woman wif a 8th-grade education. Got mixed up wif several men, all worthless. What am I gonna do on the outside, Honey? Clean houses? Work at de car wash? Make maybe $10,000 to $15,000 a year? Come on, Honey! I be makin' dat much in a month, an it be tax free. I just be more careful next time. It be dumb luck dat dey caught me!"

"Okay, Jal. Look, I'll go talk to the DA and see what she has on you. I'll file a discovery motion before I go to see her and give her a copy at our meeting. The DA's Office is pretty good at complying with my demands. You can plan on seeing me tomorrow right after lunch. Say, about 2:00."

"I ain't goin' nowhere, Honey."

Pat laughed and could not help liking this woman, even though she was a con artist.

"Until tomorrow then."

"See you at 2:00, Honey," and Jalessa put out her hairy arms and gave Pat a hug.

* * *

Pat left and went to see the Assistant DA assigned to Jalessa's case. Nancy Katman was a tough cookie. She drove a red Chevy van, rode a motorcycle, and liked to wear anything but a dress. He heard she had a pet pig named Ethel. She also had a sharp mind and was not a pushover in court.

"Hi, Thelma. Please tell Nancy I've come to see her about the Jalessa Johnson case."

"She's with someone, but you're next. Say, did you hear what happened at this courthouse yesterday? Solicitor George Franklyn was sitting in a stall in the men's room when the commode in the next stall exploded! He said he smelled something like burning rope for the ten minutes he was in there. Then blamm!" laughed Thelma.

"Sounds terrible! Did it do much damage?"

"No, not really. Most everyone except Solicitor Franklyn and the police thought it was funny."

"Come to think about it, it was funny. Can you imagine him sitting there when it went off?"

"You said no damage, so it must not have been a bomb."

"Oh no, probably some kids pulling a prank."

Yeah, a 30-year-old kid, thought Pat. Eb had visited him yesterday.

"Nancy can see you now."

"Thanks, Thelma. " Pat went into the hall leading to Nancy's office.

* * *

"Hi, I'm Pat Patton," he managed to get the words out as he looked at a hefty woman wearing a black sweater, black slacks and a beautiful big smile.

"Nice to meet you, Pat." Nancy reached out and they shook hands. "Have you met Shirley O'Kelly," asked Nancy, pointing to a young woman, who had walked into the room.

Pat was thunderstruck! There she stood - - the girl of his dreams. As they shook hands, it was as though electricity flowed from her to him. Pat noticed the top of her head came up to his chin and he could smell her perfume. She smiled at him with bright green eyes and her long blond hair swayed as she moved her head. Oh, how she filled out her white sweater and dark blue skirt. Not beautiful in a classic sense, but she was very attractive and radiated something that took Pat's breath away. Little did he realize he was having a similar effect on her. Neither one of them could speak for a few seconds.

There was a sharp contrast between Nancy and Shirley. While Shirley radiated femininity with her long blond hair, Nancy radiated charm, a sureness of her abilities, and her reputation spoke of a touch of rebel. Shirley had an air of confidence, but there was no doubt who was in charge when in Nancy's office because she was the veteran.

Finally, after what seemed like an hour, Pat was able to say, "I-I'm very pleased to meet you, Miss O'Kelly," hoping that it was Miss and not Mrs. He looked for a ring but, because of the way she was standing, he could not see her left hand.

Shirley also hesitated before saying, "S-o nice to meet you, Mr. Patton." She had caught him staring at her left hand, realized what he was doing, and moved her hand through her hair so he could see her naked ring finger.

"Pat, Shirley here was Judge Cody's law clerk. She just got word she passed the Bar and will now be working for the DA's Office. She starts as an Assistant DA next week. Shirley, Thelma or one of the other girls will show you around and I'll see you after lunch."

"See you, Miss O'Kelly." Pat gave a boyish grin.

"You, too," agreed Shirley with a sweet smile as she left.

"Okay, Pat, now down to business. Thelma said you wanted to see me about our old friend, Jalessa Johnson."

"Old friend?"

"Yes. We have been trying to get her for years. A slick customer, that one. She could con an ax from a woodcutter."

"What do you have on her, Nancy?"

"Look, I'm not going to pull any punches. We've got her dead to rights on one tire case and I'd say we have an 80% chance on the other two tire cases. Maybe as high as 90%. All of the cases are similar. Jalessa calls up a tire store and asks them what time they close. If they say 9:00, she tells them she has to work until 8:30 but could get there by 8:45. What she is trying to do is catch them as they are trying to close."

"How do you know she calls first?"

"Two different store employees recognized her voice. Back to my story. She then asks if the store has a certain tire and size in stock. Always premium top-of-the-line tires. She gets different sizes, which leads me to believe she has them pre-sold. Anyway, she tells the store employee she has someone to mount them, so she doesn't need the tires installed.

"Just to sound legitimate, she haggles over the price, telling them she should get a discount as they are not being mounted. Jalessa goes to the tire store, buys the tires using a check, shows them a phony driver's license, and has the tires put into the back of her station wagon. Finally, she drives off into the sunset, or rather the moon light in most cases."

"How did she get caught?"

"Sheer luck or bad luck on her part. She picked the wrong store where the cashier was the daughter of the woman your client was pretending to be. When the cashier saw the name and address of her mother on the driver's license and check, she immediately stalled Jalessa and called the police. Jalessa got wise and left, without the fake license with her picture and fingerprints on the plastic. An employee also got her tag number."

"Pat, a first-year law student could prosecute this case and get a conviction. The other cases are similar, but we don't have the license. However, we do have witnesses who will ID her."

"It doesn't look good for the home team."

"But, Pat, this is your big day because I'm going to offer your client a deal she can't refuse. If she decides to go to trial and loses, the judge has promised ten years on each count. That's 30 years if he runs the sentences consecutively. This case has been assigned to Judge Musselman, who said he would accept five years to serve, followed by five years of probation on the three counts. In other words, ten do five, but only because you're such a nice guy," smiled Nancy.

"Sure, but I know it couldn't have anything to do with his crowded trial calendar, could it?"

"How did you ever guess?" laughed Nancy.

"I'll pass it on to her as I know *Chain Gang* can be tough."

"Nice meeting you, Pat. Let me know if we have a deal. And - before you try it, he will not budge from the five to serve, and that is only if she is willing to plead guilty. I'm being truthful when I tell you it is his bottom line."

Nancy picked up the phone.

"Thelma, Nancy here, I'm going to lunch."

Pat saluted and left. It was a fruitful meeting, but half of his mind had been on Shirley. He had to see her again. He could not believe it, but there she was in the empty waiting room talking to Thelma.

"Well, hi there again," said Pat. *What a stupid non-original thing to say,* thought Pat.

"Hello, Mr. Patton. I was trying to get Thelma to go to lunch with me, but she can't make it."

"I'm available." *I can't believe I said that. She'll think I'm coming on too strong.*

"Well, I may be." *What a dumb answer. Might be? Hell, I'm chomping at the bit. I don't want to play too hard to get.*

"Is that a yes?" asked Pat with a big smile.

"I guess so." *There I go again, can't say anything right,* thought Shirley, running her hand through her hair.

"We can take my car, Shirley, ah Miss O'Kelly. I'm parked across the street and you won't lose your parking space."

As they were leaving, Thelma whispered, "It worked, Shirley." Shirley did not answer but turned beet red.

"What was that all about?"

"Oh, nothing," mumbled Shirley.

"We need to walk across the street to my office so I can drop off my briefcase and let Julie, my secretary, know where I'm going."

As they crossed the street, there was silence. When they arrived, Pat told Julie, "I'm going to lunch with Miss O'Kelly. Then after lunch to the airport, if I don't have any appointments."

After thinking a moment, Pat shook his head. "I forgot about Jalessa Johnson. I told her I would meet her at 2:00."

"Geez, Boss, did you also forgot the motion's calendar on the Washington case at 4:00. It was specially set and just you and Kimbrough are on the judge's calendar to argue motions. Something got your mind confused?" ribbed Julie, who was smiling and looking at Shirley. "However, you are clear for tomorrow afternoon."

How could I have ever forgotten that?

Julie, however, had easily figured it out. Pat was trying to get as much time in as he could at the airport so he could solo as soon as possible. Having Shirley with him had confused his thinking.

"Excuse me, ladies; I did not properly introduce you two. Shirley O'Kelly, I would like you to meet Julie Crawford, my secretary. Miss O'Kelly is a new Assistant DA and was formerly a law clerk."

"Nice to meet you, Shirley."

"You, too, Julie."

"Pat never told me about you."

"We just met."

As they were going out of the back door, Julie whispered to Pat, "You sure have good taste, Boss."

"Shirley, I want to introduce you to Max the Mustang. Over there," pointing to the black convertible.

"Max is a handsome car, Pat."

He opened the door for her, bowing and saying, "Miss O'Kelly."

"Do you like Mexican?" asked Pat.

"Love it."

"Okay, then it is off to the Brave Bull." They talked non-stop during the ride. When they got to the restaurant, the conversation continued at the table.

"Where are you from, Shirley?"

"Me? Well, I'm a Georgia girl, born right here in good old Jonesboro. How about you?"

"Philadelphia, Pennsylvania, or just outside of it. I grew up on a farm, although my father was an auto mechanic who had his own automobile repair business."

"A Yankee, huh?" replied Shirley, in her best Scarlett O'Hara voice.

"Guilty. But I have been a Southerner now for several years."

"An illegal alien down here from Pennsylvania, huh? Do you have a green card?"

That broke Pat up and when he stopped laughing, she asked, "How did you come to move to the Atlanta area?"

"Would you like a brief history of my life?"

"That would be interesting. Sure, go ahead."

"I'll do it, but I have to warn you, it's your turn next."

They were smiling and getting comfortable with each other.

"Fair enough. Go ahead."

"I was born in 1949 in Philadelphia. My mother stayed home with my sister and I until we were in Junior High School then got a part-time job in a bakery, more to get out of the house than anything else. My sister ended up being a telephone operator. Dad did not want me to be a mechanic and kept telling me not to work with my hands like him but to work with my head. He said working with your hands is fine when you're young but it's hard on you when you get older. I graduated from high school in '67. Then I spent almost two years goofing off, working on my Cadillac-powered 1939 Ford Coupe. I specialized in drag racing, hunting, and chasing girls. I lived with a pistol on my hip and a rifle or shotgun in my hands.

"We had a 114-acre farm but we didn't farm for a living. My dad bought a tractor and we farmed about 80 acres of the land part time but had a neighbor use his heavy equipment for harvesting the crops.

"I entered Penn State University in '70 and in '71 I got drafted. Christmas of 1971 at that, and went into the Army in January '72. After basic training, they sent me to a six-month electronics' school. Then to Thule, Greenland, for a year but I somehow missed going to Viet Nam. When I got out of the Army in '74, I moved in with my parents in Charleston, SC, and graduated from Charleston State College. In '75 I got married to a girl I met while in the Army, which was a big mistake, because it lasted less than a year. I moved to Atlanta in '76 to go to law school, and got a job with the Great Atlanta Insurance Company.

"I went to law school at night, worked at Great Atlanta during the day, and part-time at a motorcycle shop. This past January I sat for the Georgia Bar exam as a senior in law school, and darned if I didn't luck out and pass that sucker. Last June they swore me in, and here I am. How was that?"

"Very good, Mr. Patton. By the way, what is your middle name?"

"Patton"

"No. Your middle name.

"My father married a Patton, no relation, and my mother's maiden name was given to me as my middle name."

"Pat Patton Patton?" asked a laughing Shirley.

"Yes. But, please call me Pat. Now the spotlight is on you!"

"I guess a deal is a deal." Shirley made a fake pout. "I was born in '51, right here in Jonesboro, GA. My father is a doctor, medical type. My mother is a nurse. That's how she met my dad. My brother is the smart one and is a doctor. I graduated from Jonesboro High School in '69 and went to the University of Georgia from '69 to '73 where I received a BA in Business Administration. After graduation, I decided to get my masters, which I received in '75. I played on the tennis team in high school and in college.

"You mentioned guns, so you might be surprised when I tell you I went hunting with my dad and bagged two bucks. I made him field-dress them though. You know, his being a doctor and all. I am proficient with a pistol and Daddy bought me a .38 Colt Cobra. I got a concealed weapon permit when I worked as a law clerk and sometimes went out to the parking lot after working late at night.

"Then after I earned my Master's degree in Business Administration, I realized I had been in college for six years and needed to get away from it. I got a job as a stewardess with World Wide Airlines and saw the world, or at least the airports of the world. I ended up married to a pilot for 13 months. A real bad deal -- he needed a whole lot more female company than just me. I was with the airlines for two years, and then decided to go to law school. Dad wanted me to go to medical school, but doctor's hours are not for me. I graduated last year and landed a job as a law clerk until I passed the Bar, which I just did. I got sworn in Monday. So now you know everything about me, except that I moved out of my parent's house to be on my own."

I wish I did, really did, know everything. I've never felt this way about anyone before and I've just met her.

"Are you okay, Pat?"

"Oh, just thinking. You must have really worked hard."

"I did, but I had to. I'm smart, but not brilliant. I can get the grades, but I have to work for them. My dad paid for all of my college. I can't imagine how you got through it all; working two jobs at the same time you went to law school."

"Like you said, it wasn't easy, but if you want it bad enough, you can do it."

Just then the Special #2 came, which consisted of a burrito, rice, and beans, and they both got Cokes. The two of them were engrossed with each other, and before they knew it, lunch was over and they needed to get back to their respective jobs.

"Pat, I have a confession to make."

"What is it, Shirley?"

"When you came out of Nancy's office into the waiting room, ah, ah..."

"Yes?"

"I was stalling. Waiting for you. Thelma was up to her ears in it, too. She really likes you and had told me all about you."

"Wow! I'm flattered, but I have a confession to make,

too. When I came out of Nancy's office, I was looking for you. I was trying to think of a way to start up a conversation. Then when I got to talk to you, nothing came out right."

They both laughed and went back to their respective offices. Pat dropped Shirley off after getting her phone number and promising to call that evening.

* * *

About a half mile from the office, he had a flat tire, which took him over 45 minutes to jack up the car, change the tire, and drop the flat at the local gas station. As a result, at 2:30, he got back to the jail to see Jalessa.

"Say, Honey, where you been? It be way after 2:00 and I've been worried 'bout you!"

"You won't believe this, Jalessa, but just before I got to my office from lunch, I got a flat tire!"

Jalessa got real close to Pat and put one of her hairy arms around him. "Honey, you get me out of dis mess an I be gettin' you all de tires you can use!"

"No! No! Don't do that to me. Don't do that to me."

Her whole face lit up in a mischievous smile.

"Okay, Honey. Tell me what dat big bad old Assistant DA had to say."

Pat told her. She agreed that going to trial with so much of evidence against her was useless. "Set up a plea."

* * *

Pat went to the motion hearing in preparation for Sammy's trial.

That night Pat talked to Shirley for over an hour on the phone and set up a date for Friday night.

* * *

While Pat was making plans to see Shirley, Skinny was making plans to see Pat!

Chapter 16

Late November - Plans Cancelled

Skinny had everything ready to go on Friday night. He was working late in the school and waiting for Dean. Something was wrong though, because he was supposed to get word that maintenance man Larry Near was on duty. A buddy was buffing the hall and watching for Larry to come to work. Only Larry would work in the plan because all of Skinny's makeup was geared to resemble Larry, the only one who physically resembled Skinny. Dean came in and had a frown on his face.

"What's up?"

"Bad news, Skinny! Our hall man talked to an inmate buddy who works in maintenance, who told him that Near called in sick tonight."

"Damn! Damn! Damn! I was all keyed up and ready to do it!"

"Me, too. Where can I hide the makeup?"

Skinny took the stuff and put it inside an unused broken Franklin computer he had gutted. He had taken out the screws on the cover so he could slip it off. After he put the things inside, he replaced one screw to insure someone could not accidently pull off the cover and find his stash.

"Well, it's off for now. I want to do it on a Friday because our escape won't be as readily noticed. The weekend crews are laid back and not as careful."

"See you next week then, about the same time."

"No, Dean, not next Friday, 'cause that's inventory day. Everything will be screwed up and movement restricted. Most likely some of the staff will be in here, too. It will have to be Friday two weeks. Damn, Damn, Damn! I wanted out of here tonight!" muttered a very disappointed Skinny.

"Sorry, Skinny. We are good to go, just need the right time. Well, I'm going. See you either on the yard or in school Monday."

After Dean left, Skinny hid a long metal shaft he had removed from the carriage of an old typewriter kept for parts. The shaft originally had rubber rollers on it to hold down the paper. It had taken a week to hone a very sharp point on one end of the shaft. It resembled a short lethal sword.

Waiting was going to throw his escape plans into the first week of December. As he thought about it, a big smile came over his face.

December! Of course! I'll escape and then give them each a Christmas present to last an eternity!

He could feel his finger on the trigger as he thought about it.

Christmas 1980 would be their last.

* * *

Friday for Pat was just another day at the office. Julie said there was a man in the waiting room, but he didn't have an appointment. Pat agreed to see him because he said it involved both a divorce and a criminal case.

Julie showed him in. "Mr. Patton, this is Mr. Roy Davis."

"Please have a seat, Mr. Davis. How can I help you?"

"Well, I'm here to see you about two things. I'm not worried about the first one, but I want you to know I love my wife."

"I'm sure you do. However, I'm confused. What's the first *one*?"

"What *first one*?"

"You said you weren't worried about the *first one*. I'm trying to find out what that is."

"Oh, ah, I got a simple battery charge on me. I'm not worried about that one because I don't beat my wife anymore. I'm on Lithium, you see. I used to beat her, but not anymore. That's why I'm not worried about that charge. I am worried about the divorce. Mr. Patton, I love my wife and worship her like the queen she is. Even if she is living with Melvin."

"You're telling me she is now living with a man named Melvin?"

"No."

"What do you mean by no?"

"Well, uh, Melvin's not a man. At least not yet."

"Mr. Davis, you have me completely confused. Please explain."

"Melvin used to be a woman, but now is only half of one. She had an operation to remove her breasts. However, she hasn't had the operation to put an appendage between her legs yet. Oh, Mr. Patton, I can do my wife so much more good than Melvin can. I want her back!" cried Mr. Davis.

"I'm afraid, under Georgia law, if she uses the grounds that the marriage is irretrievably broken, it's all over. That's because it only takes one party to dissolve it. The judge would have no choice."

Mr. Davis looked at Pat, got up and stomped out without saying a word, slamming doors as he left.

Julie came in wondering what was going on as Mr. Davis was loudly talking to himself as he made his noisy exit to the parking lot. Pat told her the almost unbelievable story.

"Julie, it just occurred to me. That man left this office, got into a 3500-pound automobile, and is driving on the same roads as you, your family, Shirley, her family, and me. And, he is completely nuts! He surely is!"

"You can say that again. Jeez, the guy was creepy. Ah, Boss, I've got some good-bad news for you."

"Okay, let's have it."

"I got a call from Assistant DA Kimbrough concerning the Washington case. You are on *Chain Gang's* trial calendar for the second Monday in December, which is only a little over two weeks from now. That was the good news."

"Come on, Julie, what's the bad news?"

"You're number one out."

"Man, that is bad news; it surely is, as I was hoping to have more time to prepare. I know I've done a ton of work on it already, far more than I'll get paid for, but when it's your first trial, you never have enough time. So, maybe it's just as well, as I could prepare for the next year and still think of something else I need to do."

"Jeez, Boss, you have a neat way of looking at things. What a positive attitude!"

"Thanks, Julie. BecauseI don't have any appointments this afternoon, I'm going to work on the Washington case. I want you to subpoena Mrs. Washington, Mrs. Jones, and Doctor Fester. Also, a document subpoena for Dr. Fester's file on Sammy," requested Pat, taking a bite out of a Hershey Bar.

"I'll go over to the courthouse now. Rhonda can cover for me."

"Fine, Julie. I'll work on the Washington case until about 4:30. I have a hot date with Shirley!"

"You really seem to like her. First real date, huh?"

"Right on both accounts. I more than like her, and it is our first real date. We are getting to know each other fairly well though, as we have talked on the phone for an hour or so every night, and I did take her out to lunch last Wednesday.

"Tomorrow, being Saturday, I plan to spend the best part of the day at the airport. If the wind conditions are calm, I can practice hops. I did some last time and got 20 to 30 feet in the air. Tomorrow I can use the half-mile runway and get up to 50 or 75 feet. Maybe even 100 feet or so and land at the end of the runway. Then fly back and do it again and again. The wind needs to be no more than a few miles per hour or I can't practice. Usually the best time is early morning and late afternoon, but I hope to get in late from my date with Shirley. If I get home too early, things didn't go well. Pat grinned.

"I'll let you get back to work and disturb you only if somebody is threatening to give you some money."

"You're learning, Shirley, I mean Julie."

"Boy, you've got it bad. Call me if you need me.

Pat worked on the Washington case all afternoon. *The public has no idea how much work goes into preparing for a jury trial. Interviewing the DA, your client, witnesses, and in this case, a shrink.*

He was also able to talk to a bank employee, who was on the DA's witness list, and one of the police officers. Sometimes interviewing witnesses was very hard because a DA often instructed them not to talk to defense attorneys.

Later Pat called the bank and told the manager, "I understand you talked to investigators from the DA's Office. While your co-operation is appreciated, there are a few more questions."

He never said he was from the DA's Office, he just gave that impression. As a result, he learned about a teller who Sammy held at knife-point, and she talked to Pat freely.

Opening statements and closing arguments had to be prepared, as well as anticipated cross-examination questions, and questions he wanted to ask his witnesses on direct examination. Then there were voir dire questions, or preliminary questions, to ask a prospective jury member, in order to determine if the attorney wanted that person on the jury. There were also requests to charge, which was law that the attorneys would request the judge to give to the jury at the end of the trial. Of course, always in the respective side's favor. A well-prepared attorney also had to anticipate objections to evidence he presented and be prepared to argue his objections, or counter the objection of opposing counsel.

Witnesses had to be prepared in what to say, and almost as important, what not to say. They also needed to know what they could expect when the DA cross-examined them. A lot of hard work goes into trial preparation, and more hard work and tense moments when trying the case. Objections have to be made in a timely fashion, almost instantly, or you waive the right to make them. An attorney cannot come back an hour later and object to something he did not like. Overall, one devil of a lot of work went into a trial.

Pat was glad he had done most of the preparation as the month went along. He was also fortunate he had Herb, because Herb had spent several hours preparing Pat for his first jury trial. Pat had also taken Herb's advice and, early on, had sat through a jury trial in each of the four Superior Court judges' courtrooms. He had also watched one trial in State court, where misdemeanors, or lesser crimes, were tried.

Pat came out of his daydream when Julie said, "Boss, a reporter from the Clayton Daily News is on the phone asking if you have any comments on the Washington case."

"Boy, they have the scent now, don't they? Tell the reporter *no comment* at this time, except to say my client is obviously mentally ill, and I plan on showing his mental illness to the jury. I will be glad to agree to an interview when the trial is over. I do not want to compromise my client in any way by commenting on the case at this time."

"There was also a phone call from some nut-case wondering if you and Sammy would be interested in investing in a roofing nail company."

"Sure, Julie, I'll take a thousand shares of stock." Pat's unhidden sarcasm always made Julie giggle.

Pat looked at the clock. "Gosh, 4:30 already! Got to go! Do you have anything you have to do, Julie?"

"No, why?"

"Then leave early, but mark 5:30 on the time card. Here, I already cut you a check based on that. You deserve it."

"Geez! Thank you, Boss! I can beat the traffic now that I can get into my car without that *Insurance Guy* blocking me in. By the way, Boss, you know anything about that firecracker in the men's room at the courthouse? Was it you or Eb?"

"Quiet, Julie. The walls have ears."

"Enjoy your hot date. Gertrude is going to be upset by the competition."

"I'll see her Saturday and Sunday afternoon. She will have to play second fiddle to Shirley. Have a good weekend!"

"You, too, Boss!"

* * *

On the way home, Pat stopped for some beer, and once again turned on the CB radio. There they were, Pick'em-Up-Man, Sheet-Metal King, Diamond Jim, and MoPar Man.

Pat could not resist the temptation to pick up the mike.

"Breaker, breaker, any taker? How 'bout it you, sweet Pick'em-Up-Man? Did you enjoy the beer I left for you?" Pat used his Gay Blade lisp.

"No! Not you again, Blade!"

"I bought a nice pair of tight pink pants just for my s-w-e-e-t Pick'em-Up-Man."

"Please leave me alone, Blade," pleaded Pick'em-Up-Man.

"Boys, he don't sound too awful convincing to me. I'll bet he's seein' the Blade on the side." Diamond Jim laughed.

"No," corrected the Blade, "*on my tummy!*"

"See what you did, Blade? My friends are turning their backs on me."

"Would y-o-u like me to turn my b-a-c-k on you, if you know what I mean?"

"Blade, one of these days I'll catch up with you and I'll kick your ass clear over your car!"

"But, Sweetie, that's not what you did with it the other night."

"Get off the damn radio, you freaking fagot! I've had enough of you to last a lifetime!"

"I know. Remember when you said a little of m-e-e-e goes a l-o-n-g way?"

"Score, ten for the Blade and one for Pick'em-Up-Man!" announced MoPar Man.

Pick'em-Up-Man flew into a rage, cussing and pounding his fists against his dash, spittle coming out of his mouth.

Pat decided he had done enough damage for one night.

"Ta-ta, Handsome! See you lay-ter sweet pa-ta-ter."

"Nasty Pick-em-Up-Man! You might have hurt the Blade's feelings with all of that cussin'," laughed Sheet-Metal Man.

Pat was smiling as he pulled into his driveway.

"Hey, Eb, I'm home." Pat put two six-packs in the fridge.

No answer. He walked back to the bedroom and Eb's door was closed. He was about to knock when he heard moans and groans and the sound of vibrating bed springs and saw Eb's infamous sign on the door that read, "Caution- -Man at Work."

Better not knock. Eb's got him an afternoon delight. Well, I have something much, much better. Shirley! This was no one-night stand. I never felt this way about anyone before. Not even mys first wife. Man, I have it bad. I want to be with her and, of course, I want sex, but being with her, holding her, and talking with her is more important to me. I'm so afraid of doing something or saying something that could blow this relationship.

Pat took a shower and got ready to go. Still early, he decided to stop for some flowers.

Shirley's apartment complex was only 15 minutes away, and he did not have a problem finding it. Pat was very nervous as he walked to the apartment door.

* * *

Earlier that day, Shirley had phoned her best friend.

"Kathy, I'm a nervous wreck! This is no ordinary date for me. There is something special about this guy that I can't put my finger on. What if I mess it up? What if he doesn't like me? What can I wear?"

"Hold on, Shirley. You sound like a young girl going to her first dance! Of course he'll like you. Gosh, Honey, have you ever really taken a close look at yourself? You have a very attractive face, beautiful hair, gorgeous eyes and teeth, and a magnificent body, not to mention a great personality."

"Boy, do you know how to make a girl feel good! Are you sure you're talking about me?"

"Yes, I'm talking about you. As for what to wear, you do wonders for a sweater. So, why not that white one, or should I say beige, and the skirt to match. Also, the gold belt and beige shoes. And wear your hair long - - that's what most guys like."

"Oh, thank you, Kathy. I feel better already. I had better start getting ready. I'm just excited about this date and want everything to be perfect."

Shirley hung up the phone and took a shower, and then proceeded to try on several outfits before she finally settled on the one Kathy suggested. The clock stood still! She was as ready as she would ever be and she had an hour before he was due. She had left the office at 3:00 to prepare for this *big date.*

"Finally, he's here!" She had been looking out the window and saw the beautiful black Mustang pull up. Pat was wearing black slacks and a white sweater with a collar on it, and black shoes. He was carrying a gray jacket, as the night was cooling off very fast. The weather in Georgia, especially from Halloween to Christmas is hard to redice; it could be 70° or below freezing. Tonight was mild and a very mild weekend was predicted. Shirley was glad, because Pat wanted to go flying tomorrow and Sunday afternoon. Sunday morning she was going to try getting him in church with her.

The doorbell rang and Shirley jumped, even though she knew it was going to ring. Her heart was racing as she opened the door.

As Pat pushed the doorbell button, his knees got weak. He wanted to make a good impression on her.

"Hi, Shirley." He didn't know what to do - - nothing, hug her, or shake her hand.

Boy does she look good! I can't be going out with something this gorgeous. He tried not to stare at her breasts, but that was hard - - they filled out her sweater so beautifully.

"Come in, Pat." *What a hunk! I'll bet he runs and works out. A non-smoker, too!*

She didn't know what to do -- give him her hand, fly into his arms, or nothing. She played it safe and did nothing.

"I brought a little something for you." Pat pulled the beautiful bouquet of flowers from behind his back.

Shirley's eyes lit up and she could not restrain herself as she took the flowers in her left hand and wrapped herself around him with a big hug using her right arm. As she did so, Pat could not restrain himself and he put both arms around her and hugged her back. As he did, her soft breasts pressed against his chest and he felt his member expanding. She really turned him on!

They broke up the clinch and both seemed a little embarrassed.

"I brought a paper to check out a movie after we are done eating." He held the newspaper in front of his pants.

"Have a seat. I'll put your beautiful flowers in a vase."

Shirley returned and placed it in the middle of her coffee table. From where Pat was sitting, he could see her bend over the table, which showed off her buttocks. This did nothing to help his problem.

"You have a very nice place, Shirley." Until then he really hadn't looked much at the apartment. She had very good taste in furniture and the place was spotless.

"Thank you, Pat. Let me show you around."

"Just one minute. I was trying to find the movie section in the paper." He continued to cover up with the open newspaper.

Maybe thinking about a movie will help my situation.

Shirley sat down beside him and they found a movie both thought they would like. This gave the old fellow time to relax and allowed Pat to stand up without being embarrassed.

"I'll take you up on that apartment tour now."

"Okay, come on. You have seen my living room, and here is the kitchen. This next room is a second bedroom, but since I don't intend to have a roommate, I have turned it into a study. And – speaking of roommates. Do you have a picture of Eb? My best friend Kathy is available and he sounds like a hoot."

Good, no roommate. How nice!

"Ah, I'll have to get one."

"This is my bedroom. I also have a half-bath in here. The full-bath is right down the hall. As you noticed, the study also has a half-bath."

"Shirley, this place is really fixed up nice. Women seem to have a natural touch with something like this. My décor is 30-year old male and it looks it. My house just seems to have pieces of furniture in it, but yours seems so integrated, all the pieces seem to fit together."

"Thank you."

They went back to the living room and she got her coat. Pat helped her put it on and they left for the Red Lobster and supper.

* * *

Pat had called earlier and made reservations, so it was not long before they were seated. They talked, laughed, and continued getting to know each other.

"Shirley, I have never met anyone quite like you before."

"I'll bet you say that to all the girls."

"No, it's true. I feel like I have known you a lot longer than a week."

"Maybe it's because we have talked on the phone for an hour or longer every night since I met you," laughed Shirley.

"I guess that's it." A beaming Pat looked at his watch. "Wow, it's time to go to the movie theater already."

"I'm ready." Shirley got up from her chair.

The bill had been paid, but they had stayed, totally engrossed with each other and oblivious to time. They left and Pat stopped at a convenience store.

"What kind of soft drink do you like?"

"Coke would be fine."

"That's what I drink, too. Ah, look. Please don't think I'm a cheapskate when I say this, but would you mind if I got us a couple of drinks here and you take them into the movie theater in your pocket book?" cautiously asked Pat.

"No. In fact, Daddy does it all the time with Mother. He says you have to mortgage your house to get a soft drink when you see a movie."

"He sounds like a neat guy to me. Be right back."

Pat bought two drinks and each a Hershey Bar.

* * *

"Here we are." Pat pulled into the parking lot. Then he broke out in laughter.

"What is it, Pat?" asked Shirley, now also laughing.

"See that guy over there?" explained Pat, almost unable to talk, as he tried to point out a man in the crowd.

"Yes, but I don't see anything so funny."

"Look at the movie he is about to go see."

"It's a sword-fighting picture called *The Gay Buccaneer*."

Pat was almost laughing too hard to continue. The man was Pick'em-Up-Man with some little dude wearing tight pink pants! And, he had a wiggle in his walk!

"I'll tell you about them as soon as we get our tickets,

but not to *The Gay Buccaneer.*"

They got their tickets, bought the mandatory box of popcorn, and found some good seats about one-quarter of the way down and in the middle of the theater. While waiting for the movie to start, Pat told her the story of Pick'em-Up-Man and the Gay Blade. Shirley laughed so hard she couldn't talk and people started looking at her. Pat caught it and laughed, too. The movie had not started yet, so they had not disturbed anyone.

"Pat, I can't really believe you did that!"

"Oh, but I did, I did."

Shirley got closer and put her hand on his. He felt excitement shoot up through his arm.

I wonder if I was too bold, but it seemed so natural to take his hand.

She had no need to worry as Pat took his left hand and put it over hers. They looked at each other and smiled. The two of them talked a few more minutes and then the movie started.

Pat pulled his hands away and Shirley gave him a puzzled look, but Pat put his right arm around her shoulders. She smiled and got as close to this man as she possibly could.

Pat's arm started to go numb, but he didn't want to move it from around her. Finally, he had to, but then took a chance and placed it on her lap. She put her hand on his and they continued to watch the movie.

Gosh, I felt a shock wave go through me . His elbow is on my thigh and his hand is on my knee. That feels so damned good!

I can't believe I put my hand on her lap.

Too soon the movie was over.

***

As they walked to *Max the Mustang*, Shirley grabbed his arm and whispered, "Look over there! It's Pick'em-Up-Man and Sugar Britches."

Pat looked and could not believe his eyes. Pick'em-Up-Man had his arm around the little guy in pink pants and was now opening the door for him. They were in a late model Chevy pickup truck.

"I guess he thought he was safe here away from home, but it really is Pick'em-Up-Man, and I like the name Sugar Britches."

"Turn on the CB radio, Pat! Maybe you can have some more fun with him," agitated Shirley.

"You got it, Shir, you surely do."

"There he goes. Let's follow him, like in the movies, but not too far."

"Okay."

Almost immediately they heard him on the radio. He was talking to an 18-wheeler on a nearby highway. Pat cut in.

"Hey, Pick'em-Up-Man, you two-timing creep! Who is that floozy you're with? Why I'll scratch her eyes out."

"Uh, uh, is that you, Blade?" Pick'em-Up-Man sounded defeated.

"You know darn well it is and I'm upset because number one, you stood me up at the bowling alley, and number two, now you're with, that - - that - - thing that's sitting next to you!"

"It's okay, Blade. Willie and me ain't going steady. This is only a date. Are you following me? Come on."

Pat didn't answer right away because he and Shirley were laughing. He also ignored Pick'em-Up-Man's question.

"Come on back, Blade, this be the Pick'em-Up-Man. And, what did you mean by I stood you up? You stood me up. I was right in front of the *Bowl-A-Rama* for a solid hour and circled it every ten minutes! Come on."

Pat picked up the mike. "*The Bowl-A-Rama*? Sweetie, I was at the *Ten Golden Pins*."

"I'm sorry, Blade. Hey, you won't tell the guys about this will you? They don't know, but you sure have given them ideas. Come on. Pick'em-Up-Man had a pleading voice.

"Oh, go back to your floozy! I'll have to think about it. Ten Four and Out."

He and Shirley laughed until Shirley's stomach hurt.

"Pat, I had no idea what a mischievous, bad little boy I am going out with. And me, *Miss Law and Order* and all." She exaggerated her Southern accent.

"Shir, there is most likely a mischievous side of you, too!

I just haven't seen it yet. On the other hand, have I? You're the one who wanted me to turn on the CB radio and you're the one, ladies and gentlemen of the jury, who forced, yes I say, forced me to follow Pick'em-up-Man!"

"I don't know whether to plead the Fifth or cop a plea!" laughed Shirley. "And, by the way, I kind of like it when you call me Shir."

"Why thank you, ma'am. Say, there's an ice-cream place. You game?"

"Butter Pecan.".

"Boy, that's a short-cut answer." They pulled into *20 Flavors and More.*

Pat went into the store and came out with two ice-cream cones.

I have to take Shirley home now. At times like this, I hate bucket seats and four on the floor. I want to hold her. Boy would I love to put my arm around her and cup one of those lovely breasts.

I wish we would have taken my car, thought Shirley. *It doesn't have bucket seats. If he were to touch one of my breasts, I would be so embarrassed, not that he touched one, but my erect nipples would give away what I'm really thinking.*

Man, I can't even think about her without the worm turning into a snake.

They arrived at her apartment after talking all the way home. Pat got out, opened the car door for her, and they walked to the door.

* * *

"Would you like to come in for a nightcap?"

"Does a bear ... uh."

"Don't worry; I know the rest of it. Come on in.

Pat sat on the couch while Shirley turned on the record player she had preloaded with mood music. She went into the kitchen and fixed them a mixed drink, along with a bowl of potato chips and pretzels, and then sat down next to him.

"Pat, I had a wonderful time."

"Me, too, Shir. You are so much fun to be with." He gently nudged her into his arms and kissed her. She responded very passionately, and Pat found them sliding down on the couch with him halfway on top of her.

"Oh, Pat," moaned Shirley and pulled him down on top of her. They kissed long and passionately.

Without thinking, he kissed her again while he reached up and put his left hand on one of her soft breasts. He could feel the hard nipple through her bra and felt the transformation process take place. He pushed her sweater up over her bra, while sliding his hand around her back and unclasping it. Pat pulled up the bra and exposed one of the loveliest breasts he had ever seen. Her small nipples were hard as he placed his lips on one and kissed it all over. His left hand was on her thigh and then between her legs. Shirley let out a moan, and then gently stopped him. She put both hands on his bewildered face and looked him in the eyes.

"Pat?"

"Yes, Shir."

"Would you think I'm a bad girl if I asked you to spend the night?"

Pat got up and she led him into the bedroom. Neither was embarrassed now as they undressed each other. Her body was almost perfect, as was Pat's from his work-outs and running. He pulled her down on the bed, their naked bodies touching as he kissed her breasts while his finger found the soft moist opening between her legs.

"You don't have to worry, Honey. I'm on the pill," moaned Shirley.

He kissed her again, and then gently entered her. The pace immediately got faster and faster until it seemed like the bed would collapse when they simultaneously reached never-ending climaxes. Then they lay together, exhausted. Later they made love again at a much slower and longer-lasting pace. When they woke up in the morning, they did it again.

"I'm going to get a shower. Want to join me?" asked Shirley.

"I surely do, but I need to go out to Max first."

"What on earth for?"

"I have an overnight bag in the trunk with a change of underwear and a shaving kit in it."

"What? I just don't believe you," laughed Shirley.

"It's my Boy Scout training."

"Yes, I know. Be prepared!" grinned Shirley.

Pat went out and got his overnight bag, came back and took a shower with Shirley. They ended up making love again in the shower.

Shirley made breakfast and they talked. He told her he would be back and take her out, after he was done at the airport. He was not sure what time it would be, but he would call as soon as he got home.

"Pat, can I ask you for a favor?"

"Sure."

"Would you go with me to church tomorrow morning? You would have the afternoon to fly."

"Of course, Shir. I'd love to. Your church or mine?"

"You never mentioned a church. I know it might sound strange coming from a person who did what I did last night. I mean, having a man overnight and all, but I'm really not a bad person. I fell for you is all."

"I understand." Pat held her close.

"You never answered my question."

"I attend the First Baptist Church. How about you?"

"My whole family goes to the Solid Rock Christian Church in Jonesboro and I would love to introduce you to them."

"You have a deal. What time do I need to pick you up?"

"Sunday School starts at 10:00 and church at 11:00, but if you spend Saturday night here, you wouldn't have to pick me up. Hey, tonight is Saturday night. Having you here last night has my time-line confused. Well, do you want to?"

"Does a bear ...,"

"Yes, I know." She held him tighter. "You know, you could be habit forming."

"You already are! I'll call from home as soon as I get there. They don't have a phone at the airport. Speaking of the phone, I called Eb on yours to let him know what's going on. He was a worried little fellow because I didn't make it home last night. I told him I got captured by a beautiful woman who wouldn't let me go!"

"You know, Pat, you really are kind of strange," laughed Shirley.

"Since I got your invitation to spend the night, I won't go home from the airport. I'll come here instead. I can just pack what I need and put it in Max. Say, do you roller skate or bowl?"

"I sure do, Big Boy."

"If you're game, we'll try it tonight. Roller skating or bowling that is." Pat made a mischievous grin. He kissed her and left for home, thinking of her and Gertrude.

Maybe he wouldn't be so anxious to solo if he could read the future.

* * *

"Skinny, what will we do if a guard discovers our stash?"

"What do you think?" answered Skinny with a sick grin on his face.

"But I don't want to kill nobody."

"Don't worry. *You* won't have to."

This was the first time Dean was really afraid of Skinny.

Chapter 17

Late November - Solo in Gertrude

When Pat got back home, Eb was full of questions. Pat told him he was sure that he had met *the girl*.

"Eb, Shirley has it all. Look, I have to pack it up and head for the airport. If I can do a bunch of hops today, John thinks I might be ready to solo tomorrow. No big thing. I'll just take Gertrude around the pattern a few times. I hope so, because I'll be busy next weekend with last-minute preparations for the Washington trial."

"Listen to you, Pat. I've never seen you this excited. You're talking in circles. Sounds like you have two loves in your life, Gertrude and Shirley."

"I guess you're right. Man, I feel so alive. I'd have a beer if I weren't going flying."

"Why work next weekend on a law case?"

"That's right; I haven't seen you in a while. I'm first on the trial calendar, a week from Monday, on the Washington trial. I have my trial notebook finished, but I need to study and practice my opening and closing. I also need to review the rules of evidence along with trial procedures. Herb will be helping me all next week, too, as I told Julie to schedule only necessary appointments. Also, knowing trial objections is a must."

"Pat, I'm not doing anything today. Mind if I go with you and watch you fly?" asked Eb, who was sipping a beer.

"You're more than welcome to go, but you'll have to drive your truck, as I'm going to Shirley's from the airport." Pat couldn't help making a huge grin.

"So that's why you said something about packing it up,

huh?"

"Yeah, Eb, and I've got to take a suit because we're going to church in the morning. I'm going to meet her parents at church. You could meet us there if you like. Her dad is some kind of doctor, an MD I believe she said."

"Wow, the big time!

"Maybe. I think he's a regular doctor, but I would not care if he were flipping burgers at McDonalds."

"I'll skip church this time. Invite me later when you're not about to meet her parents. Go pack and I'll follow you to the airport."

Pat packed his overnight bag and suit bag with enough clothes and a pair of shoes to go to the office Monday from Shirley's apartment . . . if it worked out that way. He made sure he had an extra change of underwear and his dress shoes and socks. Next, he grabbed some Cokes and a small ice chest.

A few minutes later Pat yelled, "I'm ready."

Pat had parked in the driveway, and he had to make a real effort to get everything to the car in one trip. He already had his spare helmet, jacket, gloves, and roller-skates in the trunk. He had purchased several pair of disposable earplugs, which were in his pocket. After the first time in Gertrude, he always wore earplugs, as not only was her engine loud but also the spinning prop was even louder.

He stopped for some sandwiches and ice at a corner store, pulled into Bellah Airfield and parked beside Gertrude's hanger. Eb was following and parked beside him. They were the first ones there, but it would not be long until most of the gang arrived - - the weather was sunny with temperatures in the sixties. To top it off, little wind was present. It could not be better.

Pat had Eb help him pull up the tarp on the front of the hanger so he could untie Gertrude and get her out.

"Wow! She sure is neat. Do you think John would mind if I sat in her?"

"No. Not as long as I'm here, but don't touch anything." Eb climbed in and immediately got the fever. Pat let him dream a few minutes before he told Eb he needed to do a preflight check prior to firing up the engine. Pat had given John some money for gas and oil to fill two five-gallon cans with premixed gas, kept in the hanger. He had gassed her up the last time he flew but checked the fuel anyway.

As Eb got out, Pat inserted his earplugs, and put on his helmet. He jumped in and buckled up, because one of the other pilots had arrived. He turned on the ignition switch, pumped the priming bulb a few times, pulled the choke to *on*, advanced the throttle a little and yelled, "Clear prop," as he pulled the starter rope. The engine started on the third try. As it warmed up, Pat reduced the throttle and the choke until Gertrude was idling smoothly. This was important because a pilot doesn't want to cut power when flying and have the engine quit.

Pat gunned the throttle and taxied out to the strip. He did a series of hops about six to ten feet high. He turned around at the end of the runway and did another series of hops, but this time 20 to 30 feet high. When he got to the end, he turned around and went for broke, up 60 to 70 feet, as high as the large trees beside the runway. He flew all the way to the end of the strip and landed. Pat turned around and did it again, and was lifting off in less than 100 feet.

I can't believe this is not illegal; it's so much fun!

Finally, Pat saw several ultralights come out of their hangers, warming up, and getting ready to fly.

"Well, Gertrude, time to go back to your nest."

Pat came to a stop outside of the hanger and cut the engine, waving to the other pilots. Eb came running up to him.

"Man, I can't believe this! I have to learn how to fly one of those things."

"Eb, just a minute. I still have my earplugs in."

Pat took them out and he and Eb talked flying while they put Gertrude to bed. Afterward, Pat refilled the tank as John still might show up to fly. A micro-screened funnel was used to fuel Gertrude. It let gas flow through but would not allow the heavier water to pass. Water in the gas could stop the engine and kill the pilot. Sure enough, just as he finished, John drove up.

"How did you do?"

"I did hops for over an hour. Most of the time treetop high with a landing at the end."

"Tomorrow afternoon you can do a few for me, and if I like what I see, you can take her around the pattern."

"Around the pattern? You mean solo?"

"That's right. Don't look surprised. I'll bet you were thinking it's about solo time."

"Right, but it still sneaks up on you, you know?"

"How about helping me pull her back out. I'm going to fly some and practice a few emergency landings."

They pulled her out and in the process introduced John to Eb. John did a quick preflight inspection, put in his earplugs, put on his helmet, and got into Gertrude.

"Start her for me, Pat."

"Clear prop!" yelled Pat. She fired up the first time, as the engine was still warm.

Pat and Eb watched as John taxied out to the strip and proceeded to take off. It was beautiful! Gertrude was up there flying around the pattern at 1000 feet.

"Eb, I need to go as my sweetie is waiting, but I'm sure John would love to talk flying with you if you want to stick around."

Blowing out a puff of smoke from his cigar, Eb noted: "I have a date, but not until later. Because you're deserting me tonight, I'll see if I can get her to spend the night. She seems like a real hot chickie, so maybe I'll get to dunk my dickie!"

Pat shook his head and left for Shirley's apartment.

* * *

On the way, he called from a pay phone to let her know he had left the airport and asked if he could pick up anything. She said "no", except for some drinks, which he got.

He pulled into the parking lot and got out of the Mustang, still wearing his blue jeans, sweatshirt, and old shoes. Pat got to the door and had to put down some of the things he was carrying in order to ring the doorbell. When he was about to push it, the door swung open.

"Oh, Pat. I'm sorry I didn't get here in time. I saw you coming, carrying all those things and hurried to the door."

"That's okay, Shir. I made it."

Pat put his things down, and took her into his arms.

They kissed and looked into each other's eyes.

"You don't look much like an attorney today. More like an airplane pilot, I would think."

"Well, you look great in those gray slacks, and red sweater. I still can't believe this is happening with a good-looking and intelligent girl like you."

"I feel the same way about you. I see you brought your suit bag, so that means church tomorrow morning. I told Mom and Dad to expect us and we'll go out to lunch afterward."

"I'm looking forward to going to your church and meeting your folks. I have no family here and I miss them. I'll have to take you to Charleston some weekend."

"Do you drive or fly?"

"Most of the time I drive but sometimes I fly on Southern Airways."

"I'd love that, but I haven't even seen your house yet."

"How about next weekend? I have to spend several hours getting ready for the Washington trial. I know you're now with the DA's Office, but that should be okay as long as you check with your boss and stay away from taking cases where I represent the defendant."

"Already done. However, I got some flak from the new office manager and girlfriend of Assistant DA Dumbrowski. I talked to DA Colver Friday evening and let him know I had a date with you. He said basically the same thing, but went farther -- I am required to give you no information about any case that our office is handling and I am not to mention anything about your cases to anyone in the DA's Office."

"Sounds good to me. So why not plan to come over next weekend and bring a good book or some records. There's also the TV. I can spend breaks and evenings with you, but I have to work on the last-minute things on that case. I'm sure you understand, don't you?"

"Of course I do, and I'd love to come over, but I'll drive my car so I can go to the office Monday morning."

"Why didn't I meet you years ago?"

"Because years ago we most likely would not have been ready for this, and a good thing would have been wasted."

"Shir, you really have a good head on that fabulous body

of yours! You make perfect sense. By the way, what was the objection you encountered?"

"She thought 'too much of a conflict,' you a defense attorney and me an Assistant DA. I have to watch her as she has all of the guys wrapped around her little finger already. She is very good looking, has a great figure, and comes from a rich family. Her father is a big wig somewhere around Tampa. Wait until you see the T-bird she drives. She may be Dumbrowski's girlfriend but she's coming on to every guy in the office. I know it's not possible, but I got the impression she knew you."

"The new office manager is probably jealous of a good looking smart Assistant DA named Shirley.

"Thank you, Honey," said Shirley, running her fingers through her hair.

"Say, I like the *Honey*. By the way, I'm going to solo tomorrow afternoon. Would you want to come and watch?"

"Does a bear ... ah, what time?" smiled Shirley.

When Pat stopped laughing, he said, "Well, we need to be there no later than 4:00 or so because it's dark by 6:00 now. I really should be there by 3:30."

"I'll let Mom know we need to eat somewhere close, because we need to get out by 2:00 – 3:00. We can change clothes and go right to the airport. How long does it take to get there from here?"

"Sounds good to me. Ah, 30 to 45 minutes, depending upon traffic. The time table you set out should work, but 2:30 will be the latest we can leave."

"We'll do it."

"Let me get a quick shower and change clothes."

"Can I watch?" asked Shirley with a mischievous grin on her face.

"You dirty girl!" joked Pat.

"But I love to watch the transformation process. You know how you said it - - from a worm to a snake," answered Shirley with an innocent little-girl grin.

"Keep that up and we won't get out of here. Tell you what, Shir, I'll give you a worm's-eye view tonight. Transformation guaranteed, and there's not even a full moon. I'll even tie a ribbon on him for you."

That got Shirley going, as she joined Pat in laughing.

"Go get your shower." She playfully slapped him on his butt.

Pat took a shower and was drying off when she opened the shower door a crack. "I just want one little peek. Oh, isn't he the cutest little thing?"

"Little? You're going to hurt his feelings!"

"Do they have feelings?" Shirley opened the door wider.

"Of course they do!"

"Well, then let me tell him I'm sorry and give him a little make-up kiss." She took it in her hand and gently began to kiss it. As she did, it grew, and grew, and grew. "Imagine that. It's now standing tall," exclaimed Shirley.

Pat shook his head in bewilderment, picked her up, threw her across his shoulder, and deposited her on the bed. He reached down and pulled off her pants and panties and attacked her with wild desire. She was receptive and liked the roughness as long as it was short of hurting her. She responded with animal lust. They ended it quickly with climaxes that felt like explosions.

"Oh, you frightfully wonderful beast!" sighed Shirley.

"Me? Look who started this. I was just an innocent victim!" grinned Pat. "But if the truth be known, I can't get enough of you!"

"Well, somehow this is your entire fault, Pat. You sicked that cute little attack-trained thing on me."

"There you go blaming me again."

"We'll have to eat before bowling or skating. You pick it, or we'll miss our dinner reservations," smiled Shirley, as she looked at her watch.

"Shir, you really know how to turn things around, but I wouldn't change one thing about you." Pat wrapped her in his arms and gently kissed her.

"Oh-h-h, Pat. Keep on doing that and you'll have to sic old Waldo on me again!"

"Waldo is it?"

"That's as good a name as any." Shirley gave her innocent little-girl look.

"Shir, you had better behave yourself. Remember I'm meeting your parents tomorrow. What would your mother think of your actions here tonight, little girl?"

"She would tell you you're out of your gourd. However, sometimes I think Daddy sees through his little girl, although it's supposed to be Mom seeing through her daughter. For the most part, though, I have been a good little girl."

"Yeah, I'll bet!" smiled Pat, as he got ready.

"Speaking of being good, now that I know you better, I have been putting two and two together, and I believe you are the one who did it. It never would have dawned on me, but now it clicks."

"What on earth are you talking about? You're not making sense."

"The courthouse explosion in the men's room. Toilet blown up, half the wall blown out. The place evacuated, the police, fire company, and the FBI called. Secretaries peeing in their pants, grown men crying! You did it, Pat! You, the accused, are guilty as sin," said Shirley pointing her finger at him.

"Talk about exaggerations! A little tiny firecracker and you turn it into a stick of dynamite. Come on, Shir," ribbed Pat.

"Okay, Buster, look me in the eye, right here, Buddy, and deny that you did it!"

"Who, me?" Pat stuck out his lower lip in a fake pout.

"You did do it! I know it! You big crazy loon. You could have been in big trouble if someone caught you. Gosh I wish I had been there to see it!"

"But, Honey, you know I could never do something like that," replied Pat in a little-boy voice.

"Look, I don't know why I'm doing this, but here."

"What's this?"

"It's a key to my apartment."

"Thank you, Shir, but are you sure you want to do this?"

"Pat, this is crazy, but if you asked me to marry you right now, I would say "yes", and I've only known you for a week."

"Yes, it is crazy, but I think you know the feeling is mutual. Nevertheless, if you still feel the same way this time next year or possibly sooner, I will ask you *the question*. Shir, I really don't want to live with someone and not be married. Stay the night, yes, but not move in. If I love you enough to live with you, then I love you enough to marry you."

"Very well. Let's make this time next year Plan 'A'. But, then there is also Plan 'B' to consider." Shirley put her hands on his shoulders and looked up at him with those beautiful green eyes.

"What's Plan 'B'?"

"One hell of a lot sooner," exclaimed Shirley.

Pat put his arms around her and gave her a long, lingering kiss. How could he have been so lucky to have found her? He still had a hard time believing she felt the same about him.

* * *

They went to the bowling alley after dinner and rolled three games. Pat really was a good bowler and was on a bowling team at Great Atlanta. It was great fun but they would have had a good time doing anything together. After bowling, they went back to Shirley's apartment. Pat made a big show of opening the door for her with his new key. They put on some LP records containing love songs and talked. Neither wanted to get to bed late because they needed to get up for church the next morning. After taking a shower together, it was time for bed and lovemaking. When they were done, Pat held her in his arms and they fell asleep.

* * *

Skinny was also ready to go to sleep, but he was mentally practicing upward thrusts with his long homemade stiletto. *Patton, this one's for you!* thought Skinny as he imagined sinking it up to the hilt into Pat's chest. He smiled and went to sleep.

* * *

The next morning Shirley was going to cook breakfast, but Pat talked her into going to McDonald's for an Egg

McMuffin, hash browns, and orange juice. They would have a lot more time and could lazy-around eating breakfast. Then it was time to go to church.

As they arrived at the parking lot of the Solid Rock Christian Church, Shirley saw her parent's car and pointed it out to Pat.

Wow, a 450 SEL Mercedes! Pat pulled in beside them and they all got out of their cars. Her mother came over and gave Shirley a hug and held out her hand to Pat.

"So, this is the young man my daughter has been telling me about. I'm pleased to meet you, Mr. Patton," smiled Mrs. O'Kelly graciously.

As soon as her dad was done greeting Shirley with a hug, she introduced him to Pat. "Daddy, this is Pat Patton. Pat, my Dad."

"A pleasure, young man. Our daughter has spoken very highly of you. She tells me you are going to solo an ultralight airplane this afternoon."

"Yes, sir. I'm really looking forward to it. I can't wait until I get up there. In the air I mean."

"Yes, I do know what you mean. I'm a pilot myself."

"Oh, I forgot to tell you. Daddy has a Cessna 172 over at the South Expressway Airport. We had better get a seat in Sunday School. Mom, Dad, we'll see you later in church."

"Okay, Dear."

They went inside, and Pat watched the O'Kellys walk down the hall to the senior's class. What a good-looking couple! Mrs. O'Kelly was in her early fifties and Mr. O'Kelly in his middle fifties. He was about the same height and build as Pat, except about 20 pounds heavier. He had lost some of his hair but was a nice-looking man who carried himself well. Mrs. O'Kelly was an older Shirley -- about 5' 3" and 120 pounds, blond hair mixed with a touch of gray and green eyes. She had a nice figure.. He immediately liked both.

Sunday School was extremely interesting. The teacher had been a missionary for a number of years, had excellent knowledge of the Bible and had visited the Holy Land several times. Therefore, he spoke with authority.

Pat was impressed, and before he realized, the lesson

was over. The teacher was good, the people friendly, and the company superb.

The church sanctuary was large and seated around 1,000 people. The preacher was outstanding; he said a few things Pat did not care to hear but needed saying. His theme was that we needed to live by the standards set by Jesus, not by man. It made sense.

Funny how we humans do not like to hear about our shortcomings and what to do about them, even if it is true.

Mr. O'Kelly was one of the men who took up the offering and passed the plates containing the communion. He was a striking figure and Pat noticed everyone called him Doctor O'Kelly, with the exception of some of his close friends. Pat met many people, all asking him to come back again. He was proud to be with Shirley and her family. She had told him she had an older brother who was married and lived in Tampa, FL, where his wife's family resided. He was starting his career as a medical doctor, working for an HMO. Mr. O'Kelly offered him a job but he wanted to make it on his own.

They went out to eat at the Pampered Pig Bar-B-Q. The staff served good food and did it promptly. Pat could not get over how down-to-earth this well-off family acted. He was told that Dr. O'Kelly and his wife, who was an RN, donated time to a children's hospital and a retirement home for disabled veterans.

"Thank you very much for treating us to lunch, Mr. & Mrs. O'Kelly."

"Pat, you're very welcome, and please call me Greg. By the way, you're invited to go flying with me in my Cessna."

"And call me Grace," interrupted Mrs. O'Kelly with a big smile. "Without trying to be too presumptuous, you are both invited to our house for supper this coming Friday night."

Shirley looked at Pat. "I'm free, but I don't know what your plans are. I know you have the Washington trial to work on this next weekend. Mom and Daddy, he is first out on his first jury trial next Monday, and he'll need time to prepare for it."

"Grace...I feel a little funny addressing you like that...I

was planning on asking your daughter out anyway, so that would be fine with me. I try never to turn down a home-cooked meal. My folks live in Charleston and I only get over there once every month or two. And...Greg, I would love to go flying."

"It's a date then," Shirley told her mother.

"Say, kids. I have always wondered where the term *passed the Bar* came from. Do either of you know?"

"I can tell you, sir," answered Pat. "Many years ago they had a wooden bar separating the judge and court officials from the spectators in the courtroom. When someone was admitted to the practice of law, he was then allowed to *pass the Bar*. The term was originally used in the English legal system and copied here. The phrase has stuck over the years."

"Thank you, Pat. That's interesting."

"Shir, it's 2:15, so we had better go. But, I have to visit the little boy's room first."

As soon as Pat was gone, Mrs. O'Kelly spoke up.

"Shirley, I am impressed with your young man. He is intelligent, good-looking, well-mannered, and has a good future in front of him."

"Grace, I'll second that," added Greg.

"Thank you both. This guy is very special to me. I have never met anyone like him before. I can't believe he is still single, but I don't suppose he had much time for girls, what with having to work his way through college. Do you know that Pat worked full-time for Great Atlanta, went to law school three nights a week, and worked at a motor-cycle shop the nights he was not going to school and all day on Saturday?"

"He sounds like a very ambitious person to me," noted Greg.

"How many months have you known him?" asked her mother.

Not months, Mom, days. Ten days to be exact."

"Amazing! You two act like old friends," said her father.

"I know, because I feel I have known him for months, not days, and we have been talking almost every night on the phone."

"Well, don't rush things, dear, but my gut feeling is very reassuring. He is either a super good catch, or a very good actor. I believe, if I were you, I'd put my hooks into him." Grace winked and smiled.

"Mother, couldn't you see my claw marks?" answered Shirley also with a wink and a smile.

"One other question," asked Greg. "Does he have a wife or ex-wife and children?"

"He was married a short time, but no kids."

"Then you have the green light, sweetie. As you know, we love kids but they can be a problem when people remarry. It's rough when you hear a child tell you they don't have to listen to you because you're not their mother."

"Greg, I feel our daughter has found a man we both approve of."

Pat came back from the rest room and sat down.

"We were talking about you," informed Shirley.

"I know, 'cause like they say, I felt my ears burning."

"Mom and Daddy, we need to go because Pat needs daylight to solo."

"Be careful, Pat, and don't forget my offer to take you up in my Cessna."

"I'm looking forward to it Mr., ah, Greg. I would love to go anytime except next weekend. As Shirley told you, I'm tied up with trial preparation."

* * *

They headed for Shirley's apartment.

"I really like your parents," Pat commented, then he started laughing.

"What's so funny?" said Shirley, running her hand through her long blond hair.

"You know when your dad asked me if I wanted to go flying with him."

"Sure."

"Well, I almost said, *does a bear...*"

* * *

Upon arriving at her apartment, they changed clothes

and left for Bellah Airfield. On the way to the airport, Shirley suddenly got a feeling of dread. She could not shake it but said nothing to Pat. Soon they arrived at the airport where John was waiting for Pat.

"You sure lucked out on the weather. I have Gertrude out of the hanger, fueled up, and checked out, but if I were you, I'd rather be with this young lady than Gertrude."

"I'm greedy; I want them both. John, this young lady is Shirley O'Kelly, and she is here to watch me make a complete fool out of myself."

"Shirley, I'm John, owner of this contraption your fellow is about to fly."

"Nice to meet you, John."

"Same here, Shirley. Incidentally, what do you think of Gertrude?"

"She looks so small."

"Right you are, but sometimes great things come in small packages."

"I agree." Pat looked at Shirley. "I'm ready, John. Let's do it."

"Okay, hop in. Word is out about you soloing today because here comes the whole gang." John pointed to several cars and pickups that had arrived. "I want you to do a few more treetop high-hops, then taxi over to where you will see us standing and we'll talk a minute."

Pat did a quick *make-sure* preflight and climbed into Gertrude. He went through the starting drill and turned on the ignition switch.

"Clear prop!" yelled John as he pulled the starter rope.

Three pulls got Gertrude to fire up. Pat let Gertrude warm up, gradually pulling back on the throttle and taking off the choke. He had told Shirley to stick with John or else sit in the car and read a book. She was not the type to sit in a car while her boyfriend was up in the air in a toy airplane.

Pat taxied to the end of the runway and lined Gertrude up with it, checked the instruments, and pushed the throttle full forward. He held her onto the ground by pushing the stick forward, and when the airspeed got up to 35 mph, pulled back on the stick and lifted off the ground. He was at treetop level in less than ten seconds. Pat pulled back on the throttle and flew three-quarter of the way down the strip. He pushed the stick forward and pulled back on the throttle, always keeping the airplane over the 25-mph stall-speed. At about six feet off the ground, he flared out; keeping the nose wheel a foot or two higher than the rear wheels, touched down on the rear wheels, and then all three wheels were on the ground. He turned around and did the same thing on the way back. Pat landed, taxied over to John and Shirley, and got out of the airplane.

"How do you feel about soloing? Are you ready?"

Shirley grabbed Pat and held him close. He felt her trembling, her feeling of dread returning.

"What is it, Honey?"

"Nothing," answered Shirley nervously. "Please, just be careful up there!"

"Let's do it, John."

"OK. Put on my wrist altimeter."

Pat put what looked like a giant watch on his left wrist.

"When you take off, be sure to keep your air speed at 35 mph while climbing.

"I always do," agreed Pat with a reassuring smile.

"Keep your throttle wide open until you get to 500 feet on the altimeter, and use your stick to keep the airspeed up. If the plane bleeds off before 500 feet, push the stick forward for a less steep angle of attack, and the airspeed will come back up. People get killed stalling airplanes too close to the ground because they don't have the altitude to recover. Be extra careful making turns. I can't stress the importance to never let the airspeed get below 25 mph! Okay, go do it. Fly a right-hand circle pattern and land back here. If everything does not look exactly right, give her full throttle and do a go-around."

"Got you."

"See the 100, 200, 300, 400, and 500 foot marks on the altimeter? Fly the pattern at 500 feet."

"Please be careful, Pat," Shirley's voice registered anxiety, as she still had a bad feeling she could not lose.

Pat climbed back into Gertrude with all of the guys clapping and giving him the thumbs up.

"Okay, Gertrude, let's do this!"

"Clear prop!" yelled Pat as he pulled the rope starter from the cockpit. Pat taxied to the end of the runway, all eyes on him. He gave Gertrude some power, left rudder, and turned her around to face the long runway.

"This is it!" His mouth was dry and his heart was pounding with excitement. Soloing sounded like fun, but it was also a little scary.

If I screw up, there's no one to take over. He double-checked all the instruments. The engine sounded good.

Here we go, thought Pat as he gave her full throttle. Gertrude started to move faster and faster. Pat held her on the ground until the air-speed indicator read 35 mph, and then he pulled back on the stick. She leapt into the air. Up, up, up, he went. The throttle was wide open and he used the stick to keep a climb rate that kept the air-speed indicator at 35 mph. Before he knew it, he was above the trees and climbing. By the time he reached the end of the runway the altimeter read 300 feet. He had never been over treetop level before. He felt excited and apprehensive at the same time.

John had warned him about airspeed when climbing and making a turn. Airspeed could bleed off fast if climbing at too steep of an angle and the plane could stall if the pilot was not careful. At 300 feet, he might not have the height to recover. He was always aware of his airspeed. After making the turn, he checked his altimeter again. Wow! He was at 800 feet, and John had told him to stay at 500 feet. Pat had never made a turn before. When he looked down, everything looked different! He was not prepared for the big change in the view. People looked like ants. He was confused as to where he was.

Pat pulled back on the throttle but the airplane did not seem to want to lose altitude. Just as he was thinking, *how in the world would I handle an emergency,* the engine started to cut out.

Bam, bam, bam, it backfired! He pushed the throttle all the way forward and the engine caught, but only to cut out again. The plane lost enough power that it also started losing altitude. He was disoriented and now had engine problems!

I can't panic! That kills more pilots than anything else!

Large trees were all around the airport, which made his situation even more dangerous. Pat kept pushing the throttle in and out and the engine responded by cutting in and out in return, losing even more altitude. He made another turn and lined up on a runway, but even with the lost altitude, he was much too high to land and heading for some large trees at the end of the strip. His only hope was to go over them. In desperation, he gave it full throttle. Pat knew if he tried to land now, he would soon be out of runway and slam into the trees.

* * *

"Oh, my God!" cried Shirley as she looked on with horror.

"Pat is going to overshoot the runway and crash into the trees!" yelled John as he started running toward the trees. Pilots were getting into their vehicles and heading for Pat.

* * *

"Please, God, don't let me crash!" yelled Pat. "Come on, Gertrude. You can do it!" cried Pat.

Just then, the engine caught, but he was approaching the end of the runway and was now only about 40 feet high with 50-foot trees coming up fast! He was gaining altitude but was it fast enough?

* * *

"This is even worse," yelled John as he ran. "He's never going to make it over those trees! It would have been better to hit them lower than higher because of the fall from 50 feet ."

* * *

Shirley was running beside him and praying Pat would survive.

* * *

Suddenly, a gust of wind came over the trees and gave Gertrude enough lift to barely clear the treetops!

"Gertrude, that was close, but now I know what the *pucker factor* is, first hand!"

The engine was again running strong and Pat got back up to 500 feet. He saw cars and people returning to their original places. He turned and lined up on the main runway, but this time came in lower at the beginning of the runway so as not to overshoot it.

"Damn! We're still too high!" yelled Pat to Gertrude. "At this rate we'll run out of runway again before we get low enough to land!"

Then he remembered the spoilers and activated them. She now lost altitude very fast and he soon made a sloppy, but safe, landing.

He taxied over to John and Shirley, cut the engine, and yelled, "Yeah, baby," while slapping the stick!

* * *

Everybody was clapping and Shirley was yelling something and had tears in her eyes. She ran to him as he got out of the airplane and almost knocked him down as she threw her arms around him.

John came over to Pat, puffing from the run.

"You did it, but you gave us all a big scare when the engine started cutting out. It looked like you would hit the trees! I'm changing the spark plugs immediately as a precautionary measure."

"Pat, I was so scared! I don't want to lose you."

"Were you scared when the engine started to cut out?" asked one of the pilots.

"No. Scared wouldn't begin to cover it. More like terrified! Boy, I can see there's no substitute for experience, as I misjudged my altitude when trying to land. Everything looks so different from 500 feet. I really screwed up!"

Everyone laughed. "All pilots have war stories to tell if they fly long enough, I guess."

Shirley was astonished that Pat could joke after what had just happened to him.

Then the chanting started, "Off with your shirt! Off with your shirt! Off with your shirt!"

"I hope you didn't wear a good shirt, Pat, because tradition calls for cutting the back out of it, and inscribing the date and place of your solo flight," hinted John.

"Okay, you guys win." Pat pulled off his old shirt.

John's last statement was for the benefit of the other pilots, as John had warned Pat to wear an old shirt. He had another, better one in the car. They cut the back out of it and John wrote: *Pat Patton soloed this 29th day of Nov. 1980 at Bellah Airfield*. It was done with a large Magic Marker and all of the pilots signed it with a fine Magic Marker. This was a souvenir Pat would treasure and it would remind him of how our lives sometimes hang by a thread.

"John, we still have over 30 minutes flying time left. After you change the plugs, would you mind if I flew the pattern with the guys this time?"

"Pat, you're not really thinking of doing that again, are you?" Shirley had alarm in her voice.

John broke in, "Miss, you have to understand a couple of things. Now he has more experience and knows what to do in an emergency. If any one of these other pilots had been flying Gertrude, he would have made a routine emergency landing. We practice these types of emergencies on a regular basis. Moreover, if he does not get back into the plane right now, he will most likely never fly again. Is that what you want?"

"Of course not, and I understand what you're saying. Okay, Pat, go do it!"

"Thank you both." Pat shook John's hand while putting the other one around Shirley.

"Tell you what, Pat. Go up for 15 minutes and I'll take the last 15 minutes." John finished changing Gertrude's spark plugs. "By the way, here's a souvenir of your solo flight." He handed Pat a piece of a tree limb that had been stuck in the landing gear.

"That's one I'd rather not have. On second thought, it might be a good reminder to never take Gertrude for granted."

Pat climbed into Gertrude and yelled, "Clear prop!"

Before he took off he said a prayer thanking the Lord for letting him live another day. Now that Shirley was part of his life he was doubly grateful.

She fired up on the first pull and Pat got in line for takeoff. When the plane in front of him had a few hundred feet head start, Pat pushed the throttle all the way forward.

What a feeling! It was a combination of excitement and dread.

He took Gertrude up to about 1000 feet this time and flew around the pattern twice with the other guys before he started his descent. He was having so much fun he didn't want to go down, but John wanted some flying time in his own airplane. Pat made a sloppy landing three-quarter of the way down the field and taxied to John and Shirley.

"Fly anytime you want to, but keep track of the hours and, for the first few hours, don't fly unless there is someone else around. Just a safety precaution until you get some more experience. Also, always leave the airport with a full tank of gas in Gertrude. When the tank is full, it can't build up moisture in it."

"It's a deal, John."

"A couple more things." John strapped himself into Gertrude. "We have to depend on each other to make sure the gas is mixed properly, and if you ever have a *hard* landing, let me know and I'll do the same for you. If that ever happens, we really need to do an extra thorough check of the entire airplane."

"Okay, thanks again and we're gone."

"Pat, you looked like a little boy with a new toy up there," Shirley informed him.

"You hit the nail on the head, Shir, because that's exactly how I felt. Until the engine cut out and I aged 100 years. Perhaps it was a good thing because I will practice emergency landings over and over again until I'm as good as I can be. John has an emergency parachute that I could deploy in case of a structural failure so I guess with practice I will be as safe as you can be when soaring with the buzzards."

Pat smiled and forced a laugh.

As they drove home, they talked about going to her parent's house and church. They stopped for supper, went back to her apartment, talked, made love listening to *The Rose by Bette Midler*, and then Pat went to his house. A hard week was coming up.

If he only knew!

CHAPTER 18

December - The Parents

Pat took in several new clients because word was out that he really worked for the people he represented. The Washington's, Bobby McNew, the Andersons, Jalessa Johnson and others were flooding the county with Pat's business cards. He was also getting a new court-appointed case almost every week, and the press was starting to pick up on the *Five-O'Clock Traffic Bandits*.

Julie told him, "Jeez, they are threatening to come in and pay you money!"

He was now spending every spare hour working on the Washington trial. Herb gave him pointers and helped him consider the most common objections he could make and objections he could anticipate from Assistant DA Mark Kimbrough. He was also told what to expect from Judge Harold *Chain Gang* Musselman.

When it was apparent this case would be tried, Pat had taken Herb's advice and sat in the courtroom for several hours when Kimbrough was trying a criminal case in *Chain Gang's* courtroom. He also sat in on trials in other judge's courtrooms so he could see and hear how objections were made and how to counter them. Between what he saw and what Herb told him, he felt as ready as he could be for his first trial. The press had jumped on this case from the start with phrases like *The Five-O'Clock Traffic Bandits* to describe the case, and *The Novice Attorney* to describe Pat. Sammy and his family were comfortable with Pat, especially when he explained that even if the case were lost, Sammy could not get more time than what they had offered.

Friday came and Pat was looking forward to his big

evening, going to Greg and Grace O'Kelly's for supper. But most of all he was looking forward to being with Shirley.

* * *

Pat was not the only one with big plans for the night. Skinny was in the last stages of countdown for his escape.

Tonight is the night! I'll get out of this place or else die trying. My eyes glaze with anger every time I think of the nerve of my wife divorcing me, of all people, then marrying the jerk who stole my kids! And a neighbor at that!

And those damn attorneys who egg people on, only to line their swimming pools with more money. I'll show all of them! In the next week, houses are going to burn, and people are going to die. I could get a Brotherhood member to do them in, but I want to do it myself. Like they say, up close and personal! They will remember Dec. 5th, 1980, for the rest of their short lives!

* * *

On the way home, Pat stopped and got Shirley and her mother some flowers and a bottle of good wine for her father. Not knowing wines, he asked the owner for help in picking out a good brand and year.

Back in his car, he turned on the CB radio. Sure enough, Pick'em-Up-Man was talking to his buddies.

"Oh, you cute little old Pick'em-Up-Man. Come on, sweet thing."

"Yeah, Blade. What do you want?" asked Pick'em-Up-Man with a tired, beaten-down voice.

"How did you know it was me? Huh, handsome?"

"Who else has been harassing me these last few weeks?"

"Well, not little old me, sweetie."

"Listen to that, Sheet-Metal Man. He isn't even cussing the Blade anymore," quipped MoPar Man.

"Fellas, he has worn me out. What can I say?"

Now that Pat couldn't get a rise out of Pick'em-Up-Man,

fun was gone. So, he picked up the mike and said, "And you wore me out, too! What energy and stamina you have!"

"Sounds like the Blade beat him," said MoPar Man.

"How 'bout a truce, Blade?"

"Sealed with a kiss?"

"Hell, no!" yelled Pick'em-Up-Man.

That was more like it, thought Pat/Blade.

"Ta! Ta! Sweet Pick'em-Up-Man. I'll see you at the bowling alley and don't have anything on but a smile!"

"Why you queer SOB," yelled Pick'em-Up-Man, mainly for the benefit of his friends.

* * *

Pat turned off the radio and into his subdivision.

"Hey, Eb, I'm home."

"Who are you?" asked Eb with a cigar in his mouth and a beer in his hand.

"What are you talking about?"

"You resemble my roommate, but I haven't seen him in so long I'm not sure what he looks like."

"Okay, O Great One. I get your drift, but when it comes between you and Shir, I'm afraid there is no contest."

"On a serious note, I'm anxious to meet her, and I understand this is the weekend."

"That's right, Eb. We'll be here tonight and all weekend. I'll be working on the Washington trial."

"Well, I'll have you know, I found me a keeper, too. Her name is Jean Mickey and I will be at the young lady's apartment tonight. I hope to stay all night," hinted Eb with a smile. "When I'm with Miss Mickey, I will try to dunk my dickie."

"There is no hope for you Great One. I've got to get a shower. Shirley and I having dinner at her parent's house.

"So, no more duets, no more Diamond numbers?" asked Eb, as he blew a cloud of cigar smoke and then pushed his lip out in a fake pout. "No more redneck calls?"

"Look." Pat glanced at his watch. "A quick song, but I'm not sure if I want to do any more Diamond numbers after that last one. I feel like we were harassing some nice people."

They ended up playing three songs on the piano and drums, and afterward Pat ran for the shower. He told Eb, "No beer tonight." He didn't want Shirley's parents to smell it on his breath or clothes. He said good-bye to Eb and wished him good luck with his new playmate.

* * *

"Hi, Honey," greeted Pat as he opened the door of Shirley's apartment with his new key.

"I'm in the bathroom."

He put the wine and a couple of Hershey Bars in the refrigerator and took Shirley's flowers to the bathroom. The door was open and she was fixing her hair.

"For you, my love."

"For little ole me?"

"Yes, my dear, even if you don't give a damn!" Pat did a very poor imitation of Rhett Butler.

Shirley finally was ready. She phoned her mother saying they were on their way, grabbed the wine, and left.

"Today I got assigned my first case to prosecute. Up 'til now I was working with another Asst. DA to see how they did things, went to court with them, and handled some pleas."

"Great, Shir! What type of case?"

"You're not going to believe this, and you're not to repeat what I am about to tell you. Agreed?"

"Of course, Hon."

"Okay, here goes. Three dudes decided to rob a store. Two went in and did the job, while the third acted as a lookout on the sidewalk across the street at a bus stop. They were able to see each other and the lookout would signal in case of trouble. Well, along comes a bus and the lookout didn't know what to do. So guess what he did? He got on the bus and rode downtown!

"Meanwhile, a cruiser happened to come by and something attracted the police officer's attention. The store's outside light was signaling an SOS. The storeowner's kid was a Boy Scout and knew the Morse code. One of the cops did, too, and they caught both robbers. They ratted out the supposed lookout man because he should have tipped them off that the store-keeper's son was signaling with the lights."

"Strong case, huh?"

"On the two in the store, yes, but we anticipate some smart attorney will claim the lookout abandoned the crime by leaving on the bus. However, his buddies will testify he was standing there at the start of the robbery."

"Do they have bad records?"

"One does. Turn right at the next street and go two blocks, then left a short way to the end of the street. The house is a large brick one at the far end of the cul de sac."

They turned into the Enchanted Lake Estates, a nicer, upscale subdivision outside of Jonesboro on Lake Spivey. There was almost never a house for sale because it was an old established neighborhood and no one wanted to move once they lived there. If a person wanted to buy in this neighborhood, he would have to wait until some executive, professional, or business owner moved or died.

The houses were in the 3,000 to 4,000 square-foot range, on two to three-acre wooded lots. All were brick with many having swimming pools. The O'Kelly's lot also had frontage on Lake Spivey, and there was a community pool, tennis courts, and a putting green. In addition, there was a large clubhouse for special events, a boat-launching ramp and picnic area with a playground. All of these extras were for residents and their guests. This rule was strictly enforced, as it was a closed gated community.

The guard recognized Shirley and waived them on. They turned onto Northlake Drive, which was the O'Kelly's street, then went less than a city block to their cul de sac. There it was - - a 4,000-square-foot brick house on a 2½-acre beautiful wooded lakefront lot. As they turned into the extra-wide driveway, Pat noticed the four-car garage, boat dock, swimming pool and tennis court. Now he understood why Shirley played on her high school and college tennis teams. He had played but made a mental note to expect to be trounced when he played her.

"Shir, this place is magnificent! I had no idea you were a princess when I met you. I don't understand how you came to be such a humble, down-to-earth, loving person coming from this background. Most girls I know who had all this turned out to be the Glorias of the world."

"Thanks for the compliment, but who are the Glorias of the world?"

"Okay, you beautiful, green-eyed temptress. I'll tell you later about my experience, as well as the one Eb had, with her."

"You mean I have some competition?"

"Not hardly. She's a stuck-up snob I used to work with at Great Atlanta. But we fixed her uppity rear end."

"I've got to hear about her later. Promise?"

"Sounds good to me, Shir, and I surely will tell you about h e r . B e l i e v e m e , s h e i s n o c o m p e t i t i o n t o y o u ! However, on a serious note, if I had known you came from all of this, I probably would never have asked you out. I would have figured, wrongly of course, that I wouldn't stand a chance of getting a date. You could have any number of rich dudes, I'm sure."

"And on another serious note, that very thing has been a problem all my life. The guys from upper-class families were the ones who tried to court me, and for the most part, I sat at home because so many of them were such jerks. I preferred staying at home alone to going out with them. But, then there was you!" She leaned over and kissed him.

As he parked in the driveway, the front door of the house opened.

"Hi, Honey, and Pat."   Mrs. O'Kelly stood with her husband by her side.

"Hi, Mom. Hi Dad," greeted Shirley as she hugged them.

"Glad you could make it, Pat," welcomed Grace.

"Come in," directed Greg.

"Thank you for the invitation, Mr. and Mrs. O'Kelly, and for what I know will be a wonderful meal."   Pat extended his right hand to present Grace with flowers and his left hand to Greg with the bottle of wine. Then they all shook hands.

"That was very thoughtful, Pat."   Grace smelled the flowers. "Greg, I might go after him myself," grinned Grace.

"No you don't; he's mine, Mom!"   laughed S h i r l e y, wrapping herself around an embarrassed Pat.

"Thank you for the wine, Pat. Shirley, would you please put it in the refrigerator for me. And Pat, it's Greg and Grace."

The inside of the house looked as good as the outside.

This house could swallow mine. Life must be nice to have all of this.

Then he remembered what Shirley had said about the long hours her father put in at his medical practice. He earned it by hard work, but still it must be nice. No one gave Greg anything. Shirley said both Greg and Grace came from humble beginnings. The O'Kellys had worked for what they owned..

They went into a large den, where Pat was immediately aware of two beautiful mounted deer heads. He counted the points. One was a 10-point buck and the other a 12-point buck. Both heads were huge. Then he noticed Greg's gun cabinet, full of superb firearms. The room was about 15 by 20 feet with a real brick fireplace, expensive furniture, a large-screen TV, and a top-of-the-line stereo system.

"I love your place, Greg, and I can't help but admire your beautiful deer heads. It's hard to find racks like that! Where did you bag them?"

"Only the smaller one is mine," answered Greg.

"Who bagged the large one?"

"You're sitting next to her," smiled Greg, as he looked directly at Shirley.

"Shir, you are full of surprises! You surely are," exclaimed an astonished Pat.

"She didn't take after me," informed Grace. "I love to go with Greg camping in our motor home, but I draw the line at running around in the woods and shooting Bambi."

"Shirley, show your young man around the place while I finish with supper. Come back in about 20 minutes to help me put the food on the table while Greg and Pat talk."

"Okay, Mom. Excuse us, Dad."

* * *

It won't be long now, Mr. Patton, thought Skinny as he was preparing to walk out of Jackson State Prison.

He patted the long steel shaft hidden in his pants leg

and smiled. He was thankful the metal detectors were set up for people coming in and not going out.

The maintenance man should be here shortly.

* * *

Shirley showed Pat around the large five-bedroom house, each with its own full bath. There was a sewing room for Grace and an office for Greg. Outside there was a large screened porch and boathouse Pat hadn't seen driving in. Downstairs was a finished basement, which had a pool table, a Ping-Pong table, and another garage door, which led to Greg's workshop. It had one of every tool invented by man. The place was unbelievable.

As Pat looked around he commented, "And to think, when I first met you, I thought you were a poor little helpless thing, working to make ends meet."

"That's me," admitted Shirley, looking up at him with those lovely green eyes.

"Yeah, and then to top it off, I find you bagged a bigger buck than I have ever seen."

"That's me," agreed Shirley, this time winking at him.

Pat loved her more with each passing day. He found it hard to believe she was actually his girlfriend.

If I had placed a custom order with the Lord, the result could not have been better.

Pat looked out the window and noticed a large building in the woods with four garage doors. He had caught only a glimpse of it when they pulled into the driveway. A large pull-through shed was attached to the left side of it. The front of a large motor home was showing in the shed.

"What's in there?"

"Some of Daddy's play toys. Come quickly and I'll show you."

Pat looked in the garage door windows and saw a '57 Studebaker Golden Hawk, a '39 Ford Coupe, and a '57 Thunderbird. Shirley told him the '39 Ford had a Chevy 350 engine in it. The other cars were original. This place was like Disneyland. The '39 Ford Coupe was like the one he used to have except his had a Cadillac engine.

They returned to the den so Pat and Greg could talk while Shirley helped her mother with supper.

Greg told of his medical practice and Pat of his law practice. As they talked, Pat discovered Greg was a plastic surgeon, which explained the large house. Pat's trial came up and both enjoyed talking about flying. Greg again invited Pat to fly with him.

The women served supper, consisting of delicious fillet mignon, a baked potato, asparagus, salad, and a three-story cake, along with iced tea.

"Will you be able to make church this Sunday," asked Greg.

"I wouldn't miss it for anything. That is if your beautiful daughter will accompany me," smiled Pat, looking at Shirley.

"I might be available," teased Shirley.

They talked more after dinner, when they went out on the screened-in porch to look at the lake. The night was getting a little chilly to stay out too long, but the lake was so pretty and peaceful. They didn't want to go back into the house.

While the women did the dishes, Greg showed Pat his study and his workshop. Even though Greg was a surgeon, he was able to work both metal and wood. A man after Pat's own heart. He found himself desperately wanting to be a part of this family.

Greg led the way back upstairs just as Grace and Shirley finished the dishes. Everyone went back to the den and when Pat sat down on a love seat, Shirley was there sitting down very close beside him. That she cared deeply for this young man was obvious to her mother and father.

"What are your parents doing now," asked Grace.

"As you know, they live in Charleston. Mom is a homemaker and Dad is on Social Security disability. He has a bad back and was diagnosed with Parkinson's and Paget's diseases. He sold the Pennsylvania farm and his automotive repair business and was able to make the move and pay for a modest house. He fishes when he is able and has a small boat. Mother goes with him and enjoys fishing. They travel some but his health is not good enough for him to do a lot of driving. My sister lives in the same area and takes them with her on vacations. She is a supervisor with the telephone company. I try to talk to them at least once a week."

"They sound as though they are making the best of things. How old is your father?" asked Grace.

"He's 55 now. When he got sick, his business had been growing. He had two full-time mechanics working for him and the way things were going, he would have had to expand to a larger building with another couple of mechanics. By the time he reached 65, he would have been in great financial shape. But, with his medical problems, the cold winters were too much and he needed to move south to a warmer climate. He also wanted to be next to the ocean so he could go fishing. It all was a real shame."

"Pat's got a jury trial Monday," interjected Shirley.

"Yes, he mentioned it to me, but what type of trial is it. A DUI, or what?" queried Greg.

"No, Daddy. He's defending one of the *Five-O'Clock Traffic Bandits*," corrected Shirley, with pride in her voice.

"That case has been all over the newspapers. You mean they gave a new attorney a high-profile case like that, or were you retained by his family?" asked Greg.

"Appointed by the Court Administrator, but only because I have Herb Butterworth to help me. If I do well on this case, the press could help my career with all the radio, TV, and newspaper coverage. They have been calling the office for the past few weeks. I tell them I don't believe he is mentally competent to stand trial. I make sure I'm always polite when I talk to them."

"Do you think you can get him off?" asked Grace.

"Not a chance, but what I hope to get is a *Guilty but Mentally Ill* verdict and less time than the 20 years they are offering. They forced me to try the case by offering the maximum time for this charge. I'll attempt to show the jury and the judge that Sammy is a nice, but mentally disturbed man, and the other two dragged him into the robbery. This man actually believes he is Moses."

"We will be watching the case closely and keeping our fingers crossed for you," said Greg.

"Mom, it's almost eleven o'clock. We'll have to be going now. Pat will want to get a good night's rest so tomorrow he can work on last-minute details on this case."

"Of course, Dear. We have enjoyed having you both over for dinner. Please come back, Pat, and I must say I'm pleased to see our daughter has such good taste in men."

"Thank you very much, Grace." Pat was a little embarrassed. "And thank you for the delicious dinner, the hospitality, and for raising such a wonderful daughter."

"You're too kind, Pat," answered Grace.

"We expect you back soon, and don't forget the flying invitation."

"Good night again, everyone...And you can be sure I won't forget about flying."

* * *

Pat opened the car door for Shirley, then cheerfully hopped in himself and pulled out of the driveway. Shirley put her hand on his thigh.

"Watch it, girl, or you will start something."

"I hope you have a bed that doesn't make much noise."

"Eb probably won't be home. He will no doubt be staying with one of his many girlfriends. His latest one is Jean. Mind if I turn on the radio? I enjoy listening to the eleven o'clock news."

"Great minds always think alike. I was just going to turn it on, with your permission of course. I always listen to the news in the morning while getting dressed in the bathroom."

"Me, too!" replied Pat as he turned on the radio.

There was an advertisement, then they heard: "And now for a special announcement concerning the daring jail break of Arnold *Skinny* Anderson from Jackson Prison earlier this evening. Details are sketchy at this time. We do know Anderson was working in the Education Department at Jackson. Apparently, another inmate, whose name is being withheld pending notification of next of kin, was also involved. He either tried, or was attempting, to escape himself. Later we learned that Anderson and another inmate were missing at a routine head count. The other inmate was found dead by a search team in a closet in the Education Department."

A visibly shaken Pat turned up the volume and pulled over to the side of the road so he could concentrate on the news.

"The authorities are baffled as to how he got past not one, but three, checkpoints with electrically operated gates manned by guards. The blue Chevy P/U that belonged to a maintenance man was found in a Griffin shopping center parking lot, locked, about 20 miles from the prison. Anderson is dangerous and may be armed. Having killed already, he has nothing to lose. If you have information concerning Arnold *Skinny* Anderson, please contact your local police department. Our next story concerns . . ."

"Pat, what is it?"

"Herb did his divorce and I did the adoption of his kids," answered Pat with a wavering voice.

CHAPTER 19

December - The Escape

Earlier that Friday afternoon, Skinny had put everything in order to make his escape. Close to shift change, Dean had made him up to resemble Larry Near, the maintenance man. After school let out at 4:15, all the teachers and office personnel had left for the weekend.

Skinny told Dean he knew what Near's assistant looked like and he was ready to put makeup on him to resemble the assistant. He told Dean, "I need to use some eye shadow. Close your eyes while I apply the makeup."

Dean did as he was told and closed his eyes.

"Did you check to make sure Near was working tonight?"

Skinny said, "I checked earlier, and they will be here in a few minutes to fix the light I reported out."

Earlier, Skinny had taken out the long thin steel rod from the carriage return of the typewriter that was now in his hand as he drove it up and at an angle under Dean's left rib cage, going into his chest a good ten inches. Dean let out a gasp. He momentarily opened his eyes that registered disbelief. Death occurred even before he hit the floor.

Skinny pulled the shaft out of Dean and wiped it on a rag. There was very little bleeding. He had apparently hit his target – the heart.

Dean, you would have been excess baggage and increased my chances of getting caught. I don't understand why but I enjoy hurting and killing people. You died a good death - - quick and almost painless.

Skinny was looking forward to repeating that type killing with Mr. Near, who would be there soon. He looked at his watch ... 28 minutes to shift change. That's when he wanted to leave, right at the end of the shift change when things were confused and everyone wanted to get home.

The door opened and maintenance man Larry Near came into the main room with his small stepladder and tool box on a roll-around.

Damn! He's here already! Got to hide Dean's body.

Skinny had killed Dean in an adjoining room. He called out to Near that the light was out in the room called the closet. Skinny pulled Dean into the corner and hid him under one of the sheets he had smuggled into the Education Department.

He went over to the closet area and carefully looked in. Near was on his small ladder, checking out the light, with his back toward Skinny, who tiptoed into the room and suddenly appeared before Near, the steel shaft in one hand and a rag in the other.

"Hey! You're me!" yelled a surprised Near as he turned toward Skinny and saw his own image.

That was the last thing Near ever said, as Skinny's hand streaked upward with the long steel rod. Again, his victim could not believe what was happening, as he toppled to the floor. Skinny immediately reached into Near's shirt with the rag and put it around the shaft as he carefully pulled out the rod.

I don't want to get blood on the shirt if I can help it.

He took off Near's uniform, making sure he had Near's wallet, ID badge, and key ring. He nervously checked his watch.

Only eleven minutes until shift change! Got to hurry! He quickly undressed and put on Near's uniform and then thought about the shoes!

Man, I forgot about the damn shoes! I hope they ain't too small!

Actually, they turned out to be two sizes too big. This was an important detail he had missed, as prisoners wore black boots. The shoes were a sloppy fit, so he put on Near's socks, too.

After covering up the body with the other stolen sheet, Skinny ran to the bathroom and looked in the mirror.

This disguise is great! Even Near thought I was him! Dean really did a great job. I'll have to thank him, laughed Skinny.

He looked at his watch again. *Damn, shift change was over two minutes ago! I can't screw this up now or they'll fry me for sure!*

Skinny turned off the lights, locked the door, and headed for the first guard-controlled electric gate. He tried not to hurry.

He never had felt so vulnerable. He needed to get past three security checkpoints before he was out of the jail. The only weapon he had was the long steel rod, now stuck through his right pocket with the shaft hanging beside his leg. The handle kept it from falling down his pant leg.

Play it cool now, Skinny. Nod if they nod to you, wave if they wave to you. If they speak, mumble something. My voice isn't as deep as Near's, so I'll have to be very careful if I have to speak to someone.

He came to the first gate, stood at the red "Do Not Cross" line, and tried not to look nervous. Just then, two guards approached him from the rear.

"Hey, you!" yelled one of the guards.

Skinny froze.

"Hey, Near, you were supposed to fix . . . What? Never mind. Joe here said John took care of it."

Skinny waved his hand, barely turned around, his heart racing, and waved a thumbs-up "OK" to them.

The gate opened and he walked the short distance to the next gate on his right. He was now inside a box with gates on all four sides. The good thing was he was going out a gate opened by the same guard who let him in the box.

If the guard opened one gate, he should open this one. Skinny had another piece of luck as those two guards were going in the opposite direction, out the left gate, which had just opened. The gates were set up so only one of the four could open at any one time. He was the only one in the box now and he started to sweat.

Damn, the sweat might mess up my makeup!

He had missed the shift change and felt as though everyone was looking at him.

The gate started to open and he became instantly alert. Skinny started walking and the gate closed behind him. A long hall stretched out in front of him with another electric gate controlled by yet another guard. Skinny tried to walk as confidently as he could and was approaching the last gate to the outside of the prison. When he was about ten feet from the red line, the guard looked up at him. This was bad as he was the only one at the gate, but the guard smiled and waved. As the gate opened, Skinny smiled, waived, and walked out the gate, which led to an unlocked glass door. He pushed it open and there was the parking lot!

Skinny had been told Larry Near drove a blue Chevy P/U truck and usually parked to the right of the door, close to the building. Skinny turned right and immediately saw a blue Chevy P/U. He went over to it, looked around, put the key in the door and turned it. The door would not open! Suddenly he felt a trace of panic!

Come on, damn it!

He looked around, pulled out the key, and walked on.

Soon Skinny saw another blue Chevy P/U and this time the key worked. He got in and started the truck. Looking at his watch again, he figured he had roughly an hour until they would miss him, then another hour for the guards to search the inside of the prison. Because they knew he often worked nights, they were sure to search the Education Department and would find the bodies. He had a maximum of two hours to get out the last gate, and get rid of the truck before they started looking for it.

Larry must have been a smoker as he had cigarettes in his pocket and the ashtray is half full of butts.

Skinny pulled out a cigarette from the pack and lit it.

Man, these store-bought cigarettes beat the hell out of the hand-rolled ones I usually had to settle for in prison.

* * *

He approached the first of two electric gates he would have to drive through to get to the outside.

Once that first gate closes behind me, I'm trapped between the two of them.

He started to sweat again. Skinny held his breath as he

came to a stop before the first gate. The second gate was closing, having let out two vehicles ahead of him. The second gate closed. The first one opened. He pulled in and stopped.

Skinny took out a handkerchief. He planned to begin to cough if a guard tried to talk to him. That would partially cover his face. He stopped and suddenly realized he was trapped between the gates, along with a car behind him.

Man, the engineers really designed this place right. While one guard is checking me out, the other one is in a tower 20 feet above and controls the gates. I could kill this pig and still not get out!

Skinny checked his rearview mirror. The g u a r d o n ground level was looking in the windows of the car behind him, then at the ID of the driver. Finally, he went around the car while holding a large mirror on a long pole, with wheels on it, looking under the vehicle. He looked under both sides of the car, then approached Skinny and looked in the window.

Skinny showed him the badge while faking a coughing fit. The guard nodded and started checking under his pickup. Satisfied, he motioned the tower guard to open the gate. Skinny put the truck in gear and slowly moved through the gate.

"I'm free!" he yelled.

* * *

Driving away, Skinny turned on the radio, and ironically, Willie Nelson was singing his latest hit, *On The Road Again.* He headed toward the town of Griffin, near Atlanta because he would more easily get lost in a crowd, and he needed to settle some scores. The gas gauge read three-quarter full and he managed to scrape up $63.73 from Larry's pockets and glove compartment. For now, he was in good shape.

I know where there's a shopping center in Griffin. It should be less than 30 minutes up the road. Now if I can only make it, I can ditch this damn truck.

Skinny pulled into the Ralph Thomas Boulevard Shopping Center and parked in the last row of a grocery store parking lot. The sign said it was open 24 hours per day. He knew employees of many stores were required to keep their cars on the far end of the lot so customers would have a convenient place to park. He got out and locked the truck.

He walked quickly, looking in each car window for keys.

This is my lucky day because there sits a Ford van with the keys in the ignition switch.

He got in and started it up.

Skinny drove toward a similar van and parked near it. With a screwdriver from the glove compartment, he switched license plates with the parked van. When the owner got off work and reported the van he had driven as stolen, it would have a different tag on it. He headed north toward Atlanta.

Less than an hour later Skinny pulled into the long-term Atlanta Airport parking lot in College Park. After trying about 25 vehicles, he found a Ford Van unlocked. His luck was continuing to hold because the van had the keys in it.

People will never learn!

He found a similar van and switched plates again.

The double switch should confuse the hell out of the stupid cops! Now it's time to get armed.

He paid $2.00 to get out of the parking lot. He knew Fairburn was only about 20 minutes away and had a hardware store and a Radio Shack. It was almost dark when he parked behind the Eross Hardware store. It was closed but had night lights on.

With the lug wrench in hand from the Ford van, he pried open the door. This was a small crimeless town and the door opened easily. He wore the same rubber gloves stolen from Jackson. He doubted there would be an alarm system but worked quickly just in case. First, he took a Mossberg 500 12-gauge pump shotgun. Next came a .38 caliber revolver and a couple boxes of ammo for it and a couple of boxes for the shotgun. He put the empty boxes back on the shelf so it would not be obvious they were missing. Then two one-gallon plastic gas cans, shop rags, two flashlights, a box of rubber gloves, a hacksaw, several batteries, hunting clothes, and boots. An employee had left a pack of cigarettes and matches. "Thanks, man."

Working quickly, Skinny got a t e n t , an inflatable air mattress, and a sleeping bag out of their boxes. The boxes were also carefully put back on the shelf. He found a hatchet, a crow bar, a hunting knife, and $152.36 in petty cash. Next, he took a golf bag to hide things in and to carry his loot out to the van. He threw two cans of spray paint in the golf bag. Skinny grabbed another can of spray paint, started knocking things over, and throwing hardware and sports equipment all over the store. He wanted to make it look like the work of kids, so he spray-painted KKK, a peace sign, and obscenities on the walls.

I've already been here too long! Gotta hurry before the cops come.

He made three quick trips to the van to load the stolen goods, then closed the door and left. He went a few blocks to the back of the Radio Shack. Skinny took only a high-end police scanner and several batteries. Things were scattered and the walls were spray painted in a similar manner as the hardware store. He was there only a few minutes.

A used-clothing store was next. He took several changes of clothing, one size too large, along with three coats and an old set of clothes much too big for him. He found three uniforms, one with a gas company logo, and two pair of shoes to replace the ones he took from Near. Then he dumped the trash cans on the floor, knocked over racks of clothes and broke some interior windows. Skinny added the customary KKK, obscenities, and peace sign to the walls.

It's time to get out of town 'cause in a little while there'll be more cops here than ants at a picnic!

He headed a few miles north and stopped south of Union City at a drugstore. Skinny put on an old hat and shirt he took from the clothing store. He had the .38 tucked in his pants and several extra cartridges in his pockets. The shirttails were left hanging out for a sloppy look. He got a cold six-pack of beer, hair dye, a large mirror, comb, toothbrush and paste, and a pair of binoculars, which he had forgotten to steal at the hardware store. There was a cooler with ready-made sandwiches. He got a few, and two pair of very weak eyeglasses.

He paid for the things, left the store, got in the van, drove to another drugstore, then stopped and put the batteries in his RS police scanner. The local cops were talking gangs and

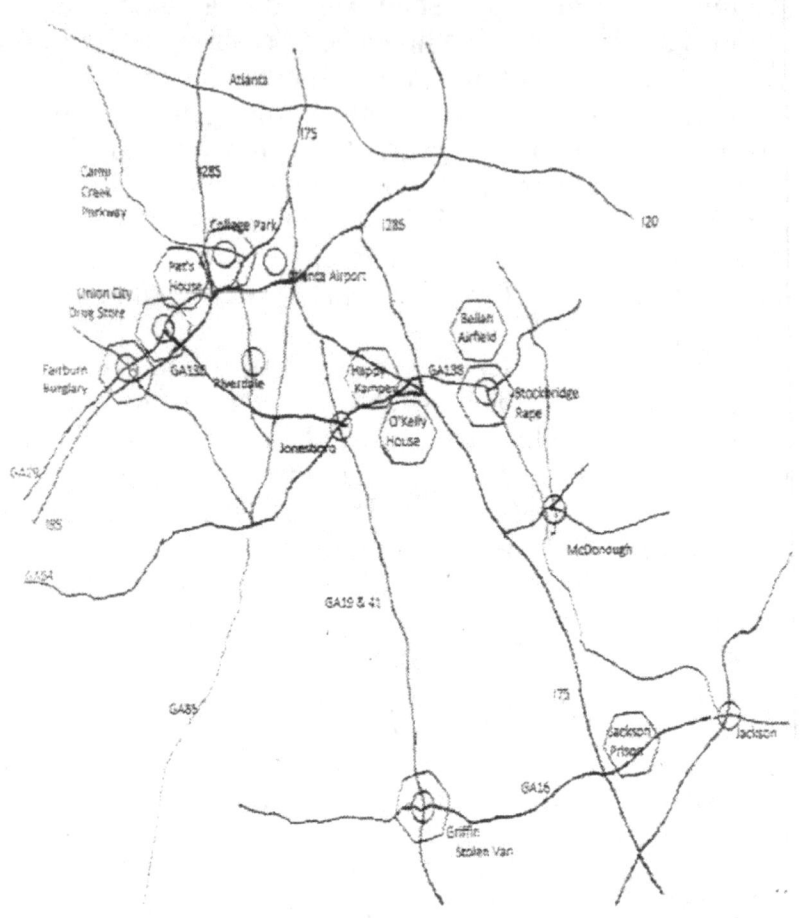

SKINNY'S ESCAPE ROUTE AND LAND MARKS

Jackson Prison-West on GA 16→Griffin-Stolen Van→College Park-Airport Parking Lot-Stolen Van-South West→Fairburn-Burglary, Hardware Store & Radio Shack-North West→Union City-Drug Store, East on GA 138→Stockbridge, Holdup & Rape, West on GA 138→Weigle's Happy Kamper Campground (about 2 miles West of I75 in Clayton County) kids. Three businesses had been broken into and all police cars were to be on a lookout for groups of kids who might be on drugs or drinking.

He changed clothes again, putting on a suit. This time Skinny bought eye makeup, a razor, a pair of scissors, several packs of cigarettes and matches. Then he got a tube of black lipstick, fake teeth, and other miscellaneous items from a shelf of left-over Halloween items.

In the van again, three police cars came speeding by as he pulled out of the parking lot. Their lights were flashing and he could see them setting up a roadblock a short distance behind him.

Man that was close! He drove away from the police roadblock with a smile on his face.

He found a gas station with an outside restroom and changed into the clothes that were much too large and made him look like a bum. Skinny put on a watch cap, pulled it down over his head and ears, then looked in the mirror to blacken out two front teeth. Finally, he put on the ugliest pair of glasses he had.

I sure don't look like me.

He had on the padding he had worn for the escape and padded his belly even more to make himself much heavier. Next, he placed strips of sheet in his mouth and under his lips to make his cheeks look fatter.

Skinny pulled out and looked for a convenience store. He headed east on Hwy 138 and was in luck, finding one in Stockbridge. He wanted to bounce around to confuse the hell out of the police. There was no way they could predict where he would pop up next. Stockbridge was only a half hour drive. At 11:00, this store was getting ready to close. There were only three cars and they were parked in back, obviously belonging to the employees. After watching for a few minutes, he saw three clerks closing up the store. The outside sign went off and the inside lights were dimmed.

The male clerk was coming toward the door when Skinny got out of the van, slammed the door into the clerk's face, and pulled out the .38 Special. He locked the door and turned a sign on the door to read "Closed." There were two female clerks and one male clerk.

He forced the male clerk to open the cash register and made all of them lie on the floor. He tied up and blindfolded the male clerk and hit him over the head with his revolver.

Wow! There's a big pile of bills here.

He would later count $2,233.00. He didn't bother with the change. Then he forced the girls to go behind the counter.

"Please don't hurt us, mister," begged one of the two female employees. "I'll do anything you want."

Hummm! She is cute, sexy, and has big boobs. The thought started getting him aroused. Skinny said nothing - - he didn't want them to hear his voice. He tied their hands behind their backs and blind-folded them with scarves from the store. He hit the worst-looking one over the head, and then proceeded to pull up the skirt and take off the panties of the one who had begged him not to hurt her. Her sweater was pulled up and her breasts exposed. She was too terrified to resist as he raped her.

She must like it as I hear her moaning.

This only increased his pace. He took only a few minutes and when he was done, he hit her over the head. The other female clerk was coming around so he hit her again, hard! Then Skinny pulled up her sweater and fondled her.

Feels so good to have this kind of power!

He got a real high from all the violence. He also liked the sex.

They were selling Boy Scout Festival tickets and that gave him an idea, so he took several of them.

Skinny cautiously looked over the counter and saw no one in the parking lot so he dragged the male clerk behind the counter. He got the keys, turned off all of the lights, and locked the door behind him. He got into the van and left, heading for a campground about 10 miles west on Hwy 138. If he remembered right, it was just past I75 in Clayton County.

The stupid cops will be checking motels. They'll never think of an escaped convict staying in a tent in a campground.

A little after midnight, he got to Weigle's Happy Kamper Campground and drove to the restroom area. He got rid of his bum's outfit in the dumpster, put on a pair of camouflage pants like deer hunters wear, and a long-sleeve flannel shirt. He washed the makeup off his face and teeth, put on a hat, a thin mustache, and a pair of red-rimmed glasses. He was ready to check in.

Skinny drove to the office but found it closed. They had a drop box for late campers to sign in where he deposited the check-in form and money for ten days. The sign said to pick any available campsite. He got one close enough to a light so he could see to put up his tent. After the tent was set up, he got the sleeping bag, air mattress, and blankets from the van. The night was cold when he went to bed to get some much-needed sleep. Skinny bundled up in the sleeping bag with blankets thrown over him.

Even this bed is better than the prison's best bunk. I'm free and it's mine!

He had a big week coming up and was tired. In the morning, Skinny would have to find a newspaper, a phone book, a map of the Atlanta area, Clayton County, and the city of Jonesboro.

They're going to be sorry for what they done to me. They'll soon know the real meaning of fear!

Skinny had a sick smile on his face as he went to sleep.

CHAPTER 20

December - Revenge

Pat and Shirley got home late Friday evening. Pat pulled his Mustang into the garage, still shaken from the news of Skinny's escape. "You have seen my castle from the outside. Now we'll do the inside. You're in the garage/shop and beyond the door on the right is the furnace/laundry room area.

"The door in front of you leads to the recreation room, and you may open it, my dear. To the direct left, through that other doorway, is my study. This is the pool table and over there the bar and card table. To your right are the stairs to the main part of the house."

"You have it fixed up so nice. I mean that. This place really looks good."

"Now I'll turn on the light and we'll go upstairs. Mademoiselle, you first." Pat bowed. "Push the door at the top of the stairs, Shir. Eb's not home. Straight in front of you is the living room and, as we keep going to the right, my piano and Eb's drums. Straight ahead is the screened-in porch."

"I'll bet you spend a lot of time out there,"

"Not really; too much airplane and road noise. We're under a landing pattern of the Atlanta Airport, which is not far away, and the house is beside a four-lane highway."

"Next is the kitchen and, to its right, my den and gun case. If you go through the door in front of you, you're back in the hall, where we came upstairs. We made a circle. The kitchen can be reached from either the living room or the den. Now down the hall and on your left is the full bath, then straight ahead Eb's bedroom. On your right is my other workshop." Pat pointed to his bedroom. "There is my main workbench." He pointed to his bed. "Eb's bedroom has the half bath but mine is

194

larger."

"You dirty old man! You should be ashamed of yourself," criticized Shirley while pushing him down on the bed.

"I am, I am, I am." Pat enveloped her in a bear-hug kiss. Reluctantly he turned her on her back, and then pulled himself up. He had a strange look on his face.

Shirley took his hand, led him into the living room, and sat him down on the couch.

"Okay, Honey, let's talk about it. And you know what I mean!"

"Right, Shir. Okay. This guy is very dangerous. You should have heard all of the things his ex-wife, Betty, told me about him. Betty! Shir, I have to call her even if it is after midnight!"

"You're right. She may not know."

Pat got Betty on the eighth ring. No, she had not heard, because they had been at the movies. She sounded very worried and thanked Pat for calling.

"I did the adoption and Herb did the divorce. Gosh, do you think I need to call Herb?"

"It wouldn't hurt. We're talking about a dangerous killer," reminded Shirley, running her fingers through her hair.

"Sounds good to me. He already killed two people in his escape. He could have tied them up but chose to kill them instead."

Pat dialed Herb's number.

"Yes, I heard the news and tried to call you but your line was busy. We need to keep our eyes open. I'll call a police friend of mine and ask that they watch Betty's house. Most likely all Skinny wants is to get away and is out of the area by now. With Skinny, however, taking chances doesn't pay."

Pat agreed and hung up.

"What are you going to do?" asked Shirley.

"Shir, I really don't think you should be around me this weekend."

"No you don't! I'm staying. A .38 is in my pocketbook, and as you found out, I know how to use it. If I were you, I'd load my guns and place some around the house where you can get at them if needed."

"Good idea, Shir. Out of sight, but where I can get hold

of one if I need it. A very good idea, it surely is."

Pat loaded his guns and placed them around the house. Then he had a Hershey Bar. Because he had a concealed weapons permit, he would make sure he was armed when he went outside. Then they went to bed and, much later, to sleep.

* * *

Skinny woke up that Saturday to a chilly morning. He had a fitful night's sleep, waking up at the slightest noise.

The newspapers will carry my prison picture, so I'll change my appearance. I'll become a redhead and keep the pads under my clothes to appear slightly dumpy, not skinny. Although uncomfortable, I'll keep the pads in my mouth. I'll also always wear a hat and glasses of some kind. In daylight, always sunglasses. Thankfully, since it is December, there are not many campers to avoid.

After he got back from the rest room, he went to the van, and picked up the hacksaw and shotgun. He cut it down to a 14-inch barrel and also cut three inches off the stock. The shotgun went into the golf bag, which sat on the front passenger's floorboard against the seat. The belt under his shirt held the .38 revolver. He kept six rounds of ammo in each front pocket of his pants and extra shotgun shells in his coat pockets. He tied the knife to the inside of his left leg, where he could easily get to it with his right hand.

What a beautiful day to stalk some folks, but first breakfast, and then I'll get some maps.

He started the van and headed for McDonalds. *I haven't had much to eat since I left my old home, so I think I'll get the Big Breakfast and an Egg McMuffin on the side.*

The only things he took with him were the police scanner, a gas can, and other items needed to torch Herb's house. He had placed all but the gas can into a grocery bag. The .38 was always with him. Skinny was traveling light because he was planning to change vehicles again.

At the third phone booth, he found a phone book chained to the booth. It did not look like it had pages torn out. His crowbar came out and soon both the white and yellow pages were his. He went to a gas station where he filled up the gas can and the van. Skinny also purchased cigarettes, matches, maps, a couple of sandwiches, drinks, a red pen, a yellow highlighter, a cooler, and some ice.

No beer today as it is a workday.

Skinny was in luck. He found the residence addresses of the Johnsons, the Butterworth's, and Smart-Ass Patton in the phone book. Next, he located the addresses on the map and circled them in red. He did the same with Butterworth's office, but he was unable to find Patton's office.

Soon fire and blood will rain! Now I'm ready to do some scouting. Let's see, Butterworth's office is closest. I've got to be careful because the cops might be staking out any of these places. Maybe not the attorneys' houses but the Johnson's for sure.

He tuned the radio to a station that had news on the top of each hour. His escape was still news as were the burglaries. The police attributed them to kids, because they believed nothing was taken, but quite a mess was made. The vandalism tied the burglaries together because all the stores were close together and spray paint was on the walls of each of them, along with symbols. Also, a holdup and rape was reported in Stockbridge.

The stupid pigs didn't find anything missing, but soon the store owners will find the empty boxes. I don't want them mothers to think 'camping' until I've left the area.

Skinny turned on the police scanner, but it reported only local accidents and domestic disputes, nothing to do with him so far. So, he headed to Butterworth's office. He didn't think anyone would be there on a Saturday, but he wanted to get the lay of the land. Skinny stayed away from his Brotherhood friends. He was sure the cops would be watching them.

The office was in Jonesboro, almost in the center of a row of attached buildings across the street from the courthouse. He drove around back and found a parking lot, which would hold about ten cars. The alley was very narrow and one-way.

Do I want to burn down his office? No! That's too impersonal. It's his damn house, his castle, his home sweet home I want!

He drove back around to the front, where he parked for a better look and saw Patton's name out front, too.

Hot damn! I lucked out - - they're in the same building. That sucker is a walking dead man!

***

When Skinny had the site clearly in his mind he left for Butterworth's house.

Located in a typical working-class Jonesboro subdivision, a mile drive from the office, it was a modest brick and wood house with a carport. He could see a car and a van in the carport. It would be easy to torch, but it was also in-between some other houses in the middle of the block. That could cause a problem. In addition, he needed a place to park.

I could pull up in the driveway on some pretext. I'll have to think about it, but I want to do it tonight. Then I'll lay low for several days and let them worry about me before I kill some people. Always the chance a cop could be hiding out on the property or even in the house. Maybe, but they didn't have much time to organize something like that. I'll have to take a chance. Also, I gotta watch out for some stupid cop driving by the house. I want them so scared they'll wet their pants just hearing my name! After a few days, they'll tend to get careless thinkin' maybe I left the area.

Butterworth's house tonight, and then I'll kill the ex-wife and her worthless husband, along with Patton, in one night. All in one swift strike! If I can do Butterworth's house tonight, I'll do the rest next Friday night, or Sunday night. Not Saturday if I can help it, 'cause they might be looking for a pattern. After I kill them, it's off to Kentucky. I like that state and don't have no friends or kinfolk there, so it should be safe. I'll find some woman to shack up with.

Skinny left to scout Pat's house in College Park. He found it on the bottom of a hill in the Newton Estates sub-division with the street branching off the main street, making a 'U', and coming right back to the main street. So, he had two ways in and out. Patton's house backed up to the Camp Creek

Parkway, a four-lane divided highway, which had limited access. The house sat on a corner lot and apparently had been a much bigger lot before the highway came through. There was a fence in back, which looked like it went all along the highway.

There's a place at the end of Patton's yard where water has washed a gulley plenty big enough for a man to get under the fence. A road borders the left side of the house and stops at the fence. It apparently went to the subdivision across the highway at an earlier time, but was cut off when the four-lane highway was built. It still left Smart-Ass Patton about a half-acre lot.

Skinny filed all of this in his memory for future use. Next, he drove down the four-lane divided highway to look at the house from the back. He had to go about a mile before he could turn around. This time Skinny was on the same side of the highway as Patton's house. He noticed several men jogging on a grass strip along the side of the road. He might want to jog by later to get a better look.

If Patton only knew I'm driving by his house, I'd bet he'd have to head for the bathroom!

Now to find the Johnson's house.

Skinny found it outside of Jonesboro, at the corner of two cross streets.

This house would have to be hit late at night. But how to get away? The back yard borders some woods, but where do they go? I'll make only one pass. The stupid pigs might be watching the house. To be safe, the next time I come here I'll have a different vehicle.

Skinny turned left at the Johnson's house and drove slowly, but not slow enough to draw attention, and immediately saw...

What! Wait a minute! Those two kids walking toward me are my two kids!

He wanted to stop and pick them up. Not that he really wanted them, but so she couldn't have them. They didn't even look as he drove past.

The woods turned out to be a five-acre tract, which apparently had not been developed.

Just as I thought. Here comes a police car going very slowly down the street. Time to get the hell out of here. I need to look more, but another day. I could park on the other side of the woods and walk to their backyard. It would be easy to find because it's beside the street. It's time to eat supper, then to Butterworth's after dark.

He found a Mexican restaurant and had one beer with his meal. After eating two beef burritos, Skinny went to his van and put on a Boy Scout leader's uniform. The sky was getting dark.

Maybe I should wait until about 1:00 in the morning, when everyone is in bed. No, I can't wait that long! Besides, how would I explain my way out if some dumb cop found me there at that early morning hour? Probably best to t go it now.

* * *

Herb, Bonnie, and family went out to eat at about the same time Skinny did. They went to the Steer Inn for a steak and salad bar.

"You know, Bonnie, going on a mini-trip this weekend may be overkill, but I don't feel comfortable staying at home, especially at night, as long as that maniac killer is on the loose. I told Pat where we will be staying and also gave him my sister, Hazel Jinks, phone number in case of an emergency. Rhonda has that information, too."

"That was a good idea and you didn't hear me argue about going, especially since we're on our way to the Pottery, and the Commerce outlet stores. I don't think the kids look like they mind going either. You could use some new shirts and ties, too."

"Right, and I get to shop for girl's clothes and records," exclaimed Beth, their 14-year-old daughter.

"Yeah, and I get to go to the sporting-goods stores and the record shops." An enthusiastic Mark, the 16-year-old son, smiled. "And check out the girls, too!"

"Let's eat and go. We've got a two-hour drive." Herb pulled on his suspenders.

They finished eating and left for a motel in Commerce.

* * *

Skinny finished eating and left the restaurant.

After I set fire to Butterworth's house, I'll change vehicles 'cause someone could get the tag number.

No one was around the van, so he got in and made everything ready to burn Herb's house. He had the Boy Scout tickets he stole from the store.

Laughing to himself, Skinny thought, *If anyone asks, I'm selling tickets to a Boy Scout fund-raising event. Like taking orders for Boy Scout cookies. Boy Scout cookies! Man, that's a good one! And me a Boy Scout leader. That's even better!*

The uniform was a little big but fit reasonably well. He got behind the wheel and smiled when he looked at the plastic gallon can of gas on the floor in front of the passenger's seat.

Skinny drove over to Herb's neighborhood and noticed that, although now very dark, the van, which was in the carport earlier, was missing and no lights were on in the house. He kept going and observing.

The storage area in the rear of the carport was constructed of wood and had the same roof as the house. If it went up in flames, unless someone got to it very quickly, the fire would destroy the entire house. Even if it didn't burn to the ground, the water damage from fire hoses would total it. What he wanted was to strike fear into the hearts of the others before he killed them. He wanted them to understand they were powerless to stop him!

Skinny parked down the street at a convenience store and took a pack of matches and a cigarette out of the grocery bag. Next he removed a rag and some duct tape. Skinny opened the lid of the gas can and stuffed the rag down into the can like a wick with the top sticking out of the plastic can. He taped it in place with the duct tape. Another piece of tape was used to block off most of the hole where the lid had been on the can so the gas wouldn't spill when he carried it. It was not foolproof but it helped. He placed the can beside the grocery bag and was now ready to go!

Carefully Skinny drove back to Herb's subdivision, first going around the block to check for cops, and then he pulled into the driveway. His heart was pounding as he got out, went to the front door and rang the doorbell, while he kept looking for a patrol car.

"If someone is home, I'm selling tickets to a Boy Scout Festival." Skinny rang the bell a second time, and then a third time. There was no answer, so he grabbed the bag and gas can from the van and went through the carport to the storage room.

The door was not locked. Quickly he went inside, risked turning on a small flashlight, and set the gas can against the wall closest to the house. Next, he took out the book of matches and lit a cigarette. When it was burning good, he placed about one-third inside the matchbook, with the cigarette touching the match heads. He laid the matchbook beside the gas-soaked rag. Skinny placed several flammable items from the shed up against the gas can and left. When the cigarette burned down to the match heads, it would ignite them, which in turn would light the wick. Finally, as the plastic container melted, it would go up in flames and so would the house. He didn't stay around to see the action - - too good a way to get caught.

I'm outa here!

Skinny drove to a different Atlanta airport long–term parking lot. This time he found a Chevy van and removed the tag. The van was backed into the parking space, so unless someone looked for the tag, no one would know it was missing.

He left and went to an area he knew had a high crime rate that was within two blocks of a large shopping center. He put the original tag back on his Ford van, so it would look like kids took it, and parked the van close to the high-crime neighborhood. He left the windows down and the keys in the ignition. He always wore rubber gloves so he wasn't worried about finger prints.

The shopping center was only a little over a block away, and he hurried toward it. Skinny didn't want to be in this neighborhood any longer than necessary. He had the .38 under his shirt but didn't want trouble, as he had a job to do. The Boy Scout leader walked all over the large parking lot on the North side of the shopping center and found a few vans with the doors unlocked, but none with the keys in them. He moved to the South lot and struck gold on his third try.

It was a Dodge van, but that was okay. He got in and drove off. A few blocks away, he found a deserted place and put on the tags, which he had taken from the long-term lot at the airport.

If my luck holds, the owner will be out of town for a week or two and it could be some time after that before he discovers the switched plates. How often do these idiots look at their license plates? How many of them know the number? By the time the plates are discovered, I'll be long gone. I'll finish my business in the Atlanta area by the weekend.

* * *

Skinny sat in his tent watching the 11 o'clock news.

Not quite like home sweet home, but it sure beats the hell out of a jail cell. With electricity, I have a small TV and a heater. It's my little home sweet home. If they catch me now, my jail cell will most likely be on death row, 'cause Georgia has the electric chair.

Finally, the reporter got to the Butterworth story.

"A mysterious fire raged out of control at the home of a prominent Jonesboro attorney, Herbert Butterworth. As you can see from the film footage taken at the scene, the house was totally destroyed, along with a car in the carport. Neighbors reported seeing a man in a Boy Scout uniform earlier in the evening. No one was home at the time of the blaze. Preliminary reports suspect foul play, as there was a strong odor of gasoline in the utility shed area. Fire Chief Ed Farmer and Arson Investigator Bobby Jinks stated they did not think this fire was an accident."

Good! I want all of them to know I did it, to know I can get to them at will. I want them to worry, to have sleepless nights, and to think about how they used me, took advantage of me, and used deceit to steal my kids. One down, three to go! In the meantime, I'll sit here and take it easy for a few days, listen to the radio and the police scanner, watch

203

TV, and read the newspaper. Let them worry, and then when I fail to come after them in the next day or two, they'll all get careless. My tent is cozy with the electric heater.

As he sat reading the *Clayton News Daily*, Skinny noticed that Patton was having his first jury trial on Monday.

Hmmm.

CHAPTER 21

Middle of December - The Trial Begins

"Mr. Butterworth, please."

"Herb Butterworth here."

"This is Lieutenant Keller of the Clayton County Police Dept. I'm afraid I have had to telephone you with some bad news. Your house has been destroyed by fire."

"Good Lord! There must be some kind of mistake."

"I'm sorry, Herb. There has been no mistake. We have known each other for years, so once I heard about the fire, I had trouble believing it myself. I carefully checked it out before I called you."

"I don't know how Bonnie and the kids will take this, but I know everyone will want to come back to Jonesboro."

"Herb, do you have any enemies? Anyone who would have wanted to burn down your house?"

"What? You mean it was no accident?"

"We don't think so."

"The only one I can think of, and incidentally the reason we were out of town, is Skinny Anderson. You know, the escaped prisoner."

"That's heavy, Mr. Butterworth! You know he killed two people during his escape, don't you?"

"Yes."

"Why would he want to get you?"

"I was his wife's attorney when she divorced him."

"Man! Soon as you get back, call me and we'll post an officer to guard you until we can get this guy."

"How did you get this number?"

Lieutenant Keller spoke as if to a child. "You're talking

to the police! Your neighbor told us."

"Yeah, ah, excuse me, but I'm kind of shook up right now and Bonnie is trying to talk to me at the same time. Look, Lieutenant, I really appreciate your help, and I'll call you as soon as I find a place to stay."

"Please do." Lieutenant Keller's voice became very serious. "This guy is nobody to fool with."

"Oh, Lieutenant One other thing. I don't know if you have met attorney Pat Patton, but he did the adoption of Skinny's kids."

"Good Lord! I heard of Mr. Patton and I'll have someone contact him immediately. He could be in real danger. We, in case you were wondering, got in touch with Skinny's ex-wife and have regular patrols going by her house. I'm also putting an officer with them as of now."

"Thanks again, Lieutenant Let me get off this phone and tell Bonnie what's going on. I'll be sure to call you when we get back."

"I'm sorry, Herb. Bye."

"What happened, Honey? You look white as cotton," observed Bonnie.

"Our house burned down!" Herb's voice was unsteady. "Lieutenant Keller does not think it was an accident."

"No! No! No! There has to be a mistake! It can't happen to us!" sobbed Bonnie, shaking like a scared child.

* * *

Pat and Shirley spent the day together working on the Washington trial. He practiced opening statements and closing arguments, and they worked on objections he might be able to make, as well as how he could counter objections the State might make. Shirley was able to help him but could not discuss what she learned to anyone else, especially someone in the DA's Office.

While Skinny was setting fire to Herb's house, Pat and Shirley were eating a late meal at the Olive Garden, where he gave her a key to his house. She was ear to ear in smiles.

They were tired and decided to go home and watch TV,

especially the 11 o'clock news. They were hoping to hear of Skinny's capture. As they watched film clips of the burning of Herb's house and listened to the announcer, they were both sure Skinny had done it. The news of the destruction of Herb's house brought cold chills to Pat and Shirley, exactly what Skinny had hoped to accomplish. They both felt vulnerable, but Shirley flatly refused to leave Pat. They went to bed but not before calling Eb at his girlfriend's apartment to let him know about Skinny's escape. They went to sleep in each other's arms, with the bedroom door locked, a chair propped against the doorknob, and their guns close beside them. They still would go to church in the morning.

About to fall asleep, Pat jumped when the phone rang. It was Lieutenant Keller telling Pat the police would be patrolling around his house several times that night and continue until Skinny was apprehended. He also wanted to put a police officer in the house, but Pat turned him down - - he felt he would have no privacy. Skinny probably had left Georgia anyway.

Pat woke up in the middle of the night and was so uptight about the trial and Skinny that he found himself in the bathroom losing his supper.

When Pat and Shirley got up the next morning, both were tired because neither had slept very well. They went to church and out to lunch with Shirley's parents but kept silent about Skinny. After lunch, they returned home for last-minute work on Pat's trial.

The Sunday night 11 o'clock news did not have anything new on Skinny; he seemed to have disappeared. However, there was new evidence the fire at Herb's house was not an accident. Reporters swarmed Herb's house and also Skinny's ex-wife. Their nose for news smelled a story concerning Skinny.

Pat left a message on Lieutenant Keller's answering machine and with Herb's sister to call him. He wanted to help in any way he could. They could stay at his house, but Pat knew Hazel Jinks, Herb's sister, had a large house and they would be welcome there. The phone was ringing.

"Hello," answered Shirley. "Herb, I'm so sorry to hear about your house. I know, he's been leaving messages all over for you to call. Okay, I'll tell him."

"That was Herb. He's at his sister's house with police protection and will let you know if he needs anything."

"He's a good guy, Shir. He surely is. You did tell him I would do anything I could, didn't you?"

"He knows that. Herb wants you to focus on the trial tomorrow. Let's go to bed. You need to sleep."

"Okay, Shir. You're right as usual. Big day tomorrow."

"Right. For me, too. I've about had it with the new office manager. She opposes any new idea or suggestion that I have. I'm about to tell her off!"

* * *

Pat was up early and went for a three-mile jog with his .22 Magnum derringer stuck in his waistband. After the jog Pat took a shower while Shirley was still sleeping. He didn't think they had to worry about Skinny during the daytime, and he had nervous energy to work off before the trial. When Shirley's clock went off, he had breakfast ready.

"Pat, you'll make someone a good wife. Let's see . . . eggs, bacon, toast, orange juice, and coffee. You wouldn't be looking for a husband, would you?" Shirley grinned.

"You mean I get to be on the bottom?" asked Pat returning the grin.

"Okay, Big Boy. It's time to go."

* * *

Pat wanted to get to the courtroom 30 minutes early. Court started at 9:30, but Judge Musselman came in at 9:00 to take some uncontested cases each morning. Pat arrived at his office just before 8:30 then walked to the courthouse.

The first thing he saw was three TV trucks parked out front, another truck from WHIT radio, and a car with *The Daily News* painted on it. They were to cover the trial.

Then he saw the pink Thunderbird parked in a reserved space for the DA's Office and it all came together. He suddenly knew the identity of the woman opposing Shirley. Shirley said she was good looking, well-built, had a rich father, lives in the

Tampa area, was disagreeable, and drove a pink Thunderbird. The license tag that read *GODDESS* confirmed it. The new office manager was Gloria!

That's all I need.

As he went in the front door, there was reporter Murray from Channel 3 trying to get her cameraman in position to get a shot of her talking to Pat.

"Mr. Patton, please give us a few words. How does it feel to be a new attorney representing one of the *Five-O'Clock Traffic Bandits*?"

Pat just smiled at the camera and kept going.

"You think you can get him off?" asked Sandi Desanto from WHIT radio.

"No comment," replied Pat, and continued on his way.

"With all the flat tires, can he get a fair trial here?" asked Vivienne Cove of *The Daily News*.

"Although I argued for a change of venue, I have faith in the people of Clayton County," answered Pat.

In reality, he had little faith in this case. There was no way Sammy was going to be found *not guilty*, and that fact was understood by both Pat and Sammy's family. This trial was not about *guilty* or *not guilty*. It was about a recommendation of the maximum sentence of 20 years by the DA's Office. Sammy simply had nothing to lose by going to trial. All the evidence to convict existed - - eyewitnesses, the money (some dyed red), the guns, the knife Sammy had used, the masks, and the getaway car. Sammy was identified as being in the bank and as one of the robbers. He also was found in the car with all the goodies.

If the press were there for a Perry Mason trial, where the real robber was sitting in the first row of the spectator seats, they were going to be sadly disappointed. Pat's job was twofold: first, do as much damage-control for Sammy as he could, and second, for his own personal career, show the DA's Office he was willing to fight for his clients and he would refuse to lay down on any case. He could've hired shrinks to counter the State's shrinks and made a fight for *Not Guilty by Reason of Insanity* but that required money, which Sammy's family did not have. Even with lots of money, a *Not Guilty* verdict was virtually impossible.

Sammy's mother and aunt had arrived early as he had asked. Pat showed them the courtroom through the window of the courtroom door. He made sure they knew where to sit, and they spent a few minutes reviewing their testimony. They talked about the judge and jury selection and what Pat and Herb thought they could expect from Assistant DA Mark Kimbrough.

The press again tried to talk to him and the two ladies. Pat had previously told them to be respectful but not talk to the press, because they could say something to hurt Sammy's case.

The time had come to go into the courtroom. Pat told both ladies they would have to leave before the trial actually started, because both sides would ask the judge to invoke the Rule of Sequestration - - the removal of all witnesses from the courtroom so a witness could not hear what another witness had said and then alter his or her testimony.

Pat walked in just as the 6' 3" tall Judge Musselman heard the last uncontested case and called for a 10-minute recess. He was stern in his courtroom but very likable out of court. He was known for *throwing the book* at repeat offenders, hence the name *Chain Gang*. He was also an expert equestrian in his spare time.

Pat went to the front of the courtroom and put his large briefcase on the defense counsel table. Kimbrough was already there and had set up his files. District Attorney Dean Colver would answer for the State when the judge called the trial calendar.

Pat went to the holding cell and briefed Sammy on what was about to take place, but Pat was not sure how much Sammy understood.

When Pat came out, a tall, distinguished looking, uniformed police officer was waiting for him.

"Pat Patton?" he asked.

"Yes, sir."

"I'm Lieutenant Keller, of the Clayton County Police Department. We talked on the phone."

"Yes, and Herb mentioned you."

"I'm sorry to bother you when you're about to go on trial, but we now have reason to believe that Arnold *Skinny*

Anderson broke into The Aurora Eross' Ace Hardware Store and is now armed to the teeth. We know at least a shotgun and a .38 Special are missing from the store. We also have reason to believe he burglarized both a Radio Shack and a clothing store. At first, we thought it was done by kids, but we are now reasonably sure he did it."

"Nice guy, huh?"

"Oh, it gets worse. We think he also robbed, at gunpoint, a convenience store in Stockbridge, beat all three clerks, and raped one of the females. Mr. Patton, she is a basket case and will be kept in the hospital for several days. This woman will need a lot of counseling to get over it, if ever. She and her co-workers also have head injuries."

"Gosh, Lieutenant, I have to have time for all this to sink in. We know he is pretty much an animal."

"There's more but before I go into that, the places that were burglarized and robbed were all over the immediate area, like a checker board. We don't know where he'll show up next. We also located two stolen vehicles. We think it's Skinny's doing. At the Atlanta airport, vehicles are turning up missing or with plates missing or switched. We're not 100 percent sure it's Skinny, but the county and airport police are working together and are watching the parking lot for stolen vehicles and anyone who resembles him."

"Now you're starting to scare an already worried me." Pat frowned.

"We also have reason to believe he burnt down Herb's house, although we can't prove it. It is possible you and the Johnsons are in very real danger until this madman is caught.

"My girlfriend and I were sure Skinny was behind the arson of Herb's house when we first heard about it."

"Here's what we plan to do - - station an officer outside in the parking lot and have a marked patrol car follow you home later. You turned down having a police officer placed in your house, but the Johnsons have agreed to it. I wish you would reconsider our offer. At any rate, we will have a car go by your house at least once per hour, at irregular intervals, until he is caught."

"Lieutenant, please notify Assistant DA Shirley O'Kelly.

She's my girlfriend and is with me much of the time. She has a right to know. I appreciate what you're trying to do."

"I sure will. I'll walk over to the DA's Office and talk with her. I don't know her but I know her father."

"Thank you, Lieutenant. Herb said you are one of the good guys, and I believe it."

Lieutenant Keller left, and Pat stood there for a minute, trying to absorb all that was said. Judge Musselman was famous for his 20-to-25-minute 10-minute breaks, so at 9:55, court was about time to start.

Shirley will be here to go to lunch with me. I can talk to her then. Why did this have to happen when I'm having my first jury trial? I was nervous enough over it. Why? Why? Okay, focus on the trial and let Lieutenant *Keller focus on Skinny.*

* * *

As Pat went into the courtroom, Sammy came in escorted by two deputies. He did not look scared, just confused as he slumped shyly into his seat. He had been allowed to wear civilian clothes and the handcuffs would be taken off before the jury came into the courtroom. That was done so as not to imply the defendant was a criminal; he was not yet convicted. The handcuffs would be put back on after the jury left.

However, every defense lawyer knows there is a big and visible sign that says, "Hey! Here sits the defendant, and he would not be sitting here if he were not guilty as hell!"

The reality is, if you are a defendant, you have to prove you are *not guilty*, even though we're all told one has to be proven *guilty beyond a reasonable doubt* to be convicted.

The bailiff announced, "Everyone please rise. The Honorable Harold Musselman is now presiding." The judge sat down and told the people in the courtroom to take their seats.

"Ladies and gentlemen, I will now call the criminal calendar."

Judge Musselman proceeded to call the cases o n t h e c a l e n d a r and each attorney stood and announced *ready*, or made another appropriate announcement. Others made excuses as to why they were not ready, such as not being able to find a witness.

"Mr. Colver, what is the first case you are calling for trial?"

"The State versus Washington, Your Honor."

"Very well. Mr. Washington is here, and his attorney Mr. Patton has announced "ready". Regarding the State versus McKnight and the State versus Newsom, the defendants and their attorneys will remain until after we strike a jury. These cases are number two and number three. If this case falls through for any reason, we will go to number two and number three if necessary. All but the first three cases are excused. After we strike the jury, numbers two and number three are excused until Wednesday morning at 9:30. Number four through ten shall be on a 60-minute standby. Mr. Kimbrough and Mr. Patton, please approach the bench."

Because assembling a jury pool cost the county money, the judge wanted to be ready to try another case if this one fell through. Many times a deal would be made with the DA and an accused would plead guilty. The jurors could then be used on another case. He wanted the next two cases ready to go as sometimes two or three cases in a row would not go to trial for any number of reasons.

Pat and Mark walked up and stood before the judge, who asked, "Are there any expected problems with this trial, or anything at all the three of us need to discuss prior to starting?"

Motions had previously been heard but neither side had additional motions, except for Pat renewing his motion for a change of venue. Pat felt this case had so much bad publicity that Sammy could not get a fair trial. Pat had earlier argued for a change of venue, but it was denied, and then denied a second time. The judge disagreed with Pat and did not think moving the trial was necessary.

"Bring in the first panel of jurors."

Three panels of 20 jurors each would be brought in, one panel at a time. The prosecution was allowed to strike 12 names and the defense 24 names *without cause* or for *no reason at all*. This was a total of 36 strikes, plus a juror could be struck for *cause*. Who knows, maybe the judge's brother, the prosecutor's wife, or Pat's father were in the jury pool. There also were other possibilities, and the judge would want an alternate juror selected in case one of the members got sick during the trial. Therefore, they had a total of 60 men and women from which the final 12, plus one or two alternates, would be picked.

Pat was given several sheets with names, addresses and occupations of the members of the jury pool, but that was all. He believed talking to each juror was necessary in order to get a feel for the person. If he felt very uncomfortable, he would strike that person, because it could be a mutual feeling.

Pat had instructed Sammy to rise when a juror came in or left the courtroom, as he wanted the jury to see respect for them from the defendant and from his attorney. He also knew he was going to get flak from the judge and Kimbrough, as all they wanted to do was hurry through this trial so they could get on to the next one. Pat couldn't care less about the time; he wanted to do his very best for Sammy and his family.

The men and women of the first panel came in and sat down in the first two rows reserved for them. They were asked a few general questions by the judge, such as, "Are any of you related to the defendant, the prosecutor, or the defense attorney?"

He then turned questioning over to Kimbrough, who asked, "Do any of you know the defendant, Sammy Joe Washington, or his attorney, Pat Patton? Are you familiar with the case?" He went on to say, "If I prove to you, beyond a reasonable doubt, that Sammy Joe Washington did what he is charged with, that is armed robbery, would any of you have a problem convicting him?" He asked more general questions. The prospective jurors had been told to raise their hands if the answer to one of his questions was positive. He also asked individual jurors questions to clarify their answers. When he was done with the panel, Pat's turn came to ask general questions to the panel at large, then specific questions.

Pat asked, "Have you ever been a victim of a crime or has any member of your family ever been the victim of a crime?" This got half of the panel to raise their hands.

Very good! I'll now be able to talk to half of the panel

individually on this one question alone.

And, he did, much to the dismay of the judge, who told him to move on two different occasions. Pat told him "Yes, Sir," then continued talking to the jury anyway. And so it went, with general and then specific questions, including, "Were you one of the drivers who got nails in your tires on I75 during the chase? Did the traffic jam cause you to be late for an appointment or to miss work?" He did not want a juror who was upset with Sammy because of the traffic jam.

Pat figured it paid off though, because he found three people on the first panel who were very upset with persons charged with crimes because of things that had happened to them or their families. He struck all three. He also struck Mary Cohen, a woman who was obviously flirting with Mark Kimbrough during jury selection, another who was married to a preacher, and a woman who was very thin, had a hawk-like face, sharp nose and never smiled. He got the feeling she would vote to convict anyone for anything.

They were finished with the first panel, so those jurors who had been questioned but not struck were seated in the jury box and break for lunch. One potential juror was struck *for cause* because she was related to the District Attorney. Five were struck by the prosecutor and eight by Pat. Of the initial 20 from the first panel, they seated six in the jury box. Six more were needed plus one alternate.

* * *

As they broke for lunch, Pat saw Shirley sitting in the back row but had not seen her come in because he had been completely absorbed in the jury selection. As they exited the courthouse, reporters were everywhere.

"You looked good, Pat. I . . ."

"Excuse me, Mr. Patton. I am Vivienne Cove of *The Daily News*. Do you have a comment for readers?"

"You'll have to excuse me, Ms. Cove, but I'm on my way to lunch with this beautiful young lady." Pat nodded to Shirley. "I will say this, though. After talking at length with Mr. Washington on many different occasions, and with his family members, I fail to see how he would have the mental capacity to orchestrate or commit any type of crime."

When Pat got through talking, he noticed Zel Murray of Channel 3 News had her cameraman recording his statement.

As they made their way out to the parking lot, two more TV reporters and two newspaper reporters stopped him. Pat gave them the same story. They got into Shirley's car because she was now with the DA's Office and had a reserved spot.

"Where to, Mr. Mason?" asked Shirley with a respectful smile.

"The local burger doodle is okay with me, Miss Smarty-Pants. You sound like the guys at Great Atlanta. They've been giving me a hard time ever since I passed the Bar. One of them even shot down one of my flying advertisements with a rubber band and paper clip. Sheer luck but Dave did it."

She made him explain *flying advertisements*. Then he leaned his head back, placed his left hand on her thigh, and commented quietly, "So far, so good."

As they ate lunch, the conversation centered on the trial, and, of course, Skinny.

* * *

Skinny sat in his tent with the small electric heater he had purchased. It was plugged into the camp site's electrical outlet. Although not uncomfortable, he wished he were in a house, or even a motel where he could watch out a window. He felt vulnerable not being able to see out of an enclosed tent with nothing to hide behind if bullets started to fly. One thing for sure, though, "The stupid cops would never think to look for me here," boasted Skinny aloud.

He turned on the TV to catch the noon news. After a few minutes of national and State news, there was Pat Patton saying, "I fail to see how he would have the mental capacity to orchestrate or commit any type of crime."

"So that's what you look like, my good-as-dead Mr. Patton. Now let's see how your mental capacity is going to hold up during this trial!"

Skinny got into his van and headed north. He got on I75,

and after stopping at a drive-through for a cheeseburger, fries, and a large Coke, he continued heading north as he ate.

About 35 miles down the road, he came to a pay phone at an exit off the expressway, on the northwest side of Atlanta. He looked at his watch, 2:30.

Skinny lucked out and found a pay phone which worked. He had looked up the Clayton County Courthouse phone number earlier, in the stolen phone books he had in the van, and dialed the number.

"Clayton County Courthouse, how may I help you?"

"Ma'am, I need to speak to Judge Musselman's secretary right away. This is an emergency!"

"I will ring her, sir."

"Judge Musselman's chambers, Dottie Albert speaking. How may I help you?"

"Ms. Albert. This is Dr. George Duckworthington. I understand you have a young attorney trying a case, ah, a Mr. Patton?"

"Yes, sir."

"I'm afraid I have some bad news, ma'am. His mother suffered a massive stroke, and his father was in a serious automobile accident coming to our hospital to see her. Oh, I have to go! They are calling me STAT!" Skinny's voice registered excitement, then he hung up.

I'm not sure his mother and father are still living, but at his age they should still be around. He got back into his van whistling The Spinners' *Working My Way Back to You,* as he drove off.

* * *

Pat was questioning a prospective juror in the second panel, when Ms. Albert appeared behind the judge and handed him a note. After the judge read the note he announced, "Ladies and gentlemen, we will now take a short break. Counsel, please approach the bench."

Pat and Mark walked up to the judge's bench wondering what was happening.

"Mr. Patton, you need to call your parents' home at once. This may be a hoax but we just received a message from a

Doctor Duckworthington saying your mother had a stroke and your father was in an automobile accident while driving to the hospital. The doctor hung up before my secretary could ask what hospital."

"Oh, no! But, if it's true, no one will be home!" Pat thought for a moment then said, "I've got the next-door neighbor's number in case no one answers!"

"Mr. Patton, you can use a phone in my office. I'll authorize the call as an emergency."

Pat went to the judge's chambers and called home. His mother answered, which startled him.

"Mom? Are you okay? Is Dad okay?"

"Pat? Sure I'm okay, and your father is watching TV."

"I'm calling from Judge Musselman's chambers. Someone called the courthouse and said you had a stroke and Dad was in an accident!"

"How cruel! No, we're both fine, Son."

"Mom, I'm going to have to go, but I'm okay now that I know the report was false. I'll call you later."

"Okay, Son. Take care and come see us soon!"

"Bye, Mom. I love you."

"Who could be mean enough to pull a hoax like that?" asked Judge Musselman.

"I might know the answer to that question, Your Honor."

Pat told the judge about Skinny and his earlier conversation with Lieutenant Keller.

"Dottie, please call the phone company and see if that call can be traced, and get Lieutenant Keller over here."

"Yes, sir!"

"Mr. Patton, are you able to continue today? If you want, we can adjourn jury selection until tomorrow morning."

"I can go on, Judge. Just give me 10 or 15 minutes to pull myself together."

"You got 'em. I need to talk to Lieutenant Keller anyway. I want him not only informed, but I also want both the Jonesboro and the Georgia State Police notified."

"Thank you, Sir. I'll be in the courtroom when you're ready."

About 20 minutes later, Judge Musselman came back in

the courtroom and motioned Pat and Mark to approach the bench. Pat had told Mark what was going on.

"The Jonesboro and Georgia State police have been notified. Lieutenant Keller said you turned down the offer of a police officer being placed in your house, so I ordered him to provide 24-hour police surveillance. No use taking chances; he could try to sneak into your house when you're not home. We will now finish with panel two then break until tomorrow morning. Any questions?"

"No, Sir," answered Pat and Mark respectfully.

They got the next six jurors plus an alternate out of the second panel. The judge swore them in and told them to report to the jury room.

* * *

Pat picked up his briefcase and met Shirley by the door.

"I heard what happened today, Pat, and I'm so sorry for you. What a cheap, creepy thing to do to someone!"

"Thank you, Shir. It just shows what a demented person we're dealing with. I'm convinced Skinny is out to get me and the Johnsons and may not be finished with Herb."

"I don't care what you say, Honey; I'm sticking with you until they get that SOB!"

"Judge Musselman ordered 24-hour surveillance on my house. I guess he's right. Herb's did burn to the ground."

"You're damn right! I just wish he were somewhere we could go after him. I feel so helpless!" blurted out Shirley.

"I know what you mean, Shir. He could be anywhere. Apparently Skinny is now an expert at disguises - - a maintenance man, a Boy Scout leader, and a bum were mentioned on TV. Did Lit. Keller tell you about the robbery and rape?"

"Yeh. He said they had good reason to believe Skinny did it. The man is an animal." Shirley voiced contempt.

"He scares me to death!"

"Mr. Patton, I understand you have a jury. How do you feel about it?" asked reporter Desanto, with WHIT radio.

"I'm Steve Futo, Channel 13 news. Any comment about the jury, or who may be after you? Is there a connection with the escaped convict?"

"I'm sure they will perform their duty to the best of their ability." Pat ignored the second question and zoomed past the rest of the press.

"We understand, from unnamed sources, the police are protecting you from Skinny Anderson!" yelled reporter Futo as Pat rushed away.

"How did the press find out about Skinny?" asked Shirley with a worried look.

"I guess Futo has a friend in the police department. What I can't understand is why a judge with the nick name of *Chain Gang* is being so nice to me."

That night Skinny's connection with Pat was all over the news.

CHAPTER 22

Middle of December - The Trial

Monday night went without incident. Shirley had insisted upon staying with Pat, and Eb elected to stay at his girlfriend's house until this nightmare blew over. He didn't mind one bit the excuse to sleep with her every night. His girlfriend didn't mind either.

Shirley got up and made breakfast, as this was Pat's big day, the start of the Washington trial. Pat was practicing his opening statement when he heard Shirley yell, "Come and get it, Big Boy!"

"You mean breakfast, too?" answered Pat with a mischievous grin.

"You know you don't have time for anything more than breakfast!"

"I guess you're right, Shir, you surely are; but I can dream, can't I?"

They finished breakfast then got into Max and headed for the courthouse. Shirley had left her car in the courthouse parking lot the night before and had ridden home with Pat.

* * *

As they left Pat's subdivision, Skinny watched from the parking lot of a nearby gas station and noticed a police car following Pat, who was driving a black Mustang convertible.

Skinny cranked up the van and headed northeast for about an hour and found a pay phone. As he drove, he was singing, *I've Been Working On His Nerves* to the tune of *I've Been Working On The Railroad*.

When he found a payphone that worked, Skinny dialed the Clayton County courthouse number while singing under his breath. The newspaper had a field day with yesterday's prank; he would give them a bigger one today.

* * *

When Pat got to the courthouse, he noticed an armed police officer stationed at the entrance to the courtroom. Pat made his way through several reporters and talked to Sammy, as well as his two witnesses. Then he sat down at the counsel table and waited. The judge came in at 9:30 and told the bailiff to bring in the jury. As they took their seats, the judge's secretary, Dottie, came in and gave him a note.

He took a deep breath and said, "Ladies and gentlemen of the jury. I'm very sorry, but something has come up that requires my immediate attention. You are excused until 10 o'clock, or until I send for you. Mr. Patton and Mr. Kimbrough, please approach the bench. Dottie, have Lieutenant Keller check this out at once and report back to me."

Both attorneys stood before the judge.

"Mr. Patton, we got a call from someone purporting to be Fire Marshal Bob Young, who said there was an explosion at your house and it created a total loss. I asked Dottie to call Lieutenant Keller for verification. Was anyone in it?"

"No, Judge. I don't believe this! But it shouldn't take long to check out as Lieutenant Keller has a car sitting at my place 24 hours per day." Pat was alarmed and disgusted.

"Pat, I certainly hope this is another hoax," said Mark Kimbrough.

"Thank you, Mark. I pray it is, too!"

A few minutes later Dottie appeared and spoke to Judge Musselman.

The judge leaned over and said, "Mr. Patton, good news! Your house is fine. Of course, the bad news is that there's a crazy man out there who has his sights set on you. Now he's also playing with me and Mr. Kimbrough."

"Could it be one of the people who got flat tires?" asked Mark while looking at Pat.

"I don't think so, and I don't think the person doing this is a nut case. I believe it's Skinny, trying to make my life miserable! And, he is doing just that!"

"Like I said, a real crazy man," remarked the Judge.

"Your Honor, with all due respect, I don't think the man is nuts. I've talked to his ex-wife at length and have come to the conclusion Skinny is a mean sociopath. He is a very evil person who does not have a conscience. What makes him even more dangerous is the fact that he is intelligent in addition to being mean. I believe he could throw a hand grenade in a daycare center and sleep like a rock that night. And, the brashness of those calls!" Pat shook his head. "I don't mind telling you both, if he's trying to get me worried, he has definitely succeeded."

"I still think there should be a man placed inside your house."

"Your Honor, I'm too private a person for that, but I will certainly welcome them outside my house, following me, or at work."

Lieutenant Keller came in the courtroom and asked the judge for permission to approach the bench, which he granted.

"Judge, as Dottie told you, we checked out Pat's house and it was fine. This time we were able to ascertain the call came from a pay phone in northeast Atlanta. The Atlanta police are going to dust for prints, but he probably used gloves. Pat, we are going to place two men at your house. There will be an unmarked car out front and one out back at the Camp Creek Parkway. The College Park police have agreed to work with us."

"Very good, Lieutenant. Mr. Patton, are you able to continue?"

"Let's do it, Judge! Maybe we can get this case tried without another interruption."

"Very well. Bailiff, bring in the jury."

The Assistant DA made his opening statement and then it was Pat's turn.

"I expect to show you Sammy Washington was not mentally competent to commit any crime, let alone bank robbery. I also expect the evidence to show Sammy thought he was Moses. He acted and dressed as he pictured Moses acting and dressing."

His opening statement was very good, and he told them he would put a psychiatrist on the stand who would tell them Sammy was mentally ill. What he did not tell them was this same shrink would also say, although Sammy was mentally ill, he knew right from wrong. This was true even though Sammy thought he was Moses and was taking money from demons.

All Pat could do was go with what he had - - which was a psychiatrist who was on the State's payroll. While the poor may get justice, the rich get a whole lot more justice. Pat didn't want justice in this case; what he really wanted was a ton of mercy. That was the only way he would get a *not-guilty* verdict. Although not probable, one person possibly could vote no in spite of the evidence and hang the jury. If that happened, the DA would certainly retry the case. Then the same scenario could happen again until the DA got tired of trying Sammy and set him free. That was even longer than a long shot.

"Mr. Kimbrough, you may now make out your case."

Kimbrough had several witnesses. He put up the arresting officer, the bank teller who Sammy held at knifepoint, the bank vice-president, and an expert witness who testified that Sammy's fingerprints were on the knife and on a picture from the bank. It depicted Exodus, with Moses leading a multitude of Jews while holding high the Ten Commandments.

Much to the chagrin of his two comrades in crime, Sammy had taken the picture off the wall and examined it, without gloves, while his buddies were trying to rob the bank. Kimbrough would call a fingerprint expert to confirm Sammy's prints on the picture.

Another witness for the State would be their own psychiatrist, who would testify Sammy knew right from wrong.

The most damaging evidence would be presented by bank security expert Chris English. He would show the jury a video of the robbery that was caught by the bank's security cameras before Sammy painted them green.

Pat's turn came to cross-examine the State's witness. He had no questions for the bank vice-president, police officer, or the expert witness. After all, he was not trying to prove Sammy did not do it. However, he did question the lovely 30-ish female bank teller. She admitted Sammy had held a knife on her but had never improperly touched her. As the jury could see, especially the men, this woman had not only quantity, but quality, as well. Any red-blooded American boy would want to touch what she had, but Sammy didn't do it. The jury listened with interest as Pat tried to paint a picture of a demented man, who was likeable, and a gentleman, but mentally incapable of committing this crime.

By the end of the day, Mark had finished with the prosecution's side of the trial, and Pat had cross-examined the witness he thought could help Sammy.

Tomorrow will be my day in the spotlight. The press is following this trial with a passion. It is getting radio, TV, and newspaper coverage, and I'm becoming a celebrity. They are playing up the fact that I'm defending one of the Five-O'Clock Traffic Bandits while Skinny is gunning for me. It makes a great news story, and because of TV and the newspapers, my face and name are now well-known. If I can make a respectable showing tomorrow, I won't be hurting for clients.

The judge dismissed the jury and Pat was making his way to the back of the courtroom through a mass of well-wishers, reporters, and other attorneys, who had come to watch the trial, when he got a message that the judge wanted to see him. He saw Shirley, who was in the back of the courtroom, and motioned for her to follow him. The judge was standing beside Dottie's desk.

"You have a phone call from an old friend and supporter of mine."

"Your Honor," said Shirley.

"Hi, Shirley."

Pat couldn't figure out who it could possibly be.

"Hello, Pat Patton here."

"Hi, Pat, this is Greg O'Kelly. We have been watching TV and I just wanted you to know we heard about the dirty tricks that reprehensible rattlesnake pulled. Grace and I want you to know you are in our prayers and we are with you all of the way. You are all Shirley ever talks about but we are really worried about her being with you."

"Thank you, sir, and speaking of your lovely daughter, she is here beside me."

"We're proud of you, Pat. Would you please give her the phone before I hang up?"

"Thank you again, and, yes, sir, here she is."

"Is that Daddy?"

"Yes, and he wants to speak to you."

"Hello, Daddy." Shirley was running her fingers through her hair.

"Hi, Sugar."

"What do you want, Daddy? I don't want to tie up the judge's telephone."

"I just have to tell you to please be careful, Honey. Don't think your mother and I don't know where you have been staying, and we will be worried to death until that madman is caught! Your mother and I urge you to stay away from Pat until they catch Skinny."

"Daddy, I just can't leave Pat alone at a time like this."

"I know, Honey, and I would be surprised if you did anything different. But your Mom and I are very concerned for your safety. You love him, don't you?"

"Yes, Daddy, very much!"

"I can look at him and tell he feels the same way about you. We love you, and please be careful. Skinny is an extremely dangerous lunatic."

"You're right, but the police have at least one car at Pat's 24-hours per day and a second at the highway in back of his house at night."

"That's a relief. Skinny would be crazy to come around there with that kind of coverage. I feel much better knowing you have police protection. Bye, Honey."

"Bye, Daddy."

"Greg is an old friend, Mr. Patton, and he seemed very concerned for your safety, and naturally, that of his daughter."

"He's a good man, Judge," replied Pat.

"Thank you for letting us talk to him," added Shirley.

"No problem. See you in the morning."

They left the judge's chambers and as they were walking out to the hall, Pat turned to Shirley, and said, "Now I know why the judge has been so nice to me."

Shirley looked up at him, reached into her pocket book, smiled and handed him a Hershey Bar. She was really getting to know him.

* * *

About 15 minutes earlier, Skinny looked over the parking lot at Pat's office and saw a black Mustang convertible he figured was Pat's.

Good! I don't see anyone around.

He took out a plastic gallon can of gasoline with a soaked rag in the filler hole and sat it under the gas tank of the black Mustang. He had taped a lit cigarette tucked into the pack of matches like he had done at Herb's house. It would ignite the gas can within 10 to 15 minutes. Next, he calmly walked back to the van and drove ten minutes up the road to a phone booth.

* * *

As Pat and Shirley were heading down the hallway, Dottie ran out of the judge's office and yelled, "Just a minute, Pat! I got a call from a man named Adam Teller who said, 'I'm in the horse business, and just cooked Patton's Mustang.' I know it makes no sense, but that's what he said."

"Shirley, are you thinking what I'm thinking?" exclaimed an alarmed Pat.

"Excuse us. We have to go!" yelled Shirley as they ran out of the courthouse. Smoke could be seen coming from the parking lot behind Pat's office, and then they heard a loud explosion.

"No! Not your beautiful Mustang!" yelled Shirley as they ran.

The police had already blocked off the lot. Max was hardly recognizable as a car. The explosion and fire also had destroyed cars on both sides of Max and damaged two more. Luckily, Herb's building was unharmed.

Several minutes later Lieutenant Keller walked over to them. "Pat, as soon as I was told this was your automobile, I put out a call for all cars to be on the lookout for Skinny. What a blatant act! The Jonesboro Police Department is only a block away, which means they got here within a minute or so. The State police have been notified."

"Thank you, Lieutenant" Pat had a tear in his eye. "That damn guy won't let me alone!"

"It doesn't look that way. I have to tell you the truth; I'm very concerned for your safety. We're dealing with a very brazen and dangerous man. And the jerk knows about me, as Dottie told me he used the name Adam Teller."

"Honey, you have fire insurance don't you?" asked Shirley.

"Sure, but I bought Max when he was only a few years old. Skinny just killed part of me. I'll never get another one like him! All the insurance company has to do is replace Max with a 1965 Mustang, or pay me the equivalent price. I'll never get one in the same shape as Max. Shir, I'm plain sick about this. I wish I could get my hands on that guy!" "So would a couple hundred law enforcement officers and numerous members of his victims' families," replied Lieutenant Keller.

"This can't be happening! It's a bad dream; it has to be!" wished a stunned Shirley. "I'm glad you were low on gas."

"I know, Hon. The tank should have been full as I almost always fill up when I get down to ¼ of a tank. I no longer feel things always happen to someone else. I'm now sure of one thing though. There is absolutely no doubt in my mind that Skinny is after me. Shir, I would feel better if we didn't see each other until the authorities get this guy. I think he has more than burning up my car on his mind!"

"Not on your life, Buster! Would you leave if he were stalking me?" asked Shirley defiantly.

"You know I wouldn't."

"So there! Case closed. I'm not exactly a helpless female, you know."

"I really don't want to get into the middle of this, Shirley, but Pat's right," agreed Lieutenant Keller. "I believe his life is in danger and yours, too, if you're with him. Again, please let us put an officer in your house like we've done with the Johnsons."

"My mind's made up, Lieutenant" Shirley was adamant.

"Sorry, Lieutenant, but I do appreciate the two police cars at my house. That should deter him."

A crowd had gathered and the reporters closed in as soon as Lieutenant Keller was finished talking to them.

"Mr. Patton, Sandi Desanto, WHIT radio. Is it true the police suspect Arnold Skinny Anderson of burning your car?

"I believe you would have to ask Lieutenant Keller or Capt. Kefauver about that."

"Sir, Vivienne Cove of the Daily News. Was this your car, and who do you think burnt it up?"

"Ms. Cove, yes, it was my car, and I think we both know who did it."

"Mr. Patton, Steve Futo, TV Channel 13 News. What are your comments concerning your car. Was this Skinny's work?"

"I believe he destroyed Max. Now please excuse us, ladies and gentlemen."

Herb, Julie, and Rhonda were standing outside the back door of the office, looking visibly upset.

"Pat, we're all so sorry about Max. We all know how you felt about that Mustang," consoled Herb.

"When are they going to get this guy? First Herb's house and now Max!" Pat was very angry now.

"Geez, Boss. Let me give you a big hug." Julie.As she hugged him, her breasts pushed into Pat's chest. Any other time that might have been enjoyable, but the loss of Max and the presence of Shirley undermined any pleasure.

"Sorry, Pat." Rhonda also gave him a hug.

"Thank you, all of you. Yes, I loved my car, but it was nothing compared to Herb losing his house."

"Here comes Lieutenant Keller again," said Shirley.

"Pat, I talked to Fire Chief Ed Farmer and...Herb, I didn't see you there. Anyway, you both need to know the fire investigators think Skinny used some kind of timer when he set both of the fires. They're not sure how he did it, but he was able to plant the gas cans, escape, and in both cases, later start the fire. We were on ready when your car went up in flames, but no Skinny. I'm telling you, within minutes we had the area within a mile of here ringed tight with police, but we still didn't get him. This gives even more credibility to the theory he used some kind of timer."

"Thank you, Lieutenant" Pat sounded resigned.

"I'd like to roast that sucker over an open pit with an apple in his mouth!" Herb told them.

"I know how you feel, but the apple isn't necessary," replied Pat.

"I'll buy the charcoal," volunteered Julie.

"And I'll provide the BBQ sauce," chimed in Rhonda.

"I'm sure the fire chief would be willing to donate a defective fire extinguisher," offered Pat.

"I'll get the matches," agreed Shirley.

"Now that we got that off of our chests, I guess I need a ride home. Shirley?"

"You got it, Hon. I'm glad I parked at the courthouse or he might have gotten mine too."

"We'll see y'all tomorrow." Pat sounded very tired.

"You present your side tomorrow?" asked Julie.

"Right, if I can get into the courtroom. You can imagine the coverage my poor burnt-up Mustang is going to get. It should be standing room only tomorrow. I hope I don't make a complete fool out of myself."

Shirley never told anyone Pat was so uptight before the trial that he got physically sick. Thinking of Skinny didn't help any either.

"Relax. We all feel that way on our first jury trial," commented Herb, pulling on his suspenders.

* * *

Pat and Shirley went to eat at The Golden Corral and then headed for home. A police car followed them. Pat felt like he was going to be pulled over at any time, because he was not used to having a police car tail him.

Shirley called her parents to let them know what had happened to Pat's car. After that, Pat had a concerned call on his answering machine from his mother as the 6 o'clock news in

Charleston also covered the story. This trial was also tied in with the manhunt for Skinny.

Suddenly the security doubled during the trial as the police thought Skinny might try something at the courthouse. Not only were there two police cars at Pat's house, but a patrol car sat at the entrance to his sub-division, 24 hours a day, watching all cars going in and out. The police ran tag checks over the radio on any cars they didn't recognize. They not only had unmarked cars in the Johnson's subdivision but also had an armed police officer in their house. Herb got similar treatment. Obviously, the police wanted Skinny in the worst way.

Pat called his mother and father to say he was okay, and then he cleaned and oiled his .44 Magnum. He loaded it and took the gun with him everywhere he went, even to the bathroom. Shirley did the same with her .38 Special. He hoped he would not have to shoot it indoors because he would probably have ringing in his ears for days; .44 Magnums are very loud.

"Shir, I'm going to go over my closing argument one more time, and then just sit on the couch, put my arm around you, cuddle up and watch some TV. I'm never going to be more ready and I need to relax."

"That's a good idea, Honey."

Pat went into the den and started practicing his closing argument. When he was half-way through, he heard a beautiful rendition of Tchaikovsky's First Piano Concerto. It sounded great, even on his old upright. He went into the living room and there was Shirley at the piano. Truly, this was an amazing woman.

If I live to be a hundred, I will never be able to play like her.

He stopped what he was doing and stood beside her as she went into Beethoven's Moonlight Sonata.

He could not help himself, but when she was done, he wrapped himself around her and gave her a long lingering kiss. He was hopelessly in love with this girl and wanted her forever. She responded and they started making love on the floor beside the piano.

When things were really heating up, there was a loud banging on the front door and a deep male voice yelled, "Open the door! Police!"

Pat jumped up, running across the room holding up his pants, turned the porch light on for five seconds and shut it off again. Then he repeated the sequence.

He yelled, "All is okay! Look at the porch light!" The officers outside looked for it every hour while Pat and Shirley were up. A light on in the living area meant the porch light needed to come on at the top of each hour, or they would investigate why Pat didn't signal them.

"Just checking, Mr. Patton. Better to be safe than sorry."

"Thank you, officer." Pat grit his teeth.

Pat looked around but Shirley had disappeared into the bathroom. As he looked down he muttered, "No snake after that; more like a short piece of limp spaghetti!"

Pat went to bed and Shirley soon joined him. "I love you very much, Shir."

"And I love you, too, Pat. More than you know. Please don't let anything happen to you. I have waited so long, I couldn't bear to lose you now!" Shirley had tears in her eyes.

"Don't worry, Honey. I'll always be here for you," replied Pat as he held her tightly. "You are a truly wonderful and amazing person."

"I feel the same about you."

Then the four of them went to bed. Pat, Shirley, .44 Magnum, and .38 Special. Frightened would not begin to explain how they felt.

* * *

Earlier that night Skinny watched the 6 o'clock news and the 11 o'clock news as he sat safely in his tent.

I have all them mothers worried now! I'll take them all out this weekend and then be on my way. Let them stew until then. They stole my kids and now I'll steal their lives!

He decided it was time to change vans again.

I'll do it tonight.

Skinny went to the van and dressed in a suit and tie.

232

This time he went to a private, long-term park-and-ride lot. After about 45 minutes, he found another van and took it. He wanted another Dodge but he had to settle for a Ford.

Well, maybe no one will notice I've had three different brands. At least they're some shade of red.

He switched plates from the Dodge with another van in the lot. Then Skinny found a 1977 Chevy van, the same color as the Ford he was driving and switched plates again. He felt that should protect him and drive the cops nuts. He hated having to park the Dodge where the Ford had been parked, but the lot was almost full. He backed it in the parking spot so the tag would not be visible from the road.

"One hour?" asked the parking lot attendant. "You decided not to go?"

"Yeah, I sat there for almost an hour and thought about the fight with my girlfriend. Then I decided I would not give in to her after all. I'll try to get the money back on my ticket."

"That's the spirit." The attendant gave him a thumbs-up sign.

Skinny stopped to eat, still wondering what possessed people to leave their keys in their cars. He hoped that the owner of the Ford van was out of town until at least the weekend.

"Damn, I won't get back to the campsite until 2 a.m. or after."

* * *

Wednesday morning, Don Weigle, the owner and manager of the campground, was making his rounds with one of the groundskeepers, picking up trash bags in an electric golf cart. He noticed the man in Tent Site 16 had a red Ford van. His job required him to notice things at his campground.

I could swear this fellow has had two or three, yes, three different vans since he has been here. A Ford is parked there now, but earlier in the week, he had a Dodge and maybe a Chevy. Could be he had a car, too, but it's hard to remember.

"Leroy, you notice anything different at Tent Site 16?"

"You mean that bright red van?"

"Right."

233

"Looks to me, it does, dat man, he trades cars almost every day. Never saw no one do dat before."

"Me neither."

When he got back to the office, he called Lieutenant Keller.

"Hi there, Lieutenant, Weigle here, from over at the campground. I got something for you to check out. Probably nothing, but I got a man over here who's had two or three different vehicles and he's not been here a week."

"Thanks, Don, but we're up to our necks in alligators right now with this Skinny guy. I'm sure you heard about him on the news."

"Yeah, I sure have. I hope you catch him. Also burnt down a house and set a car up in flames, didn't he?"

"He sure did, or at least we think it was him."

"Say, it was a lawyer's house and a lawyer's car, wasn't it?"

"Right on both counts,"

"Then he can't be all bad, can he?"

"Ordinarily, I'd laugh at a lawyer joke, but I know both of these men, and they are good people. I think that damned Skinny is going to try to knock off at least one of them, and Clayton County's police force, as well as the Jonesboro Police Department and the State police force, are trying to stop him. The Georgia Bureau of Investigation also has a team out trying to nail him. I just hope we get it done before another life or more property is lost. If I find that killer, I hope he is trying to escape! Our manpower is being taxed to the limit."

"I know what you mean, Lieutenant."

"Most likely be a day or two until we can get a car out there. You didn't get a tag number, did you?"

"No, but I'll get it and call you back."

"Okay, Don. We'll check out the tag and see if it is a stolen vehicle. That's the best I can do for you right now, but like you said, it most likely is a false alarm. Just to be safe, don't be too obvious getting the tag number."

Don, and his wife Donna, got back in the golf cart and Don told Donna he wanted her to drive up and down several aisles, so as not to look suspicious, and he would get the tag number.

"Here we go, not too fast. Okay. I got it! A 1979 Ford van, license number 4693SV."

"Except for the color, it's very similar to the one we have here at the campground," added Donna.

Don kept repeating it to himself. However, he did not write it down until he was at the end of the aisle because, as the Lieutenant said, he didn't want to look obvious doing it. He called Lit. Keller back, but he wasn't in. A clerk took the message, and tossed it on Lieutenant Keller's desk. However, unknown to her, it fell behind the desk and landed on the floor.

"I marked it on the calendar to check back with Lieutenant Keller in two days if we haven't heard from him," commented Donna.

CHAPTER 23

Middle of December - Patton for the Defense

As they left to go to court, Pat and Shirley waved to Officer Madoni in the unmarked car in front of the house. The officer followed him and informed Officer Harry Holden in the car behind the house that Pat was being escorted to court. Officer Holden acknowledged the radio call and said he would make sure no one came near Pat's house without his checking each visitor.

"I really miss my Mustang, Shir. Max was with me a number of years. He surely was. This rental car may be newer but it's not Max."

"Sorry, Honey, but maybe you can get another one. Oh, and when you were in the shower, Eb called. They are up to their eyeballs in work at the shop and he can't get off to watch the trial."

* * *

Reporters were waiting at the courthouse. Sammy had few supporters, except for the gas station and tire dealers, who made money on flat tires. And, yes, the tow truck companies.

"A few questions, Mr. Patton. Any comments on the destruction of your car?" asked TV reporter Steve Futo with a smile and knowing look.

Pat thought about this and decided he might be able to force Skinny's hand.

"Mr. Futo, as you know, the house of my friend and fellow attorney, Herb Butterworth, was burned to the ground. Yesterday, my car was deliberately set on fire across the street in my office parking lot. Those were the acts of a coward! I refuse to be intimidated by him and will now go into court and attempt to help a very nice but mentally ill man."

The media went wild! Everyone knew who Pat referred to. He had called Skinny a coward on TV. That had statewide implications and very likely national ones as well, because the wire services picked up the story.

He and Shirley went to the courthouse with TV cameras following them.

"Pat, why did you do that? Skinny is sure to come after you now!" exclaimed Shirley, who could not believe what she had heard.

"Shir, he is already after me. I want this to come to a head now, so we can lead normal lives. My comment may make him careless. I'll be ready for him tonight, and I want you away from the house.

"No, Pat, I won't do it!"

"You must, Shir. Look, please, just for tonight. If he doesn't try for me tonight, you can come back. Okay?"

"I don't want to leave you, Honey!"

"Just this one night. I'll set a trap for him. If he comes after me, like I think he will, I'll get him. You have to understand, I can't look out for both me and you."

"I can take care of myself." Shirley thought a minute. "Okay, Pat, but only one night. But, I'll worry myself to death. I'm telling you right now, there is no way in Hell I'll stay away tomorrow. I may not even stay away tonight."

"Okay, Shir, just one night." Pat hugged her.

"I've got to report to the DA's office and then I'll come back to watch you." Shirley's eyes were tearing. "I'll call Kathy and ask her to stay with me tonight."

Pat went up to the courtroom and again had to dodge reporters. Desanto, Murray, and Cove were especially persistent and Futo obviously had inside connections in the police department. Pat set up his files at the counsel table and made sure he had a pitcher of water and a paper cup. He also asked a deputy to give one to Sammy. There wasn't an empty seat in the courtroom. Next, he went to the holding cell and talked to Sammy, attempting to explain what was going to transpire.

Pat found Sammy's mother and aunt, who both knew they would be called as witnesses. Once more he went over what was expected of them and how they should act on cross-examination.

As he finished talking to them, Dr. Alex Fester came in. Pat reviewed information about his background, experience, and education, which would be needed to qualify him as an expert witness.

Mark sat at the prosecutor's table and Pat took his place at the defense table. They brought Sammy in and sat him next to Pat. You could hear mumbling of *Five-O'Clock Traffic Bandits*. The bailiff had everyone rise as Judge Musselman came in a doorway located behind his chair and sat down. All were told to take their seats.

"I call the State versus Washington. Are both parties ready?"

The attorneys answered "Yes."

"Mr. Patton, you may proceed," ordered the judge.

Pat had told Dr. Fester he would be called first, so he could go back to work.

"Your Honor, the defense calls Dr. Alex Fester."

He swore the doctor in, qualified him as an expert witness, and proceeded with his questions.

"Dr. Fester, did you examine Sammy prior to this trial?"

"Why, yes I did."

"In your professional opinion, is Sammy mentally ill?"

"Why, yes he is," said the doctor, fidgeting and stroking his beard. "But, it is also my opinion that he knew right from wrong."

There was noticeable mumbling in the courtroom.

"But, Doctor, is it not true that Sammy has periods when he actually thinks he is Moses?"

"Well, yes he does."

"And, Doctor, is it not your professional opinion that Sammy actually thought he was robbing demons and not working men?"

"Well, yes, that's true." The doctor pulled his collar.

"Then how can you conclude Sammy knew right from wrong?"

238

"Well, because, in my opinion, he knew he was robbing a bank. If demons owned the bank, robbing would still be illegal.. That includes being robbed by Moses."

The Judge had to bang his gavel to stop the laughing after that statement. Pat knew coming into this trial he was not going to get much out of this witness, so he did not ask any more questions.

When Pat finished with Dr. Fester, Mark had his turn to cross-examine. The Assistant DA pointed out the aspect of knowing right from wrong, as Pat knew he would.

When Mark finished with Doctor Fester, Pat called Mrs. Washington to the stand. The sound of her name caused some of the jurors to move forward in their seats.

Pat swore her in and had her go over Sammy's background.

"And you mean your son actually thinks he is Moses?"

"Yes, Sir, but not all de time, just most of de time."

"Would he dress a certain way when he thought he was Moses?"

"Yes, Sir. Most of de time."

"Please tell the judge and the jury how he dressed."

"Yes, Sir. Well, Sammy done has him dis Moses outfit dat he wears."

"Go on, Mrs. Washington. Please describe it."

"This be most embarrassin', but okay. He be haven a pillowcase with holes cut out for de arms and de head. He first puts it on, den he wraps a sheet round him and ties it wif a piece of rope. Next, he puts de white towel on his head. You know, he like wraps it around his head like dem Arab fellows does. Den he has dis special stick. Does I have to tell you about that? It's most embarrassin'."

"Yes, Mrs. Washington, you do." Pat used a calming voice.

"Okay, Mr. Patton. He, my boy, he thinks dat stick be a snake and de snake be tellin' him what to do. Mr. Patton, Judge, Sammy ain't no robber; dem two hoods tricked him into doin' it!"

"Objection, your honor," interrupted Mark. "I would like the court to instruct this witness to just answer the question."

"Sustained," said Judge Musselman. "Mrs. Washington, please just answer Mr. Patton's question."

"Yes, Sir."

After looking at the faces of the jurors, Mark wished he wouldn't have made the objection. He was right, but the jurors were clearly in tune with this poor woman, who was trying to help her son. Obviously, there was not one dishonest bone in her body. He would not object again, because he did not want to turn off the jury.

"Now, Mrs. Washington, after he is dressed like Moses, what does he do?"

"He goes outside and den walks around. Talks to people and de animals, and to himself."

"What does he wear on his feet?"

"Nothin'. He be goin' barefooted."

"Surely he wears shoes when it's cold in the winter."

"No, Sir, he be goin' barefooted den too."

"Why?"

"You has to ax him dat."

"Has your son ever been in trouble with the law before?"

"Oh, no Sir, he be a good boy."

"I understand your silverware came up missing. Is that correct?"

"Yes, Sir."

"Tell the judge and the jury what happened to it."

"I looked out of de window and saw Sammy be throwin' my silverware up in the air, one piece at a time. I went out and ax him what he be doin'. I was tryin' to save what was left, but that boy, he done throwed all of it up in de air. He told me that he was throwin' it up to heaven fer de angels to use. Aunt Trish, ah, Ms. Jones, was there and saw it, too. Her and me, we looked and looked in de tall grass and weeds, but only found 'bout half of it."

"Mrs. Washington, I have no other questions."

"Your witness," said Judge Musselman to Mark. He asked her a few questions but was afraid to ask too much. He had the gut feeling the jurors were very protective of her. When Mark was finished, Pat called Aunt Trish to the stand.

"Your Honor, I now call Ms. Jones, known as Aunt Trish."

The courtroom buzzed as she came into the room and took the stand. Pat swore her in and asked several questions about Sammy's childhood and about his belief that he was Moses. When he was done with her background information, he got into some specifics.

"Aunt Trish, is that what everybody calls you?"

"Yes, Sir."

"Is it all right if I call you that?"

"Sure, Mr. Patton, dat be my name."

"Aunt Trish, does Sammy smoke?"

"No Sir, but he sure does like to play with dem cigarettes."

"What do you mean by that?"

"Dat boy, he be . . ."

"You mean, Sammy, the defendant, don't you?"

"Yes, Sir. As I was saying, dat boy Sammy, he would light filter-tip cigarettes, and he be puttin' dem all over de house. On de window sills, on de table, on de dresser, and everywhere. It's a wonder dat boy didn't burn down his mama's house."

"Would he lay them down?"

"No, Sir, every one of dem would be set on de filter-tip end and de lit end jus' be stickin' straight up."

"Aunt Trish, do you have any knowledge of Mrs. Washington missing her silverware?"

"Yes, Sir!"

"Please tell the ladies and gentlemen of the jury about it."

"Yes, Sir. I be over at my sister's house when we be lookin' out de window and be seein' that boy throwin' dem forks, spoons, and knives up in de air. We found some of it in de weeds, but he done lost lots of it. His mom and I axed him why he be doin' dat, and he told us dat he be throwin' dem up to heaven fer de angels."

"Thank you, Aunt Trish. Did you ever see Sammy in his Moses outfit?"

"Oh! Yes, Sir, many times."

"Please describe it for us."

"Well, he done cut out one of his momma's good pillowcases, you know, cut holes fer his head and arms. He puts dat on, den he wraps a sheet around him and den wraps a towel round his head. Den he gets dat stick out of de closet. He be thinkin' it's a snake what talks to him, and it's his boss, just a tellin' him what to do."

"What does he wear on his feet?"

"Nothin'. He be goin' barefooted."

"How about in the winter?"

"He be goin' barefooted den too. He done never wore no shoes when he was dressed up like Moses."

"Why was that, Aunt Trish?"

"He says Moses didn't wear no shoes."

"Did you ever watch him when he was wearing his Moses outfit? When he was walking around outside?"

"Yes, Sir."

"What would he do?"

"He would walk around and talk to people. Mostly children, but he would also talk to animals. You know, dogs, cats, birds, even fish. And, of course to de stick what is a snake."

"What does he say to them?"

"Mostly he preaches, you know, Bible stuff."

"Aunt Trish, have you ever had reason to visit him in the hospital?"

"Yes, Sir! He be put in de Grady Hospital fer some kind of evaluation, and when we, his mom and me, went to see him, that boy be standin' on his head in de hallway."

"Aunt Trish, have you ever seen him hurt anyone?"

"No, Sir."

"To the best of your knowledge, has he ever been arrested before?"

"No, Sir."

"Have you ever known him to steal from anyone?"

"Heavens, no! Dat boy he be givin' anyone anything dat he has. He never take nothin' from no one."

"Thank you, Aunt Trish. No other questions of this witness, Your Honor."

Mark asked her a few questions and the judge told Pat to call his next witness.

Pat called Sammy to the stand and the courtroom went wild. The judge had to calm them down by banging with his gavel. Pat swore Sammy in and all visitors were on the edge of their seats.

"Would you state your name, please?"

"Does dat mean I has to tell my name?"

"That's right, Sammy."

"Okay. My name's Sammy Joe Washington, but I'm really Moses."

"Where do you live?"

"I stays wif my mama, and sometimes I stays at de mountain."

"Is your mama's house in Riverdale, Clayton County, Georgia?"

"I thinks so."

"You heard your mother and aunt testify that you threw your mama's silverware up in the sky. Did you do that?"

"Yes, Sir."

"Why did you do that, Sammy?"

"I was throwin' it up to the angels so dat dey could have some nice silverware to eat wif."

"Throwing it up where, Sammy?"

"To heaven. De angels, dey stays up there, you knows dat, Mr. Patton."

There was laughter in the courtroom.

"Did they, the angels, get the silverware?"

"I don't know. I guess so, but ma mama and aunt says dat dey found some of it in de weeds."

"How do you think the silverware got in the weeds, Sammy?"

"I don't know. Maybe de demons tossed it back down!"

"You also heard testimony you were standing on your head when your mother and aunt came to visit you in the hospital. Is that true?"

"No, man! Dat ain't how it happened."

"Sammy, please tell the judge and the jury what you think happened."

"Dey be walkin' on der hands."

The judge had to bang his gavel several times to quiet

the laughter.

"Wait a minute, Sammy. Are you telling this court and the jury your mother and aunt came into the hospital to see you and they were walking on their hands?"

Again, there was laughter in the courtroom.

"Yes, Sir, dat's da way it be happin'."

"Okay, Sammy. Let's go to the cigarettes. You heard testimony you lit filter-tip cigarettes and stood them upright on the filter-tipped end all over the house. Did you do that?"

"Yeah, man."

"Why did you do that?"

"Man, it be incense. Everybody done knows it be burned in de Temple."

"You mean your mother's house was the Temple?"

"Yeah, man. Moses be burnin' incense in de Temple."

"Sammy, you know a man named Jerome Smith, also known as Rodent?"

"Yes, Sir. He be Mr. Rodent."

"And you know a man named Willie Cason, also known as Serpent."

"Yes, Sir. He be Mr. Serpent."

"Did you go with them and rob the Merchants and Farmers Bank, taking money put there by hard-working people?"

"No, man."

That brought loud undertones from the courtroom.

"You didn't take money from the Bank?"

"We didn't take no hard-workin' people's money. Man, we done took money from demons who be gonna use it for evil things!"

"Sammy, please explain what you're talking about to the court and to the jury."

"Okay, Mr. Patton, but I done told it to you before."

"That's right, Sammy, but those 12 people over there in the jury box need to hear it, too."

"Whatever you says, Mr. Patton."

"Go ahead, Sammy, tell them about the demons."

"Well, you knows, de Bible has angels and demons. Mr. Rodent and Mr. Serpent done told me dat de demons be takin' over de Bank who was gonna use de money fer evil things. Dey ax me to help dem take de money from dem demons and dey was gonna give me $200. I could buy me a new bicycle, some candy, and all kinds of neat things, and be a fightin' dem demons at de same time. I wouldn't take no money from no hard-workin' peoples, but I would take money from dem demons."

"So when you took, or helped to take the money, you're saying you didn't know it belonged to hard-working people. Is that right?"

"Dat's right, it didn't! It belonged to dem demons."

"How do you know that?"

"Mr. Rodent and Mr. Serpent, dey done told me."

"What did they tell you would happen if you told anyone about this?"

"Dey told me dat a lightin' bolt would come out of de sky and hit me and der be nothin' left but ashes."

"Did they tell you what would happen to the money you got from these demons."

"Yes, Sir!"

"Well, Sammy, what would happen to it?"

"Mr. Serpent, he be gonna give it to de angel."

"Except for $200?"

"No, Sir. They be paying me $200, out of der own money. All of de demon money goes to da angel."

"Are Mr. Rodent and Mr. Serpent good people?"

"I don't know. I be startin' to believe that they might be demons demselves dat tricked me. I don't know. I'd ask de snake but dey wouldn't let me bring him wif me." A very confused sounding Sammy caused a noticeable laughter in the courtroom.

"Are you talking about the stick you keep in your closet?"

"Yes, Sir, but it be turnin' into a snake and he help wif things dat I gots to think out."

"Sammy, back to your Moses outfit. When you wore it, what clothing did you put on to make your Moses outfit?"

"First I puts on de shirt . . ."

"Would that be a pillowcase with holes cut out for your head and arms?" interrupted Pat.

245

"Yes, Sir. I puts on de shirt, den I wraps de linen robe round me, den my turban. I den puts de sash round me and I gets my staff and I goes out."

"When you go out, what would you do?"

"I'd walk, man, I'd walk."

"Where would you go?"

"To de mountain, man, to de mountain."

"How long would it take you to get there?"

"Two weeks, man, 'bout two weeks."

"What would you do when you got there?"

"Talk to de animals, man, talk to the animals."

"What kind of animals were there?"

"Lions, tigers, giraffes, and like dat."

"Was anything else there beside the animals?"

"Yes, Sir. Der be angels, and demons, man."

"Did you talk to the angels and demons?"

"No, man! I talked to de angels, but I done battle with dem demons!" said Sammy in a very excited manner.

"Thank you, Sammy. No more questions, your honor."

As Pat watched the jurors, he could sense they were sympathetic toward his client, but was it enough for a *Not Guilty by Reason of Insanity* verdict?

"Your witness, Mr. Kimbrough."

"Thank you, Your Honor. Just a couple of questions on cross." *I get the feeling the jurors are getting to like Sammy, even though he obviously robbed the bank. I've got to be careful on cross-examination.*

"Mr. Washington, my name is Mark Kimbrough, the prosecutor in this case. Do you understand that?"

"I knows dat you be da guy what's tryin' to put me in de jail."

Sammy's comment brought so much laughter in the courtroom that the judge called for order several times.

"Well, that's close enough, Mr. Washington. You have admitted to robbing the Farmers and Merchants Bank. Is that correct?"

"No, Sir. I jus' helped Mr. Rodent and Mr. Serpent takes money from some demons what were goin' to do some evil bad things wif it."

"What kind of things?"

"I don't know. Bad things."

"You said that if you told anybody about all of this, a lightning bolt would come down and fry you. Is that correct?"

"No, Sir. I said dat dey told me dat I would be turned into ashes. No fryin'."

"Okay, but you would die from a lightning bolt, correct?"

"Dat's right, Sir."

"Then, please tell the judge and the jury why you told about it anyway?" asked Mark with a smirk.

"Because Gabriel said it be okay to tell."

"Gabriel? Who in the world is he?"

"You not been no Bible readin' man. I can tell, 'cause anyone who be readin' de Bible knows who Gabriel is." Sammy had a very serious look on his face.

Several people in the courtroom nodded their heads in agreement, including some of the jurors.

"Your Honor, would you please instruct this witness to just answer the questions."

"I will, Mr. Kimbrough, but I'm afraid you walked right into that one. Mr. Washington, please just answer Mr. Kimbrough's questions."

"Yes, Sir. De Angel Gabriel. De one what talked to Mary. She be de mama of Jesus, you know."

This brought uncontrolled laughter from spectators in the courtroom. Judge Musselman again banged his gavel loudly several times for order.

"Quiet, quiet! Quiet in the courtroom!" admonished Judge Musselman.

"You may continue, Mr. Kimbrough."

The Assistant DA had learned an important lesson. He had to be very careful when questioning Sammy. Sometimes less is better than more.

"No more questions of this witness, Your Honor."

"Call your next witness, Mr. Patton."

The defense rests, Your Honor."

Again, the courtroom became very noisy.

"We will break for lunch now, and then take up the

matter of jury charges, and closing arguments. Will the two attorneys approach the bench, please? This court is adjourned until 1:30 PM."

Pat went up to the judge's bench along with Mark.

"I want to thank you both for a very clean trial. As you know, the press has been watching this one very closely. Here is a list of my standard charges to the jury." Judge Musselman handed both attorneys several sheets of paper. "Any additions to these will be considered in my chambers at 1:30. I want both of you to be there at that time. Mr. Patton, thank the Lord we did not have any more interruptions by our good friend, Mr. Anderson."

"You can say that again, Judge. This will be one trial I will never forget."

Both attorneys thanked the judge and made their way out of the courtroom.

* * *

"Pat, you did an excellent job. Sammy will go to jail, but you gave the judge and the jury several things to consider."

"Thank you, Mark, and you likewise did a superb job laying out the evidence against Sammy. See you for proposed jury charges at 1:30."

"Mr. Patton, just one request. Please tell our listeners what will come next in this trial," asked reporter Desanto.

"Okay. I'll try to explain the procedure as best I can. In a criminal trial, the jury decides the facts but the judge decides what laws to apply to the case. The law the judge gives the jury is called a charge. The judge usually has several laws he charges all juries with, but if an attorney wants him to charge the jury as to some other law, the opposing attorney would have a chance to argue against it. The judge could approve or deny it. Judges have charges on many subjects, and they sometimes can also be talked into giving language used by the Court of Appeals or the Supreme Court when they ruled on a similar case. The attorneys must dig up this information and then convince the judge to use it. Judges are very careful to consider all proposed charges, because if they refuse a valid request, the case could be overturned on appeal. I want the judge to give the charges of *Not Guilty by Reason of Insanity*, and *Guilty But Mentally Ill.*

"Thank you for explaining that to our listeners."

Pat met Shirley at the back of the courtroom. As they went out the door, other reporters attacked him like a school of piranha. Also present were two uniformed police officers. One said he had orders to follow Pat to lunch and then back to the courtroom.

"Mr. Patton, do you have any comments for Channel 3 viewers?" asked reporter Zel Murray.

"Our viewers would love to have an update on the remark you made to them this morning about Skinny being a coward," interrupted Zel Murray

"And our listeners would, too," replied Sandi Desanto as she followed Pat.

"All right, ladies, you win. I reiterate my view that Skinny is a coward. He sneaks around burning down houses, setting cars on fire, and raping innocent young convenience store employees. He will be caught and the law will deal with him. As to the insanity defense, you heard the doctor testify that my client is mentally ill. I will not comment further on the trial as it is not over yet and I would not want to do or say anything that could possibly jeopardize my client. No other comments, ladies."

* * *

"We need to go somewhere private, Honey," whispered Shirley.

"Right. With a police escort yet."

"How about Palombo's Little Italy?" suggested Shirley.

Sounds good to me. Great food, quiet, and good service."

They made their way to Pat's rental car and as soon as they got there, they were stopped by Lieutenant Keller.

"Hi, Lieutenant Join us for lunch?"

"I appreciate the offer but don't have the time right now. I'm very busy trying to protect a certain attorney from a killer. It seems he called the killer a coward on what I now believe are newscasts going nationwide.

"I take it you think I shouldn't have done it."

"You think right, but it's your life."

"But, Lieutenant, Pat felt he had to bring this thing to a head, or else he (and I) would have to look over our shoulders the rest of our life wondering if Skinny was there."

"Shirley's right. I couldn't stand wondering if I'm going to be blown away every time my doorbell rings."

"That may well be true but you're taking one hell of a chance. Pat, you never killed anyone. This guy could murder someone in the kitchen and then eat lunch with the victim's body lying on the floor. That wouldn't bother Skinny. Remember, you called the killer a coward on TV. Think of Shirley. I mean, the danger you're putting her in."

"He's already asked me not to spend tonight with him."

"How about tomorrow night, and the night after that?" asked Lieutenant Keller.

"I'm a big girl now, and I can take care of myself."

"Look, Pat, since you'll be there alone tonight, I'm going to hide an extra man somewhere and hope we can sucker him in."

"He can hide in my storage shed if you want. The officer could put a chair by the door, and with it cracked, he could see the whole back side of the yard."

"That's a good idea, Pat. I'll get someone out there today."

"Here's a key to the storage shed. I have a spare at home. He can set up any time he wants, and tell him there's a folding chair in the shed."

"Thanks, Pat. Hey, see you two later and be careful."

They had lunch and returned to the courthouse at 1:10.

CHAPTER 24

Middle of December - The Verdict

Skinny had been watching TV when Pat's comments about him being a coward came on the news. He became momentarily enraged but then turned cool and calculating.

Damn attorney ain't gonna make me do nothin' impulsive. I'm gonna stick to my game plan, but I'm also gonna gut shoot that SOB. Let him die slow-like, just like Doc told me. As for you, Ms. O'Kelly, I hope you're as good-looking in real life as you are on TV, because you and me are gonna have us a little party. I'm gonna wait until Saturday night, and then go for the kill. First my ex and her new husband will die, then Patton, and then his girlfriend immediately after our little party. They'll never suspect I would hit both of them in one night!

* * *

The two attorneys met with the judge at 1:30. He got the charges of *Not Guilty by Reason of Insanity*, and *Guilty but Mentally Ill*. Mark did not fight it, as he was certain Sammy would be found guilty and that would be a win.

Pat had to give his closing argument first, since he put Sammy on the witness stand. He argued for *Not Guilty by Reason of Insanity*. If not that, then certainly they must find him *Guilty but Mentally Ill*. He pointed out Dr. Fester's testimony wherein he diagnosed Sammy as mentally ill. The argument of no intent to commit a crime because of lack of mental capacity also was used. He talked about the testimony of Mrs. Washington and Aunt Trish, as well as Sammy's own testimony and demeanor when he took the witness stand. Pat told them, to put it bluntly, Sammy was and is nuts! However, he certainly is not dangerous. He had no intent to rob a bank, only taking money from demons who wanted to do bad things with it. He was also a gentleman with the bank teller.

Mark pointed out the evidence against Sammy, particularly his own admission that he was part of the stickup crew. He told the jury it was against the law to rob banks, even if the person thought the bank tellers were demons and the money belonged to them.

When Pat and Mark were finished, the judge charged the jury. He told the jury there was a law against armed robbery, and what the law said. Then he told them how to apply it to this case. Judge Musselman told them all 12 would have to find Sammy guilty beyond a reasonable doubt in order to convict. Just thinking Sammy was guilty was not enough. The State had to prove it. He also told them about the law concerning *Not Guilty by Reason of Insanity* and *Guilty but Mentally Ill.*

When the judge finished, the jury retired to the jury room to deliberate. Pat and Mark could not leave the courthouse until the end of the day or until after the jury reached their verdict.

"Sammy, it's up to the jury now, but no matter what happens, all of us - - you, your mother, and your aunt - - did our best. If nothing else, we showed the DA we will not stand for you being forced to plead to the maximum sentence."

"Mr. Patton, no matter how dis case come out, I knowed you did yo best fer me, and I 'preciates it."

A deputy escorted Sammy back to a holding cell. He would be brought back when the jury reached a verdict.

Pat talked to Mrs. Washington and Aunt Trish. They were very nice people and thanked Pat for doing his best for Sammy. Shirley and Herb met Pat in the back of the courtroom and Shirley gave him a big hug, congratulating him on a job well-done. He let the deputy know he would be in the snack bar in case the judge wanted him, or the jury came back with a verdict.

"Pat, I talked to Margie Loftin, the court reporter, and also Doris English, the bailiff. Both thought you did an outstanding job." Herb smiled his appreciation of Pat's success.

Then they were inundated with reporters asking questions.

"Sorry, ladies... gentlemen, I can't comment on the trial while the jury is out. I'll be more than happy to do so when it's over. As far as Mr. Anderson is concerned, a man who picks on women and ambushes men is a coward. He doesn't have the guts to come out and knock heads, man to man!"

The reporters ran to get Pat's latest comments and film to their editors.

"If that doesn't bring Skinny out tonight, nothing will." Pat had a worried look on his face.

"Pat, I wouldn't want to be in your shoes." Herb was very concerned for Pat and Shirley.

"I know, but he's after me. The sooner we meet the better. I want to be able to get my life back together."

At 5:00, the judge said: "Ladies and gentlemen of the jury, since you have indicated you have not yet reached a verdict, I have called you back to inform you that you are dismissed until 8:30 tomorrow morning. I have considered putting you up in a motel for the night because of the amount of press coverage this case has generated, but I will let you go home to your husbands and wives. I do caution you, however, not to talk to anyone about this case outside of the jury deliberation room. The press will pester you, but I will take a very dim view of any of you talking about this case to them. You're not even to discuss the trial among yourselves outside of the jury deliberation room. Any questions? No? Then you are excused until 8:30 tomorrow morning. Court will start at 9:00, but we want you to be here early and be accounted for prior to starting your deliberation. Ms. Albert, please instruct all parties in Case Number Two to be here at 9:00 to begin jury selection while this jury is deliberating. Have a good night."

* * *

Pat had supper with Shirley, then he went home by himself in the rental car. He arrived under police escort, prepared to wait for Skinny. Pat confirmed Officer T. J. was in the storage shed by walking by and talking to him without looking in his direction, in case Skinny was watching. T. J. was armed with a riot shotgun and a .38 revolver.

Pat checked his .44 Magnum, had a beer, went to bed, but couldn't sleep. About 1:00 AM he heard something. Was Skinny trying to break into the house? The noise was not loud. It sounded as though someone was trying to pry something open! He grabbed his .44 Magnum, and then slowly, and quietly, tiptoed to the back of the house near Eb's bedroom. The prying noise was definitely louder there.

Did the police officer hear it? Pat started tiptoeing down the basement stairs, but he would not go outside. The last thing he wanted was for him and the police officer to start shooting each other. As he slowly and carefully made his way down the stairs, the prying noise got louder! His heart started beating faster and a bead of sweat appeared on his forehead.

I'm ready for you, Skinny!

Pat silently made his way to the door that led from the recreation room to the laundry room. He slowly opened it. The door creaked and the prying noise stopped. He waited for what seemed hours but only a minute or two had passed when the noise began again. He crept into the laundry room. It got louder. Pat looked out the window and could see the barrel of a shotgun slowly poke its way out of the storage room door.

He slowly opened the door leading from the laundry room to the garage, and the noise could be heard coming from outside the garage door. He looked out the garage door window, as T. J. came out of the storage shed. Then Pat caught a glimpse of a raccoon trying to pry the lid off his garbage can. The coon saw the police officer and ran off into the night. Pat's heart was beating frantically and he was sweating.

What a relief!

He saw T. J. walking over to the garbage can, but the officer could not see him in the dark house. A streetlight in front of the house lit up the driveway, and while not bright, was good enough to see.

He went upstairs and back to bed with the .44 Magnum beside him. Skinny never showed up.

* * *

Pat went to court Thursday morning, red-eyed from not getting a good night's sleep. Shirley and Herb met him at the office as he drove into the parking lot, eating a Hershey Bar, still with a police escort.

"Oh, Pat, I was so worried about you! You're not getting rid of me tonight! I don't care what you say!"

"You win, Shir. I'm too tired to argue about it."

He told her about the coon, and they both had a laugh.

"Now they have a police car at my sister's house," said Herb. "Ever since he burned my house down, my wife has been afraid of almost everything. The police car is a welcome sight. They even had a man inside the house last night."

"Let me guess. Because of my comments, right?"

"You got it, Pat."

"Look, Herb, I never meant for any additional hardships to be placed on anyone else. You know that."

"I know, partner, but that's not always how it works. Don't worry about it though, because the sooner they get him, the sooner we can all rest." Herb pulled his suspenders.

They went to the courthouse and Judge Musselman sent the jury back to deliberate while Pat and Shirley went to the snack bar. The DA had let Shirley follow this case from start to finish.

Pat was national news. He had been an attorney for less than a year and was already the most famous attorney in Clayton County, if not Georgia. The combination of the trial of one of the *Five-O'Clock Traffic Bandits* and Skinny gunning for him while Pat was attempting to try the case made good news. Viewers, listeners, and readers wanted more.

* * *

At 11:30 the jury had reached a verdict.

"Mr. Foreman, I understand you have reached a verdict. Is that correct?" asked Judge Musselman.

"Yes, Sir."

"Will the defendant please rise."

"Mr. Foreman, would you please publish the verdict."

"Yes, Sir. We the jury find the defendant, Sammy Joe Washington, *Guilty but Mentally Ill*."

"Thank you, Mr. Foreman, and the rest of you ladies and gentlemen of the jury.

Pat polled the jury, asking each one of the jurors individually if that was his or her verdict, and was it still their verdict. No one had changed their mind.

"You are now excused," said Judge Musselman. "If you would like, you may stay for the sentencing phase or you may leave. You are now free to discuss this case with anyone you choose. We are ready for the sentencing phase of this trial."

* * *

"Would the defendant please stand. Mr. Washington, this is a very unusual and difficult case. You should be placed in a mental institution so you can get the help you need. Unfortunately, Georgia does not have a mental hospital with barbwire around it, where I can place you for the duration of your sentence."

The entire jury stayed and hung onto the judge's every word.

"It is a real shame, but we are placing more and more people in prison, who really belong in a mental hospital. Both attorneys, in my opinion, did a very fine job. Mr. Kimbrough proved, beyond a reasonable doubt, that you committed the crime for which you were charged. On the other hand, Mr. Patton has convinced me you're not a criminally minded bad person, and you are mentally ill. So what do we do with you? We cannot let you go around holding up banks because you believe demons are going to do evil things with the money. Conversely, I do not believe you are a hardened criminal who deserves to have the book thrown at him. Georgia law dictates at least a seven-year sentence for armed robbery. I am totally against minimum sentences set by the legislature because they put people like you in the same category as a hardened criminal. However, my hands are tied and I have no other choice.

Therefore, it is the order of this court that you serve a total of 10 years as follows: the first seven years shall be in prison, followed by three years of probation. The jury found you *Guilty but Mentally Ill.* I will place a strong recommendation in my order that you receive all the mental health help that is available. Good luck to you. Court adjourned."

Pat shook Mark's hand and gave Sammy a hug.

He then made his way out of the courtroom with Shirley at his side. He looked for Mrs. Washington and Aunt Trish and made his way toward them but the news media swamped him, wanting to ask questions.

"What are your comments on the trial," asked reporter Desanto, for WHIT radio.

"I think the jury did their duty, the prosecutor was a gentleman, and the judge did all he could for my obviously mentally ill client. He gave Sammy the least amount of prison time the law allowed. I would also like to add that Attorney Herb Butterworth was an indispensable aid to me in preparing for this trial and Shirley O'Kelly was one of my biggest supporters."

"Any comments on Mr. Anderson?" asked reporter Murray for TV 3.

"I hope he is apprehended soon, so we can get on with our lives."

"One more question Mr. . ."

"Please excuse me," interrupted Pat. "This has been a very trying week. No pun intended."

"Mrs. Washington, do you have a comment?" asked reporter Desanto.

"Yes, ma'am, Mr. Patton here is de bestest attorney in de whole wide world. Dey wanted my boy to go to de prison fer 20 whole years, but he gots it down to seven."

"He worked hard fer ma nephew and we 'preciates him very much!" added Aunt Trish.

Pat thanked the ladies and whispered to Shirley, "Let's get out of here."

* * *

They made their way to the office, escaping two more reporters. Julie was waiting for him.

"Jeez, Boss. Since this trial hit the news media, it has been *take a number* to get an appointment to see the great Patrick Patton."

"Pat, I have a feeling your fees just doubled." Herb made a big smile and extended his hand.

They better, 'cause I need to shop for a ring." Pat grinned at Shirley.

"That would be a nice Christmas gift." She beamed, running her fingers through her hair.

"Herb, I could not have done it without your expert help. Thank you."

Pat left in his rental car, and Shirley followed in hers. They made their way to Jerome and Mickey's Steak House, followed by Officer Julius Eross of the Clayton County Police Department. Pat treated the waiting officer to a steak dinner. They ate, went home, took a shower, made love, and collapsed, deep in a fitful sleep in each other's arms. There was no talk about her staying in her apartment. A chair was propped against the door and they both slept with their guns.

They waited for Skinny, but he never came.

* * *

Late Thursday afternoon, Skinny noticed the black man who worked at the campground looking at him several times, but when Skinny looked back, he pretended to be looking at something else. Skinny's danger antennas went up and red flags flashed in his brain.

Something's not right. As much as I hate to change my plans, I'll have to do it tomorrow night and get out of here. I'll break camp early in the morning, spend the day somewhere else, and then hit both my ex-wife and her new stud at the same time. And, yes, I'll get that smart-ass attorney, all in a blitz, just like Hitler did in World War II. While her boyfriend is laying there gut shot, Shirley will be lying with me! They'll never know what hit them! Then it's out of here for good, thought Skinny as he sang *Santa Claus Is Coming to Town.*

CHAPTER 25

Late December - Payback

Friday morning Shirley got up and made breakfast. She and Pat had slept lightly as Skinny was on their minds.

"Shir, I don't feel right us living together like this without being married, do you?"

"No, Honey, I don't, but this situation with Skinny has thrown our lives into turmoil. Everything has accelerated."

"We need to get married. I love you so, and now that I've gotten used to you being beside me when I wake up, I don't ever want to let you go. I was serious about a ring for Christmas, Shir."

"Sweetheart, I can't think of a present I would rather have." Shirley kissed him. "I love you very much, too! Say, maybe I could get Gloria to be my Maid of Honor."

"What?" exclaimed Pat. Then he realized she was pulling his leg.

"How do your parents feel about it? We have only known each other for a little over a month."

"They like you. In fact, Daddy told me not to let you get away. By the way, they know I'm staying with you here at your house."

"Gosh, Shir, this is not working out like I planned. I wanted to date you for at least six months, and then propose. Get married maybe six months later. You know, do it the way everyone else does. But, as God is my witness, I can't wait, and I have never been surer of anything in my life!"

"Lets' see, Christmas is next week. You can give me an engagement ring then. Mom and I can plan the wedding for as soon as we can get everything together. I'm sure Kathy would want to help, too. After all, she is my best friend. How's that sound?"

"Like music to my ears!"

"Won't Eb miss you?"

"I guess, but he'll just have to find another roommate. Knowing him, it won't be hard, and the next one will probably be female. It might even be Kathy. They are both like pups out of the same litter and need to meet."

"Look at the time! I'm going to play assistant DA today, and from what Julie says, you have a *pick-a-number-to-see-Patton* day ahead of you."

"Right. Let's get out of here. I'll take a cup of coffee to Officer T. J. in the storage shed, but they won't be able to spare a man again tonight."

They left with a police car following them. Pat picked up a newspaper, and the Washington trial was still front-page news. As they hugged goodbye, Shirley remarked, "So you haven't mentioned *him* either?"

"No, but I sure can't get *him* out of my mind."

"Maybe things got too hot for Skinny and he left the area," suggested a hopeful Shirley.

"He plain scares the hell out of me," said a worried Pat.

"Well, you'd never know it the way you called him a coward on TV."

"That was to end this waiting game, but it failed. Didn't you see my knees shaking?"

"See you at lunch, Honey. I love you!"

"Love you, too, Shir! Bye!"

* * *

Lieutenant Keller was waiting for Pat at his office.

"Well, Pat, your little game with Skinny didn't pan out Wednesday night or last night, did it?"

"No, Sir, but I had to give it a try."

"He may have left the area, but we can't be too careless. He also may be waiting for a chance to strike again."

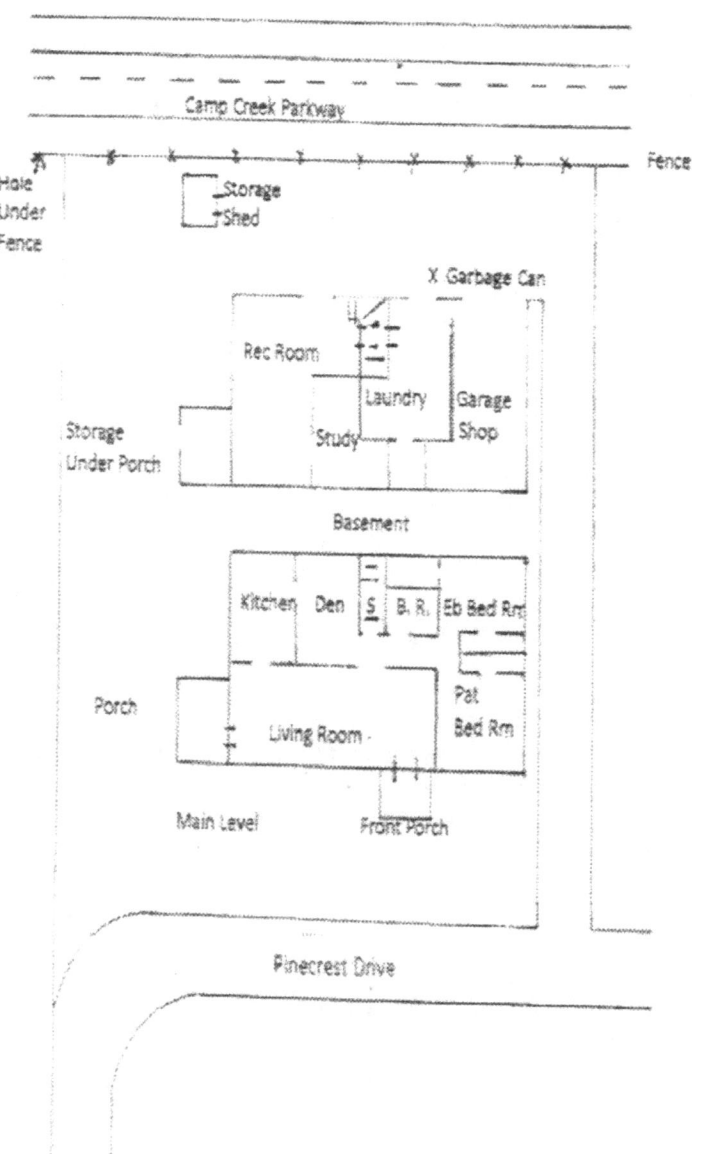

Floor Plan of Pat's House
Main Floor and Full Basement

"I get the message, Lieutenant, and I appreciate it."

Lieutenant Keller left and Pat sat down with Julie, going over numerous messages. Two TV reporters and three newspaper reporters had called wanting interviews. Forty-three people had called to set up appointments in the last three days.

"Julie, here I am, a new wet-behind-the-ears attorney, who has no idea what he is doing, and thousands of people think I'm Perry Mason."

* * *

Skinny got up early and broke camp. He was paid up for two more days but decided to let them have the money.

I always wanted to see Georgia's Stone Mountain, and I'll do it today. First, I need to change vehicles. That black guy could've gotten my tag number. This time I'll get a car, something inconspicuous but fast.

He saw what he wanted in a strip shopping center. As he looked around, Skinny found a plain two-door 1971 Dodge with chrome badges that told him it had the big 440 V8 engine. Next, he went to Stuart's Foreign Auto Parts and bought a small hammer-type dent puller and a couple of screwdrivers. He only intended to keep the Dodge for one night, so he didn't need the keys. He had a coat hanger in the van. The Dodge was parked close to a road at the end of the parking lot. He parked the van at a neighborhood bar in an empty parking lot, and then picked up the puller, coat hanger, and screwdrivers. The weather was cool, and his coat covered them and the .38 pistol stuck in his belt.

As Skinny walked to the Dodge, he looked all around. It most likely belonged to a person who worked in the mall and would not be missed until 5 o'clock at least. He scanned the lot and no one was looking, so he stuck the coat hanger in the weather stripping and pulled up the lock button on the window frame. He opened the door, then after looking around again, put the end of the dent puller in the ignition switch and yanked the slide hard. The lock popped out.

Most drivers are stupid. They don't know that the

majority of ignition locks are held in with only a small pin.

He inserted a screwdriver in the hole where the lock had been and turned it two clicks. The first click was the accessory position, the second the ignition mode, and the third start. He pumped the accelerator pedal, turned the switch one more click, and the car fired right up.

Man, that 440 engine sure sounds good! I remember reading it puts out over 300 HP.

Skinny drove to the bar parking lot, pulled in beside the van, and loaded all of his gear into the Dodge. He left the van with the window down and keys in the ignition switch, hoping someone would steal it. He was now off to Stone Mountain State Park, about a 45-minute drive. He was glad the windows were tinted, because he wanted to check his guns in the daylight. Tonight they would feel his stinger!

* * *

"Lieutenant Keller, I'm glad you're back. I found this on the floor behind your desk when I was cleaning." A young woman handed him a phone message. "It's from the manager of the Happy Kamper Campground, Mr. Weigle."

"Thank you. Gosh, this is dated yesterday morning."

He immediately gave it to his sergeant. "Please run this license number immediately." In a few minutes, it came back as belonging to a red 1977 Chevy van. Lieutenant Keller grabbed the phone.

"Hello, Don. Lieutenant Keller here. Look, I just got your message. A cleaning lady found it behind my desk. I ran the tag and it goes to a 1977 Chevy van. Are you sure it was a '79 Ford?

"Yes, 'cause I own one just like it."

"That's funny. It belongs to a 1977 Chevy but it's not coming up as stolen. Is the guy still there?"

"No, Lieutenant. He broke camp early this morning. Left without anyone seeing him or checking out with us. He still has a day or two paid in advance. He never asked for a refund, which is unusual."

"Don, please refresh my memory as to why you called

me in the first place."

"Well, the guy was acting strange, but nothing I can put my finger on. Leroy, one of my men, and I both noticed he had two or three different vehicles while here."

"What did he look like? It could be a license plate switch."

"Well, Lieutenant, that's also what's funny. The first time I saw him, he looked chubby and then suddenly he was skinny..."

"Skinny! When did he get there?" cut in the Lieutenant, sounding very excited.

"Let's see..., he checked in at 12:43 AM Saturday morning."

"Thanks a million, Don. If I'm right, you had an escaped killer there! That's not long after Anderson escaped. Bye!"

"Sergeant Purdy, I think Skinny is still in the area. I want all area law enforcement agencies informed that a man believed to be the escaped killer, Arnold *Skinny* Anderson, was at the Happy Kamper Campground as early as this morning. He was driving a red 1979 Ford Van, Georgia license number 4693SV. He has left the campground. Make sure Captain Kefauver is informed, and notify the officers at the Butterworth and Johnson residences. Use the phone. Not the radio. He is armed and very dangerous. I'll call Patton."

"Yes, Sir. Right away!"

Lieutenant Keller sat down and called Pat's office.

"Hello, Mr. Patton's office. This is Julie. How may I help you?"

"Julie, this is Lieutenant Keller. I need to speak to Pat. It's urgent."

"Yes, Sir. Right away."

"Hi, Lieutenant."

"I have a strong reason to believe a man who left the Happy Kamper Campground this morning, the one located in Clayton County, was Skinny. He was driving a stolen red 1979 Ford van. I've notified all area law enforcement... What? Hold on, Pat. Thank you, Sergeant. Pat? Hey, one of our officers just located the red Ford van in the parking lot of a local bar right here in Jonesboro! He apparently switched vehicles again."

"Thanks, Lieutenant. I'll be sure to be extra careful."

"I've got to hand it to you, Pat. You don't sound very scared."

"I'm not scared, Lieutenant, I'm terrified! Just think! Here I am, little ole me, trying to do battle with an invisible, cold-blooded killer who obviously wants to do me in. Yes, terror is the word. But - - I can't let it immobilize me."

"Pat, I put out an all-points' bulletin to all area law-enforcement agencies with our latest information on him. Our net is tightening. Again I do advise you to be very careful. I will have two men at your house again tonight. One in front and one in back. We don't have the manpower to keep the third one in your storage shed. Skinny should have left the area, but who knows . . . no one can tell what that killer will do. I also told my men I want stolen car reports to be top priority, as it may be Skinny at work."

"Thanks, Lieutenant. You're on top of things. I'll call Shirley and warn her."

He immediately called her.

"We had better be alert tonight."

"You got that right, Shir."

"When you get done there, come over to the office and we'll go to lunch. No escort this time, but two men will be looking after us tonight. They're also keeping an officer at the entrance of the subdivision on duty 24 hours a day. They're instructed to check tag numbers of any cars they don't recognize as belonging in my neighborhood."

"I'll be there. Oh, and Daddy called and asked me to bring you over to the house for supper Saturday night. He sounded mysterious and said it was important."

"Okay, Shir. See you when you get here."

* * *

Skinny was at Stone Mountain State Park, looking at the pictures of the Civil War heroes carved into the side of the granite mountain.

What a site. Lots of people here, and nothing but stupid Park police. The perfect place to hide out for the day. I wish I had time to stay longer.

He found a secluded spot, cleaned and reloaded his guns while singing, *There Will Be a Hot Time in the Old Town Tonight.*

When done, he went to the train station, ate lunch and watched some men on horses, painted to look like Indians, gallop by the side of the train trying to scare visitors.

I would love to ride the train and blow away a few Indians. Man, wouldn't that be something to see?

* * *

Pat and Shirley ate lunch at the Brave Bull.

"For a Mexican restaurant, that was a v e r y good cheeseburger." Shirley licked her lips and wiped her mouth.

"You're right. I used to come here often and get a big slice of sweet onion on it with a big spoonful of the hot sauce they serve with the chips. Ready to go?"

"I'll get the tip." She put two dollars on the table.

"I wish you wouldn't do that, Shir."

"Well, we're practically married anyway," replied Shirley with a big smile.

"You talk to your parents yet?"

"No, I want to do it in person tomorrow night. Why don't you ask Daddy for his daughter's hand in marriage when we go over there? He won't bite."

"I know, Shir, but the thought of it is scary. I think I'd rather face Skinny than your father," laughed Pat.

"You big baby!" replied Shirley, also laughing.

"You win, tomorrow night it is. I'll drop you off at the courthouse. I'm going to stop to see Sammy at the jail. I really feel sorry for him. He's a nice guy who got used by two punks. I don't know how he is making out without his snake to tell him what to do. Shir, he does not belong in jail."

"I agree. See you after work, Honey." She leaned over and gave him a kiss.

"Speaking of work, I had a talk with Gloria. She will not be giving you any more problems. Miss Golden Butt doesn't want daddy to know she was caught performing a sex act on her boss in his office. If the newspapers got a story about his

266

daughter doing something like that, it could destroy his chance of going higher up the political ladder. There is also the possibility of her losing her present job."

Shirley smiled and gave him a deeper kiss.

* * *

Pat went to the jail. They let him visit Sammy at his cell.

"Hi, Sammy. You doing okay?"

"Yes, Sir. Dey real nice to me here, but I miss Mamma and Aunt Trish. I wants to thank you fer yo help. Mamma say dat you be savin' me a bunch a time. I be missin' my snake but dey not be letin' me bring him in here. Dey won't let me bring my Moses clothes in here either."

"I wish I could've done better, Sammy. They allowed me to bring you this Bible. Look, it has a lot of pictures in color and the words aren't too awfully hard to read. I hope you get hours of enjoyment reading it."

Pat handed Sammy a children's Bible, easy for him to read and illustrated in color.

"Oh, thank you, Mr. Patton." Sammy looked through it for a minute and smiled.

"Lookee here, Mr. Patton. I be readin' what it say in Exodus 10:22–23. 'And Moses stretched forth his hand toward de heavens; and der was a thick darkness in all of De Land of Egypt... But, all de children of Israel had light in der dwellings.'"

He read but with great difficulty. As he finished, Sammy raised his hand and looked up. When he did, all the lights of the cellblock went off, except for the one in his cell. The deputy came running over.

"Sit tight, Mr. Patton. We had a temporary power failure and will have the lights back on in a minute or two. I don't understand how the light in this cell could still be on."

After a few minutes, the lights came back on and Pat left dumbfounded. Was it just a coincidence?

* * *

Pat went back to his office and saw three new clients. He talked to Herb for a few minutes while he waited for Shirley. Pat told Herb what happened at the jail and Herb shook his head in wonder. Then he said, "In God, all things are possible."

Around 5:10, Shirley arrived.

"Any news about Skinny?"

"Yes, Shir. The lieutenant called me this afternoon and said the police were working on several stolen van cases and traced three of them to the airport long-term lots. Some had license plates that belonged on a different vehicle. It's driving them nuts. One of the three didn't even know his van had been stolen. They were all out of town on business trips. The police traced the VIN number on the last van to the owner because it was sitting in the parking lot of a bar. When the owner of the bar arrived, he noticed it, and saw the driver's side window open and the keys still in the ignition switch. Looked as though someone wanted it to be stolen, which may be the case, because Skinny is believed to have taken it. The tag number and description matched the report given by the manager of the campground. The guy who owned the plate on the van that was found at the bar had no idea his plate was switched."

"Are they sure it's him?"

"No, but 90% sure. Everything fits."

"Ready to go home?"

"I guess so. We need to get some rest because we have to be on our toes this weekend, in case Skinny didn't leave town."

* * *

There it is, thought Skinny. He was looking at Geleta's Costume Shop, which he found in the phone book.

"Good, it's closed." He drove around back looking for an alley. He located it and easily found the back of the shop, next to the end.

No one around.

He pulled in the back parking lot and got out with a tire tool, a credit card and a small flashlight.

The building was old, so the door was easy to open in a few seconds, using only the credit card. Skinny was counting on no alarm in a place like this and he was right. In a few minutes, he found what he wanted. A police uniform, which included pants, shirt, and a hat were a little big, but fit him. Looking around he found a belt with holster that had a flashlight holder, handcuff holder with handcuffs, a wig, mustache, police badges, and police insignias. He grabbed a dark blue jacket, like the police might wear, gathered up the stuff and got out of there, locking the door behind him.

Geleta shouldn't discover the missing stuff for quite some time because she has the place filled to capacity with all kinds of stuff. If she didn't have it, it didn't exist.

Skinny drove to a shopping center and parked. He put on the uniform, which had the rank of sergeant on it.

"Looking good!" At 8:30, he left for the Johnson's house. As he drove, Skinny whistled, *Whistle While You Work.*

CHAPTER 26

Late December - Skinny's Visit

Skinny looked in the mirror. *Even my own mother wouldn't recognize me with this wig and mustache.*

He drove to the street before the Johnson's subdivision. Skinny again checked both guns and put the .38 in the police holster. Then he put the sawed-off shotgun on the floor beside him, stock up, so that he could get hold of it very easily. The gas gauge was checked - - almost full.

* * *

John and Betty Johnson were at home with their two children. They were watching *The Sound of Music* on TV. Elliott Fogelhorn, of the Clayton County Police Department, was with them. In addition to the officer in front of the house, a patrol car went through the subdivision every hour at irregular intervals. Officer Fogelhorn had the Johnsons keep all the window blinds closed at night. He would not let anyone go to the door without him, his hand on his holstered gun. He also made visitors slip ID under the door before he would open it. He had a riot shotgun beside a chair he sat on.

The Johnsons had a typical three-bedroom, bath-and-a-half, brick house, with a carport. Coming in the front door, the couch and the TV were on the right, not visible from the outside. One had to be inside the front door in order to see it.

* * *

Skinny parked his car on the next block, on the side of the road. Several cars were parked the same way, so it wouldn't look suspicious. He got out and held the shotgun beside his right leg. It was always loaded and he had put several extra loads of buckshot in his right pocket. Twelve rounds of .38 Special ammo were placed in his left pocket. His knife was handy and the flashlight was in the belt loop that was made for it. He did not want to use the flashlight unless it became necessary.

There was a path worn through the woods, made by children taking a shortcut to the street out back. He carefully made his way to the Johnson house. Skinny took the flashlight in his left hand and planned to shine it on his face if confronted by a police officer.

If some cop hiding out in the woods stops me, I'll just tell him I'm one of the reinforcements.

He had to go about 100 feet through the woods, but there it was, the Johnsons back yard. Man, was he lucky - - no fence and no dogs. He walked slowly to the edge of the yard but then silently ran in a crouch through the yard to the back of the house. He could hear the TV and voices coming from inside.

"Hey you, halt! Stop! Stop now! What are you doing here?" shouted Officer Headman, with his gun drawn.

"I'm one of the reinforcements." Skinny shined the flashlight on his face. "Captain Kefauver told me to patrol in back of the house to make sure the escaped convict didn't come in the back way." Skinny knew all the police officer's names from listening to his scanner.

Officer Headman partially relaxed when he saw the uniform, but was still on guard, because he did not recognize this officer.

"I'm familiar with every man in the Clayton County Police Department, but I don't know you," stated Officer Headman as he approached Skinny.

Skinny yelled, "Put that gun down! I'm on loan from the Atlanta P/D until we can get Anderson. Your captain asked my captain for help." Skinny smiled as he held the shotgun lazily at his side.

"Well, we can sure use some, Sergeant. I'm Officer Headman. I came from out front to take a leak back here when I saw you. Do you know Officer Fogelhorn? He's inside."

Officer Headman was now completely relaxed - - a big mistake. Before he knew what happened, Skinny swung the butt of the shotgun up and hit him square in the chin. The officer went down hard but Skinny again slammed the butt of the shotgun into the head of the almost unconscious man.

Now I know there's only one man in the house to worry about, and I know his name.

Skinny cut the phone lines.

He went to the front door, took the safety off the shotgun, and rang the doorbell.

The 00 buckshot should really tear them up at close range.

Officer Fogelhorn came to the door with Mr. Johnson behind him. "You're talking to a police officer. Who's there?"

"Officer Jones here, Officer Fogelhorn. Officer Headman asked me to check on the Johnsons. I'm part of the reinforcements from Atlanta P/D."

"I never heard anything about that!"

"We got assigned today; probably not enough time for you to get the word. Can I come in?" asked Skinny while shining a flashlight on his face and uniform for the benefit of the officer.

"I guess it's okay." Officer Fogelhorn opened the door. His big mistake was forgetting to ask for ID to be slid under the door. Skinny shot him in the middle of his chest. The man behind him, Mr. Johnson, stood in frozen disbelief.

"Mr. Johnson?" teased Skinny, now looking at his former neighbor with an evil grin.

"Y–y–y-yes," answered a terrified Mr. Johnson.

Skinny smiled and shot him in the chest. Before he fell, Skinny shot him again in the stomach. He burst into the room, and there she was – – his ex-wife. She had jumped up from the sofa and was looking straight at him.

Got to do it and get the hell out of here. Been here too

long already and gunfire will be heard by the neighbors.

"Hi, Betty." Skinny aimed the shotgun at her. "Did you really think you could get away with divorcing me! You don't divorce me, I divorce you! You ain't getin' my kids! I'm their father forever!"

As he was about to pull the trigger, both of his children jumped up from the floor and grabbed their mother, sobbing, tears running down their faces.

"Please, don't hurt our Mommy," they pleaded.

He had no reservations about killing Betty, but even Skinny could not kill his own kids. He ran from the house.

At least I wasted her worthless husband. I'm their dad again!

Skinny ran through the woods, his flashlight now leading the way. He got to the car and drove off, pushing the speed limit without going so fast as to draw undo attention.

"Now, for that Smart Ass Patton. You'll get yours tonight!" Skinny's voice was very angry and determined. "You have less than an hour to live."

* * *

Pat and Shirley had finished watching *Shane* on TV when the phone rang.

"Lieutenant Keller here. Pat, Skinny just paid a visit to the Johnson's house. He hit one officer in the head with a blunt instrument and shot another one in the chest. He also shot Mr. Johnson. Mrs. Johnson and the children are okay, but we don't know the condition of Mr. Johnson or the officers. He reportedly used a shotgun, so it does not look good. I'm leaving for the Johnson's house now but wanted to warn you. We believe he has skipped town or is now trying to leave after the shooting. However, in an abundance of caution, I'm calling you to be on your toes. He's crazy enough to head straight for your house."

"Thank you, Lieutenant I'm aware that no one can predict what that animal will do."

"We had our radio dispatcher alert both the officer in back of your house and the one in front. I have also sent another car to the entrance of your subdivision and have instructed the officer to check out all suspicious vehicles coming or going. He's Officer Billy Waters and is familiar with the neighborhood, as he has patrolled it for the past two years."

"I can't thank you enough, Lieutenant. Did anyone see Skinny's vehicle when he left the Johnsons? Hold one second, Lieutenant Shirley wants to know what's going on."

Pat briefly told her and then had her get on the extension phone.

"Lieutenant, Shirley's on the other phone."

"Okay, back to your question. So far no one has been found who saw Skinny's vehicle, but you can be certain of two things: one, it is stolen, and two, we're working the neighborhood hot and heavy, trying to get leads."

"I'm sure you're right, Lieutenant, about Skinny leaving, but we'll act like he hasn't," said Shirley.

"Got to go. Be careful. Bye."

"Hon, do you really think Skinny has left the area?"

"Hell, no! Hold onto you gun."

* * *

Officer Ricky Siniard was on patrol and noticed the car in front of him going a little over the speed limit with one taillight out. He called in the tag number and it came back stolen. He had no idea Skinny was listening to the conversation on his scanner. Siniard told dispatch his location and that he was going to pull the car over. He turned on his blue lights. Skinny saw him in the rearview mirror.

"Oh, hell! The one time I didn't swap plates." He pulled over, put the long pointed rod up his left sleeve, waited until the officer got out, opened his door, and got out.

"Hi, Officer." Skinny smiled..

"Get back in the car and keep your hands where I can see them," ordered Officer Siniard, matter-of-factly. "What is this? You're a police officer?" Siniard had a puzzled look on his face when he saw the uniform.

"Your Captain Kefauver called my captain and I got

assigned here on temporary duty. We found a stolen car and since all the wreckers were busy, I was told to take it to the impound lot," lied Skinny.

"But, that's against regulations."

"The Captain knows that, but with all of the manpower being used on the escaped convict case, you know . . . Anderson, he has to take some shortcuts just to keep his head above water."

Skinny sounded so convincing that Officer Siniard dropped his guard allowing Skinny to get within striking distance. Another serious mistake!

No cars now!

Revenge flashed in Skinny's brain, and so did the steel shaft. He quickly buried it 12 inches into Officer Siniard's chest. Skinny pulled him into the police car, turned off the lights, and propped him up to look like he was sitting behind the wheel. His head slumped, so Skinny straightened it up using the officer's billy club. The bottom was stuck under his shirt and the top stuck into his almost-too-large hat. He removed the portable blue light from the police car and took it with him.

Damn, now they got the tag number! I need to stop and get another tag or another car.

About 2 miles up the road he found a shopping center and was able to change tags with another Dodge. He reloaded the shotgun.

Man, will the poor SOB who owns that car have some explaining to do. Skinny was laughing thinking about it.

* * *

When Willie Smith, a mild-mannered, thin gay man came bopping out of the shopping center a half-hour later, he was met by seven police officers with drawn guns. They handcuffed him and placed Willie under arrest for auto theft and murder. Suddenly there was a yellow puddle where he was standing. It did not take long to realize they had the wrong man.

Skinny was lucky that Officer Ethel Felix decided to cruise all the parking lots in the area looking for stolen vehicles, because this diversion brought him some much-needed time to complete his task.

The police knew a total of three police officers, and maybe more, had been murdered. They were sure it was Skinny, as Officer Siniard was stabbed in the same manner as the two men at Jackson State Prison.

Unknown to Skinny, in less than two hours from the time he stole the tag, the police had the new tag number. Now an all-out search was about to take place. All Clayton County Police Department officers were called in from days off and vacations. The chief was trying to contact everyone on the force. They wanted Skinny in the worst way. The officers on the Clayton County police force were brothers and sisters, knew and liked Officers Foglehorn, Headman, Franklin, and now Siniard. Each of them wanted to be the one who found Skinny trying to escape and resisting arrest. They wanted to save the taxpayers some money.

CHAPTER 27

Late December - The Showdown

Skinny got through the police net closing around him and decided to drive down the Camp Creek Parkway on the opposite side of the road from Pat's house. Sure enough, there was a county police car parked behind the house, just off the highway. Skinny remembered, at the far end of the property, there was a way to get under the fence. His original plan was to pretend he was a jogger. However. at 11:30 PM, he surely would get stopped when he got near Pat's house.

Time for my alternate plan.

The police scanner had been full of talk about the murdered officers and that Skinny was the prime suspect.

Throwing all caution aside, he went about a mile until he was able to make a left-hand turn and go in the opposite direction on the divided highway.

The press made a big deal out of Pat not accepting an officer in his house, which is probably true, but I have to be careful. It could be a trap. I'm sure there is a cop in front of the house. Time to take drastic action.

Skinny pulled up behind the Clayton County police car parked behind Pat's house, flashing the blue light for two or three seconds, and turning off the engine and lights. He got out with the pointed steel rod up his left sleeve. Skinny had heard the names Lieutenant Keller and Capt. Kefauver mentioned on the police scanner. Now he knew they had his tag number.

I've got to move fast! Make the hit and leave! Find

another car, and get the hell out of this state as quick as I can.
But, I have to kill Patton first! And then there's Shirley, my
party girl!

Officer Price Jacobson got out of his car to see what was
going on. His hand was on the grip of his .38 Special service
revolver. He also had a riot shotgun in the car. He was alert and
very wary. He knew at least one fellow officer had been
murdered and two others were wounded and may have died.
Jacobson was taking no chances. He hadn't been told about
another police officer being sent there.

"Hi!" Skinny quickly introduced himself. "I'm Officer
Jim Sanders, one of the reinforcements sent by Atlanta to help
you guys out. Lieutenant Keller asked me to stop and check on
you and . . . ah . . . what's his name out front?"

"Gilstrap."

"Yeah. Gilstrap, that's it. The Lieutenant told me he was
still trying to get a man in the house. Did Patton ever consent to
it?"

"No. Say, you're asking a lot of . . ."

"Look over there in the yard!" Skinny pointed. "That
looks like a man by the porch!"

The officer turned to look. "I don't see any - - - ahhhh,"
cried Officer Jacobson, as he fell to the ground with 12 inches
of steel shoved up into him.

Skinny quickly stuffed him behind the front seat of the
patrol car, as he could see a car coming. He took his shotgun,
flashlight, wire cutters, bolt cutters, a pry bar, and crawled
under the fence. He had to disable the cop in front of the house,
or if he was too hard to get at, kill Patton and get away before
the cop out front knew what happened. The latter would be
a last resort. He was humming *A Hunting We Will Go* as he
made his way toward the house.

After Skinny crawled under the fence, he noticed all the
blinds and curtains were drawn. He could not see inside.

A quick shot through a window would be nice, except
I'd miss my party with little Miss Tight-Ass. I could set the
house on fire and kill Smart-Ass Patton when he comes
running out. However, that would take too much time, and
100 cops would be here before I could get away.

"Time, time, time," muttered Skinny.

Another cop could show up at any time. I hope that won't happen because I want to gut-shoot Patton and spend some quality time with my party girl. I'll try not to shoot him with my shotgun. If I can, I'll put a .38 right where Doc said it would kill him slow and with a lot of pain.

He sat the tools on the ground in back of the house and walked boldly over to the patrol car in front of the house, shotgun over his shoulder.

"Hey, Gilstrap! I'm here, so you can take a break."

No answer. He walked up to the car and could not believe what he saw. Gilstrap was fast asleep, snoring away. Skinny opened the door very slowly, and just as Gilstrap woke up, he went back to sleep again when the butt of the shotgun struck him in the head. Skinny hit him again.

"Stupid pig!" spat Skinny at the unconscious officer.

He pulled the car keys and Gilstrap's guns, and threw them as far as he could. Then he ripped out the mike cord to the radio, handcuffed Gilstrap to the steering wheel, and ran to the back of the house.

I hope Smart-Ass Patton has a ladder in the storage shed. He opened the storage shed with the aid of his flashlight and bolt cutters. Skinny found a ladder and quietly put it up against the screened porch, which had its floor about eight feet off the ground. He found the telephone line and cut it.

* * *

Pat and Shirley were in bed, but neither could go to sleep nor were they interested in lovemaking. Pat was very uneasy and had a bad premonition.

"Shir, I can't shake this bad feeling I have, right here in the pit of my stomach."

"I have the same feeling, Honey. If Skinny does not show up tonight, and he would be crazy to do that, I think he'll be gone for good."

"You're forgetting he got Johnson with an officer in the house and another out front."

"No, I didn't forget; I'm just trying to make us feel better."

The phone rang.

"Hello, Pat speaking."

"This is the Great Eb."

"Well, you old rascal. What are you up to? Dunkin' your dickie?"

"I was worried about you, man. I was watching TV and they broke in with a news bulletin saying Skinny shot two cops and his former wife's husband. Now they suspect him of killing a police officer, who apparently stopped him only a few miles from your place. Be care . . ."

Click!

"Eb? Eb? Are you still there? Eb?"

"What's wrong, Honey."

"The phone went dead. Shir, get your gun in your hand and turn off all the lights! I don't like this."

Before she could get to the switch, all the lights went out.

"He's here, isn't he?" asked Shirley with a shaky voice.

"We've got to keep quiet, Shir! We need to be quiet and get in a corner. We don't want to shoot each other," whispered Pat as he gripped his .44 Magnum.

* * *

At the Clayton County police headquarters, the radio operator tried to call Officer Jacobson, but couldn't reach him.

"Lieutenant Keller, Sir, I tried and tried, but I can't reach Officer Jacobson at Patton's house!"

"Try . . . who's the other officer we sent there?"

"Gilstrap, Sir."

"Try him."

"Yes, Sir," answered the dispatcher as she tried again. No answer.

"He does not respond either, Sir."

Lieutenant Keller immediately called Pat's home phone number.

"No answer! The operator says there's trouble on the line. Get all cars in the area of the Patton house to go there immediately! I want at least two cars in front and two in back. I want cars ready to block all roads in and out of that area!"

"Yes, Sir."

"Alert College Park and the State police. Also try to notify the GBI team, but don't be in a hurry to do it...this case is our baby."

"Yes, Sir."

Keller told the Captain he was on his way to Patton's house, then notified the dispatcher where he was headed.

"Lt, the car we had at the entrance of the subdivision is on its way. He'll be there in just a minute."

"Good. I'm gone!"

"Just a minute, Sir." The dispatcher's voice cracked as tears appeared in her eyes.

"We just got word that Officer Siniard was apparently found murdered in his patrol car. It has to be Skinny!"

"Thank you. Goodbye," yelled Lieutenant Keller running out.

* * *

After Skinny cut the telephone line, he was able to pull out the meter head, which turned off all electricity to Pat's house. As he went up the ladder to the screened porch, he thought, *I was lucky to have found one in the storage shed.* With his knife, Skinny cut a large hole in the screen. He crawled through the hole and tried the door leading from the porch to the house. Because there was no outside entrance from the porch, the door was not very secure It easily opened with some help from a credit card.

Bingo! It didn't make much noise. I need to create a diversion. Now we'll soon see who's a coward!

He went back through the hole in the screen, down the ladder and walked quickly to the garage door. Skinny took the pry bar and forced the lock open. He raised the garage door by pushing it open as far as he could to create a *loud* noise.

That smart-ass attorney will think I'm in the basement, thought Skinny as he hurried back to the porch. He went up the ladder and back through the screen. Very slowly and quietly, he opened the door, and removed the safety from his sawed-off shotgun before he went inside. The drawn curtains did not completely stop the illumination from the streetlight outside. The front door had three small windows, which also allowed light to flow into the room.

Skinny found himself in the living room/dining room area. He was getting aroused thinking about what he was going to do to Shirley. The room seemed to be about 10 feet wide and about twice as long. At the other end of the room, to his right, was the main entrance door. Directly across the room from it was an open doorway, which he thought might lead to a hallway. Maybe to the bedrooms. He could see another door beyond it, probably to the basement or a closet.

I can't wait too long, but let's see if this turkey moves. He had a twisted, evil smile on his face.

Maybe I should have brought along a turkey call, he thought with a smirk.

He pointed the shotgun at the doorway and waited.

* * *

A few minutes earlier Pat was talking to Shirley.

"Shir, he's in the basement!" whispered Pat. "To go from the garage to the stairs, he has to first go through the door to the laundry room, then through the door to the recreation room. He would have to turn right to come up the stairs, but the door to the recreation room opens out and to the right, toward the stairs, from the laundry room. If I'm at the stairs with my .44 Magnum, I can shoot through the door when he opens it. He won't be able to swing his shotgun, or a pistol for that matter, around on me, because the door will be in the way. Wait here but stay in a corner."

"Do what you have to do, Honey, but please come back to me. This guy's a killer. You aren't."

Big mistake! He played right into Skinny's hands.

Pat quietly tiptoed in his stocking feet to the basement door and carefully opened it. As silently as he could, he started down the stairs, listening as he went. The door from the recreation room to the back yard had a window letting in enough light from the outside to see the steps.

Skinny had heard but not seen him in the hallway. He silently made his way a little closer to the doorway, which he looked through into the hall. The basement door was across from him and open. He could see the outline of Pat from the waist up, slowly descending the stairs.

Skinny took two more steps and was in the hallway.

As his finger tightened on the trigger of his shotgun, he yelled, "Hey, smart-ass attorney! I've got something for you!"

Boom! Boom!

Skinny thought, *something's wrong!* After the second gunshot, he reflexively jerked and pulled the trigger on his shotgun. He managed to turn his head and saw Shirley standing about 8 feet away with her barking .38 Special.

At the sound of the shots, Pat whirled around and saw Skinny silhouetted against the light coming in from the windows of the living-room.

Skinny, with great difficulty, was trying to raise his shotgun at Shirley. She was getting ready to shoot him again.

Although Pat caught a round of buckshot in his left shoulder, he was able to bring up his .44 Magnum and shoot Skinny in the chest, knocking him back into the living room. The image of Shirley was the last thing Skinny ever saw.

Pat slowly struggled up the stairs with his gun pointed toward Skinny lying on the floor, twitching. Blood was running down Pat's shirt and Skinny was a bloody mess. Shirley came into the living room with her .38 Special pointed at Skinny and then proceeded to kick him in the balls, again and again.

Pat knocked away the shotgun and removed the pistol from Skinny's holster. They treated him like a poisonous snake that still might be alive. Blue lights were now flashing from both the front and the rear of the house as Pat held Shirley, tears of relief rolling down her face.

"Pat, you've been shot!"

He had trouble hearing her because his ears were ringing from the gunshots.

"I'll be okay. You saved my life, Shir! He tricked me and I was a dead man!" Pat was very shaky and emotional. They slumped to the floor in each other's arms.

CHAPTER 28

Late December - The Day After

The next day was Saturday, so Pat and Shirley went to her parents' house for the evening meal as planned. The night before, Greg and Grace wanted to rush to the hospital but Pat had already been discharged and Shirley told them she would see them the next evening. Shirley drove because Pat had his left arm in a sling. They pulled in the driveway and Shirley's mother and father ran out to meet them.

"Hi, kids. Boy, you don't know how worried your mother and I have been about you!" With that, Mr. and Mrs. O'Kelly both enthusiastically embraced Shirley and Pat. They were careful not to bump Pat's arm.

"My baby, I was so afraid for you," exclaimed Mrs. O'Kelly, as she held onto Shirley. "Your brother called to make sure you're okay. He was going to fly here if he was needed. I told him the District Attorney gave you a week off with pay, as you are required to go through counseling, like police officers when involved in a shooting."

"I'm fine mother."

"Skinny was to evil like Mother Theresa was too good," commented Mr. O'Kelly. "Thank you for taking care of my little girl, Pat."

"He was the most evil man I have ever known, and you're welcome, Sir, but I think it was your little girl who took care of me. But...we could not have survived without His help."

Mr. O'Kelly whispered something in Shirley's ear.

"Pat. Daddy has something for you."

They held hands and walked to the back of the house

with her parents.

"Like it, Pat? It's yours," stated Mr. O'Kelly.

"I can't believe this!" exclaimed Pat.

"Shirley, look at this!"

Sitting there was the most beautiful sight Pat had ever seen - - a 1967 Mustang convertible, fully restored, with a highly modified Ford 351 Cleveland engine.

Epilogue

Officer Fogelhorn and Mr. Johnson, although seriously bruised, survived because they were wearing bulletproof vests. Officer Headman was hospitalized with a concussion and released five days later. Officer Siniard was lucky no vital organs or arteries were hit and, after a long hospital stay, should recover. Officer Gilstrap is alive but has been in a coma ever since Skinny hit him on the head. He has a wife and two children who he does not recognize and is not expected to recover. Officer Jacobson will never get to see his new baby girl, born three weeks later, as he was pronounced dead on arrival at Clayton General Hospital.

Mrs. Johnson, her two children, and Mrs. Butterworth are all in long-term counseling. Herb sometimes wakes up with nightmares although he has learned to cope with his thoughts of Skinny and what his terrorism did to his wife. Bonnie is afraid to go anywhere at night without Herb's presence.

Pat's shoulder wound was not serious and he made a fast and full recovery. He and Shirley are both practicing law and plan to be married in the near future. Greg insisted on putting new carpet in the hall and living room where Skinny died. Pat and Shirley both get cold chills when thoughts of Skinny enter their minds.

The newspaper said his body would be interred in the paupers' cemetery on Tuesday. As the grave diggers worked, a lone man watched from the shadows of an ancient tree. He looked angry, as he alternated clenching and unclenching his fists and stating, "I'll get them for you, Skinny!"

About the Author

For 26 years, the author had a law practice. He became an attorney, at age 36, the hard way, by working his way through college and law school while holding down a full-time job as an avionics technician and working part-time in a motorcycle shop.

In 1980's Georgia, attorneys got their start by signing up to represent people on the indigent list. Our Constitution states that no one charged with a crime who faces substantial jail time will be denied an attorney. If the accused cannot afford one, the state will provide legal representation. Except for large cities, public defenders were almost unheard of, so representation came from B a r members. The author represented well over 100 criminal defendants, also handling adoptions, divorces, bankruptcies, wills, personal injury and various other cases.

Prior to becoming an attorney, he was a farmer, store clerk, part-owner of an automobile salvage yard, draftsman, electronics technician, motorcycle mechanic, professional welder, board operator at a TV station, customer relations representative for a photocopy company, and management trainee for a well-known insurance company. Hobbies have included hunting, boating, flying ultralight airplanes, roller and ice skating, motorcycles, bowling, antique automobiles, scuba diving, weightlifting, jogging, softball, hypnosis, and traveling.

The author has been published nationally, written numerous newspaper articles and several novels to be published. Except for a few humorous scenes, he strived to make prison and the practice of law as realistic as possible. Now retired, he lives on a lake in Georgia.

Coming Books

in the

Adventures of Pat Patton Series

<u>Evil in the Shadows</u> continues the story of a maturing Pat, not only in his respect for others but also in his romance with Shirley. True cases, humorous and sad, from the writer's experiences as an attorney will continue to educate the reader in the judicial system. This time, Skinny's brother, a more depraved and cruel killer, hunts Pat, and now Shirley, too, for revenge. This novel is now available on Amazon.com as a traditional book and on Kindle.

Mr. Clean: Serial Killer will be available early in 2018. Pat is only one of many who a serial killer is out to eliminate because they are, in his mind, unclean. He likes to play cat-and-mouse before the kill

If you liked *Death to the Novice Attorney*, a five-star review on Amazon.com would be very much appreciated.

The author is available for speaking engagements on writing and self-publishing, the U.S. Constitution and other political subjects as well as law topics.

He will respond to you at rogerfen@bellsouth.net.